Bumps

Zoë Barnes

PIATKUS

First published in Great Britain in 1997 by
Judy Piatkus (Publishers) Ltd of
5 Windmill Street, London W1

First paperback edition 1997

*A catalogue record for this book is available
from the British Library*

ISBN 0 7499 3030 6

Phototypest in Times by Intype London Ltd
Printed in Great Britain by
Mackays of Chatham Plc

Prologue

How it all began...

'I might have known you'd over-react,' said Gareth Scott sourly.

Taz stared back at him, open-mouthed. Behind her, a warm June breeze fluttered her living room curtains, filling the flat with fragrance from the flower beds beneath the open window. Bees buzzed; lawnmowers droned lazily in gardens vibrant with flowers; cats dozed in the sunshine. But she didn't notice any of it. This had just become the worst day of Taz Norton's life.

It took her a second or two to get her breath back.

'Now hold on, Gareth. Let me get this straight. It's my birthday, you've just told me you've been two-timing me with my flatmate – how am I *supposed* to react?'

The question hung in the air, sizzling with rage.

Melanie, who until now had been almost cowering behind Gareth, tried to touch Taz's arm. Taz shook it off with a venomous glare, and Melanie shrank away.

'Please Taz... I don't want us to stop being friends.'

The ludicrousness of it all made Taz burst out laughing.

'Friends? Is *this* how you treat your friends, Mel? No wonder you haven't got any.'

'Oh Taz, please Taz, you don't know how sorry I am about all this, we never *meant* to...' protested Melanie, flinching.

Every cliché in the book, thought Taz bitterly. Every bloody cliché. How could I be so blind?

'Oh I see. So this just kind of *happened*, right? You just

1

fell into bed with each other and couldn't help your-selves?'

'Not exactly, but . . .' Melanie looked across at Gareth, her eyes pleading with him to help her. Taz didn't give him the chance.

'But nothing.' Taz took a deep breath, held it, then let it out slowly. 'Just tell me how long this has been going on.'

'Since . . .' Melanie stared down at her feet. 'Since that party at Chippenham.'

The sting of betrayal bit a little deeper into Taz's soul.

'The charity ball? The one I gave you my ticket for because I had to work late?'

Melanie nodded dumbly.

'I'm sorry,' she whispered, hanging her head. 'Really sorry.'

'We've been seeing each other for about three months now,' said Gareth helpfully. Taz rounded on him, all guns blazing.

'I may be blind, Gareth, but I can still add up.'

For a couple of seconds they were eyeball to eyeball. Then Gareth turned his treacherously handsome face away, making some pretext of looking at the clock on the mantelpiece.

'We should really be going,' he commented. 'If we want to miss the worst of the traffic.'

'You *bastard*,' hissed Taz, hurting so violently that all she could do was turn her back on Gareth and Melanie.

Her eyes swept around the ground-floor conversion she'd shared with Melanie for over two years, ever since the two of them arrived in Cheltenham, ready to conquer the world. Everything had gone so well for them, Mel getting the advertising job she'd always dreamed of and Taz steadily climbing the management ladder at Seuss & Goldman, Cheltenham's premier department store.

And then along came Gareth Scott: twenty years older than Taz, good-looking, powerful, sexy. Everywhere she looked were remnants of a nine-month affair that should never have happened. Expensive wallpaper chosen by

2

Gareth. Sofa-bed with wine-stained cushions, on which Taz and Gareth had spent so many uninhibited Sunday afternoons. Porcelain figurine of a naked dancer: a present from . . . who else?

'For God's sake Taz, must you be so childish?' snapped Gareth. 'This thing we had – OK so it was a lot of fun, but it was just physical, we knew it was never meant to last. We were always going to see other people . . .'

'You mean *you* were always going to see other people,' said Taz tartly. 'You just conveniently forgot to mention it to me.' She glanced at Melanie. 'I wonder who'll be next on the list.'

Gareth snorted, raking his slightly-greying hair back from his forehead with exasperated fingers.

'Can't you get it into your head, Taz? It's completely different with Melanie.'

'We love each other, Taz,' pleaded Melanie. 'Gareth's got a new job and we're going away together.'

Melanie clung to Gareth's arm, her soft grey eyes silently pleading for forgiveness. You manipulative bitch, thought Taz.

'I think it's time you went,' said Taz quietly.

'But I need to get the rest of my things,' protested Melanie.

'Now,' said Taz. 'Before I forget what a nice, reasonable person I am.'

Gareth picked up Melanie's overnight bag from the settee.

'Come on Mel darling, you don't need anything from here,' he said, stooping to kiss Melanie's cheek with such tenderness that Taz knew it was meant as a final snub. 'I'll be taking care of you from now on.'

The door of the flat closed with a soft click. Footsteps receded, then there was the sound of a car engine; and Taz was alone. She stood and stared at the living-room wall for a long time before picking up the remains of her birthday cake and slinging it violently at the wallpaper. Gareth's wallpaper. The cake slid slowly down, leaving oily trails of melted butter icing.

'Sod off Gareth. See if I bloody well care.'

Her eyes were dry as she flopped down onto the carpet and hugged a cushion to her chest. Minky, her cat, slunk in from the kitchen and rubbed up against her legs, mewing and purring for food; but Taz didn't even notice.

It was at least half an hour before she got up and went into the kitchen, where she ate a whole family bag of tortilla chips. And another ten minutes before her eyes strayed to Gareth's empty coffee cup, still sitting unwashed on the draining board.

But a few seconds after that, she was sobbing into the empty bag.

Chapter 1

'You'll get fat,' commented Taz, with a sly wink at her friend across the outdoor finger buffet.

Binnie Lethbridge – soon-to-be ex-manager of Seuss & Goldman's china department – glanced down guiltily at her seventh mini-quiche of the afternoon.

She and Taz looked at each other, then down at Binnie's stomach, extravagantly balloon-like beneath her floral maternity smock. Then they both fell about laughing.

'Fat, yeah, right. Like anybody's going to *notice*.' Binnie ate yet another, rounding up the crumbs with a quick flick of her tongue. 'Mmm, yummy. Oooh.' She pulled a face and shifted uneasily from one foot to the other.

'I think I need the loo again.'

'Again!'

'Wait till you're pregnant, then you'll understand. Here, mind my plate for me will you? And don't scoff all the crostini. I'll be back in a mo.'

Taz yawned and consulted her watch. Still only half past two. Just how long could it take to finish a croquet match?

Behind her, the manicured lawns of Cheltenham Croquet Club quivered to polite applause as yet another wooden ball was thwacked through a coloured hoop. It was all very English, complete with crustless cucumber sandwiches, white drill shorts and individual mandarin pavlovas, but it wasn't very Taz. Taz Norton was far more at home at the sharp end of a business deal, doing her damnedest to prove that she fully deserved to be Seuss & Goldman's youngest departmental manager.

She tried to force herself to take an interest in the game.

After all, she'd been sent here to represent the store, she ought at least to *look* as if she was enjoying herself.

'I bet you enjoy a good game don't you, m'dear?'

The touch of a hand surreptitiously fondling her bottom nearly made Taz Norton jump out of her skin, and sent half of Binnie's crostini flying. She spun round and found herself glaring at a middle-aged Lothario in a beige linen suit.

'Excuse *me*?'

'Croquet.' The smile under the clipped moustache was verging on a leer. 'Do you play? You look like a . . . sporty sort of a gel.'

Yeah, thought Taz, suddenly wishing her smart green skirt was a couple of inches longer. She treated him to the kind of polite, sub-zero smile she used on awkward customers at work.

'Sorry, no. I've never had the inclination.' She prayed that Binnie would hurry back. How many times could one pregnant woman go to the lavatory in an afternoon?

'Ah. So few ladies do these days. But you appreciate the *game* of course?'

'Croquet? Of course.'

Taz wished she could be sure he was just talking about the Seuss & Goldman Croquet Challenge. Creep, he ought to be ashamed of himself.

'And it's such a wonderful day out for you ladies, isn't it? Showing off your new summer frocks.'

'Wonderful.' Her smile was so fixed it was becoming painful.

Taz's gaze wandered over his left shoulder. Rescue me, Binnie, she willed silently. But there was still no sign of her.

'Actually, this isn't just a day out for me, it's work,' she confessed.

'Really?' In the distance, shouts of 'well played!' rose above well-bred applause.

'Yes, I'm here to represent Seuss & Goldman.'

'S & G, eh? Well, well.' The mention of Cheltenham's most prestigious department store prompted the moustache to twitch with renewed interest. A snap of the

6

fingers. 'I say, you're the company secretary's daughter, aren't you? Knew I'd seen you somewhere before . . .'

Taz played her ace.

'I'm a departmental manager.' She relished the look of astonishment this provoked. 'In charge of menswear. Now, if you'll just excuse me . . .' To her relief, she had just caught sight of Binnie. 'I think my colleague is calling me over.'

Refilling her plate, Binnie bit into a vol-au-vent and nodded towards the retreating figure of the man in the linen suit.

'Honest Taz, I leave you for five minutes and you're chatting up blokes. Mind you, you've got good taste.'

'You're kidding. Who *is* that?'

'You don't know? That's Angus Cornforth, you know, the Goldman family lawyer.'

'Good God.' Taz stared after him. He was now chatting to a couple of girls from the Ladies' College, his arm round one and his free hand heading straight for the other one's bottom. 'He goosed me!'

'You're well in there then,' grinned Binnie. 'He obviously likes you.'

'You mean he likes anything in a tight skirt.' Taz eased a finger under the waistband of her brand-new Betty Jackson suit. 'I knew I should have bought the fourteen, I can hardly breathe in this.'

'You look great. Anyhow, you have to suffer to be beautiful.'

A few more pastry-crumbs fell onto Binnie's dress, but she didn't bother to brush them off. Taz wondered if being pregnant shrivelled up the bit of your brain that made you care what you looked like because lately Binnie Lethbridge looked like she'd swallowed a Laura Ashley bed-settee. It had been quite painful to witness her dramatic transformation, from foxy to frumpy in under seven months.

'You could do worse than Cornforth, you know,' Binnie went on. 'He's filthy rich.'

'I don't care if he's the Sultan of Brunei. I've had

enough of older men to last me a lifetime, thank you very much.'

'I thought you were . . . you know . . . over him.'

'What do you think?'

'Well, it's not every group finance manager who redecorates your living room then buggers off to set up home with your flatmate.'

There was an awkward silence. Binnie sipped lemon squash and surveyed the match on court. 'Well played! Did you see that roquet?'

'What?'

'Roquet. It's when you make your ball hit somebody else's.'

'Oh.'

'You see, when the out-player missed, the in-player roqueted his ball, stopped it out into court and got a rush on her partner's ball.'

Binnie laughed at the look of complete bafflement on Taz's face.

'Sorry, I used to play a bit at university.' She patted her bump with a swollen-fingered hand. 'In the days when I could still see my feet. So . . . have you heard from Gareth since he ran out on you?'

'No. But Melanie rang up last week.'

'No! The cheeky little madam.'

'She wanted her hi-fi system back.'

'Well I hope you told her where she could shove it.'

'Actually I told her I'd sold it.'

'And have you?'

'Course not.' Taz giggled. 'But I reckoned it was about time I had a new hi-fi.'

'Nice one,' said Binnie approvingly.

Taz turned and gazed out at the court, but she was seeing Gareth and Melanie on the day they'd told her they were leaving Cheltenham. Together. To think that she hadn't suspected for a moment. That was what really pissed her off – letting him . . . no, letting *anyone* put one over on her.

'So,' said Binnie. 'Still with Gareth is she?'

'As far as I know. She didn't say where they were and

I didn't ask. Good riddance to bad rubbish.' Taz stretched her aching neck, closed her eyes and leaned her head back, letting the sun bathe her tired face. Her hat was making her head itch, and she yearned to take it off. What with the Gareth business and the summer sales about to go into overdrive at Seuss & Goldman, lately she'd been feeling a bit run down.

'At least he never moved in with you,' pointed out Binnie, 'and it could have been worse.'

Taz took a glass of fresh lemonade from the buffet, and rolled the cool glass over her burning skin.

'Oh yeah? How?'

'You could have married the cheating scumbag.' Binnie grinned.

'Don't be silly,' laughed Taz. 'I'm only twenty-five. I'm not letting some guy con me into staying home and washing his socks while he goes off and becomes vice-President of Lonrho.' She realised what she'd said and turned quickly back to Binnie. 'I didn't mean you and Jim . . .'

'It's OK, I know what you meant. I don't mind giving up my job. I thought I would, but I've got the baby to think about, and Scotland's a great place for a kid to grow up.'

'Wouldn't you be bored, just being at home? You could find a job up there. When the baby's older.'

'I guess. But on Jim's salary we don't need the money any more, and Jim's mother's dead set against child-minders. To be honest, it's funny but since I got pregnant I just don't . . . well . . . care about work the way I used to.' Binnie chuckled. 'That's hormones for you. I used to have shoulder-pads like that woman out of *Dynasty*, the one who was always falling into bed with Dex Dexter.'

'Alexis.'

'That's the one.'

Taz squinted into the sun. At thirty-seven Binnie looked fat, bloated, uncomfortable . . . and curiously happy. The poor woman had haemorrhoids, varicose veins, high blood pressure and permanent backache, yet in spite of it all she looked so contented, like a prize Jersey cow in calf. Taz shuddered. She'd never be like that, not her. No way.

Never in a million zillion years.

It was drizzling half-heartedly by the time Taz had dropped Binnie off at home and driven back to Seuss & Goldman. In the staff car park, Taz threw her hat onto the back seat, then eased undone the button on her skirt. Bliss. At last she could breathe again.

The victorian gothic facade of Seuss & Goldman loomed like a benevolent vulture over the broad, tree-dotted expanse of Imperial Gardens and the Promenade. Over the hundred and twenty years of its existence, the buildings had been added to from time to time, sometimes in unexpected ways but always sympathetically; incorporating the domed remains of the old Winter Gardens after the war, and acquiring a rather fine glass atrium and new offices during the expansion of the Eighties.

But in all that time, the essence of S&G had never really changed. It had become a byword for quality, and not just in Cheltenham. In the last thirty years, Seuss & Goldman had opened stores all over the UK and on the Continent, and now the board had their eye on the other side of the Atlantic. As a matter of fact, so did Taz.

There was no doubt about it, Taz had done well to get onto the S&G graduate training programme. That was four years ago, when she was fresh out of redbrick uni with a 2:1 in French and Business Studies and a head full of dreams. In those four short years she'd risen from dogsbody to head of menswear – not bad for a girl who'd failed GCSE Maths. She'd learned a lot in those four years. The dreams were still there, as powerful and compelling as ever; they were just a bit more realistic.

A glance in the mirror verified that her bobbed brown hair was neat and tidy, and a quick slick of lip-gloss refreshed her flagging make-up. Time to face the troops.

Walking up the access road at the rear of the store, past the almost invisible entrance to the food hall, Taz pushed open the door which led to the security lodge.

'Afternoon, Joe,' she nodded to the grizzled guard on

the desk as she signed for her name badge. 'How's your wife's leg?'

'Champion, miss. Surgeon fixed her veins up a treat.'

Pinning on her badge, Taz walked across the lobby to the staff staircase, almost colliding with Ted Williams, the slimy second-in-command from the food hall, heading for the incinerator with bags of out-of-date crisps.

'Been dodging class have we?'

Taz confined herself to a brief smile and a nod; there was something about Ted that made her flesh creep. Climbing the back stairs took her quickly to the first floor, and into the Deco splendour of the menswear department. *Her* department. That thought gave her a childish thrill of pride every time she walked onto the sales floor.

She paused for a moment to survey her realm. To the left was men's formalwear, the stock rather too densely packed together on account of lack of space and too many ornate pillars. She'd have to get something done about that. Beyond formalwear were countrywear and Cara Mondini's sports and leisure Department. To Taz's right was men's casualwear, rather brighter and less crowded than formalwear, with more space and innovative styling. This led eventually into computing and electrical, but the last of the Polo jackets marked the limit of Taz's jurisdiction.

There wasn't time to stand and ponder. There was work to be done. As she headed for countrywear she knew that something wasn't quite right. For a start, there was no sign of Marion Grey, the senior sales consultant. And the sound of raised voices was coming from one of the cashpoints . . .

Long before she reached the sales desk, Taz spotted Kate Avery, her new eighteen-year-old trainee, practically barricaded behind the till as a smartly-dressed woman waved a credit card in her face.

Taz felt more than a twinge of annoyance. Where on earth was Marion? And there was no sign of Leroy McIntosh either. Honestly, you couldn't turn your back for ten seconds without everything falling to bits. Taz took a deep breath and clicked on a professional smile.

'Excuse me. Is there a problem?'

Kate turned a flushed face towards Taz. A face that screamed, 'Rescue me!'

'Oh, Ms Norton. This lady . . .'

'I demand to see the manager. Now!' said the customer, eyeing, Taz disdainfully.

'I *am* the departmental manager.'

'Oh.' The booming voice softened by a couple of decibels. 'I see.'

'Can I help, Mrs . . .?'

'Seward. Verity Seward. I wish to purchase a cashmere sweater for my husband, but this halfwitted girl says there is a problem with my credit card.'

'I see. Well, whatever it is I'm sure we'll soon have it sorted out.'

Taz glanced at Kate. Poor kid, she looked like she wanted to shrivel up and die. But one of the first lessons any management trainee needed to learn was how to avoid being bullied by overbearing women with golf-club accents. She took the gold Amex card and dialled through. It was just as she'd thought. The Sewards were well over their card limit and had fallen behind with their monthly payments. So much for the Jaeger suit and the Gucci bag.

'Apparently, the card company requires a nominal payment of ten pounds before your purchase is authorised.'

'But that's preposterous . . .'

'This sort of thing does happen occasionally.'

'Well it has never happened to me.'

'I'm sure it's nothing serious,' said Taz soothingly. 'Or the company wouldn't authorise the transaction at all. So, if you could just make this one small payment . . .'

With extremely bad grace, Mrs Seward unzipped her purse and took out a neatly-folded ten-pound note.

'Thank you so much.' Taz passed the banknote to Kate, together with a note of the authorisation code. 'Now Miss Avery will process your sale.'

Afterwards, Taz drew Kate to one side, asking, 'Are you OK now?'

'I'm sorry. But she was so rude! I just . . . panicked.'

'You get customers like that, I'm afraid. They lose their temper because they're embarrassed. The trick is not to let them intimidate you into doing the wrong thing. But always be polite. Let them *think* they've got the upper hand.'

'It's so difficult.'

'It gets easier with practice, I promise.' Taz thought of her own first day as junior management trainee. She'd been given the job of cleaning the costume jewellery, took all the price labels off then couldn't remember which one belonged to which necklace. 'Don't worry. Everyone makes mistakes.'

'Even you?' Kate looked doubtful.

'Especially me. But don't tell anyone!'

Particularly not Marion Grey, thought Taz as she saw the senior sales consultant bustling over from the men's changing rooms with an armful of trousers. Marion was fifty-three, had been at Seuss & Goldman since she was fifteen, and acted as if the store was her own personal property.

'Kate, don't stand around doing nothing, make yourself look busy. In my day ... Oh. Miss Norton.' Marion's expression was not so much apologetic as disdainful. 'You're back then.'

'I left early. Mrs Lethbridge was feeling a bit under the weather, so I took her home.'

'Oh the poor dear, I'm sorry to hear that.' Taz knew that Marion had a soft spot for Binnie. Binnie was, after all, doing what women were supposed to do: giving up her high-powered job to have babies and feed her husband home-made casseroles. Exactly what Marion herself would have done, if she'd ever found a man brave enough to marry her. 'She should be at home with her feet up, in her condition. Letting women work right up to the birth, it's not right.'

'I'm sure she'll be fine once she's had a rest. Anyhow, she's going on maternity leave next week.' Taz looked Marion up and down. 'I thought I asked Leroy to take charge of the changing rooms while you supervised the sales floor.'

13

'Yes, well, you did, but I thought it would be better if Leroy tidied up the stockroom, and then that nice gentleman from Bishop's Cleeve came in, enquiring about ready-to-wear suits . . .'

'Marion!' hissed Taz. 'Your job is here on the floor, and if I ask you to do something, I expect you to do it. Is that clear?'

'I was only using my initiative,' she sniffed.

'Yes. I appreciate that. But I'm sure you also appreciate how important it is for us all to pull together as a team.'

Even Marion couldn't think of an answer to that one.

As soon as she could, Taz went into the departmental staff-room to catch up on paperwork. It was quite a contrast to the relative luxury of the sales floor. A small rickety, table served as a desk; cracked lino didn't quite cover the bare boards; and a calendar hung forlornly on a wall which hadn't been repapered since 1976. Taz chuckled as she sat down. If the customers saw this, it would really open their eyes.

The phone rang. Taz picked up the receiver.

'Menswear, Tasmin Norton speaking. Oh, hi Nikki.' Taz got on well with Nikki Fraser, the store manager's PA. 'Look, it's not about those quarterly sales figures is it? I'm still collating them.'

'No, not that. Ms Latchford wants you to come up to her office at five thirty today.'

Taz had a sudden sinking feeling. A royal summons, to the boss's office? Such an unusual event could spell only one thing: trouble.

Four heads jerked round as Taz knocked on Diana Latchford's door and stuck her head inside.

'You wanted to see me? Oh.' Taz hesitated at the sight of three other departmental managers, already huddled around the oval table at the far end of Diana's office. 'Sorry, I thought . . .'

Diana Latchford was standing by the window, a cool late-forty-something in mauve Escada; her hair greying gracefully. Behind her a huge picture window looked out onto the tastefully grand buildings of the Queen's Hotel and the Ladies' College beyond. She glanced up as the door opened, but scarcely interrupted her flow.

'... a carefully-balanced mix of new and established product lines. And that is why – do come in and help yourself to a coffee, Taz – that is why all next year's promotional events are going to be so important.'

Taz poured herself a black coffee from the percolator. Hmm, Blue Mountain, *must* be something important. She parked her bum between Ken and Cara Mondini. Brendan Ryan from womenswear graced her with a brief grunt but he was too busy hanging on Diana's every word to pay her much attention.

Diana pushed back her perfect sleeve to glance at her Cartier wristwatch.

'Well, seeing as we're all here now we may as well start. I need to be at a meeting by seven thirty.'

'Nikki's not taking minutes then?' asked Cara.

'There's no need, I want to keep this informal.'

Diana took her seat at the table. She had a coffee too, but, in her own white bone-china cup with gilded edging, with no lipstick stains on the rim. Diana Latchford was the nearest thing in retailing to the Immaculate Conception.

'Naturally, you've all read the memo about the new Los Angeles store.'

'Is it still on schedule to open in March?' ventured Taz.

'If the works are completed on schedule.' Diana pursed her lips. 'And they will be, if the site director values his life.'

'So when's the precise opening date?' Ken fiddled absent-mindedly with his Biro, doodling on his blotter. He looked every inch what he was: an ex-pork butcher from Tewkesbury, hopelessly out of his depth.

'Provisionally, we're looking at the fifth of March,' cut in Brendan, jabbing buttons on his electronic organiser. 'Subject to confirmation by the board later this month – that's right isn't it?'

Diana eyed Brendan in the way a schoolteacher eyes up a know-all pupil. Brendan even looked like a

15

schoolboy, with that floppy fringe and that fresh, clean-cut complexion.

'Quite so. Now, as you know Seuss & Goldman has invested heavily in this exciting venture and it is vital that we gain maximum benefit from publicity on both sides of the Atlantic, particularly as we're planning to open in New York in eighteen months' time.'

'I thought it was going to be Chicago,' said Cara, a former tennis champion and still impressively svelte at forty-three.

'Then perhaps you should re-read the last information sheet from head office.' Diana cleared her throat impatiently. 'Now. We have decided that next year's in-store spring promotion will have an American theme. And that is why I am asking you, as key departmental managers, to come up with a range of ideas.'

'Us?' said Ken blankly.

'There's an American amateur basketball team coming over on an exchange visit next spring,' commented Cara, leafing through her diary. 'They'll be playing exhibition matches in Cheltenham. I suppose there might be a chance for some kind of tie-in . . .'

Brendan wrinkled his nose.

'Basketball? God no. What S & G customers want are *culture* and *style*. Theatre sponsorship, a quality in-store shopping experience . . .'

'Culture and style? You mean like Wally the Wombat?' Laughed Ken.

Flush-faced and annoyed, Brendan rounded on Ken.

'You know as well as I do, Wally the Wombat was a product-led promotion for a new high-yield Australian range of . . .'

'Brendan, Wally the Wombat was a midget in a fun-fur suit, handing out free samples of face cream.'

Cara joined in, enjoying a rare opportunity to embarrass Brendan.

'That's right. And what about that "simply darling" Shetland pony? The one that peed all over Santa's Grotto. I'm not sure I'd call *that* a quality shopping experience.'

'Surely,' Taz cut in, 'we can appeal to a wide range of

customer preferences, without losing touch with traditional S&G values?'

'Sounds great in theory,' sniffed Brendan. 'But just you try making it work.'

'Look, this is a great opportunity,' She persisted. There's room to set up a whole range of events. This is a key store opening, we need to sustain customer and media interest over more than just a day or two. Here and in the US.'

'Precisely.' Diana Latchford jotted a few notes in her diary. 'The fact is, Cheltenham is the original S & G store and its flagship. All our stores will be staging an "American Week", but head office expects something *special* from us. What I want is at least a week's worth of linked events and promotions, culminating in a transatlantic catwalk show, showcasing the best of British and American fashion design.'

Taz shot a glance at Brendan. Suddenly he was looking a lot happier at the prospect of another small step towards the glittering summit of his career. As he was fond of reminding people, Brendan Ryan knew more about fashion than anyone else at Seuss & Goldman. He had been senior merchandiser at head office before being called on to transform womenswear from stuffy gentility to the epitome of hip. He'd done a pretty good job, and never let anybody forget it.

'US high fashion. Right, I see Ralph Lauren of course.' He made frenzied notes. 'Donna Karan – and Klein, Tommy Hilfiger, and with my connections in the business I just *might* be able to persuade one or two of the top catwalk models . . .'

'Good, fine,' interrupted Diana. I'm sure you'll all come up with wonderful ideas. Now, I have to leave or I'll miss the group Finance meeting, but we'll get together again in a few days' time. Nikki will call you to arrange when.'

Brendan didn't look best pleased to be interrupted in mid-flow, but gathered up his organiser and shoved it into his pocket. Taz repacked her bag and followed Cara and Ken to the door. Her mind was already back home, stretched out in a decadently hot bath with a really trashy novel.

'Hold on a moment will you, Taz? I'd like a word.'

Taz's hand dropped from the door handle. Her heart skipped a beat, then made up for it with three in rapid succession. Uh-oh. She'd been right about the trouble after all.

'Yes. Right. Sure.' She listened to footsteps and polite chatter receding along the corridor to the lift; getting further and further away, like her Black Lace and her jasmine bath oil. 'What did you want to see me about?'

Diana finished packing her briefcase and swung it up onto the table. Her expression gave nothing away.

'I've been keeping an eye on your work,' she said finally. 'I like what I see.'

Taz allowed herself a cautious exhalation of relief.

'Thank you.'

Diana kicked off her comfortable work shoes and squeezed her toes into a pair of smart black courts.

'You've nothing to thank me for. It was my predecessor who promoted you, and if it had been up to me . . . well, let's say I don't often take chances with people and you *are* still very young and relatively inexperienced.'

'I can't help being twenty-five,' pointed out Taz, a tad peevishly. 'If you like, I'll pretend to be thirty. Surely what matters is whether or not I can do the job.'

Diana smiled. Taz coloured up.

'Did I just say something funny?'

'Not exactly. It just occurred to me that you sounded like me at the same age, convinced everyone was out to stab me in the back and determined to stab them first. Mind you, I was right, they *were* out to get me.' Seeing Taz's expression, she laughed. 'Relax. I'm already convinced. I've seen the quarterly sales returns for your department and frankly, I'm impressed. Which is why I've decided to take one of my rare chances.'

'Chances?'

'On you. I'm thinking about putting you in charge of the American promotion. The whole shebang. Reckon you can handle that?'

Gobsmacked, Taz ran through a range of facial expressions that would have done credit to Jim Carrey.

18

'Well?'

'Yes. Yes, of course I can. But what about Brendan? I thought . . .'

Brendan was not going to like this one little bit. He was five years older than Taz and ran womenswear like the paramilitary wing of Christian Dior. Brendan had masterminded every one of the last three in-store promotional events. And he was not going to take kindly to being ordered about by Taz.

'Never mind our Mr Ryan. Leave him to me. What I'm asking you, Taz, is are you ready for this? Can you take it on and make a success of it? Because if you can't say yes right now I'm going to ask somebody else to do it.'

'Yes,' said Taz, pulling herself together. 'Yes, I'd be glad to do it. Thank you.'

'Don't thank me.' Diana took a delicate sip of her very black coffee. 'Just get out there and make a good job of it. And prove to me that you deserve your next promotion.'

Chapter 2

'Mroaw.'

Taz groaned and rolled over in bed. The clock on the bedside table said eight thirty, but so what? It was Saturday today: the one precious Saturday off she'd managed to cadge in the last six months. And she wasn't getting out of bed for anyone, cats included.

'Oh Minky, no! It's too early ...'

A blue-grey head appeared over the top of the duvet.

'Prrrp. Ee-ew.'

Taz surrendered to the insistent nudge of a cold nose, and swung her legs out of bed. Oooh, steady. The room was spinning out of focus, and she felt vaguely nauseous too; in fact she'd been feeling generally 'off' for days now. Must be some kind of tummy bug, there couldn't be any other explanation for it.

'All right, all right!' She thrust her arms into her dressing gown. 'Minky, you're a greedy pig.'

She plodded into the kitchen, hotly pursued by Minky, who hindered every movement by winding round and round her legs.

Taz stretched up to get the last can of cat food from the top shelf of the cupboard. She gagged as she peeled back the ring-pull and spooned tropical mackerel in aspic into Minky's dish.

'Oh God they've left the eyes in.' She held the dish just above Minky's head, holding her breath and trying not to look at it. 'Look, are you absolutely sure about this?'

Brr-brr.

Uh?

Brr-brr, brr-brr.

That wasn't Minky, that was the phone, dammit. Taz groaned. Now she was *never* going to get back to sleep.

Where had she put it? Somewhere in the bedroom . . . Taz fumbled about and snatched up the cordless phone from under a pile of last night's clothes. Yawn.

'Yeah?'

A soft Northern Irish accent greeted her from the other end of the line.

'Tasmin, dear, is that you? It's Mummy.'

'Mummy?' Taz suppressed a groan.

'Are you all right, Tasmin? You sound peculiar.'

'I'm fine, Mummy. I was just having a bit of a lie-in.'

'You're not ill, are you?'

Taz rubbed her tummy. It was settling down a bit now, she'd be fine when she'd had a cup of tea.

'No, of course not.'

'You'll give yourself a headache, lying in bed all day.'

'I told you, I'm fine.' Mummy and Dad might have taken early retirement a year ago, but for them the day still started at six thirty and fifteen minutes extra consti-tuted a lie-in.

'Anyhow, your father's gone to the clinic with his knee.'

'Poor Dad! Is it his cartilage again?'

'It's something and nothing, he just likes that young physiotherapist making a fuss of him.' Isobel Norton lowered her voice to a conspiratorial whisper. 'Did you get it for me?'

'Get what?'

'The jacket! For the Bennetts' garden party. It's next week you know, and you did say you'd try . . .'

Taz thought guiltily of the ornate evening jacket she'd bought for her mother from Seuss & Goldman's summer design event. She'd had it two weeks but had put off going to see her parents in case they gave her the third-degree and it all came out about Gareth.

In the nine months she'd been seeing Gareth, she'd managed to keep him and her parents resolutely separate. Not because they'd have disapproved of him. On the con-trary, Mummy would have adored him with his 'mature'

21

good looks and commanding personality; and he was exactly the kind of alpha male her father wanted to see protecting his little girl. Which just went to show how wrong parents could be.

'Oh. Yes, actually I did manage to get it for you.'

'Oh Tasmin you're a darling. And with your staff discount it's quite good value really. Mind you, quality is always worth paying for, it's just a pity your father doesn't see it that way.'

'So what does he reckon to you spending three hundred pounds on a jacket?'

Isobel gave a little nervous laugh.

'You don't think I'd tell him, do you? I've said I'm getting one from Marks & Spencer. You know what he's like, he'll never tell the difference.'

Taz suppressed a chuckle. After thirty-odd years of marriage, her Mum and Dad still behaved like kids.

'I'll make sure you get it for the party,' she promised, thinking longingly of the duvet.

Her tummy had started making curious gurgling noises. It *must* be a bug. Or something she'd eaten. Lazy Saturdays meant pain au chocolat and endless cappuccinos, but all she felt like today was nibbling on a dry water biscuit.

'The thing is,' Isobel went on. 'I was wondering, could you bring it over this morning, while your father's out?'

'Mummy . . .'

'It'd be ever so kind of you, you wouldn't mind would you? I mean, it's not as if you're doing anything else . . .'

'Well, actually . . .'

'I knew you wouldn't mind. See you in about an hour then? Don't be late, you know what your father's like, you could set your clock by him.'

After she'd rang off, Taz went wearily into the bathroom. As she ran a bath she caught sight of herself in the mirror over the sink. Her usually glossy brown hair was flat and dishevelled, her oval face rather pale and puffy about her dark brown eyes.

'Taz Norton,' she told herself sternly, 'you're twenty-five years old and your Mum can still wrap you round her little finger. How on earth are you ever going to get to be chairman of Seuss & Goldman?'

It was almost nine by the time Taz was ready to leave. As she stepped out from her ground-floor flat into the cool passageway of the converted Victorian villa, she could hear all manner of argy-bargy coming from the garden.

To her surprise, she saw that all her neighbours were there: Roland and Simon, the gay couple from upstairs who liked to move their furniture about at three in the morning; Al the Elvis impersonator from the attic flat; even that strange foreign couple from the basement. And there were other people there too – two blokes in overalls, one with a pneumatic drill, and a third sitting in the cab of a van, munching on a bacon sandwich.

Nobody seemed very happy. In fact it looked like a lynch mob.

'It's not good enough, I've got to get to work!'

'Look, mate, it's no good mouthing off at me . . .'

'If you don't move your lorry and fill up that hole . . .'

Taz edged her way past. 'If you'll just excuse me, I need to get to my garage.'

This met with hollow laughter from all sides.

'You won't be able to use your car today,' replied Simon with a glare at the three workmen. 'The bloody cable TV people have dug a hole right in the middle of the front drive. We're all blocked in till Monday.'

Which is how Taz came to be delivering a designer evening jacket to her mother in the top box of her 1956 BSA Gold Star.

Inconvenient or not, it was the perfect day for a motor-bike ride. Hazy sunshine, warm as toast, a cooling breeze and an open road. Terrific. As she coasted out of Chel-tenham and powered into the Gloucestershire countryside, Taz mentally thanked her father – not for the first time – for having wanted a son.

Being presented with an only daughter, Bill Norton had done what any practical man would: he had brought her up as if she *was* a son. By the age of eleven she could strip down a carburettor, by thirteen she could adjust the suspension on a Honda 250; and on her sixteenth birthday her dad had plonked her on the seat of a BSA Bantam, kick-started it at the top of a steep hill and told her to hold on tight.

From that moment on, Taz had been hooked on bikes. Big ones, little ones, noisy or smelly or oily, she loved them all. Perhaps unsurprisingly, Isobel did not share her enthusiasm.

Taz took the A46 and headed on south-west through Leckhampton and Shurdington, past Crickley Hill and the remains of the Roman villa near Upton St Leonards. This part of the world was very different from the Wirral suburbs where she'd grown up, but there were a lot worse places you could live. Bill and Isobel Norton had fallen in love with the Cotswolds and retired early to a cottage in Painswick. The fact that Taz worked at Cheltenham S&G was a complete coincidence – at least, that was what Isobel claimed.

A couple of miles outside Painswick, Taz noticed the engine starting to cough. It did that sometimes, when the petrol tank was less than a quarter full.

'Don't you dare die on me,' she whispered as she eased the bike into a garage.

She dismounted, took off her helmet and shook her hair free. Now that she was off the bike, and the exhilaration of speed was gone, she felt faintly peculiar again. She took deep breaths. It would pass. Determinedly she unscrewed the fuel cap and started filling the tank.

And hey! Here was something to take her mind off her stomach. The young mechanic who strolled out onto the forecourt was six foot three of blond testosterone, appetisingly tanned beneath his white cutaway tee-shirt, and with just a romantic oil-smear on one cheek to prove that he knew his way round an engine.

'Hi.' The smile lit up a double row of Hollywood teeth, set in a hunkily square jaw. 'She's yours?'

A bear's paw of a hand smoothed down over the petrol tank of the Gold Star and along the still-warm leather of the seat.

'Used to be my dad's, till he injured his knee. I've had her five years now.'

'Runs well?'

'Usually. Bit temperamental though, I have to nurse the engine along sometimes.' She finished filling the tank and slotted the hose back onto the side of the pump.

'What a beauty.' Piercingly blue eyes looked straight into Taz's. 'Live round here, do you?'

'The other side of Cheltenham. Charlton Kings.'

'Yeah? Whereabouts?'

'Cow Lane – just off the Ham Road.'

Taz moistened her dry lips with the tip of her tongue. Her throat was dry, too. She was doing something she hadn't done in ages, not since before Gareth. She was flirting!

'You should come to the classic bike rally at Stroud,' said the mechanic, ever so casually.

'I might do that.' Taz tried to sound casual too. 'When is it?'

'A fortnight on Sunday. I'll be there, I've got a prewar motorcycle combo entered in the concours d'élégance.'

Taz met his smile dizzily. She felt a bit ... woozy. Not quite right. And he wasn't *that* breathtakingly gorgeous.

She was going to say 'I'd love to,' but at that moment the most dreadful thing she could imagine went right ahead and happened.

'I ... I'm sorry, I think I'm going to ...'

Before she could even turn away, a sudden spasm of nausea overwhelmed her. And she the next thing she knew, she threw up. Right there, in the middle of the garage forecourt. All over the blond mechanic's brown DMs.

'Bloody hell, woman!'

When Taz managed to look up, the come-to-bed eyes had turned to tempered steel.

'Right,' he said from between clenched teeth. 'I'll go and fetch a bucket of disinfectant then.'

Isobel Norton was not overly impressed to see the BSA

Gold Star coasting to a halt outside her immaculate choc-olate-box cottage.

'Tasmin!' She came out onto the doorstep, as usual dressed as if she was going to church, even on a Saturday morning; her faded auburn hair so firmly set and sprayed in place that it would have taken a hurricane to dislodge it. 'Why aren't you in the car?'

'It's a long story.'

'You haven't crashed it and not told us?'

'Don't be silly, Mummy.'

'But what about my jacket?'

'See? It's absolutely fine, Mummy,' said Taz as she handed over the neatly-folded cellspare package.

'You're sure? Well, you'd better give it here, we don't want oil all over it, do we?'

Taz let her mother rabbit on. Since she had retired as receptionist at the local surgery, Isobel Norton was feeling the lack of somebody to boss around. Dad had to put up with it seven days a week; once every couple of weeks Taz could just about tolerate.

She ducked to avoid hitting her head on a hanging basket, and stepped inside the cottage. The smell of Sheen made her retch, though there was nothing left to bring up. She took long, slow, deep breaths. Her mother scruti-nised her with a critical eye.

'You're looking very pale. You should eat more spinach.'

'I'm fine!' Taz tried not to think about spinach.

'You're ill, aren't you? You've not got those terrible period pains again, have you? You really ought to see the doctor in case you're anaemic . . .'

Isobel's words struck an unwelcome chord. Taz's heart missed a beat, then started racing.

'No, no, Mummy, there's nothing wrong with my periods.' Except, whispered a little voice inside her head, you haven't had one since Gareth left. Five weeks ago. She tried hard to discipline her own overactive imagination. 'Guess what, Mummy, Diana Latchford's putting me in charge of next year's spring promotion. The American Week.'

'That's nice dear,' said Isobel vaguely. 'Have you got a boyfriend yet?'

'No, Mummy. Nobody special.'

'You mustn't neglect your social life, you know. Work isn't everything. And you don't want to get left on the shelf, not if you want to have a family.'

'No.' Taz swallowed hard. 'Why don't we go and see what this jacket looks like on you?'

Out of its cover it looked like a dog's breakfast, but even in her middle years Isobel Norton had a certain wild Irish chic that could carry off emerald-green velvet sprinkled with seed pearls and diamanté.

'What do you think?'

'It looks great. Very ... dramatic.'

'You're not just saying that? I don't want to let Daddy down, you know.'

Laughing, Taz promised her mother: 'You'll be the belle of the ball.'

The squeak of the front gate made Isobel jump like a startled faun. Hastily she wriggled out of the jacket and made a grab for a discarded Marks & Spencer carrier bag.

'Here, put it in here before he sees.'

'Mum – it's *your* money you're spending!'

'Do it, Tasmin. Please.'

By the time Bill Norton came into the living room, limping slightly in his favourite golfing trousers, Isobel was sitting on the sofa and Taz was in the kitchen, filling the kettle. She popped her head out of the kitchen.

'Hello Dad.'

'Hello sweetheart. The Gold Star's not quite given up the ghost yet then?'

'I'm looking after it for you, Dad, don't you worry.'

'Don't suppose I'll ride it again, not with my knee like this,' Bill grunted.

'Tasmin's got some news,' cut in Isobel. 'She's been given a special job to do at work, something about springs.'

'The spring promotion, Mummy. I've been put in charge of the American Event.'

'Good girl,' beamed Bill Norton. 'We'll soon have you

beating Branson at his own game. Wish I'd had the same chances when I was your age.'

'Yeah. I know.' There was an ache of uneasiness inside Taz. She covered it up by arranging teacups on a tray. Suddenly she didn't want her Dad to be so proud of her any more, to expect such great things of her. Suddenly she was afraid that she might let him down.

Isobel flounced off the sofa and fetched the M&S carrier bag. Bill glanced idly at it.

'That's the jacket you've been going on about then?'

'That's right, what do you think?' She slipped into it and paraded in front of her husband. 'Well?'

Bill Norton chuckled.

'If that's Marks & Spencer,' he said with a wink at his daughter, 'I'm a Dutchman's uncle.'

Chapter 3

Sunday dawned warm but overcast. Not the greatest of weather for Binnie and Jim's farewell barbecue, but it might improve by lunchtime.

Taz was still feeling rather overcast herself. She decided to perk herself up with a visit to the paper shop. She'd buy a couple of really juicy scandal-rags, next week's lottery ticket, and of course a respectable paper too, so she could pretend to read the business supplement.

She wriggled inside her tee-shirt as she walked. This new bra was a bit tight, she was sure it hadn't been when she bought it. And these jeans – they felt like they'd been sprayed on. Certainly she'd not been eating properly since Gareth left, and she knew she ought to take better care of herself. You couldn't live on crisps and takeaways, and expect to get away with it.

Maybe that was why her period was so late: eating the wrong things, late nights, stress . . . yeah, that would be it. That and the tummy bug.

She spent the rest of the morning lounging about on the bed, sipping mineral water and browsing through famous people's sex-lives. Glancing at the clock, she saw that it was nearly twelve. Time to get ready for Binnie's party.

Taz wandered into the bathroom, only to find Minky balancing on the toilet seat, head stuck halfway down the bowl.

'Minky! That's disgusting. Naughty girl.'

The cat slunk away, leaving a trail of wet footprints. Why did cats invariably prefer nasty smelly loo-water to

29

nice clean tap-water? Come to think of it, why did nice sensible girls like Taz Norton always prefer two-faced bastards like Gareth Scott?

Showered, waxed, deodorised and powdered, Taz felt ready to face the world. She took her three favourite party dresses out of the wardrobe, and rummaged in her underwear drawer for her Wonderbra. The phone rang.

'Taz? Hi, Binnie here. All set for the jamboree?'

'Of course. I've got a bottle of rosé, is that OK?'

'Fine, as long as you don't tempt me with it,' laughed Binnie.

'Why's that?'

'I'm on the wagon, Taz. A well-behaved mum-to-be.'

'Yeah.' Taz hesitated, desperate to broach the subject but not knowing how or where to begin. 'Binnie . . .'

'What?'

'Oh, nothing.' She cursed herself for bottling out for the umpteenth time. 'Do you want me to bring anything else?'

'Just yourself. What are you going to wear?'

'I'm not sure. The green, maybe.'

'How about that apricot slinky thing? You always look good in that.'

'Tarty, you mean!'

'I do not! But as it happens we've got one or two unattached hunks coming today. You might as well make the most of it.'

'Do you *ever* stop matchmaking?'

'Humour me. I'm an old married lady with varicose veins, it's one of the few pleasures I have left.' Binnie chuckled. 'Apart from wild sex orgies. Not.'

'I'll be there about one, OK?'

'Too right you will. And Taz. Take my word for it, the apricot thingy looks great.'

Taz put the phone down and surveyed the three outfits on the bed. There was the green silk two-piece, cool and ever so slightly sophisticated; the colour brought out the tiny flecks of green in her brown eyes, and the slim line of it was flattering. Then there was the white halter-neck mini, but maybe that was too Club 18-30, not quite the thing for a dull day in Battledown.

And finally, there was the apricot slinky thing. Taz held it up to the light and it shimmered expensively. It was a close-cut, low-necked sheath dress, quite short and designed to be worn with heaps of attitude. Binnie was right, it could look terrific and it fitted her like a second skin, but . . . Oh what the hell, she'd try it on.

The first problem came with the Wonderbra. Not to put too fine a point on it, she didn't seem to need it any more. Taz stood in front of the mirror and stared. How could somebody's chest swell up so much in such a short time?

The Wonderbra made her look so obscene, she took it off and flung it onto the bed. One of her usual stretchy bras would have to do instead. With a sense of foreboding, she wriggled into the apricot dress. It was a mistake, she knew that the minute she tried to do the zip up. She managed to get it as far as her shoulder-blades, but that was that. The bottom half of her was more or less the same shape and size as normal, but those breasts . . . It was unbelievable, like it had happened overnight. All of a sudden, small-breasted Taz Norton had the cleavage other women paid three thousand pounds for. And frankly she wasn't at all sure she wanted it.

Half an hour later, Taz emerged wearing the white halter-necked dress and feeling conspicuous. It fitted OK, but didn't leave a great deal to the imagination. Nor did it help to hear one of the cable TV men whistling 'June is busting out all over' as she got into the taxi.

'Taz! Taz darling! Come and meet the gang.'

Binnie swept across the lawn like a galleon in full sail, trailing several small children behind her. In the distance, Seuss & Goldman's china and glass department were trouncing sporting goods at rounders, despite the best efforts of Cara Mondini.

'Hi Binnie,' said Taz as they embraced.

'This is Amy, and Tom, and Emma – oh, and that's Kezia, with her finger up her nose. Don't do that, darling, it's not nice.'

'Whose . . .?'

'My sister Lana's, she's extremely fertile.'

'So I can see. So, are you and Jim planning your own football team too?'

'No fear. Contraception's a wonderful thing. Go and see Uncle David, kids, he's going to do a lovely Punch and Judy show.' She looked up. 'What happened to the slinky number?'

'It doesn't fit me any more. Round the bust.'

'Really? Well, I couldn't help noticing . . . I mean, you are a bit more . . .'

'Yes. Yes, I know. Can we talk about something else?'

Binnie's eyebrows shot up, but she said nothing.

Jim was over by the barbecue, showing off to an audience of friends and neighbours with a big pair of tongs and a striped apron. Shrieking kids were running about and crawling all over the burger buns, but he just beamed at them indulgently. He grinned at Taz and Binnie's approach, and wriggled his spectacles up his nose.

'Ankle-biters, don't you just love 'em?'

'Hi, Jim.' Taz held out the bottle of rosé. 'I thought this might help the party along.'

'More wine, fantastic! Put it with the rest and pour yourself a drink. Venison burgers'll be ready shortly.'

'I'll just stick with the drink, thanks.'

One of Binnie's friends sniggered, 'Very wise. Last time I came to one of Jim's barbies, the sausages were still frozen in the middle.'

'You OK, Taz?' hissed Binnie.

'I'm just not that hungry.'

'But you always eat like a horse!'

'Well, today I'm eating like a hamster.' Taz took a Twiglet and bit off the end, then poured herself a glass of fresh orange juice, tipped in a few cubes of ice and took a sip, grateful for the sensation of cold on her tongue. The weather was still overcast, but the air felt hot, clammy and heavy.

'We're moving on Friday,' said Binnie, out of the blue. Taz looked across at her. She seemed wistful, even sad. 'We've almost finished the packing. Jim can't wait.'

'You're not regretting it, are you?'

There was a long silence.

'Course not.'

'Are you absolutely sure?'

Binnie patted her bump.

'How could I possibly regret this? I'll miss you, though.'

'You too.'

All of a sudden, Binnie grabbed Taz's arm, almost making her spill her drink.

'Sorry, but you've *got* to look over there. Over by the tree. What do you reckon?'

Taz shaded her eyes and gazed across the landscaped vastness of Binnie and Jim's back lawn, towards a group of five or six people, chatting under the sycamores.

'The one in the white trousers?'

'No, not him, silly – the one next to him. The young, dark and utterly irresistible one, don't tell me you haven't noticed him.'

'He's OK I suppose.' Better than OK, even, thought Taz. Tall and tanned and a touch sporty, in that open-necked shirt and those well-cut grey shorts. A squash player, maybe. 'Nice legs.'

'His name's Tony. Come on, I'm going to introduce you.'

It was no use protesting. Binnie had a firm grip on Taz's arm, and for a heavily pregnant woman she had a surprising turn of speed.

'Hi, everyone, this is Taz. Taz, this is Avril, Heather, Peter, Mike ... and Tony. Tony's an architect in Oxford. Quite the rising star.'

The minute Tony switched on his electric smile, Taz knew she hated him. He was just like Gareth, only younger. Powerful, ambitious, sex-on-a-stick and utterly indifferent to anything beyond his own immediate appetites.

'Pleased to meet you,' she lied politely. Tony took her hand, held it lingeringly, and for one horrible moment Taz thought he was actually going to kiss it.

'Lovely to meet you too.' He sounded like he meant it, even. The rat.

33

'Is this the Taz you've been telling us about?' asked Heather. From the look of pure jealousy in her grey eyes, it was obvious she'd already established squatter's rights on Tony. 'The one who works in a shop?'

'Taz is a manager at Seuss & Goldman,' said Binnie grandly.

'Only a departmental manager,' Taz pointed out hastily.

'She's recently been promoted. In fact Taz is really going places, aren't you Taz?'

'I'm sure she is,' purred Tony. He patted Taz's hand. This time she snatched it away. 'You're obviously a very talented young woman, Taz, you shouldn't hide your light under a bushel.'

Heather's eyes narrowed to bitchy slits. They locked onto Taz's breasts, straining at the white halter-neck dress that had fitted so modestly such a short time ago. Then they flicked back to Tony, whose gaze was fixed there too.

'I wouldn't have thought she was the sort to hide anything,' Heather sniffed meaningfully. 'She's got everything up front.'

'I beg your pardon?' said Taz, her cheeks crimson.

'Button it, Heather,' snapped Tony.

'Why the hell should I?'

'Because you're embarrassing me – and our friends.'

'And what do you think you're doing to me? God, Tony, you may be a fool for any bimbo with big tits, but this is the last time you're making a fool out of me!'

Taz stared back in horror. Normally she would have fired back some scathing riposte, but somehow Heather's nastiness had wormed its way into a part of her that was tender and sore and afraid.

'Can I get you another drink, Heather?' suggested Binnie soothingly.

'Excuse me,' said Taz faintly, blinking back tears. 'I just . . . I just need to . . .'

And with eyes stinging she turned tail and fled back to the house, ignoring the startled looks of middle-class bores with ketchup round their mouths.

The inside of Binnie's house came as quite a shock. It was

34

empty and echoing. Boxes lay all over the bare wooden floors, some sealed up and labelled 'Dungarrow, via Inverness', others standing open with little packages of crumpled newspaper lying alongside. Rolled-up carpets leaned against the walls.

Taz closed the French doors behind her and stood for a few moments in the living room, remembering last Christmas, when Jim had perched on the lid of the grand piano and sung the 'The Good Ship Venus' in his Father Christmas boxer shorts. After sinking a whole bottle of cherry brandy, Binnie had declared that life was for drinking, shagging and spending money. Not necessarily in that order.

Things had changed since then. Taz's hand strayed to her flat, ordinary, innocent-looking stomach. Maybe things were going to change a lot more before they all got much older.

Moments later Taz turned to see Binnie, red in the face and sweating in her pink maternity smock.

'Kitchen. Now.'

'Why?'

Binnie's steel grip came down on Taz's shoulder and steered her into the kitchen. She closed the door and leaned back against it.

'Sit.'

Like a puppy in a Barbara Woodhouse video, Taz sat, plonking her bottom on one of Binnie's antique Windsor chairs.

'What's got into you, Taz?'

'Nothing. I told you.' Taz drummed her fingers on the table.

'Come off it. You don't burst into tears for nothing. Normally you'd make mincemeat of a thick bitch like Heather.'

'You might have told me she was Tony's girlfriend.'

'I had no idea. He only split up with Avril a month ago.' Binnie took a carton of orange juice out of the fridge, fetched two glasses and pulled up a chair. 'Here. Have a drink. It's not beer but you can cry into it if you like.'

Taz managed a laugh and a sniff. She searched for a tissue in her handbag but she'd forgotten to bring one.

'I'm not crying.'

'You were though. Your eyes are all puffy. Look, tell Auntie Binnie what's up and we'll sort it out together.' She tore a sheet off a roll of kitchen towel. 'Here, blow into this, it's horrible having snot dripping out of your nose.'

Taz blew her nose and wiped it.

'I guess I'm just not feeling at my best just now.'

'Man trouble?'

She shook her head.

'Then what exactly?'

'I'm . . . not feeling very well. That's all.'

Amazement registered on Binnie's apple-cheeked face.

'But Taz, you *never* let anything get you down! Not ever. Not even on that management course, when you had viral pneumonia!'

'Well I'm feeling ill now. OK?'

'So what's wrong?'

'Nothing much. A tummy bug or something. It'll pass.'

Binnie gave her a long, hard look.

'Forgive me for calling you a liar, Taz, but stop bullshitting me, will you? And get a move on, I'm moving to Scotland next week.'

'If I tell you . . .' she began.

'If you tell me, I'll get a megaphone and broadcast it to the whole of Battledown, what do *you* think?' Binnie put her arm round Taz's shoulders. 'Don't you trust me?'

'Yes, but . . .' Taz trembled, it was like being a kid again. 'For God's sake don't breathe a word, Binnie, promise me you won't.'

'Not a word. I promise.'

'Oh Binnie.' Before she'd even got the words out, Taz dissolved into sobs. Sobs she'd been suppressing for too long, the way she'd been blanking the truth out of her mind. 'Binnie, I think I'm pregnant.'

Binnie was silent for a few seconds. Taz tried to stop crying, but now the truth was out it was as if her body had to get rid of its tension too.

'Oh Taz,' sighed Binnie, reaching for the rest of the kitchen roll, 'I was afraid you were going to say that.'

'You knew?'

'Not knew, no. But I was beginning to wonder. I've been through it all, you see, I know what it's like.' She considered for a moment. 'Let's not jump to conclusions, though. What makes you think you're pregnant?'

'I'm a fortnight overdue.'

'OK.'

'I keep feeling sick.'

'Uh-huh.'

'And throwing up.'

'In the mornings?'

'And later, sometimes.'

'And what else?'

Taz looked down at her breasts. They seemed monstrously large, she could almost imagine they were swelling up even as she looked at them.

'These. They're turning into Zeppelins.'

'Fair enough. But that doesn't prove anything, does it?'

'It does to me.'

'Well there's only one way to be sure.'

'I can't go to see the doctor, I can't!'

'All right, two ways. You'll have to do a home pregnancy test. Come on.' Binnie hauled Taz to her feet.

'Come on where?'

'We're going to get you a pregnancy testing kit.'

'But it's Sunday! And what about the barbecue?'

'Jim'll keep things going till we get back, he probably won't even notice we've gone.'

'Where are we going?' demanded Taz as Binnie's battered Volvo hurtled through the satanic intricacies of the Cheltenham one-way system.

'The out-of-town supermarket. They've got an in-store pharmacy.' Binnie swung round the bend and headed out of town. 'But it shuts at four, so I'll have to put my foot down.'

'Why can't I just wait till tomorrow and get one from Boots?'

'Because you won't.' Binnie threw a stern look at Taz. 'I know you. You think if you ignore something it'll go away.'

The supermarket car park was a congested nightmare. Binnie finally found a parking space and they began walking towards the automatic doors.

'Do we have to?'

'Yes. You'll thank me for this one day.'

The in-store pharmacy was located just behind the furthermost checkout, beyond the bubble baths and face creams. A white-coated youth with a face like rhubarb crumble was standing behind the counter, fiddling with the condom display.

'Go on then,' said Binnie brightly, pushing Taz forward.

'I can't! Look at him – he's about sixteen!'

Binnie gazed heavenward and muttered a prayer for strength.

'You're a departmental manager, Taz Norton, not Mavis flipping Riley.'

'I know, but couldn't you . . . please?'

'Oh all right then. If I must.'

Binnie marched up to the counter. The spotty dispenser finished arranging his condoms and started fiddling with his greasy hair.

'Can I help you, madam?'

'Yes.' Binnie's gargantuan bump collided with the edge of the counter. 'I want a pregnancy testing kit.'

The youth blinked, then eased his collar away from his throat. His eyes travelled down to Binnie's mountainous stomach.

'Haven't you left it a bit late?'

Five minutes later Taz and Binnie were back on the road, with Taz clutching the tiny parcel.

'I think I'm going to be sick.'

'No you're not. Think beautiful thoughts.'

'All I can think are pregnant ones. And they're not beautiful at all.'

'You're probably not pregnant anyway.' Binnie laughed. 'First time I thought I was expecting, I rushed out and bought a kit, and before I'd even unwrapped the blessed thing, my period started. What a waste of eight pounds ninety-nine.'

The Volvo sped towards Cow Lane, drawing up just short of the driveway to Shepcote House. Minky was sitting in the front window of Taz's flat, trying to catch a butterfly through the glass.

'I'll have to drop you here, what with that hole in the drive.'

'Can't you come in for a few minutes?'

'I'd better get back. Even Jim may have noticed I'm not there by now.'

Taz stepped out onto the pavement, the box in her hand. Roland and Simon stopped playing frisbee on the front lawn and waved at her. She was sure they could tell just from the look on her face what she had in that box. She hesitated.

'See you before you go?'

'Of course.'

'Binnie . . .'

'What now?'

'Thanks.' Taz's throat felt abominally dry as she spoke.

'Don't thank me. Just do that test, first thing tomorrow morning. Do you promise?'

'I promise.'

'See you soon then, Taz. Oh, and Taz? Don't think I didn't see you crossing your fingers behind your back.'

The following morning, Minky was off her food and so was Taz. At six thirty, Taz was on her knees in the bathroom, gazing gloomily down into the depths of the lavatory bowl, wondering if this nightmare was ever going to end.

She wiped her mouth and got up. There was no avoiding the small blue box on the shelf over the sink. PREGSURE: when you need to know TODAY.

Did she need to know – today or any other day? Was ignorance really bliss? She hesitated, then remembered her promise to Binnie and unwrapped the box. She hardly needed to read the instructions, the whole thing was a lot simpler than the last time she'd had to use one of these things. That had been when she was seventeen, her panic the result of a fumbled sexual encounter at a friend's party. Now it was so darned easy.

Almost as easy as getting yourself pregnant. Pee onto a stick thing and wait a couple of minutes to see if it changed colour.

She went into the kitchen and filled the kettle, but the water was still tinged brown with sediment and in any case, she'd lost her taste for tea. The seconds ticked by, then the minutes. It was time, but her feet were rooted to the spot. Minky jumped up on the work surface.

'Prrrup.'

'Bad pussy, get down.' But her heart wasn't in it. She stroked Minky's velvety back, and it arched in simple pleasure, the tail leaping to attention. Why couldn't she be a cat too?

Steeling herself, Taz turned and walked into the bathroom, clicking the light on. She didn't really need to look; she already knew that the stick thing had changed colour, that sunshine yellow had become gothic black, and so had her entire life.

Pregnant.

Her heart raced. She felt dizzy, sick, tearful, afraid. And ashamed of her own stupidity for allowing this to happen to her. Oh God no. She stared at the tiny stick in her hand, remembering the words from the instruction leaflet: 'There are very few false positives.' And then Diana Latchford's voice, sterner still: 'Prove to me that you deserve your next promotion.'

For several minutes, Taz sat in the living room and stared at the telephone. By now it was past eight o'clock and if she didn't get a move on she was going to be late for work. But somehow that seemed laughably insignificant right now.

Her fingers grabbed hold of the receiver. Binnie, she had to phone Binnie, she would know what to do. But no. Binnie had already done enough.

Taz Norton, she told herself, you've let other people run your life for you for far too long. Now it's time to get a grip on yourself.

She dialled the number of the surgery. After an interminable number of rings, a woman's voice answered, coolly
distant.

'Surgery, can I help you?'

'I need to see a doctor.'

Pause. The sound of turning pages.

'Thursday at half-past five, with Doctor Aziz.'

'No, you don't understand,' said Taz, this time with
more insistence. 'I need to see a doctor. Today.'

Chapter 4

Four forty-five? How on earth was she going to wait until then?

Taz could still hear the doctor's receptionist telling her how incredibly lucky she was to get an appointment at all at such short notice. But four forty-five, that was over eight hours away! Taz forced herself to take long, deep breaths. All she had to do was get through this one ordinary Monday, and by a quarter to five everything would be sorted out. Like it had never happened.

So just keep your head, Taz, she told herself as she smoothed the wrinkles from her tights and walked out onto the sales floor; focus on what you have to do, and everything'll be just fine. Gareth's history; you're far too smart to let him mess up your life.

'Morning, Miss Norton.'

Leroy McIntosh, immaculate as always, stepped out from behind the cash desk. It never failed to amaze Taz how her formalwear specialist managed to wear the S&G regulation charcoal grey suit and white shirt like it was Yves St Laurent. Discreet enamelled cufflinks added a touch of colour to his crisp shirt-cuffs, dazzling white against the rich chocolate brown of his skin. Twenty-four but agelessly stylish, he looked every bit as cool, keen and competent as Taz knew him to be.

'Morning Leroy. Marion,' she added with emphasis, trying to provoke some kind of positive response.

But the grey-cardiganed figure went on impatiently rearranging a rackful of polo shirts. There were times

42

when Taz found Marion's growing uncooperativeness not so much infuriating as unnerving.

'I don't know why you don't lay down the law to visual display, they're not doing their job properly,' muttered Marion. Leroy raised one perfectly-groomed eyebrow, but Taz avoided his gaze.

'If you have any constructive comments I'll be happy to take note of them.' The last thing she wanted today was a big confrontation, but Marion Grey had a special talent for getting up her nose. 'You know how much I value staff input.'

Except from you Marion, she thought, and wondered if her words had sounded as hollow as they felt. She glanced at her watch; eight twenty-five. 'Right. Flash meeting with *everyone* in five minutes, I want to go over last week's sales figures.'

By eight thirty a small crowd had gathered by the central cash desk in men's formalwear. Having so many part-timers made it difficult to get to know everyone individually, and keeping an eye on both Kate and Justin, Taz's newly-promoted assistant departmental sales manager, made life even more hectic than usual; so these daily flash meetings gave her a chance to pounce on any small problems before they turned into major crises.

'OK, is everyone here? Justin's coming in late today, he's at the dentist. Where's Kate?'

'Personnel sent down for her', said one of the part-timers. 'Something about a mistake in her tax code.'

'Fair enough, I'll speak to her later.' And to personnel for that matter. It was naughty of them, they knew how important flash meetings were. 'Now, sales figures. The good news is, last week we met our sales target . . .'

'Thought so,' said Leroy with a sideways look at Marion – who made a point of loathing everything he liked, on principle. 'I knew those coloured formal shirts would go down well. Dressing down for Fridays is the biggest new style trend since picture ties.' Once Leroy got going there was no stopping him. Taz nipped him in the bud with a hard stare.

'Like I said, we met our target, but only just.'

'Which is a brilliant compared to this time last year,' pointed out Leroy, like Marion a survivor from the old regime. 'We never had a bonus once in eighteen months.'

'Maybe so. But doing OK isn't good enough – I've a lot of faith in you as a sales team, and I'm confident we can do much better.'

'But how?' protested Pauline, thirtysomething mum of two school-age boys, and a dedicated clockwatcher who did twenty-one hours a week and not a minute longer.

'By working harder.' Taz ignored the muted groans. 'Working together. Through more skilful merchandising. Overall we're still underperforming in formalwear, Leroy, and as product specialist I expect you to take a special interest in promoting sales. So where are we going wrong?'

'You can't sell people what they don't want,' protested Leroy, on the defensive now. Some of these 'English classics' lines are old hat. What about getting in more Versace – or Armani?'

'Traditional quality tailoring is what our older gentlemen demand,' snapped Marion.

'But it's the younger customers we should be targeting, Marion,' cut in Pauline, shaking her blonde bob in disbelief. 'They're the ones with the money.'

'And the retired colonels won't be around for ever,' pointed out Leroy. 'Nor will S&G, if we don't move with the times.'

'We have to look to the future, that's true,' nodded Taz. 'And the new casualwear is selling well. But we can't neglect our more traditional customers either.'

'We're already doing precisely that,' sniffed Marion. 'When I started at Seuss & Goldman it was one of the few really first-class department stores outside London . . .'

'And it still is,' stressed Taz patiently. 'But we have to be prepared to try new things. So if you have any bright ideas I want to know. I mean that,' she added. 'This is a team, not a one-woman show.'

'In the meantime, I want the autumn-weight suits moved to the front of the sales floor, just behind the sale racks. Leroy, Pauline, you take charge of that. Marion, reposition the shoes and sort out some summery accessories to brighten up the display. Meanwhile, I'll ask Justin to call S&G Edinburgh, and find out how they're displaying "English classics" there – they're outselling everything else.'

'What about the "Summer Holiday" promotion?' Pauline nodded towards the the customer lifts at the far side of the sales floor. Crammed into a gloomy corner, just out of sight, was an elaborate mock-up of a beach scene, complete with several hundredweight of sand, dummies in designer swimwear and Ray-Bans, two sunloungers and a red jet-ski.

'We'll be winding it up this week – visual merchandising are coming to dismantle it on Friday, ready for the Autumn Event.'

'Which means we need to be ready with the sweaters and the Timberland boots?'

'Correct. In fact, there should be a delivery of winter-weight Viyella shirts tomorrow morning, so Pauline, I want you to check those into the stock room as soon as they arrive from goods receiving. Right. Any more questions?'

No one replied. Taz could feel the restlessness in them, their eyes flicking towards the clock on the wall, their feet shuffling on the monogrammed carpet. Soon it would be nine fifteen and the doors would open on another day. A run-of-the-mill Monday for everyone else in the world, or that was how it seemed to Taz. But a day that had the power to change her life for ever – if she let it.

'Fine, that's all then.' Taz took a deep breath. 'Oh – just one thing. Could you stay behind for a moment, Marion? I'd like a word.'

Marion opened her mouth as if to protest, then shut it again, her thin lips pressed very tightly together. Everything about her body language expressed hostility.

'Now then Marion, what's this all about? You seem very unhappy in your work. I can't just let that pass. I want to help.'

Marion's watery grey eyes grew narrow with suspicion. But she couldn't resist rising to the bait.

'I *love* my work, I take a real pride in it. It's my whole life. You know that.'

'So why the long face?' Taz tried hard to sound sympathetic. It wasn't easy. 'Something must be wrong. It matters if my staff are miserable in their work. Maybe we should think about a transfer . . .'

'But I've been in menswear for twenty years!' And I should be assistant departmental manager, said the reproachful eyes; not some jumped-up kid like Justin who thinks he knows everything because he's got an A level. 'It's not the work.'

'What then?'

'If you must know, I don't like the way things are going. Seuss & Goldman isn't the store it used to be . . . it's . . .'

'Changing?'

'Cheap. That's what it is. All this shoddy ready-to-wear rubbish, it's cheapening the image of the store.'

'It's making money, Marion. And that's what selling is all about. It's your job – and mine. We should be working together on this.'

'Are you saying I don't know how to do my job? Is that what you're saying?' retorted Martin, bristling.

'No, Marion, I'm not. You're an efficient sales consultant and we all value your experience. But you must appreciate that if you're unhappy that's going to come across in your work. Customers notice . . .'

'I see.' Marion drew herself up, very stiff and unbending. 'Well I'm sure I've never neglected my customers in any way, Miss Norton.'

Taz knew she ought to make time for a longer interview, somewhere private and more relaxed, where she could winkle the truth out of her bit by bit. But Marion Grey wasn't the only person who mattered around here – and she certainly wasn't the only one with problems.

'Look, Marion, we'll talk about this properly when we both have more time. Think about what I've said. If you have a problem, any problem, you can come to me and it won't go any further. Right now I've got to ring central purchasing about those green polo-neck sweaters.'

'Like I said. Shoddy,' said Marion, who had naturally

been the one to notice that the green polos all had one arm longer than the other.

'I'm going into the office to make that call. Send Justin to me when he gets here, would you? I need him to deputise for me at the management meeting this afternoon.'

At this, Marion's ears pricked up.

'But you *never* miss the management meeting.'

'Not as a rule, no. But today I have another . . . commitment.' Before she'd thought about what she was saying, Taz had added, 'A medical appointment.'

'Really?' Marion was hanging on every word now. 'I've noticed you've been looking tired lately. And there was that tummy upset you had last week. Nothing *serious*, I hope?'

Butterflies gambolled in the pit of Taz's empty stomach. Just how much more had people noticed? And how much had they guessed? Nothing, she told herself, you're just being paranoid. She offered Marion what she hoped was a relaxed smile.

'Nothing to worry about,' she replied, avoiding Marion's inquisitive gaze by giving the central display stand a critical once-over. 'For heaven's sake get that tidied up before Mrs Latchford comes round.'

It was almost four o'clock before Taz was able to hand over her paperwork to Justin and go to fetch her coat.

If she hadn't felt so relieved to be escaping, she'd have been overwhelmed with guilt. Missing one of the weekly management meetings unless you were at death's door was very much frowned upon, and this was the first time since she'd joined Seuss & Goldman that she'd failed to do what was expected of her. Taz's dedication to her career had always verged on the fanatical.

But there were some things that couldn't wait. Taz picked up her car keys and thrust them into her pocket, walking quickly down the back stairs to the security desk, an island of dented Victorian mahogany rising out of a sea of stained green carpet. This was something that customers never saw – the unglamorous enclave between the rubbish compactor and the basement stairs.

'Playing hookey, Miss N?' enquired the security guard archly as she signed out and deposited her name badge in its designated pigeon-hole.

'Fraid not Brian, just a meeting I have to go to.' She tossed the pen onto the desk. 'See you tomorrow.'

She stepped out of the artificial twilight into the afternoon sunshine. For the first time all day, she was alone with her thoughts – not the company's thoughts, not Marion's moans or Leroy's frustrations. Her heart pounded as she walked briskly towards the staff car park.

Just as she was opening the driver's door her pager went off, bleeping suddenly and insistently as it hung from her skirt belt. Damn and double blast. Her reflexes screamed at her to run straight back to the security lodge, find out what the crisis was and sort it out. That was what Taz would do – at any other time. After a moment's hesitation, she did the unthinkable.

She switched her pager off.

I'm pregnant, doctor, it was an accident, I want a termination.' For the umpteenth time that day Taz rehearsed what she was going to say, but no matter how she phrased them, the words sounded cold and clinical. She steered out of the car park, into the one-way system. Only half an hour to get to the surgery, better get a move on.

'I can't have this baby, it would ruin my career.' Was she really this selfish? Come on, Taz, she told herself, this has nothing to do with selfishness and everything to do with being sensible, practical, grown-up. You're meant to be a manager, not a mother. At least, not yet. What would Diana Latchford do in this situation? Silly question. Diana Latchford would never let this happen to her in the first place.

She stopped at a pelican crossing, watching the tide of humanity sweep across the road as she waited for the lights to change. 'I'm sorry, doctor, but I've made up my mind. I'm just not ready for this. I *have* to have the pregnancy terminated.' That was all there was to it.

But like little black demons doubts whispered treason inside her head. All the way up the London Road towards Charlton Kings, she was trying desperately not to listen.

You'll regret it.

No I won't.

It's Gareth's baby too, don't you think you ought to tell him?

It's not a baby, it's an accident.

Are you sure you know what you're doing? You can't change your mind later.

Shut up, shut up, SHUT UP!

Arriving five minutes early at the surgery, Taz was in such a state that she stalled the car right in the middle of the driveway. By the time she'd calmed herself down and found reception, it was bang on her appointment time. An Irish girl with a telephone receiver cradled under her chin checked her in.

'Name?' Then into the receiver, 'Was that Erythromycin or Indomethacin, Mrs Bailey? Name?' she repeated, slightly louder.

'Oh – Tasmin Norton.'

'I know, Mrs Bailey, but if the doctor says . . .' The green eyes flicked up again. 'All right Miss Norton, take a seat in the waiting room.'

Taz pushed open the swing door and stepped straight into Hell – or at least, that particular sub-department of Hell reserved for small children and their harassed mothers.

Weren't doctors' surgeries supposed to be oases of tranquility? Not this one, obviously. Voices snapped, snarled, giggled, squealed, shouted, cajoled and stage-whispered. Toy trucks crashed into each other. A plastic trumpet squeaked its one, ear-splitting note again and again and again.

'Sophie, put that down. I won't tell you again.' Fingers prised a copy of *Country Living* from between small, determined teeth. 'Now spit it out. *All* of it.'

A tired-faced, plumply pregnant brunette in faded denim dungarees made a lunge for a laughing baby who was crawling determinedly towards Taz's ankles.

'Craig, don't you dare!' She smiled apologetically at Taz. 'Sorry love, he's got a thing about red shoes, don't know where he gets it from.'

Taz managed a faint smile, pushed aside a plastic Power Ranger and sat down. Babies. Babies everywhere, you couldn't move for them. Ones with teeth and ones with pink slobbery gums, ones that roared and ones that hiccupped . . .

'Have you been waiting long?' Taz asked the young mum as she gathered up her smaller baby and grabbed the end of Craig's Peter Rabbit reins.

'Oh no, only about three quarters of an hour. It's usually a lot busier than this.'

Taz's heart sank a little deeper. Craig crawled to a protesting halt and sat up on his fat little bottom. His blue eyes stared up, round and unblinking, into Taz's face, as if to say, 'How could anybody not want me? How could anybody not want their own gorgeous, cuddly, innocent little angel?' Then he sneezed, and a thin trail of green snot trickled down over his upper lip.

'Oh dear, that didn't go on your shoes did it? He's a bit snuffly today.' Craig's face disappeared behind a large paper tissue.

Taz picked up a magazine but hardly knew what she was staring blankly at. Her aching head was filled with the sound of children giggling, squealing, shrieking and sobbing, and above the cacophony her own voice, repeating over and over again, 'I've made up my mind, doctor, I want a termination.' I do. I do. I do!

Slowly her eyes drifted up the wall to a poster. A baby-food poster. Toothless gums parted in an ecstatic smile as a spoonful of mashed banana loomed into view. Next to it, a handwritten notice proclaimed: 'Mums! Don't forget baby's Hib vaccination.'

Half-hypnotised, Taz started as a hand touched her lightly on the arm. An old dear in a winked knowingly at her.

'Your first time is it? The minute I saw you I thought, it's her first time, she looks like a scared rabbit.'

'Sorry, I'm not with you.'

'The mum-and-baby clinic. Your first, is it? Not to worry, you'll be fine. I've got three you know, two boys and a girl.'

'Actually, I'm not . . .' began Taz, but the old lady was too busy rhapsodising to notice.

'Boys are easier of course, but every mum wants a little girl to dress up, doesn't she? What are you hoping for? You and your husband must be so pleased . . .'

A door opened at the far side of the waiting room and a male voice called out, 'Tasmin Norton?'

'Here.' She stood up and took a shaky step forward. Legs turning to jelly, she followed the doctor into his office and closed the door behind her.

'Hi, I'm Dr Flowers. Take a seat.' He looked a bit like a baby himself, thought Taz. Fat, pink and almost bald, except for a halo of ginger fuzz that extended from ear to ear round the back of his head.

'Thank you.'

For some unaccountable reason Taz was shaking all over as she flopped down onto the orange plastic chair. The gonk on the doctor's desk peered accusingly at her over the top of a half-finished mug of coffee. A bluebottle buzzed idly round her head, but she couldn't summon up the energy to swat it. Quite suddenly, she felt completely drained.

'Now, what can I do for you? I understood from my receptionist that it was urgent?' Dr Flowers had his prescribing pen at the ready, hovering eagerly over the pad.

'I . . .' began Taz, but the words just dried up in her throat. This was madness. She'd been over this a hundred times in her head, she knew exactly what to say.

'It's OK. Take your time.' The doctor laid his pen on the desk top, sat back and folded his hands. His voice was so calm, so kind, so understanding that it struck an unexpected chord in Taz, releasing a flood of pent-up tears. 'It's all right, have a tissue.' He handed her the box and she seized a handful. 'Whatever it is you won't shock me.'

'Doctor I . . . I'm having a baby,' Taz managed to blurt

51

out through halting sobs. 'And I . . . I just don't know what to do for the best.'

Afterwards, sitting in her car in the car park, Taz stared disbelievingly at the scrap of paper in her hand: the telephone number of Steffi Parkes, the 'absolutely super' lady who ran local childbirth classes for the Mother and Child Trust.

Childbirth classes? Ante-natal checks? Urine samples and blood tests? How on earth had she come to this crazy change of heart?

She sat back in the driving seat, taking long, deep gulps of air. So. According to Dr Flowers she was roughly eight weeks pregnant, which meant that she must have conceived three days before Gareth left her for Melanie. Well. Quite some leaving present. She pictured the last time they'd made love. How Gareth had cradled her in his arms as they lay in her bed, and kissed her on the nose and told her she really must learn to take life less seriously . . .

Didn't she have every reason to hate this tiny, embryonic life growing so silently inside her? 'Your baby's about an inch long,' that's what Dr Flowers had said. *My baby*! A peculiar shiver of exhilaration ran up and down her spine, replaced a moment later by anger, inextricably mixed up with fear.

'I suppose you think you've won, do you?' she murmured as her eyes drifted momentarily down to her mysteriously flat stomach. 'Well listen, little baby.' You needn't think I'm going to love you, because I'm not.

'I'm *not*.'

Being brave was all very well in the doctor's surgery. Facing up to the world took a lot more guts. But Taz knew sooner or later she was going to have to tell people she was pregnant, before they worked it out for themselves. But not yet. She wasn't ready yet.

The following morning, Taz got up two hours early, spent half an hour in the bath, and forced herself to keep down a whole two rounds of dry toast. If she was going

52

to fight the world and win, she wasn't going to do it on an empty stomach.

Sunlight poured in through the windows as Taz went back into the bedroom. Rising up above the cluster of houses, Ham Hill glowed in the summer sunshine, a stone-built cottage golden on the skyline and woolly sheep dotted about the fields. There were, as Binnie often said, a lot worse places you could live.

Minky sat on the end of the bed and washed her whiskers as Taz selected something special to wear, something that would make her feel good, confident, in control. What about the brown dress and jacket? She turned to Minky for a verdict. Minky turned her back and rolled over.

'Wah.'

OK, so not the brown. It would have to be the grey then; very S&G, a tiny bit severe, but she could jazz it up with that pink sleeveless top and it would look just fine.

Taz arrived at work three quarters of an hour early, to do some action planning before everyone else arrived. But as she walked through administration and into men-swear, she realised that she wasn't alone after all. Diana Latchford was standing in the middle of leisurewear, deep in conversation with Patros Nikephoros, the visual mer-chandising manager. Neither of them looked particularly happy.

'Ah. Tasmin,' said Diana meaningfully. The way Patros was looking at her over the top of his trendy oval spec-tacles reminded her of a judge pronouncing sentence. 'I'm glad you're here early.'

'I thought I'd try and get some preparation done before the hurly-burly starts. Is something wrong?'

Patros let out a dry laugh and scratched his dark head with the end of his pencil. Everything about Patros was dry: his politics, his wit, his sarcasm.

'If you'd been here yesterday afternoon you'd know that. But I understand you were too busy to grace us with your presence.'

'I was . . . I had an appointment.'

'Is your pager working properly? We tried bleeping you.'

53

'I'm sorry, I must have accidentally switched it off. But I asked Justin to stand in for me. Has something happened?'

'If you take a look at the Summer Holiday display,' said Patros, 'you may notice something different about it.'

'Someone,' added Diana Latchford, 'has stolen the jet-ski.'

'The *jet-ski*?'

'Security saw them on CCTV. In fact, half the store saw them carrying the jet-ski into the lift. Seems everyone thought they were workmen employed by S&G – nobody thought to stop them and ask.'

Oh my God, thought Taz. The one time I'm not where I should be, look what happens . . .

'But it was chained down.'

'Haven't you ever heard of bolt-cutters?' sighed Patros.

'And what about the police?'

'Notified, of course,' said Patros. 'I expect they'll go through the motions when they stop laughing.'

'But we're insured – aren't we?'

'Thankfully, yes,' nodded Diana. 'But this is extremely embarrassing for the store – we had the jet-ski on free loan from Hammerhead Sports, and it was due for return on Friday.'

'Head office are not going to be pleased,' observed Patros. 'Particularly if this gets into the local paper. Someone should have been supervising that display.'

'Oh come on,' protested Taz. 'Be reasonable. If you put a five-grand jet-ski in a cramped corner by the lifts, where nobody can see it from the main sales floor, what do you expect?'

'I expect you to do your job,' sneered Patros with a flick of his wavy black hair.

'And you're saying I'm not?'

'If you're not here to keep an eye on your staff . . .'

'Displays are *your* responsibility, Patros, not mine. My responsibility is to sell clothes and make money for this store.'

'Why don't you wait for me in my office, Patros? We'll check the paperwork again over a cup of coffee. I just want a quick word with Miss Norton,' Diana said tactfully.

'If I were you, I'd have several.'

Taz watched Patros stalk off towards the stairs in a cloud of Armani cologne. Damn, damn, damn.

'I'm sorry about the jet-ski,' Taz said quietly. 'I would have been here yesterday afternoon . . . but believe me, it was unavoidable. I had to see the doctor.'

'It's not like you to miss a management meeting.'

The pause which followed was far more meaningful than the words. Taz read Diana's expression without difficulty. It said: 'You don't have to tell me if you don't want to, but it might be better to tell me than to let somebody else find out.'

'Whatever you tell me won't go any further, I hope you can trust my integrity.'

'Yes, of course, it's just . . .' She glanced back over her shoulder.

'Don't worry. There's no one else around.'

Taz could hear the blood pounding in her ears. Everything around her seemed slightly odd and not entirely real; an exact copy of reality.

'I'm pregnant.' The words left her in a rush of breath that left her gasping and dizzy.

'Ah.' Was that a flicker of disappointment on Diana's face, or was Taz imagining it? The faulty ceiling fan above her head cast shifting shadows on the general manager's face, making it difficult to focus on. The blades turned round and round: drone, stutter; drone, stutter. 'Exactly how pregnant?'

'Eight weeks. Or so.' Actually eight weeks, three days and fourteen hours, thought Taz, silently cursing Gareth's name to eternal and excruciating damnation.

'Ah.'

They both knew the significance of what Taz had just said. Another thirty-two weeks took you up to the end of March. Only a week before the start of the spring sale, and just three weeks after the opening of the new American branch of S&G.

'Oh Taz,' sighed Diana, very quietly and very wearily. It was the first time she'd ever called her Taz, not Tasmin or Ms Norton. 'Taz, you really believe in doing things the hard way, don't you?'

'It was a mistake. A really stupid one.'

'And the father?'

'We're not together any more. And no, I'm not going to tell him.'

'But you're keeping the baby?'

'It's not what I intended, but . . .' Taz nodded.

She waited for the explosion, but it didn't come. Diana stroked back her stylish hair with a hand which sported five perfectly varnished ovals.

'And what about the spring promotion? The American Event? Still think you can cope?'

To her surprise, Taz heard herself reply: 'I know I can. If you'll let me.'

'Why shouldn't I? OK, so you're pregnant, it's not a hanging offence. And of course, officially I don't even have to know – you're not obliged to tell me until a few weeks before you want to take maternity leave.' She paused. 'You're coming back of course? After the birth?'

'There's no way I could give up my career! Not for anyone.'

Diana's lips twitched as though they were about to smile, then thought better of it. 'You realise I won't be making any concessions?'

'I wouldn't want you to.'

'Fair enough. As long as we understand each other. Then I'll look forward to receiving your action plan for the American Event. Oh, and Taz?'

'Yes, Mrs Latchford?'

'Make damn sure you get all the maternity benefits you're entitled to.'

Over the next week or so, Taz began to get used to the idea of being pregnant. She even got round to booking herself onto some ante-natal classes. If she was going to have a baby, she was going to do it properly, the way she'd always done everything.

But there was one thing she hadn't done. Perhaps the hardest thing of all: telling her mum and dad. She knew it was absurd, knew she should have told them long ago; but every time she reached for the phone she thought of something much more important that needed doing right away. She'd cleaned the oven twice already – and it wasn't even dirty in the first place.

On her next day off she finally plucked up the courage to do it. As she dialled the number she'd almost convinced herself that it would be all right after all, that she'd been worrying about nothing. If she could get used to the idea of motherhood, then Mum and Dad could get used to it. too. They'd often talked about how they'd love to have grandchildren. They'd just be having them a bit earlier than they expected.

'Yes?' said her father's voice.

'Daddy? It's Tasmin.'

'Hello, sweetheart. When are you coming round to see us, it's been ages.'

'Soon, Daddy.'

'So, what is it you want from your old dad?' chuckled Bill.

'What do you mean?'

'Come on, Tasmin, you only ever call me "Daddy" when you're after something. Bike broken down again, has it? Need a bit of extra cash to tide you over?'

'No, nothing like that. Daddy . . . I've got something to tell you.'

'Go on.'

'You mustn't be upset . . .'

'Tell your old dad, sweetheart, it can't be that bad.'

'I'm . . . pregnant, Daddy. I'm expecting a baby.'

She held her breath, almost hoping that he would shout at her, because that would be predictable and perhaps even deserved. She'd been naughty, he would tell her off: she would cry a little and then they would be friends again, all the bad things forgotten.

'Daddy? Dad, did you hear me? I'm having a . . .'

Click.

She stared at the receiver, for a few moments not quite believing her own ears. Surely he wouldn't put the phone down on her. They must have been cut off.

She dialled again. And a third time, a fourth, a fifth. But every time she got nothing but an engaged tone.

'Oh Daddy,' she whispered into the receiver, knowing that he couldn't hear her. All at once she was five years old again. And all because Daddy was angry with her, so angry that he'd taken the telephone off the hook, and she had no way of knowing if he'd ever forgive her.

Chapter 5

Painswick looked even prettier than usual, the age-smoothed Cotswold stone of the cottages mellow in the Sunday evening sunlight. Lobelia, pansies and geraniums spilled and trailed out of hanging baskets, and the warmly scented air buzzed with dragonflies, dipping low over well-tended garden ponds. In the distance, a single bell tolled for Evensong at the village church. Taz however wasn't in the mood for artistic appreciation.

Drawing up outside her parents' house, Taz saw the lace curtain flick across, then back again. So they were at home then. Her throat felt dry and constricted as she hurried up the path. She wasn't looking forward to this, but the sooner it was sorted out, the better.

Before she had time to knock, the door flew open. Isobel Norton had an oven glove dangling from one hand and a pair of kitchen scissors in the other. She did not look thrilled to see her daughter.

'Mummy, I—'

Before Taz had had a chance to say anything mean-ingful, Isobel dragged her inside and shut the door behind her, with such force that the lilies on the hall table all shook their heads in protest.

'Tasmin, for heaven's sake, what on earth have you been saying to upset your father? He hasn't spoken one word to me in the last two hours.'

Without waiting for a reply, Isobel bustled off towards the kitchen, Taz trailing in her wake. The whole cottage seemed filled with the scents of beeswax polish and home-cooked dinners, the same comforting smells that had greeted Taz every day when she came home from school. Isobel Norton had never believed in working mothers.

The smell of cooking grew almost overpowering as Isobel took an earthenware dish out of the Aga and removed the lid. With short, irritable scissor movements, she snipped fresh sage leaves into the chicken casserole.

'I know you must have said *something* to your father on the telephone, but goodness alone knows what it was.' Isobel slammed the lid on the casserole dish and slid it back into the oven. 'You haven't wrecked that precious bike of his, have you? You know what he was like that time you ran over a stone and bent the forks . . .'

'Dad won't tell you what's wrong?'

Taz fingered a wooden spoon lying on the kitchen table. That wooden spoon must be even older than she was, she could remember licking cake mixture off it when she couldn't have been more than . . . well, no more than a baby.

'You know your father,' sighed Isobel. 'He takes umbrage at something and the next thing you know, he's in that shed of his tinkering with oily bits of metal.'

At that moment the back door clicked open and Bill Norton came in from the garden.

'Carrots,' he grunted, dumping a trug of freshly-pulled veg onto the worktop by the door. Then he turned to go back out, and saw Taz. Her heart somersaulted in her chest, the spoon clattering out of her fingers onto the table.

'Daddy.'

Their eyes met.

'Oh. It's you.'

Taz knew that look. It had been the same when she'd told him that, no, she didn't want to try for Oxbridge because – whatever he might think – she wasn't clever enough. And besides, it just wasn't *her*. He'd given her that selfsame look when she'd told him he had to stop living out his own ambitions through her.

'Bill darling,' coaxed Isobel. 'Tasmin's come to sort out this silly disagreement you've had.'

'Disagreement?' Bill laughed sarcastically. 'That's what she's calling it, is it?'

'Bill – Tasmin.' A note of exasperation was creeping back into Isobel's voice. She fought it down with the kind of steely determination she'd used when entertaining her husband's more difficult business associates. 'Why don't we all sit down and have a nice glass of wine while you tell me what's going on?'

'Yes,' said Bill, now looking Tasmin straight in the eye. She squirmed. 'Why don't you tell your mother exactly what you told me?'

Isobel looked quizzically at Taz, before fetching white wine and three classes.

'Go on, dear,' said Isobel, pushing Taz down onto a chair.

'Yes, go on,' said Bill, ignoring the glass of wine his wife had put in front of him. 'Tell your mother what you've done. Or isn't it true, what you told me?'

'It's true,' said Taz softly. 'I wish it wasn't, but it is.' She felt her heart contract in her chest, her father's anger and disappointment so oppressively tangible that she could scarcely breathe.

'*What* is true?' demanded Isobel. 'Will somebody please tell me what's going on?'

Taz laid her hand over her mother's.

'I'm having a baby, Mummy.'

Isobel's eyes opened wide in a stare of ultimate horror and disbelief. This was something far too dreadful to be assimilated on a first hearing.

'No, no, that's not possible. You wouldn't be so stupid.'

'It's true, Mummy. I know it's not what you wanted for me, and I know how disappointed you'll be, but . . .'

She tried putting her arm round her mother's shoulders, but Isobel seemed too shell-shocked to notice. She just kept on shaking her head and repeating the same words, over and over again.

'It's not true, it's not true, it *can't* be true.'

Gradually, Isobel subsided into a kind of stultified silence. Nobody said anything. They all avoided looking at each other. The grandfather clock in the hall measured out the ponderous seconds in heavy, sluggish clunks. Taz stared down at her wine glass, suddenly realising that she couldn't have any wine, not even if she wanted it. Not now she was pregnant. Getting drunk was just one more thing she'd not be doing again for a long, long time.

Hand shaking slightly, Isobel raised her glass to her lips and drained it.

'The father – he'll be standing by you, of course?'

'He doesn't know about the baby. And I'm not going to tell him. We weren't . . . close.'

At this, Bill slammed his fist down on the table, so hard that the bottle skipped half an inch across the surface and Taz nearly jumped out of her skin. His face paled with rage.

'Not close!'

'Daddy, please . . . don't shout.'

'You were close enough to let him get you into trouble,' Bill hissed.

'It wasn't like that.'

Taz paused, having to make a conscious effort not to hyperventilate. She needed a paper bag to breathe into; no, she needed a very large bottle of vodka, some Valium . . . and a new set of parents. What was it about parents? How did they invariably contrive to turn any difficult situation into pure mental torture?

'Oh really?' There was a distasteful sneer in Bill's voice now.

'Yes, really. Not that you'd understand. And besides.' She found the defiance to return her father's disgusted gaze. 'It's my business.'

'You're my daughter. It's my business if you choose to ruin your life after everything I've given you . . .'

'I'm a grown woman. And you don't own me.'

Isobel poured herself another half-glass of wine, then as an afterthought topped it right up to the brim.

'Oh Tasmin. Tasmin, how could you?' Her faded green eyes flicked up at a sudden dreadful thought. 'You can't possibly keep it, of course. I suppose you'll have to have it adopted.' Her fingernails tapped against the stem of the wineglass. 'If you're discreet . . . we could send you on a long holiday to your aunt in Tuscany . . .'

'Mother.' Taz gripped her mother's hands and forced her to look into her face. 'Stop trying to organise my life for me. I've already made up my mind. I'm having this baby and I'm keeping it.'

'But Tasmin – you can't. People would . . .'

'I'll get by. This is the Nineties, not the Fifties. And I couldn't give a damn what people think or say. But I do care about you.'

'If you cared about me and your mother,' replied Bill, 'You'd not be throwing your life away.'

'Throwing it away? Daddy, this is going to be your grandchild. And plenty of single women manage a baby and a career.'

Bill Norton got slowly to his feet, scraping the legs of his chair on the floor. Not one flicker of sympathy softened the granite mask of his face.

'I've heard enough of this, I'm going out.' He reached for his battered tweed hat.

'Daddy, please – don't go!' Taz reached out her hand but he brushed it aside. 'We need to talk.'

'I've nothing more to say to you.'

Taz knew it was useless trying any more. Bill was already trudging down the garden to his shed, his back stooped like a man who has suddenly aged ten years in the space of a few moments.

'Oh Mummy,' she sighed, sinking back onto her chair. 'Mummy, I never meant it to be like this.' She looked up. 'You understand, don't you? I never intended to get myself into this situation, but . . .'

Isobel wasn't listening. She was clearing away the glasses, bustling around in a swirl of Liberty print skirts.

'You won't be staying for dinner then?'

'Mummy, are you listening to me?'

Without turning to look at Taz, Isobel kept on babbling nineteen to the dozen, as though keeping up an eternal monologue might absolve her from the need to think.

'It's probably best if you don't stay. God only knows when your father will calm down, I'll probably have to throw his dinner in the bin.' She put on her rubber gloves and started scrubbing frantically at a Pyrex dish. 'Perhaps I can freeze it – do you think it would freeze? I expect so, if I let it cool down properly . . .'

'Mummy, listen to me. I love you and I love Daddy, but I'm not your little girl any more. I'll make my own mistakes and when I do, I'll take responsibility for what I've done.'

'Why, Tasmin?' Isobel swung round, suddenly quivering with righteous anger. 'Why are you humiliating us like this? Have you any idea what people will think when they find out our own daughter is an unmarried mother?'

Taz gaped. She'd never quite appreciated the sheer depth of her mother's social snobbery.

'This isn't about what people think – it's about a baby. Your grandson or granddaughter.'

'An *illegitimate* baby, Tasmin. How could you *do* this to us, when we sacrificed everything to give you the best that money could buy?'

In that moment, Taz came perilously close to shaking her mother till her teeth rattled.

'Would you rather I had an abortion? Is that what you're saying?'

Her mother remained silent. Taz snatched up her handbag from where it lay, beside the stove. It had been a huge mistake coming over; she should have guessed it would all end in histrionics, with everyone blaming everyone else.

'If that's all you have to say, I'm going. I just thought you had a right to know, that's all.'

As she turned to go, Isobel straightened up and turned round.

'Tasmin.'

A faint flutter of hope made Taz halt in her tracks.

'Give it time. It's . . . it's a lot to take in . . . and you might change your mind . . .'

'I might. But I won't. Tell Dad he knows where I am if he wants to talk.'

A week passed. Bill Norton couldn't have kept his distance more determinedly if pregnancy had been contagious. Taz cried a little, ate a lot of Dime bars and pickled gherkins, threw up, dusted herself off and got on with life. No matter how much she was hurting inside, she could still pretend that she didn't care.

Wednesday saw the first fortnightly meeting of the American Event committee. Taz knew, the moment she walked into the seminar room, that she was in for a rough ride. Cara Mondini was sitting on the window-ledge, chain-smoking and reading a copy of *In-Line Skater*; Brendan Ryan was calling Bruce Oldfield, very loudly and ostentatiously, on his mobile phone; and as for Ken Harris, he hadn't even bothered to turn up. Taz's heart sank another few notches as she set eyes on Ted Williams, Ken's consummately slimy ADSM.

'Hi,' grinned Ted, swinging his feet casually down off the table. There was something vaguely reptilian about that shiny, blunt-featured face, and those long-fingered hands with their prominent knuckles. 'Ken's too busy to come.'

'You mean he couldn't be arsed,' said Brendan, switching off his phone. He glanced at his watch. 'Right Taz. I can give you half an hour, my Ralph Lauren supplier's coming at three.'

'You'll give me as long as I need,' said Taz coolly. 'This is a keynote event for S&G, we have to get it right.'

'Important for you, sure,' agreed Brendan. 'But then you're Diana's blue-eyed girl, aren't you?'

Ted winked and scratched his ankle. Taz couldn't help noticing that he was wearing slightly grubby white socks.

'Taz wants a result, stands to reason. But what's in it for the rest of us, eh?'

'Shut up, Ted,' sighed Cara, elbows on the table and a Marlboro between her lips. 'This has to be done so let's just get on with it. So – what's the master plan, Taz?'

Taz turned over a page of the flip chart to reveal a list of dates.

'Right. March for fifteenth to the twenty-second. I've talked to promotions at head office, and that's the key week we're looking at. The Los Angeles store opening has been moved to the twenty-first, so what we want is a varied programme of celebrations, culminating in the New World Fashion Event on opening day.'

'I thought D-Day was the fifth,' observed Cara.

'Some problem with a public holiday – bit of a cock-up by the men in suits,' smirked Brendan, the fount of all knowledge.

'Anyhow, Brendan,' continued Taz. 'Promotions have agreed in principle to fund a transatlantic fashion event, with full media coverage of course. They'll be taking care of the publicity and PR. At this stage, I'm looking at a late-afternoon or evening event here in Cheltenham, to coincide exactly with the US opening and their fashion show.'

'Afternoon?' Cara wrinkled her nose doubtfully. 'Will there be enough interest?'

'Should be, luckily it's a Saturday. And Mrs Latchford's considering keeping the store open till midnight on opening day, if we can get enough staff to volunteer.'

'What about follow-up?' demanded Brendan. 'Any spin-offs to maximise sales?'

'We'll be showing in-store videos of the British and American shows, to sustain interest in the New World designerwear range over the following month or so. But what I really need at this stage . . .' Her eyes travelled over the three faces in front of her. 'What I really need is more input from you.' She folded her arms and waited. 'Well?'

Cara gazed vacantly at her notepad. Brendan folded his arms and stared right back. Ted chewed gum. Taz contemplated mass murder.

'For pity's sake, you must've come up with *something*. Ted – how about you?'

'Ken says head office are sending him some new American-style corn-dogs, he'll get the checkout girls to dress up as cheerleaders or something.'

'And that's it?'

'Don't look at me, I'm just passing on the message.' He shrugged.

'Cara?'

'Well, I checked, and the junior amateur basketball team is definitely over that week, but we'd have to organise some opponents for them.'

'Shouldn't be too difficult to find a few school teams to play them then. Can you look into that?'

'Yeah. I guess. But let's face it, Taz, a team of American kindergarten kids would slaughter any local teams we could scrape together.'

'How about persuading the British Olympic team to play an exhibition against them?'

Cara looked uninspired, but agreed, 'Well . . . I'll have a go, if that's what you want.'

Taz counted silently to ten. If you want something done properly, jeered a voice in her head, do it yourself. On the face of it, it hardly seemed worth bothering with Brendan, he was always so smugly unco-operative, just willing her to fall flat on her face. And if he found about the baby . . .

'So. Any bright ideas, Brendan?'

'This is your party, Taz, I wouldn't want to tread on your toes.'

'How very thoughtful. Do I take it that means you haven't thought of anything either? Forgive me Brendan, but I thought you were supposed to be the fashion expert around here.'

'I bow to your superior product knowledge,' said Brendan, smiling daggers.

'Right. I see. Interesting concept of team working you have.' Taz mentally took Brendan's precious product knowledge, rolled it up and shoved it where the sun didn't shine. 'Dump Taz in it right up to the neck and watch her sink. Is that the general idea?'

'Oh come on, Taz,' protested Cara, 'Calm down. You know Brendan, he just likes winding people up.'

But calming down was the last thing Taz felt like doing. She felt constantly nauseous, her father had practically disowned her, she was absurdly nervous about going to her first ante-natal class, and now the whole world was thumbing its nose at her.

'OK, look. And listen, all of you. Either you stop

messing me about and work with me, or I start telling you what to do. Is that what you want? To be treated like you can't even wipe your own bottoms without a list of instructions?' Three pairs of eyes looked back at her. No, stared back at her. She knew she was getting over-emotional and she hated herself for it. 'Because believe me, if you want to act like kids I'll be more than happy to treat you that way.'

Taz didn't wait for a reply, just ripped the page from the flip chart and tossed it onto the table. Then she concluded, 'Think about it. Next meeting two weeks today. And I want to see some changes of attitude. Right?'

As she stormed out of the seminar room, slamming the door behind her, she just caught Ted's voice following her down the corridor.

'Poor cow. It's her hormones you know.' And, hormones or no hormones, she very nearly went right back and flattened him.

There was no respite on the shop floor. After a swift face-wash and a prayer for patience, Taz returned to menswear to find Kate and Leroy in a huddle over the PDQ machine.

'It did it again,' said Kate. 'Just then. If you wait, it'll do it again.'

'Do what?' demanded Taz, directing an old lady back down the escalator to ladies' special occasion hats.

'It's the credit card machine,' said Leroy. 'It keeps . . . beeping.'

'It's supposed to.'

'Not *all* the time, surely,' said Kate. And as if to oblige, the machine started up again, giving out a series of six shrill squeaks before quietening down to a kind of ominous purr. 'And there's something else wrong with it too . . .'

A man in a brown suit was bearing down on the cash desk with an armful of Argyle socks.

'Can you tell me if these are one hundred per cent virgin wool?'

Taz smiled and discreetly prodded Leroy in the ribs.

'Mr McIntosh here will help you, he's our formalwear specialist.'

' . . . because they're no good at all if they're less than a hundred per cent, they make me sweat and I get this fungal infection . . .'

Once Leroy had guided the customer out of earshot, Taz took a closer look at the machine. 'Right. How long has it been like this?'

'About two hours, I think. It started while you were talking to the buyer about those Burberry raincoats.'

'Why on earth didn't you tell me before?'

'You were busy. And then you had that meeting to go to.'

A second outbreak of beeping, louder and faster than the last, set heads turning all over men's formalwear.

'Well this won't do, I'll have to ring the bank. Hang on, what's this?' She reached down and picked a long strip of paper off the floor.

'Oh, that. I tore it off, it just kept on coming out of the machine, even when we weren't using it.'

Taz had a feeling of imminent doom as she scanned the printout: nine sets of identical figures, the same card number, the same authorisation code. And the same amount every time: £136.99. Something was very, very wrong.

'Right, Kate. The first thing you do is unplug that machine. Take it off line. Now. Then ring the management office and tell them what's happened.'

She went into the stockroom to dial up an outside line.

'Control centre. Emma speaking. Can I help you?'

'This is menswear at Seuss & Goldman, Cheltenham. We have a serious fault with one of our PDQ machines.'

'We'll try and get someone out to you sometime tomorrow . . .'

'You'll get someone out to us today. Within the hour.'

'I'm afraid I can't possibly authorise that unless it's urgent.'

'Urgent! It's charged some poor customer nine times for the same purchase! Now will you please get your engineer here straight away, and in the meantime, consider the last eight transactions null and void. Oh, and I'd be grateful if you'd confirm that in writing to our store manager, Mrs Latchford. Is that clear?'

'Er . . . yes. I'll get on to it right away.'

'Thank you.'

Taz breathed a sigh of relief as she replaced the receiver. At least she hadn't completely lost her touch. Now all she had to do was contact the unsuspecting customer.

At six forty-five, when any sensible person would be driving home to a warm cat and a TV dinner, Taz was driving across Cheltenham to the house of a woman she'd never met.

She'd only spoken to Steffi Parkes briefly on the telephone, but already Taz was having second thoughts about 'childbirth preparation' classes. Reassuring comments about 'getting to know your own body' and 'putting yourself in control of the most beautiful experience you will ever have' made her feel faintly queasy. She and Binnie had always joked about touchy-feely New Age earthmothers, and she was already picturing Ms Parkes in a kaftan and ankle-bracelets, breastfeeding twins while preparing a nourishing chickpea ragôut.

Her expectations were somewhat dented when she turned into Ranelagh Crescent, and discovered not a tepee but a Lutyens thatched villa, surrounded by mature gardens and with a red sports coupé in the drive.

Joining the three cars already parked on the road outside, Taz got out and headed towards the front door. A stockily-built, dark-haired woman in red jeans and a black tee-shirt was already waiting on the doorstep, plump arms cradling a bundle which at first looked like a baby but on closer inspection turned out to be a four-pack of toilet rolls and a fluffy hand-towel.

'Hi,' said the woman, cheeks dimpling in a smile which made the corners of her brown eyes crinkle. 'I'm Dee. Your first class is it?'

'Does it show?' giggled Taz nervously.

'Don't worry, you'll be fine. Steffi's wonderful, she puts

70

everyone at their ease. And I'm an old hand,' she added. 'This'll be my fourth time.'

'Four!' And I'm panicking about coping with one, thought Taz, with a sudden awful vision of unexpected quintuplets, their mouths springing open simultaneously like the beaks of baby vultures. 'How on earth do you manage?'

Dee laughed, shaking a straggle of black curls out of her eyes.

'It's instinct. Just relax and you'll be fine.' She rang the doorbell a second time. 'Come on Steffi, I'm dying for the loo. Emergency supplies,' she explained with a comedy grimace at the bundle. 'You'd be surprised how much loo roll half a dozen expectant mums can get through in one evening.'

'Mmm. I can imagine. I seem to be spending half my life in the bathroom. Oh – I'm Tasmin Norton, by the way. But everyone calls me Taz.'

'Everyone except your mum, eh?' If Dee noticed the slight squirm of discomfort, she didn't show it. 'I mean, the whole world calls me Dee but not my mother. She says, "You're a good Polish girl and your father and I baptised you Danuta, so you're Danuta in the eyes of God". Parents, eh?'

'Parents,' agreed Taz with a barely audible sigh. 'With my luck I'll turn out just like my mother.'

Footsteps sounded in the hall, and the door opened. An elegant woman in a burgundy silk blouse, black trousers and patent loafers greeted them with a peck on either cheek.

'Dee, darling, so glad you decided to come. We do so need the experienced mums as well as the first-timers. And you must be Taz! I'm Steffi, come in and make yourself comfy. We were just organising some coffee and nibbles.'

Slightly shell-shocked, Taz followed Dee and Steffi past signed horse-racing prints displayed on terracotta rag-rolled walls, and a revolting but probably priceless bronze of a stag at bay. At the end of the hallway, they turned right into an immense bay-windowed living room.

Balanced and squashed into settees and armchairs, around a kind of carpet-mosaic made up of mattresses and exercise mats, sat an assortment of mums-to-be; plus two thirtysomething men Taz took to be significant others, and a middle-aged woman with a tight perm who looked as though it was requiring every ounce of her strength not to take over the class and lick them all into shape.

'Hi everyone, this is Taz,' beamed Steffi.

'Hi, Taz,' came back the reply. It was like being the new girl on your first day at school. There was even a kind of uniform: they had all turned up in the only jeans they could still squeeze into, teamed with a baggy tee-shirt.

Steffi was busy organising things.

'If you could just make a tiny bit more room by you, Chloë . . . that's lovely.'

Yes, they all looked remarkably similar . . . except one, thought Taz, with a twitch of amusement as she and Dee squeezed onto one of Steffi's opulent leather sofas, between a willowy, faintly neurotic-looking blonde and a squat woman with acne. There was a rebel amongst them. And this one was sitting right next to the schoolmarmish woman with the perm, which only added to the bizarre effect.

The kid – for she couldn't be out of her teens – looked as if she'd graduated straight from school uniform into skintight Lycra. She wore a sleeveless orange vest with a zip running up the front, clumpy shoes with soles like tractor tyres, a nose-stud and – just to finish off the overall look, acid-green cropped leggings which matched the colour of her pony-tailed hair.

Mmm. Definitely different. And not very happy either, to judge from the way she was sitting, elbows on knees, eyes staring down at the tasselled corner of the hand-woven carpet. Poor dumb kid. She ought to be out raving, not having babies. For some reason she couldn't quite fathom, Taz felt intrigued by the girl; as though neither of them quite belonged here, and almost as if that sense of isolation formed a tenuous link between them.

Steffi started off the session by clapping her hands, making her heavy gold bracelet rattle opulently.

72

'Right. Now we're all here, let's talk a little about what we're going to be doing. I'm delighted that you've all made a positive decision to attend the course . . .'

'Some of us didn't have any choice,' muttered the girl with the green hair, casting a venomous look at the woman sitting next to her.

'Mandy,' hissed the woman with the perm, colouring up slightly. 'Mandy, we agreed at the case conference that this was best for you and the baby.'

'Oh we did, did we? I don't remember anybody bothering to ask me what I thought.'

'Shall we have that coffee now?' enquired Steffi in the middle of a silence as thick as blackstrap molasses. 'The biscuits are home-made, why don't you try one, Taz?'

The first ten minutes consisted of decaffeinated coffee, mineral water, fruit juice, high-fibre vitamin-enriched biscuits and a shower of leaflets, with titles from 'Breastfeeding Is Best' to 'What If I Don't Love My Baby?'. That's all I need, thought Taz, putting the last leaflet to the bottom of her bag. All this physical stuff is hard enough to live with, I can't handle psychology as well.

'We usually begin by getting to know each other,' said Steffi, perching on the arm of a chair, coffee-cup poised halfway to her subtly lipsticked mouth. Her eyes scanned the room, hoping for enthusiastic eye contact, but only Dee returned her smile – and Dee had already been through this three times before, thought Taz.

To give her her due, Steffi was indomitable. She would probably have carried on with her childbirth class on the deck of the sinking *Titanic*. And the smile never slipped, not once.

'It's important, I think, to tell each other a little about ourselves. The more we know each other, the better we'll trust and confide in each other. And when you're having a baby you really do need someone you can trust.'

'OK. I'm Steffi, I'm thirty-eight years old and I have two children, Micha and Alexander, aged four and two. I used to work in financial services but I gave up after Alexander was born. Training as a childbirth counsellor offered me a chance to stay at home, but fulfil my need to have another role beyond that of mother. There. That wasn't so bad, was it?' She sipped her coffee and passed round the plate of biscuits a second time. 'Dee – you've been to my classes before, why don't you start the ball rolling?'

Dee sat slightly forward in her seat. After four or five management training courses, Taz was used to this kind of embarrassing getting-to-know-you exercise, but had never grown to like it. By contrast, Dee seemed to lap it up; you couldn't help but admire her self-assurance.

'My name's Dee Wiechula – that's short for Danuta in case you were wondering. I'm thirty-seven, single, and I'm mum to Denny, who's three, Petula, who's four, and Emma-Louise, who's coming up to six. I run the Green Café in the High Street, but as far as I'm concerned being a mother is my job – it's the most important job in the world.' She patted her tummy. 'And I'm really looking forward to welcoming this little one into the world. Actually, they think it may be twins!'

The ice broken, people began talking more freely. You could feel relaxation seeping into the atmosphere, and it had nothing to do with the whale music playing softly on the sound system. Taz listened to all the little stories, so insignificant yet so important to the teller. There was Wendy and her husband Kevin, so inseparably devoted that they even wore identical tee-shirts and trainers; Lynette, who'd been trying for a baby for ten years and was almost in tears of ecstasy as she told everyone that she was fourteen weeks pregnant; and Priti, whose husband Raj seemed alarmingly convinced that their baby was going to be a boy.

'My name's Chloë,' began the quivering blonde next to Taz, her white hands neatly folded in her lap. 'Chloë Baxendale. I'm thirty-one, and I got married last month to Clive. Clive's working late tonight,' she explained, silently pleading with the others not to judge her husband harshly. 'He has the family business to run.'

'And do you work, Chloë?' enquired Steffi.

'Only in a china shop, part-time. I expect I'll be giving it up soon, I don't really know.'

'And when's your little one due?' enquired Dee with a friendly pat on Chloë's hand. To Taz's surprise, Chloë coloured up and looked away.

'I'm ... er ... about four months pregnant,' she said in an embarrassed whisper. 'Clive and I were engaged for two and a half years, we were waiting for the right time to get married.'

Steffi moved quickly on. To the glowering vision in orange and green.

'How about you, Mandy? Why don't you tell us about yourself?'

'Yes, go on, Mandy,' urged the woman sitting next to her, nudging her elbow in a maternal sort of way. She didn't look like her mum though, thought Taz; didn't sound like her, either. There was nothing remotely middle-class about Mandy.

Mandy shook the hand from her elbow and poked the ball of chewing gum into her cheek.

'All right then. If that's what you want.' The brown eyes held a hint of malicious intent. 'I'm Mandy Robson, I'm eighteen, the condom split and my dad said if I didn't get rid of the little brat he'd throw me onto the street.' Drinking in the shocked silence, Mandy cast a glance at the red-faced woman next to her. 'Oh yeah. And this is Irene Watkins, she's my social worker. She reckons I'm not fit to have a kid, but since she's a forty-year-old virgin ...'

'Mandy, for goodness' sake!' snapped the social worker. 'Look everyone, I'm really sorry ... she only does it to shock people.'

But Mandy was studiously ignoring her. Taz caught her eye briefly and thought – though she wasn't sure – that Mandy actually winked at her. The cheeky little cow.

'Taz?' Steffi Parkes' voice brought her back to the present. 'Would you like to tell us a little about yourself?'

'OK. I'm twenty-five, I'm single and I work as a depart-mental sales manager at Seuss & Goldman', she began. At this, a smile spread across Mandy's face.

'Seuss & Goldman? I nicked a pair of jeans from there once. They didn't fit though, I took 'em back and got a refund. Joke,' she added for the benefit of Irene Watkins. 'I wouldn't be seen dead in there, it's for old fogeys.'

But Taz wasn't so sure it was a joke. Something in Mandy's expression made her suspect there was a lot more to Mandy Robson than met the eye.

After the class, Dee invited everybody back to the Green Café for more decaff and organic oatmeal flapjacks. Perhaps unsurprisingly only Taz and Chloë took her up on the invitation, Mandy disappearing in the direction of her social worker's 2CV, her former bravado not much in evidence. In fact, thought Taz, she looked for all the world like a kicked dog on the end of a too-tight leash.

'This is where you live?' enquired Chloë tremulously as Dee unlocked the door of the café, which was situated at the undesirable end of Cheltenham High Street, in what was euphemistically known as a 'Neighbourhood regeneration area'. A distinctive smell of boiled lentils and soy sauce wafted out.

'I have a flat above the café – and there's another flat on the second floor, but I let it out.'

'If you have any more children, you'll need all the extra space you can get,' commented Taz with humour.

'So I'll manage,' said Dee with a shrug. 'You can't have too many kids, the more you have the more joy they bring you.'

'You really think so?' asked Chloë doubtfully.

'I know so. Now, what's it to be – coffee, tea, fruit juice?'

'Just a glass of water would be nice,' said Taz. 'And a sit down. I'm feeling worn out after all that.'

She sank gratefully onto one of Dee's bentwood chairs. The colour scheme was a bit savage, naked plywood stained with green wood-preservative, and the smell took some getting used to, but there was a cosy homeliness about the café. She decided she liked it.

'Still, it was entertaining,' commented Dee, going to take a bottle of spring water from the fridge.

'That girl!' exclaimed Chloë, shaking her head. 'You know, I don't think she's ready to have a baby, she's not nearly mature enough.'

'But then neither am I,' replied Taz darkly.

'If it comes to that,' said Chloë, 'Is anyone ever really grown-up enough to be a mother? It's such a huge step to take. One minute you've met a man you quite like, the next . . .'

Dee seemed to think this was the funniest thing she'd ever heard.

'But having babies is the most natural thing in the world!' She tipped mineral water into three glasses. 'As natural as . . . as having sex!'

'Which is something I don't suppose any of us will be doing again for a while,' remarked Taz.

'Don't you believe it,' winked Dee, raising her glass. 'Cheers. Here's to a happy, healthy, *sexually active* pregnancy.'

At that moment Taz's pager went off inside her handbag. For once she'd almost forgotten about the world of work, the world she carried around with her and thought about constantly, even when she wasn't at Seuss & Goldman. What could possibly have happened, to make them page her at this time of night? Had there been a break-in at the store? A fire? Had all the PDQ machines got together and raided the Bank of England? Oh please, don't let it be some disaster caused because Taz Norton's mind had been on her uterus instead of her job . . .

She took out the pager and read the number; a mobile phone number she didn't recognise.

'Excuse me, I need to make a call . . .'

Dee pointed to a door marked 'Private, Staff Only'. 'There's a phone through there, on the right.'

'I'll pay for the call of course.'

'Forget it. But try not to make too much noise, the kids are asleep upstairs.'

Taz hurried through the door to the phone. She dialled up the number. A sleepy voice answered.

'Lethbridge – yeah?'

'*Jim*? Jim, is that you?'

'Oh, Taz. I've been trying to get you.' The sound of a suppressed yawn. 'You weren't at home, and Binnie kept going on about letting you know.'

Panic clutched at Taz's stomach.

'Is something wrong? Binnie's not ill is she?' She strove to keep her voice down, cupping the mouthpiece in her hand.

'Not ill, she's had the baby. A fortnight early, but it's OK. Little girl, just under six pounds. I'm at the hospital.'

'Jim, that's wonderful!' And the funny thing was, she really meant it.

'Yeah.' In her excitement, Taz hardly noticed Jim's less than ecstatic reaction to the birth.

'And Binnie, how's she?'

'A bit sore. Her blood pressure was high, they had to induce her. But she's fine. Look, I'll have to go, I'm knackered, been on my feet since five a.m.'

'Send me a photo – and tell Binnie well done.'

They said their farewells, the phone line clicked and went dead. Taz leaned back against the corridor wall. It felt cool and slightly moist through her thin tee-shirt.

Her hand slipped to her stomach, just beginning to show the first, faint signs of the tiny life growing within. What was it the baby book had said? 'You're fourteen weeks pregnant and your foetus is about the size of a mouse . . .' A mouse. But this was a baby, a growing, living baby, just like Binnie's. And if this small life had begun as a mistake, in doubt and anger and recrimination, she was going to make sure that it came into the world with all the love she could manage to give it.

Fourteen weeks. She paused, waiting for her heartbeat to slow down before going back into the café to join Dee and Chloë. In another six months or so it would be her, not Binnie, in that hospital bed. Her with her baby son or daughter in her arms. That thought took a lot of getting used to.

But for the first time since the pregnancy test, she had begun to feel as excited as she was scared about the birth; and that had to be a good beginning.

Chapter 6

Christmas was coming, and Taz was getting fat.

As September and October passed by and late summer became autumn, Taz began to feel that she had passed a watershed. Having the whole business out in the open and dealing with people's occasional hostile comments was turning out to be a whole lot easier than coping with their sly smiles and malicious gossip.

Being 'outed' brought a kind of freedom. Taz had given up casting wistful glances at the now-unwearable size twelve suit hanging on the back of her bedroom door, and had surrendered to comfy size fourteen shift dresses under navy-blue jackets, huge and masterful bras which held her in a kind of breath-squeezing bear hug, and shoes which were only half an inch short of being completely flat. Her only lingering regrets were getting too big to ride the BSA Gold Star . . . and failing to make things up with her parents.

She had come almost to look forward to her one evening a week at Steffi's house, wallowing about on a mattress on the floor and practising bizarre breathing exercises. More than that, she had come to enjoy the after-class chat at the Green Café, with Dee and Chloë and – on one or two occasions – even the outrageous Mandy Robson.

They would probably never have become friends under any other circumstances, but pregnancy was something that could only truly be understood by somebody else who was experiencing it.

As the business of being pregnant took up more and

more of her time and energy, the business of being a good manager became harder and harder. The American Event was far fiddlier and more time-consuming than Taz had imagined it would be.

Over all of this loomed the spectre of the monthly sales figures. There hardly seemed time to fret about the ugly silence which had fallen on relations between Taz and her parents.

The October clearance sale inevitably gave way to the first week of November. Elsewhere, the world might be gearing up for fireworks round the bonfire, but when November dawned at Seuss & Goldman, out came the tinsel and the holly.

The day after Santa arrived in his grotto, riding through Montpellier in a sleigh pulled by *real* reindeer, something happened to put a definite dampener on Taz's festive spirit.

'Customer in young designerwear, Leroy. Marion, prop up that display, it's leaning over. We don't want it falling on someone's head.'

Taz watched Marion walk sullenly across to the polystyrene snowman and jab it ill-temperedly back into place. Marion's normal sourness was slowly turning into a kind of silent, black resentment. But every time Taz tried to broach the subject, Marion pursed her lips and demanded, 'Can I go back to work now, Miss Norton? If there's nothing else? I have such a lot to do.'

As Taz was standing at the top of the main escalator, looking down at the enormous Christmas tree rising up from the middle of the glass-roofed atrium, Diana Latchford came silently up behind her.

'Tasmin? Tasmin, a word please.'

Taz swivelled round. The look on Diana's face was more formal than usual, and she had Gerry, the assistant store manager, with her. Gerry Rothwell was scrupulously fair, straight as a die, but no one could accuse him of being over-friendly. He nodded dourly.

'Ms Norton? Mrs Latchford and I have come to check your Christmas displays.' His gaze lingered for a moment on Taz's stomach, then swept away, covering the whole department in a single panoramic snapshot. 'I take it all went smoothly?'

'Well . . .' Taz followed Gerry's gaze. The department looked OK to her, though that top-heavy snowman in a case perhaps didn't quite come up to her usual exacting standards. 'We were here till nine o'clock last night, finishing off. As you can see, all the decorations are up.'

'Hmm.' Diana took a few steps forward and cast critical eyes over a display of stocking fillers: gold-plated golf tees, novelty cufflinks, silver cases for business cards. 'I don't like this, you'll have to move it.'

'But . . .' Damn, thought Taz. She'd spent three quarters of an hour moving that display round the department, trying to find the best place for it. Wherever you put it it stuck out like a sore thumb. 'Any suggestions?'

'It's up to you where you put it,' Diana replied. 'It's my job simply to tell you I don't like it. Now, show me what you've done with the new designer collections we've just got in.'

'I've put the Cerrutti and Lauren over here, by the balcony rail. There's plenty of light to show off the colours, and the Tommy Hilfiger next to the denim . . .'

Gerry Rothwell shook his head.

'You can't put it there, it's a blind spot in the CCTV system and this is high-value merchandise. Remember what happened to that jet-ski. Is it all security tagged?'

'Most of it. We don't have enough tags to do everything, so we've concentrated on the most expensive items.'

'Fair enough. But you'll still have to move the display. Maybe swap it with outerwear.'

'But that's where it was before,' protested Taz. 'And it wasn't selling.'

'Then find another solution.' Gerry scribbled something down on the notebook he habitually carried around with him. 'That's what we pay you for.'

Taz was beginning to feel hot, bothered and slightly upset. It didn't help that Marion was watching her from behind a rack of Yves St Laurent suits. Leroy was trying not to listen, but she could tell from the embarrassed way he was showing a customer a pair of trousers that he knew what was going on.

Don't take it personally Taz, she scolded herself: criticism comes with the job. That's one of the first things you have to learn when you start out in retail management. Your bosses tell you you're crap and you have to keep on proving you're not, until finally you're so successful that you're promoted above them, at which point you start telling them they're crap instead.

'So – what about the rest of the displays?' She held her breath, then played her trump card. 'I took advice from visual merchandising of course.'

'Of course.' Diana nodded. 'Yes. They seem OK.'

Scarcely were the words out of her mouth than the polystyrene snowman fell head-first onto the carpet about six inches in front of a startled customer.

Horrified, Taz lunged forward, saying breathlessly, 'Sir, I'm so sorry. Are you all right?'

'Yes, er, fine, thank you. But that's a bit dangerous, isn't it?'

'I'll have it fixed immediately. You're sure you're all right?'

She watched him glide away down the escalator, cursing her bad luck, worse judgement and a lost sale.

'Marion, get this cleared up straight away. Then call visual merchandising and ask them to send someone to take down that canoe. It's a safety hazard.' She turned back to Diana. 'I'm so sorry . . .'

Diana laid her hand on Taz's shoulder.

'Into your office. Now. We need to talk.'

Taz's minute departmental office was situated just behind the gentlemen's personal shopping suite. As the door closed behind her, it occurred to Taz just how much like a cell it was.

'You wanted to speak to me.'

'Sit down. You look like you need to.'

'I'm fine. Really.' Taz stood up straight and pulled her stomach in, folding her hands over it. That way, she hardly looked pregnant at all.

'I'll get straight to the point, Tasmin. You're not performing as well as I've come to expect you to perform. I need to find out why that is.'

'I've been working hard on the American promotion.'

'I appreciate that, but it's meant to be a team effort – thought you'd have learned about the need to delegate by now.'

'Yes,' said Taz. 'You're right, of course.' Inwardly she was thinking, it's all very well delegating when people cooperate with you; it's not quite so practical when they're all willing you to fail.

'I'm disappointed, Tasmin. Your departmental sales figures are down for October. And I need to know that you have a hundred per cent commitment to the day-to-day business of your department, irrespective of any other projects you may take on.'

'We still made our target,' Taz protested. 'We came in clearly under budget.'

'True, but it was still a poor performance compared to September and August. You've set yourself a high standard Tasmin, and if you do any less than brilliantly it will be interpreted as failure.'

'I have no intention of failing,' said Taz with controlled anger.

'I'm glad to hear it. And then there's the matter of the staff rotas and time-sheets.'

'What about them?' Taz felt a twinge of unease. It was no use lying to herself; she knew she hadn't been spending enough time on routine administration.

'There are one or two irregularities. For example, last month one of your part-timers is recorded as working a full thirty hours, yet the staff rota shows she took an extra day's absence which wasn't recorded as annual leave.'

Taz silently cursed her own negligence.

'I'm sorry, that was an oversight. Pauline had a domestic emergency and needed extra time off. Colleen covered for her and she's working off the hours this week.'

'It's not the way we do things at Seuss & Goldman.'

Diana's expression softened slightly, the cutting edge fading from her voice.

'Listen, Taz. You have a very demanding job. Perhaps it's proving too much for . . .'

Taz saw red. After all that flannel about backing her all the way, Diana was stabbing her in the back.

'For what? For a woman in my "condition"? Is that what you're saying, that I'm not up to my job any more?'

'No I'm not. I'm not saying anything. I'm just asking you to think about it.'

'I've thought about it plenty. And I *can* do this.'

'I hope you succeed. For everybody's sake.' As Diana laid her hand on the door handle, she added, 'Don't forget to move those displays, will you? And if you can have that sales report on my desk by tomorrow.'

'You'll have it by this evening,' replied Taz. She wondered how on earth she was going to manage it, but she would. If she had to, she'd work flat out to prove Diana Latchford wrong.

And she did. Instead of coming in at eight thirty, Taz started getting up half an hour earlier and starting work at eight. She'd never left the store before six thirty, but now it was more like seven, some nights much later. On a couple of occasions she found herself leaving with the security guard when he went off at nine.

Oddly enough, even though she was tired, fat, and ached all over, Taz was beginning to get back her old fire. She had something to prove. Just because she was pregnant didn't mean she was some kind of fluffy-brained invalid.

Having this baby wasn't going to mean the end of the life she'd fought to make for herself. Taz knew she wasn't going to let her career slip away. And she was going to make sure everyone else knew it: Diana, Brendan, Ted . . . and her mum and dad too, if they ever grew up and stopped putting the phone down on her.

One grey Saturday morning in November, Taz arrived at work to find a memo from Diana Latchford in her pigeon-hole. 'It has come to my attention that menswear stock has overflowed into the fashion accessories stockroom. Ensure that excess stock is transferred to your department by 1100 hours Tuesday, to make room for incoming deliveries.'

'There's nowhere to put it,' protested Marion as Taz pushed her into the goods lift and they jolted up towards the third-floor stockrooms.

'Then we'll have to find somewhere, won't we?' Privately, Taz shared Marion's doubts. There really wasn't anywhere in the department to put two whole racks of formal suits, and the menswear stockroom was piled high with cartons of underpants sent in error from central buying, which now refused to have them back. '*Won't we?*' she repeated, as Marion just kept staring ahead of her, her face set in a permanent scowl.

'What's that?' Marion blinked and looked up.

'I said, we'll have to find room for this stock in the department. If the worst comes to the worst, I can probably persuade Kate to take the stocking-fillers.' At the end of her menswear placement Kate had been seconded to assist the manager of the in-store Christmas shop.

'I suppose,' said Marion, following Taz out of the lift.

Taz ran her bar-coded name badge over a wall scanner and the stockroom door clicked open. The recent refit had brought all kinds of new technology to Seuss & Goldman; you had to be adaptable to keep up with it all.

'Are you *sure* there isn't something bothering you, Marion?'

'What? Oh. No, nothing. Where's this stock then?'

Taz indicated the two rails of suits.

'It's no good taking all that down. There's nowhere . . .' Marion began again.

'For goodness' sake, Marion, don't you listen to anything I say? Now, help me out with it – or do I have to do everything myself?'

Taz's mounting exasperation wasn't helped by the fact that the goods lifts were only just big enough to take two six-foot clothes rails, and there was an inch-high step to negotiate to get them in. Taz cursed the eccentric layout of the store. Whoever had planned its redevelopment in the early Nineties had obviously not thought much about the people who would have to work in it. The stockrooms were miles from the sales floor, the staff canteen was little more than a dingy corridor, and pagers had a habit of going off when you were nowhere near a phone. When *I'm* chief executive of Seuss & Goldman, Taz told herself firmly, things are going to change around here.

The lift jolted its way back down to the first floor, the door sliding only half open so that Taz had to jam her leg in it to stop it closing on several thousand pounds' worth of gentlemen's quality suiting.

'Take that rail over to formalwear. You and Leroy will have to find a way of squeezing the stock in. I'll see if I can put up a display at the far side of young designerwear – these four-button single breasteds are quite trendy. I'll be over in a bit to help you move the stocking-fillers to the Christmas shop.'

Taz pushed her clothes rail through the department, towards the young designerwear collection. Diana Latchford might not approve of her solution to the stockroom problem, but if so, tough. They'd just have to hope there was a sudden run on suits.

'Pauline? Marcus? When you're free.'

Pauline finished dusting one of the mannequins and came over. Marcus finished off a sale, bagging up not one but an impressive three Ralph Lauren shirts. He was only a Saturday assistant, a seventeen year-old in the middle of A levels, but Taz could see he had what it took to get on. The customers liked his relaxed approach and trendy blond haircut. That was part of the satisfaction of her job, matching the right sales assistant with the right section.

She gathered Pauline and Marcus around her.

'I'm afraid we have to get this rail of suits on display asap, there's nowhere else to put them. I've rung visual merchandising and Mr Nikephoros is sending down an extra end display unit. Think you can handle setting it up?'

'Miss Norton?' Taz turned to see one of the temporary student workers heading towards her. 'There's a customer asking to see the manager.'

'Why? What's the problem?' Taz's stomach formed a knot.

'I don't know. She just came into the department and said could she speak to the departmental manager. She didn't seem angry or anything, but she wouldn't tell me what it was about.'

'All right, I'll come. Where is she?'

'Over by ties and socks.'

Apprehensively, Taz made her way back towards formalwear. It struck her, not for the first time, how easy it would be to run a department if there weren't any customers to mess things up ...

But this was no ordinary customer. Taz saw her standing by the tie display, a slightly-built figure with greying auburn hair, a blue Eastex suit and a Dior scarf. A scarf identical to the one Taz had brought back from her last student trip to Paris ...

'Mum? Mum, what on earth are you doing here?'

Isobel Norton turned slowly to greet her daughter. Her expression was calm and perfectly pleasant, but her eyes seemed sad and more than a little wary; fearful even as she said, 'I'm not banned from shopping at Seuss & Goldman, am I dear?'

'N-no, of course not.' Taz instinctively drew her jacket across her stomach, feeling her mother's gaze burn into her. 'But – you asked to see me?'

Isobel held out two ties, one a yellow and red paisley print, the other patterned with diagonal stripes in green and grey.

'You know your father's taste better than I do, dear.' Her voice trembled slightly as she spoke, and she seemed to find it difficult to meet her daughter's gaze head-on. 'Which of these two do you think he'd wear?'

Taz couldn't suppress a faint smile. On his last day at the bank, Bill Norton had come home and made a bonfire of all his ties. With perfect pragmatism, Isobel had gone straight out and bought him some more.

'I don't know. The yellow and red, maybe? But he's not a tie person really, is he?'

'No. No, you're right, perhaps I should go for cufflinks

instead. You always were closer to him than I ever was.' She laughed softly. 'I used to be jealous, you know. You were such a pretty little girl, so . . . innocent. Butter wouldn't melt.'

Taz touched her mother's hand and Isobel looked up. The gaze was steady this time.

'How are you, Mum?'

'I'm fine.'

'And Daddy?'

The eyes dropped down again.

'I'm really sorry, Mum, but . . . I really want you to accept this baby, *both* of you.'

Isobel reached out and gently pushed aside Taz's hands, so that her jacket fell open, revealing the bump underneath. She laid her right hand on it, asking, 'Have you felt it move yet?'

'Not yet. But I've seen the scan. Oh Mum, you should see it – it's got arms and legs and a nose, like a complete person in miniature. Come with me, next time I go to the hospital.'

'Oh Tasmin dear, I don't know.'

But Taz had seen the glimmer of love, even covetousness in her mother's eyes; and something told her that, in spite of everything, there was no way that Isobel Norton could fail to love her unborn grandchild – or resist the urge to interfere at every possible opportunity.

'Think about it. At least come and meet me in town for a coffee sometime. We can talk.' She paused, then added, 'Bring Daddy too.'

Isobel chose to ignore Taz's plea, as Taz had feared she would.

'You are eating properly, aren't you? And getting plenty of iron? Guinness is good if you're anaemic . . .'

'Yes, Mum.'

'Do your exercises, and make sure you get a proper sit-down every afternoon. If you don't put your feet up for an hour or two you'll get shocking varicose veins.'

'I'll be fine. But Mum . . . Mum, I really need to sort things with Dad too. Make him understand.'

Isobel let out a long, slow, whispering sigh.

'These socks are nice, dear. Shall I get him a pair – to go with the tie?'

Desperate to elicit some kind of response, Taz put her hands on her mother's shoulders.

'Mum. It'll be Christmas soon. You know how you and Daddy always come over for the day. Will I be seeing you again this year?'

'I don't know dear,' Isobel whispered. 'I wish I did, but I really don't know.'

'I wouldn't worry about your Dad,' said Dee, passing round mugs of hot chocolate. 'He'll come round.'

'I'm not so sure,' said Taz, drinking in the mug's warmth, more than welcome on this wild and wet November evening. 'He's like me – pig-headed.'

'My mother was so pleased when I told her about the baby,' said Chloë, stirring her chocolate reflectively and licking the spoon.

''Course she was pleased.' These were the first words Mandy had uttered since Taz had persuaded her to come back to Dee's after the meeting. She'd been positively passive all night. 'You've got a fella.'

'So have you,' pointed out Dee. 'What did you say his name was . . . Dave, wasn't it?'

'Yeah.' Mandy jabbed her index finger into the middle of a ginger biscuit, shattering it like ice on a pond. 'Dave.'

'Isn't he happy about the baby then?' asked Chloë, her blue eyes fixed with more than usual interest on Mandy. 'Isn't he looking forward to being a father?'

'It was a crap idea comin' here,' said Mandy abruptly, getting up. 'I'm off home.'

'Don't go.' On a sudden impulse she couldn't quite explain, Taz laid her hand on Mandy's arm. More surprised than annoyed, Mandy stared down at her.

'Stay and have a chat, Chloë didn't mean to upset you, did you Chloë?'

Cloë blinked back, mystified as only the very middle-class could be.

'Of course not. I didn't know I had. What did I say?'

'Oh shut up,' said Mandy without much energy. She looked down at Taz. 'Just for a bit then.'

Mandy sat down heavily, her growing bump jiggling underneath her Metallica tee-shirt: the one, Taz recalled, that Mandy said belonged to Dave. Normally she favoured little stretchy crop-tops that strained to contain her swollen breasts, or tight mini-dresses in colours that made you wince. She was wearing that faded old tee-shirt like a comfort blanket.

'I didn't think much of tonight's class,' observed Taz, keen to stick to a safe topic. 'Steffi didn't seem quite . . . well . . . with it.'

'She's getting divorced,' said Dee, pausing between mouthfuls of cake. 'Didn't you know? Caught her husband with the woman who does the ironing.'

'No!' Chloë clapped her hand to her mouth.

'Kicked him out in his underpants. Mind you, she won't go through with the divorce. It's not the first time it's happened, she always takes him back. Says they have to stay together for the kids.'

'For the money you mean,' said Mandy. 'What is he, an accountant or somethin'? She's not stupid.'

'Oh, I'm sure it's nothing like that,' said Chloë, who would have given Bluebeard the benefit of the doubt.

Well I'm not, thought Taz, but didn't say so.

The sound of footsteps coming down the back stairs halted Dee in the middle of an exposé of Steffi Parkes' love-life. She grinned.

'That'll be Adam, my tenant – you know, he rents the upstairs flat.'

'Is he nice?' enquired Chloë.

Dee gave a dirty laugh as she crammed the last morsel of cake into her mouth.

'Almost worth dieting for. But only almost.'

A young man walked in. Not just any young man though, thought Taz with the kind of rush of interest she was sure mothers-to-be weren't supposed to have. He was, quite simply, a hunk. How else could you describe someone who was a lithe six-four, golden-haired with a

90

crinkly smile that somehow managed to combine strength and vulnerability?

He strolled into the café, a sports bag under his arm. He looked understatedly athletic in black Levi's and a rugby shirt, the sleeves casually rolled to reveal fine golden hairs that glistened as they caught the light.

Dee got up and grabbed him by the arm, urging, 'Adam, come and say hello, don't be shy. Ladies, this is Adam Rolfe.'

'You never told me you were having cake,' grinned Adam, picking a stray currant off Dee's plate. 'I'd have come earlier.' His voice was nice too, thought Taz dreamily, her eyes travelling up from Adam's smiling mouth to his twinkling grey-blue eyes.

Dee busied herself with the introductions.

'This is Chloë.'

'Pleased to meet you.'

'And Taz.'

'Short for Tasmanian Devil? I shall have to watch my step,' Adam joked.

'Tasmin actually,' babbled Taz, who couldn't think of anything witty or even sensible to say. 'But I hate it.'

'I don't. It's nice.' He actually sounded as if he meant it.

'And this is . . . Mandy. Mandy, don't you want to say hello to Adam?'

Mandy showed not the faintest spark of interest. Dee nudged her and she pulled a face.

'Hello to Adam.'

'Adam's a solicitor,' said Dee, as proudly as if she'd been his mother. She even fiddled with the collar of his rugby shirt, a gesture which he must have hated but put up with with remarkable good humour.

'Really?' Chloë pricked her ears up. 'One of the big practices?'

'Actually I work at the local law centre. Private practice never really appealed to me.'

His eyes met Taz's, only briefly, but long enough for Taz to feel a shameless shiver of pleasure. You silly girl, she told herself, don't you ever learn? Five months pregnant and you're still trying to pick up blokes.

91

'So you're a saint too,' she murmured. The words escaped before she'd had a chance to realise what she was saying.

'Heck no, strictly a sinner,' replied Adam, the smile lopsided and slightly self-deprecating. Taz wondered, with an ache of hopeless lust, exactly what that might mean. 'Anyhow, must go, the court's booked for nine-thirty.'

Pity, thought Taz, watching the door rattle in its frame as it closed behind Adam's retreating back.

'Told you he was nice,' said Dee smugly.

'So . . . are you and he . . .? I mean, is he the father?' asked Chloë. Good question, thought Taz. Dee made no secret of the fact that her three kids had two different fathers, not that she could have if she'd wanted to as they were also two different colours. Compared to Dee's, Taz's own love life seemed quite tame.

'Hardly. He's not my type,' laughed Dee.

'Then who . . .?'

'Oh, Carl and I split up months ago. I'm with someone else now, I'll have to introduce you some time.'

But Taz was still thinking about Adam Rolfe. Idiot, she told herself; but sometimes even single mums-to-be needed to dream.

It was late. Rain was pelting down out of murky sky. Taz stood in the doorway of the Green Café and pulled up the collar of her raincoat. Good job the car wasn't parked too far away.

Taz wished she'd brought an umbrella; still, a bit of rain wouldn't hurt. She was about to make a run for it when she noticed Mandy hanging back.

'Not going home?'

Mandy stared up at the rain.

'Only missed my bus, haven't I? I'll have to walk now.'

'Where do you live?'

'Hollybush Estate,' said Marion, looking evasive.

'But that's two miles away! And all you've got is that little denim jacket.'

'So what if I have?' she sniffed.

Taz noticed for the first time that her eyes looked pink-rimmed and puffy.

'Have you been crying?'

'What's it to you?'

'Maybe I can help.'

'You all think you're God incarnate you lot, don't you? Well you're bleedin' well not, so keep your stinking nose out of it, all right?'

Taken aback by this outburst, Taz fumbled in her pocket for a tissue. If she wasn't much use as an amateur psychologist she could perhaps try the practical approach.

'All right. Whatever you say. Here, use this, it's clean.'

Mandy hesitated, then took the tissue and blew her nose.

'It's nothing. I'll sort it out myself.' She started walking out into the bucketing rain, the heavy droplets bouncing off her hunched shoulders. Taz set off in pursuit, her boots making squelching noises on the wet pavement.

'Come with me, let me give you a lift home.'

Mandy stopped and looked at her.

'What – to Hollybush?' She spoke the word as if it was the far side of the moon.

'To wherever. I'm not having you wandering about in the rain. Come on, the car's in the Henrietta Street car park.'

Mandy didn't reply, but shrugged and started trudging along beside Taz, hands in the pockets of her rust-coloured denim jacket.

'Are you all right, Mandy?'

'You're not my social worker, butt out will you?'

'OK. Like I said, I only wanted to help. And I couldn't help noticing . . .'

Mandy looked up sharply, her rain-dampened face small and childlike in the sodium glare from the street lamp overhead.

'Noticin' what?'

'That you've been crying.'

Mandy bit her lip.

'This your car then?'

Taz nodded, unlocking the passenger door.

'Not much cop, is it?'

Taz slid into the driver's seat, catching her reflection in the rearview mirror. Her hair was plastered in wet strands to the side of her face. She looked like a drowned rat.

'It doesn't suit you,' said Mandy once she was in.

'That hairstyle. You should have it feathered at the sides so it's softer round your face.' Her voice tailed off into a mutter, as though annoyed that she had been caught out showing enthusiasm. 'I did a hairdressing course once.'

'Is that what you do now?'

'The salon chucked me as soon as I got to seventeen – too expensive to keep me on, see. I've been doing a bit of cleanin'. S'pose I'll have to stop soon, what with the baby.'

She laid her two hands flat against her stomach. And then, to Taz's complete amazement, Mandy started to cry.

'Mandy! Mandy, whatever's the matter?' She tried to slide her arm round Mandy's sodden shoulders, and this time Mandy didn't shrug her off. Her whole body was shaking with sobs.

'It's Dave, innit?'

'Dave? What's wrong with him? Is he ill?'

'He's in the nick. They said he's been doin' burglaries again, didn't they? Only this time he didn't do it but they're goin' to send him down anyway, I know they are . . .'

'Oh.' Taz hardly knew what to say. 'Look . . . maybe it's not that bad. He might get off. Or maybe they'll let him off with a caution or something.'

'He's had one already.' Mandy wiped her eyes on her sleeve, and sniffed loudly. 'So've I, that's why the social services are sniffin' round, see. Dave thought it'd be a laugh to nick a car and go for a ride. Dickhead,' she said, but there was more affection and sadness in her voice than anger.

For a moment, Taz thought Mandy was actually going to open up, then she shook back her green rats' tails.

'Are we goin' or what then?'

On the drive across Cheltenham to the Hollybush Estate, they talked about everything but Mandy. They talked about hairstyles, disposable nappies, football, motorbikes. It was as if the oyster-shell which had almost opened up had suddenly snapped shut again.

Hollybush was even more dismal than Taz had expected it to be. The dark, windy, rainy night didn't help, but, this place couldn't look friendly even if the sun was beating down out of a cloudless sky. Row upon row of identical houses stared out with empty eyes, some boarded up and deserted, others boasting wrecked cars in the front gardens or black burn marks where some bored teenager had tried to burn the whole lot down. Over the whole sorry mess loomed three dilapidated tower blocks, relics from the Sixties that somebody had forgotten to pull down.

'Lovely, innit,' commented Mandy. 'Been here before have you? Didn't think so. You should see the look on your face.'

'Have you always lived here?'

'Yeah. Course.' Mandy laughed. 'Did you read in last week's paper? They're going to graze sheep on the grass over there, to make it look more friendly. Poor bloody sheep, they won't last five minutes, people round here can't afford roast lamb.'

'Where do you live?'

'You can drop me here if you like.'

'It's OK, I'll take you right up to the door.'

'Like I said, drop me here. I'll walk the rest of the way,' insisted Mandy defensively.

Taz stopped the car and Mandy got out, her tatty rucksack hanging limply from one shoulder.

'Thanks for the lift. Sorry I can't ask you in for coffee, I haven't got any. Besides, you wouldn't like where I live.'

'Try me,' said Taz bravely, though she was pretty sure that Mandy was right.

'You'd better get a move on,' Mandy called back over her shoulder. 'Stay here more than five seconds and they'll have your hub caps.'

Taz watched her walking into the distance, head down, taking short, quick steps that made the rucksack bounce against her back. Strange girl. And intriguing. For every protective layer you peeled off, there were another ten you'd probably never get through.

And as she drove away, she thought of the book she'd seen peeping out of the top of Mandy's rucksack. What was a girl like Mandy Robson doing with a copy of Gabriel Garcia Marquez?

Chapter 7

Taz was just hauling herself out of the bath on Saturday evening when the doorbell went.

That would be Al from upstairs, on the scrounge again. Trust him to turn up now. She wriggled into her dressing gown and slippers, casting a quick glance into the hall mirror to check that she was decent.

'OK, coming. Hang on a minute.' She wrenched the bath-cap off her hair and tossed it onto the telephone table. 'Just a mo, the door sticks.'

Off came the safety chain and the door juddered open. Outside, on the landing, slouched a gum-chewing punkette with green hair and orange lipstick.

'*Mandy*?'

'Come any time, you said.' At the café, last week. So I'm here.'

'Oh. Yes, I suppose I did.' But I didn't really mean it, thought Taz guiltily. And you and I both know it, which is probably why you're calling my bluff.

'Well?' The ball of gum changed cheeks. 'Can I come in then, or what?'

'Y-yeah, of course. If you don't mind the mess. I haven't vacuumed for a week.'

'Nice place this,' observed Mandy as she swanned off down the hallway without so much as a by-your-leave, sticking her head into each room. She erupted into the living room and flopped down on the sofa. 'Disgusting wallpaper though, all those stripes, makes you go cross-eyed.'

Taz looked at the wallpaper in a way she'd never done

before. It was the expensive designer wallpaper Gareth had chosen specially for her. Now, for the first time, she saw that it was completely hideous.

'And what's that brown stain? You got damp or somethin'?'

All the sponging and scrubbing in the world hadn't got rid of the oily brown skidmark where the birthday cake had hit the wall. Taz had meant to strip the entire wall and repaper with the spare roll she'd kept, but somehow she'd never quite got round to it; and eventually she'd learned to stop seeing the stain.

'Actually it's buttercream. There was a bit of an accident . . . with a cake.'

'Must've been some party,' commented Mandy with a grin.

'It was my birthday.' Taz wondered why she was telling Mandy any of this. She ought to feel angry that the pushy little tart had barged in on her lazy Saturday evening, which she'd planned to spend with *A Hundred and One Dalmatians* and a box of Milk Tray. But if anything, she felt relieved. 'Do you want a cup of tea or something?'

'Got any fruit juice? I don't fancy tea any more, it gives me heartburn.'

'Yeah? I'm like that with strawberry yoghurt.' Taz walked through into the kitchen. 'Orange all right?'

'Fine.' Mandy followed Taz into the kitchen, where Minky was trying hard to get into the fridge. 'Cool cat.'

'That's Minky. Minky, say hello to Mandy.'

'Prrp.'

'I was wondering if I ought really to find her another home. I mean, with all this talk about toxoplasmosis . . .'

Mandy laughed and – not without a certain amount of difficult – bent down to scoop the cat into her arms.

'She wouldn't get rid of you, would she? Not a cool cat like you.' Mandy scratched the end of the cat's nose, and Minky rolled over in her arms, in a shameless display of sensual abandon.

'Get rid of her? No. No, you're right, I'd cry my eyes out.'

'And if you were goin' to catch anything you'd have

caught it by now. Besides,' Mandy scanned the kitchen, 'you're messy but you're not that dirty.'

'Well ta very much I'm sure!' Taz swung round with two glasses of orange juice, not quite decided whether to laugh or pour it over Mandy's head. Mandy was generous with her backhanded compliments. 'Do you want to drink it here, or shall we go through?'

'Here's fine. I like other people's kitchens.' Mandy hauled herself up until she was sitting on the worktop, swinging her trainered feet and several inches of purple striped sock. 'Ours is like a cupboard. Even the cockroaches have put in for a transfer.'

Taz drew up a chair and sat down. She looked up at Mandy, her hair gelled into droopy green spikes that made her look like a dejected circus clown.

'Your mum and dad still aren't happy about the baby, are they?'

'Dad says if I don't chuck Dave for good, he won't have anythin' to do with me or the baby.'

'And your mum?'

'She shouts and cries a lot, but she always ends up doin' what Dad wants.'

Taz sensed Mandy's anger and despair, teeming perilously close beneath the hard surface.

'You could move out, find a place of your own.' As soon as she said it, Taz knew it was a stupid thing to say.

'Oh yeah. And where am I goin' to get the deposit?'

'There's your cleaning job.'

'They laid me off yesterday, said now I'm gettin' big I won't be able to do the job properly.'

'Oh Mandy. I'm sorry.' Taz knew better than most how it hurt to be told you were no use any more, just because you were pregnant. 'What about Social Services?'

At this, Mandy's head jerked up and her hand moved to her belly in a protective reflex.

'I'm not lettin' them take it away from me. This baby's mine.'

The ferocity of Mandy's response stunned Taz. She'd thought of the girl as apathetic, even hostile, towards the thought of being a mother; and yet here she was, clasping her unborn child and hissing defiance like a mother cat.

'But they wouldn't – would they?'

'What do *you* think?'

Taz didn't reply. She and Mandy went on looking at each other for a few moments. Mandy's gaze slid down to a book lying on the draining board by the sink, where Taz had dropped it.

'*Being a Mother – Naturally* – I've read that one.'

'Really?' Taz felt a surge of relief as the tension snapped.

'It was crap. Hippy rubbish, all lentils an' meditation.'

'Still, there's a lot to be said for . . . you know . . . natural methods. Like Steffi says.'

'You reckon? I'm not into pain myself.'

Taz laughed, 'Me neither. Give me an anaesthetic and wake me up when it's all over. Do you want a biscuit?'

Mandy helped herself to a Hob-Nob from the tin. 'I shouldn't though, I'm gettin' fat. Any more on my bum and I'll have to wear maternity gear.' She wrinkled her nose. 'Mothercare, God, I don't know how you can stand all that polyester.' She looked Taz up and down. 'Want to know somethin'?'

'What?'

'You look shagged out.'

'I'm fine!'

'No you're not, you've got spots and there are bags under your eyes.' As Mandy got into her stride, Taz had the uncomfortable sensation of being scolded by her mother. She was also beginning to feel rather less than glamorous. 'You're a bit fat as well, maybe it's fluid. You want to watch that.'

'Yes, I know, but . . .'

'What did they tell you down the hospital?'

'Well . . .' Taz squirmed guiltily. 'Actually I had to miss my last clinic appointment . . . there's so much on at work.'

Mandy couldn't have looked more disgusted if Taz had announced that she had a full set of Michael Bolton records.

'You *missed* it? How could you *do* that? What about the baby?'

'It's OK, I'll go to the next one.'

'You bet you will. 'Cause I'm goin' with you.'

Taz stared at Mandy.

'You're what?'

'You heard.' And that was the end of that. Mandy unplugged the kettle, took it over to the sink and filled it up. 'You want to descale this, it's gone all furry. Now, where's your teabags? Better have two sugars, you look like you could use the energy.'

Taz was going to say 'But I don't take sugar,' but there didn't seem a lot of point. Mandy had turned into the human tornado and, in a funny kind of way, Taz sort of liked it.

More out of habit than anything else, Taz reached down the box of Milk Tray from the kitchen cupboard. It was a full pound box, plenty big enough for two.

'Mandy . . . Have you got anything planned for tonight?'

'Nothing special, why?'

'Don't suppose you like *A Hundred and One Dalmatians*, do you?'

Things were hectic at Seuss & Goldman, the pace of work hotting up with each day that brought Christmas one step closer.

Without Kate, Taz found herself relying more and more on Leroy and Marion. Justin would be OK once he'd settled in, but he was still learning the ropes. Annoyingly, Marion seemed more distracted than ever, Leroy kept having to ask for half-days off at short notice, and Pauline – well, Pauline was reliable enough as long as neither of her children had measles, but she wouldn't have worked one minute of overtime even if you'd put a gun to her head. And as for the temporary Christmas staff, all they cared about was the money.

Wednesday was Leroy's day off, and with Marion seconded to help out the flu-stricken china and glass department, staffing was especially tight. After lunch, Taz gave Justin his instructions for the rest of the day.

'You know what to do with that delivery of Galliano jackets?'

'Get them out asap.'

'Yes, but make sure visual merchandising prepares the stand first. Patros told me he wants to do something with fun-fur and rollerblades. Oh – and if I'm not back by the end of trading, you'll have to cash up and make sure the tills go up to the cash office. And don't forget to hand in the till tag at security, or there'll be no float tomorrow . . .'

Taz was just about to tell him it all a third time, to be on the safe side, when Alice, one of the students, beckoned her over.

'Call for you. In the office.'

She went into the office and picked up the phone.

'Menswear, Tasmin Norton speaking.'

'Taz, it's Cherie. Cherie Hooper, remember?'

Taz remembered all right. She and Cherie had been on the S&G management programme together, only Cherie had been too much of an individual to fit in. She'd left after six months, taking all her quirky brilliance with her, and walked straight into the manager's job at the Gloucester branch of Heroes Menswear.

'Cherie! How are you?'

'I'm great. And you?'

'Er . . . terrific.' Or at least, thought Taz, as terrific as a person could be with swollen ankles and hormonal itching.

'I heard congratulations are in order. When's it due?'

'Somewhere around the end of March.'

'And you're coming back to work afterwards?'

'Too right I am. I'd go crazy at home all day. Now, Cherie, what can I do for you?' Taz glanced at her watch. 'Only I've got a meeting in ten minutes.'

'It's about Leroy McIntosh's application.'

'Leroy? Application for what?'

'For the assistant manager's job, here at Heroes.' A cold shiver ran down Taz's spine. So *this* was why Leroy had been having so much time off lately.

'Oh.'

'I take it you didn't know then.'

102

In the short silence, Taz pulled herself together. OK, so Leroy hadn't told her he was applying for jobs, but then he was by no means obliged to, and in a similar position she'd probably have kept her mouth shut too.

'Let me guess – you want a reference?'

'On the nose. Leroy really impressed us at interview, but we need a second opinion. What do you reckon – could he handle it?'

For a split second, Taz fought the temptation to say, 'No, Leroy's hopelessly immature, he's not ready for that kind of responsibility yet.' But that would be barefaced lying. She took a deep breath.

'Yes, no question. He's been here three years and I know he's about ready for a change. He's thorough, responsible and creative. I'd be sorry to see him go, but whatever you offer him you'll be getting a bargain.'

'Thanks Taz, that's all I needed to know. Good luck with the baby – rather you than me.'

Taz felt curiously empty for a few moments, as though someone had died, or a close friend was moving away. She'd come to regard Leroy almost as a permanent fixture, and that, of course, was not just unwise but careless too.

With two minutes to spare, she walked into the seminar room – and breathed a sigh of relief as Brendan and Cara greeted her with what looked like genuine smiles. If only she could say the same for Ted, with his sly grin and piggy eyes.

'Morning Cara, Brendan. Ted. Ken not here again?'

Ted opened his Filofax at a page covered in meticulous pencilled notes.

'Ken's in Wiltshire, looking at sausages.'

'Lucky old Ken,' sniggered Cara.

'He asked me to deputise for him and report back. You'll be circulating full minutes to him, of course?'

'Of course.' Taz cursed Ted's love of procedure. 'But this is essentially informal, and we have a lot of work to get through, so let's keep the paperwork to a minimum. Now Brendan, shall we start with you? How've you been getting on?'

She hardly dared hope that Brendan would be ready to

cooperate. But it seemed that their endless, acrimonious squabbles had got somewhere at last, and his old enthusiasm was clearly resurfacing as he called up a page of text on his portable PC.

'The arrangements for the fashion show are coming along fine. Head office can supply as much catwalk and staging as we want. We've got Imperial Gardens for the whole of that afternoon and until midnight, with an all-weather canopy in case the weather lets us down.'

'I'm liaising with my opposite number in America, as you suggested.' Brendan nodded an acknowledgement to Taz, who chalked up an invisible point scored. 'And we've agreed to concentrate on using the professional catwalk models in the American event. We'll stick to semi-pros and some of the younger members of staff for the Cheltenham show.'

'Good idea,' said Taz, for once in full agreement with Brendan. She jotted down a few details. 'It's the American show which will get most of the publicity.'

'And people find professionals intimidating sometimes,' added Cara. 'They want to know what the clothes are going to look like on real people. If you like, Brendan, I'll ask some of my girls and boys if they want to model – they have the right athletic look for sportswear.'

'Yeah, thanks, great idea. We have some great new swimwear designs lined up.'

'And how about the sporting events, Cara?' Taz turned her attentions to the next item on her list. 'Any luck with the basketball team?'

'All under control. The appeal in the local paper worked out well – so far we've got ten families offering accommodation, so we only need a couple more. Oh, and I'm looking into that idea you had for a fancy-dress softball game in aid of disabled kids.'

'Fine. So, Ted – any news on Ken's plans for the food hall?' Taz had a sense of foreboding as Ted cleared his throat, unfolding a concertina of Filofax paper, covered with a giant flow-chart.

'He's working on the catering, you'll be getting that interim report from him next week.'

'I'd better,' said Taz grimly. 'Or I'll be pinning him to the wall by his earlobes. And yes, Ted, you *can* tell him I said that. Now, what else?'

'I've come up with an idea,' announced Ted. 'A good one. In fact, the promotions manager at head office is so keen, he wants us to go ahead with it right away.'

'He what!' Taz's mouth fell open. 'You're telling me you've gone over my head to the promotions manager, without even consulting me?'

Ted's voice was soothing, his smile redefining the meaning of 'smug'.

'Cool it, Taz, it needed acting on straight away and you weren't around. You were at the ante-natal clinic I think . . .'

'Right. You'd better tell us all about this marvellous idea, hadn't you? Or is it so wonderful you've decided to keep it to yourself?'

'Now why would I do that?' Why indeed, thought Taz; when you can show us all what an unbearable little smart-arse you are. He cleared his throat. 'As you probably know, before Seuss & Goldman I worked in the travel industry – in fact, for a company which specialised in arranging complimentary overseas trips as incentives for sales executives who met their annual targets.'

'Go on.' Taz tried staring him out, but nothing seemed to unsettle Ted.

'I had a word with my former employers, and they were happy to donate a family trip – for two adults and two children – to Los Angeles. All they're asking in return is a little publicity.'

'Anyhow, I rang up the promotions manager, and he agreed that we could run an in-store competition – the winners to travel to Los Angeles in March and cut the ribbon at the store opening.'

He sat back in his chair, arms folded, and waited for the applause to start.

You're right, thought Taz, it *is* a good idea. You sneaky bastard. You've obstructed me all the way, you've gone behind my back, and now the promotions manager thinks you're the best thing since Wonderbras. Why, it was almost worthy of Gareth.

'So – what do you think?' enquired Ted with oh-so-innocent curiosity.

'I think . . . it's a great idea, Ted. Well done, credit where credit's due.'

But the words almost stuck in her throat.

If Mandy Robson said she was going to do something, she did it. And sure enough, the following Tuesday morning found her on Taz's doorstep. She wasn't about to take no for an answer.

'Got your sample?'

'Yes.'

'Been takin' your iron tablets? And are you sittin' with your feet up, like the doctor said?'

Taz looked at Mandy.

'What is this – twenty questions?'

'Somebody's got to take care of you,' sniffed Mandy. 'It's obvious you're not takin' care of yourself.'

She stalked off towards Taz's car and Taz followed, complete with briefcase packed with sardine and peanut butter sandwiches, a half-finished sales report, clean knickers and a paracetamol bottle full of wee. If the top came off the bottle she'd be in real trouble.

'Hurry up Taz, we'll be late.'

'Late!' she scoffed as she tossed her briefcase onto the back seat and squeezed in behind the wheel – a manoeuvre which was becoming more and more of an Olympic event. 'No one ever gets seen on time at that place.'

'That's because they give everybody the same appointment,' said Mandy wisely.

'Why on earth would they do that?'

'God knows.' Mandy treated her to a good hard stare. 'So the doc won't be kickin' his heels when daft cows like you don't turn up for their check-ups?'

As it happened Taz was right, they needn't have rushed. Outpatients was crammed with a chaos of large stomachs, baby buggies and baffled, fractious toddlers. A notice on the wall proclaimed: PATIENTS WILL BE DEALT WITH AS QUICKLY AS POSSIBLE. THIS CLINIC IS RUNNING APPROXIMATELY ONE AND A HALF HOURS LATE. The 'one and a half hours' bit was untidily handwritten, on a piece of yellowing cardboard that looked as if it had been around for a very long time.

'One and a half hours!' groaned Taz. 'I can't wait that long, I've got the rep from Junior Gaultier coming at eleven. I'll have to go.'

'Look Taz, everybody has to wait. It's what havin' a baby's all about. Why should you be any different?'

'All right, all right. I know.'

Taz sank down onto the last empty chair and picked up a magazine. She resigned herself to getting through every back issue of *Horse and Hound* before earning the right to leave Purgatory.

'You got a birthin' partner yet then?' asked Mandy out of the blue.

'No. I haven't really thought about it.'

'What about your fella?'

'I haven't got one, I told you. He doesn't know I'm pregnant and as far as I'm concerned that's just fine.'

'I s'pose,' said Mandy reflectively, bending forward to look at her toes over the smooth arch of her stomach. 'What about your mum then?'

'I don't know. Maybe. I think she's coming round, but if Dad doesn't see sense ... To be honest, I'm not even sure I'd want her there when I have the baby. What about you?'

'Dave's in the nick.'

'I thought he was out on bail.'

Mandy shook her green locks dispiritedly. Her roots were showing, a mousy mud-brown against the emerald dye.

'Went and got drunk an' threw a punch at a copper, didn't he? He's in Gloucester Prison on remand. It could be months ...'

Taz squeezed Mandy's hand, as encouragingly as she could.

'He'll get off. If he really is innocent.'

'I just wish I could have him for Christmas, that's all.'

Mandy's eyes lingered on the decorations strung across the ceiling; every time the door opened, a gust of cold air shook the red and gold tinsel stars, making them dance.

'There's always next Christmas.'

At that moment a tiny girl in a pink dress tripped over Taz's feet, fell flat on her nose and burst into great, hacking sobs. Taz looked down at her, wanting to do something but paralysed with ineptitude.

'Where's her mother?'

'In the loo. She'll be back in a minute.'

'Oh.' The child tottered to her feet, holding out fat arms for comfort. Tears cascaded down a red and puckered face.

Mandy let out a grunt of exasperation.

'Well go on Taz, pick her up and give her a cuddle.' She winked. 'If anybody needs the practice, you do.'

At five thirty prompt on Christmas Eve, Seuss & Goldman closed its doors and let out a collective sigh of relief.

'Thank God *that's* over,' tutted Patros Nikephoros as he trundled a skip-load of cut-price sweatshirts out of the lift and onto the sales floor. 'I tell you, it gets worse every year.'

'Sold out of socks by lunchtime and not a cufflink left in the place,' commented Leroy, helping Alice to put up a sign which read:/30% OFF OWN-BRAND SUITS WHILE STOCKS LAST. 'I've never known a Christmas Eve like it.'

'You've only been here five minutes,' sniffed Marion dismissively. 'You don't know anything worth knowing.'

And Marion went back to her sullen cashing-up, leaving Leroy wondering what he'd done to get up her nose this time.

'Well I *love* Christmas,' chirruped Alice, with all the artless enthusiasm of a twenty-year-old student with a pocketful of holiday cash. 'It's the happiest time of the year. Did I tell you Daddy's buying me a car?'

'Only about twenty times,' replied Pauline through clenched teeth.

Leaning over the balcony rail, Taz surveyed the ground

floor, slowly emptying of its few, last-minute customers. A pre-recorded voice announced in perfect BBC vowels that 'The store is now closed, but don't forget that the Seuss & Goldman New Year sale begins on the twenty-seventh. We hope you have a very merry Christmas with Seuss & Goldman.'

A small, ginger-haired boy in a red duffel coat, with mittens dangling on elastic from the sleeves, was hanging back, trying to drag his mother towards one of the displays. How old was he? Two and a half? Three? 'Mummy, Mummy, want *that*.' 'Come *on*, Peter. If you're not good, Father Christmas won't bring you any toys.' And then he was gone, dragged on the end of his protesting arm past the giant Christmas tree and out into the inky twilight.

As far as Seuss & Goldman was concerned, this marked the end of Christmas: from here on in it was the New Year sale and then downhill all the way to Easter and the new summer swimwear collection.

'Better get our skates on,' said Taz, trying to ignore her burning feet, ricked neck and the niggling ache in her stomach. She rubbed the small of her back; that ached, too. All she wanted right now was to sink into a hot bath. 'We can't go home until we've got all the sale stock out. Justin – you take care of accessories with Fiona and Pauline. Alice, you can help Leroy with formalwear.'

'How long for?' said Alice, her face falling.

'Until it's done. I expect we'll be finished about nine or half-past.'

'But I've got a party to go to at eight thirty, I've brought my dress with me and everything.'

Taz shrugged. It might seem harsh, but maybe it was time Alice realised working in a shop wasn't just an easy option for people who hadn't got the talent or the social advantages to do anything else.

'Sorry, but that's the rule. Everyone stays until the displays are ready – the sale starts in three days. If you don't stay, you don't get paid.'

Alice muttered something to Wendy about it being 'barbaric' and 'not in her contract', but nobody paid her much attention. They were too busy rotating stock, helping

Patros to set up the new racking, putting out sale items and hanging up signs.

The atmosphere relaxed as the pace of work hotted up. Somebody produced a radio and tuned it to a carol service. Leroy sang along to 'Away in a Manger' in his light baritone, turning it into acid jazz. Two slightly tipsy juniors from visual merchandising danced with paper hats on their heads as they dressed up two mannequins in end-of-line Yves St Laurent baseball jackets and Dolce & Gabbana jeans. Everyone except Marion pretended not to notice when they giggled and fell over their own feet. Voices called to each other over the top of the music.

'Patros – can you get someone to do some more "ten per cent off" tickets, we're going to run out.'

'Can somebody hold the other end of this? It's falling down.'

'I knew these shirts wouldn't sell, the minute they came into the store. Everybody knows big logos don't sell.'

'Tell me about it. They had "clearance sale" written all over them.'

Taz contemplated the end of a long red and white silk banner, which needed to be draped across the entrance to the department, just at the top of the main escalator.

Picking up the end of the banner, she put her foot gingerly on the bottom rung of the stepladder. Balancing was more difficult than she'd thought it would be – with her bump sticking out, she had to go up backwards, one hand holding on, the staple gun in her pocket and the other hand grasping the banner. By the second step, she was wishing she hadn't bothered; she was more grateful than she'd ever have admitted to be rescued by Leroy.

'Miss Norton . . . please. You shouldn't be doing that.'

She looked down at him, a trifle sheepishly.

'You might hurt yourself. Let me, eh? Please?'

Instead of chewing his head off, she got down and handed him the staple gun. She wondered when he'd get round to telling her about the job at Heroes. In fact, she almost asked him outright. After all, the sooner she knew when he was planning to leave, the sooner she could get used to not having him around to rely on.

But there was no easy way of asking; and besides, there was so much to be getting on with. Time was ticking on, and people were restless to get off home to their families, to tuck up their children and kiss them goodnight.

Taz wondered about her own mum and dad. Was she being foolish to hope that they would turn up tomorrow morning on her doorstep, the way they always did, with a bottle of Dad's horrible peapod wine and a pressed ox-tongue in a cake-tin? Mum hadn't said yes ... but then again, she hadn't said no either.

Even working flat out, it wasn't until almost nine-thirty that Taz was completely satisfied with the sales displays.

'All done,' she sighed, plonking her bottom gratefully on a chair which seemed to appear from nowhere. 'Well done everyone, you've done brilliantly and I'm really grateful. Now, for goodness' sake get off home and have a wonderful Christmas. You too Justin,' she added to the hovering face beside her.

'But the gloves still need tagging . . .'

'I'll get here early on Thursday and do them. Now clear off! The lot of you!'

Cards and pleasantries were exchanged, coats collected from the cloakroom, and everyone was set to go home when the lift doors slid open. Out stepped Diana Latchford with something in a square cardboard box. Gerry Rothwell was a couple of paces behind, hands in his pockets and as coldly expressionless as ever.

'Tasmin, you're still here.' Diana Latchford nodded her approval. 'We were hoping to catch you before you left.'

Taz cursed silently, mentally picturing herself still in the store at midnight, watching Santa fly over Montpellier in his sleigh while she moved the sock display for the fifteenth time.

'What's wrong?'

'Why should anything be wrong?' Diana set the box on top of the counter by the tills. 'Mr Rothwell and I have simply come to give you your Department of the Year award.'

'My . . . what?' Taz had heard all the words, but they just didn't register inside her head. Alice gasped. Marion

111

looked bored. Leroy let out a whistle and grinned like a Cheshire Cat.

'Open the box,' said Diana.

A ripple of excitement ran around the sales assistants.

Taz lifted the lid off. Inside lay a Waterford crystal bowl engraved with the words: 'Seuss & Goldman UK. Department of the Year'. She slid her hands underneath and took it out, carefully cradling its precious fragility. This was like a wonderful dream, and like a dream, it didn't make one atom of sense.

'But . . .' she began. But Brendan! she was thinking. He's turned right round inside six months. It ought to be Brendan who's getting this, not me.

'But nothing. Really, it was a very easy decision to make, wasn't it Gerry?'

Gerry Rothwell nodded and smiled. He looked as if it was causing him great pain, but yes, he actually smiled.

'There was no contest,' he said. 'The performance of menswear over the last year has been outstanding.'

'And the credit for that,' added Diana, 'has to go to you, Tasmin. It's not been easy for you, and I admit at times I wondered how you'd manage; but that was my fault, not yours. Well done – and here's to the next twelve months.'

Euphoria struck through her exhaustion like a shaft of sunlight breaking through storm-clouds. Taz lifted the bowl and, with tears of pride and delight brimming in her eyes, she turned to face Leroy and Marion, Pauline and Justin, and all the others she'd blessed and cursed and bullied and cajoled through the year.

'This belongs to you,' she smiled. And she meant every word.

The funny thing was, the baby seemed to understand what was going on too. For at that very moment Taz felt a mighty kick right in the middle of her tummy, as Norton Junior gave a victory roll. A kick that was as stubborn and as single-minded as Taz herself.

'Ouch!' She stumbled. Diana swiftly relieved her of the bowl, setting it safely back on the counter.

'Are you all right, Tasmin? You're not ill?'

'Couldn't be better,' Taz smiled. She'd done it at last, proved that she could be pregnant and still run the tightest department in the store. And this was a perfect, crowning moment.

But even in her moment of glory, Taz knew the hardest part was yet to come.

Chapter 8

Taz lay dozing on the sofa, a half-eaten sandwich on the floor beside her and three identical pairs of lemon-coloured bootees lying side by side on the mantelpiece. People weren't always as imaginative as they might be in their choice of Christmas presents.

She was dreaming – about the baby. Instead of being born in the usual way, it was having to fight its way to the outside world through a mountain of non-sexist yellow knitwear.

The telephone rang, and Taz jolted into wakefulness.

'Mmm?' she enquired sleepily.

'If that's a man you've got there with you, put him down right now!'

'Binnie!' With a certain amount of difficulty, Taz swung her feet onto the floor and propped up her aching back with a cushion. 'Happy Christmas . . . well, Boxing Day.'

'Is it?' Binnie yawned. A yawn that sounded like it came from the heart. 'It hasn't sunk in yet.'

'Well you must be very tired,' volunteered Taz inanely. 'With the new baby . . .'

'Tired?' Binnie laughed. 'Listen kid, you don't know the half of it. You will soon though,' she added with good-humoured malice. 'So how's things?'

'Oh, you know. Fine really.' Taz thought of her still-groaning fridge. 'Two pound of sprouts and nobody to eat them.'

'Your mum and dad didn't turn up then?' Binnie sounded outraged, but Taz herself was pretty much past caring. If that was how Bill and Isobel wanted to play it, fair enough.

'Nope. I had Christmas dinner with Roland and Simon. I've never had devilled tuna roulade before. So tell me – how's Amy?'

The warmth and enthusiasm came back into Binnie's voice.

'Fantastic. Gorgeous. Perfect. I love her to bits.'

'And what's Scotland like?'

'God knows. Most of it's under two feet of snow. I haven't been out since last Thursday.'

'And Jim? He's OK?'

'As far as I can tell,' grunted Binnie. 'He's on a bloody oil rig.'

'An oil rig! At Christmas?'

'Apparently it's a very important oil rig and it's never heard of statutory bank holidays. So me and Amy are stuck with trying to entertain the three old hags from *Macbeth* – Jim's mum, Granny Jean and Great Aunt Shula. You'll meet them when you come up for the christening.'

'I'm not sure I want to!'

'Just make sure you pack a flak jacket,' said Binnie pointedly. 'They're rabid Presbyterians, the lot of 'em. Now quick, tell me all the gossip – we should have ten minutes before Amy wakes up for a feed. Have you got a bloke yet?'

Taz thought this was the funniest thing in the world. Ever.

'Hardly! I'm seven months pregnant!'

'So what? Go on, tell Auntie Binnie.'

Taz hesitated. Her eyes flicked to the TV screen.

'Binnie . . . I was thinking . . . about the christening.'

'You *are* still coming?' Taz thought she caught a note of panic in Binnie's voice, but it wasn't like Binnie to lose her cool. She was always so capable, so in control of everything. 'Promise me you've not changed your mind.'

'Yes, of course I'm coming. But I was just thinking – maybe it's not such a great idea for me to be Amy's godmother. What with me being single and pregnant ... people are bound to talk ...'

Binnie's voice turned to tempered steel.

'Now listen here, *Mizz* Norton. I had a heart-to-heart with the minister and he said if I'm happy, he's happy. Amy's going to have godparents she can be proud of, and if Great Aunt Shula doesn't like it she can lump it. Got that?'

Defeated, Taz flopped back onto a pile of cushions.

'Got it.'

'I can't wait to see that woman's face,' said Binnie. 'I've had nothing but earache since the day Amy was born. You'd think nobody else in the world had ever breastfed. Mind you, I'm not winning any prizes,' she added ruefully. 'You'd think with breasts this size I'd be lactating gold top by the gallon. Now wouldn't you?'

'Well ...'

'Only *now* I find out it doesn't work that way. And poor Amy gets half-suffocated every time I try to put her on the nipple. I don't know which of us ends up more exhausted.' And as for sex – 'I'm never *ever* going to do *that* again.'

'Oh Binnie,' giggled Taz, helpless with laughter. Binnie Lethbridge was the last person she could imagine embracing celibacy. Or at least, the last person behind Dee Wiechula. 'You don't mean that!'

'Oh yes I darned well do. It's like sitting on razor blades. I tell you Taz, it's a cruel world and the blokes get all the lucky breaks. Speaking of which, how's things at S&G? Is my department missing me yet?'

'Of course!'

'Keep lying to me, I like it.'

'It's the truth. Mike Collins made a real hash of the reorganisation, they've moved him to electrical goods and brought in someone from Birmingham. Profits are down almost five per cent since the summer.'

'You really know how to boost a girl's ego. So what's doing in menswear?'

'We got Department of the Year ...'

'Congratulations! I knew you could do it.'

' . . . Marion is still biting everybody's head off . . . oh, and did I tell you about Leroy? He was offered assistant manager at Heroes in Gloucester. And do you know what? He *turned it down*!'

'Well, well, well,' Binnie said slyly. 'I wonder why.'

'What's *that* supposed to mean?'

'Nothing. Only that he fancies you.'

'He does not!' Taz was grateful that Binnie couldn't see her expression.

'If you say so. But I bet he bought you a Christmas present.'

Taz coughed embarrassedly. So what if Leroy had bought her a present? Everyone in the department bought presents for everyone else, it was traditional. OK, so Leroy was the only one to buy her something that wasn't for the baby . . .

'You know what?' she countered. 'I think motherhood has addled your brain.'

Binnie exploded into hollow laughter.

'Just you wait till *you're* up to your elbows in dirty baby-wipes and your mother-in-law's bending your ear about nappy-rash.'

'Yeah, well – that's not likely to happen to me, is it? I haven't even got a boyfriend, let alone a mother-in-law.'

'Ouch. Sorry. Foot in mouth. The thing is, Taz, I've only had three hours' sleep in the last seventy-two and I'm starting to *enjoy* daytime TV. Take no notice of me.' Binnie started fussing and clucking like a distracted bantam hen. 'Oh no, I think I can hear Amy crying . . . hang on, no, it's OK, it's the radio. What train are you getting when you come up?'

'I don't know yet, I'll have to check the timetable.'

'Well don't forget to ring and tell me, so Jim can come and pick you up from the station. He might as well make himself useful for something,' she added darkly. 'Oh – and bring some apricot and date bread will you? You can't get it up here.'

Brrring. Brrr-ing, brr-ing.

The sound of the doorbell caught Taz unawares. It was Boxing Day teatime, with the dusk closing in around the hills, a time for dozing off with mince pies and a sitcom, not for unexpected calls. Maybe she'd left something at Roland and Simon's.

'There's someone at the door, Binnie, I'll have to go . . .'

'Remember, no chickening out of the christening.'

'No, no, bye, see you soon.'

'Bye.'

Taz got to her feet and walked to the front door, as quickly as her expanded girth would allow; squeezing past the jumble of unopened cardboard boxes of baby equipment.

The bell sounded again, just as she managed to get the door open.

'Hello, dear. Can I come in?'

'*Mummy*!' Tax gasped.

Isobel must have seen the spark of astonished pleasure in her daughter's eyes, for her look of apologetic embarrassment turned to a tentative smile.

'It's a bit cold out here on the doorstep . . . oh, what a lot of boxes, are they things for the baby? You've not bought a pram have you? You do know it's bad luck to bring a pram into the house before the baby's born?'

Taz drew her mother, still chattering nervously, into the hallway and closed the door behind her.

Isobel met her daughter's gaze.

'I've been a silly woman, Tasmin. I let your father bully me into not calling you yesterday. I'm sorry.'

'It's all right, Mummy, really it is.'

'He's so stubborn, he just won't budge.'

'I know.'

'He knows he's in the wrong, but he's gone so far he doesn't know how to say sorry.'

They looked at each other, smiled stupidly, tried a nervous arm round the shoulders that turned into a clinging hug.

'Cup of tea?' enquired Taz, leading the way into the living room. The nine-inch-high tinsel tree on top of the TV set – the sole concession to Christmas decorations in the entire flat – suddenly seemed every bit as festive as the giant Norwegian spruce in Trafalgar Square.

'That'd be lovely.' Isobel reached into her pocket and took out a square package, wrapped up in red paper tied with gold ribbon. 'I got you this.'

Taz took it, kissing her mother on her lightly-powdered cheek. It smelt of Yardley's Lavender.

'Thank you!'

'It's not much – just a silk scarf and a bit of scented soap. I just thought . . . everyone will be buying you things for the baby, and I don't suppose you've much spare money to spend on yourself.'

It didn't matter that the silk scarf was expensively hideous, or that the overpowering flowery scent of the soap made Taz's oversensitive stomach squirm with discomfort. All that mattered was that her mother had remembered, had thought about her. Had *forgiven* her.

'Where's Dad?' asked Taz, clearing a space for her mother on the sofa.

'Sulking in front of *The Great Escape*.' Isobel met Taz's quizzical look, and smiled. She hadn't smiled much lately, thought Taz. It suited her. 'And I'm going to let him stew in his own juice for a few hours. Maybe it'll bring him to his senses.'

Snow, snow; sheep, sheep, snow.

As the Inter-City chugged north, the landscape became increasingly devoid of human habitation. And the laden sky was almost whiter than the hills on which it rested, threatening still more snow.

Taz was beginning to wonder if it mightn't have been wiser to stay home, after all. She knew for a fact that Mandy thought she was barmy – she'd told her so – and Isobel was full of lurid anecdotes about mums-to-be having to be rescued from remote Scottish hillsides by helicopter. Only Dee had been positively encouraging. 'Make the most of it,' she'd said firmly. 'It'll be the last holiday you get in a long time.'

Probably the last holiday ever, mused Taz. This motherhood lark was proving more expensive than she'd ever imagined, and the baby wasn't even born yet. Three hundred pounds for a baby buggy! You could have three weeks in Malta for that, or practically an entire lifetime at Butlin's, as Al had been quick to point out. Ah well, she'd just have to pray for a massive pay-rise at her annual appraisal.

The January sales had passed in their usual blur of activity. Weary as she was, Taz had enjoyed the hurly-burly. She'd always loved the special buzz of the sales. You didn't even have to try to sell people things – the merchandise practically wrapped itself up and walked out of the door. Funny to think that, come the July sales, she'd be on maternity leave . . .

'Fraser! Fraser, will you move yoursel'?' A thin-faced woman picking her way between the seats dealt a less-than-gentle nudge to the four-year-old in front of her, and he promptly tripped over Taz's jutting foot. 'Watch where you're goin', you stupid bairn.'

'Oh – sorry,' said Taz, hastily withdrawing her foot. 'Is he all right?' But the harassed mother wasn't listening. A bony red hand swatted the boy's right ear and he let out a sullen yowl of protest.

Taz shuddered and watched the small boy being towed by the earlobe to a distant lavatory. She wondered if she might end up like Fraser's mother, nerves frayed to snapping point.

Gingerly, she eased her stomach into a slightly less uncomfortable position. God (a bloke) had clearly not designed pregnant women for rail travel. If you sat in one of the 'airline' seats, the flip-down table cut into your bump like a giant bulldog clip. The only alternative was to share one of the bigger tables with three foreign students, assorted backpacks and a big slobbery dog. Taz had opted for the bulldog clip, resting her individual fruit pie on her stomach and praying that the baby wouldn't kick out suddenly and send it flying across the carriage.

After changing trains twice and leaving Edinburgh far behind, Taz had only three thoughts left in her head: bath, bed, and food – all at once if possible. Although it was only mid-afternoon when the little regional shuttle rattled into a tiny station somewhere under a snowy mountain,

Taz was confident she could sleep for a week, a fortnight if pushed.

She was the only person getting off at Dungallow, and the only sign of life was a thin plume of smoke rising above the roof of a distant croft. There was no porter, no ticket collector – and no Binnie. As the train slid slowly out of the station, Taz began to feel the first stirrings of panic. It was completely, utterly arctic here, fit to freeze your toes right off; and snow was beginning to tumble lazily out of the bleached, grey-white sky. What if she'd got the day wrong? Why had she forgotten to bring Binnie's phone number with her? She rummaged in her pockets, it had to be here somewhere . . .

A voice somewhere to the left of her shouted, 'Taz! Taz, don't you *dare* pick up that suitcase! Jim, don't just stand there, pick up Taz's suitcase.'

Taz swung round to see Binnie storming towards her through a little white wicket gate. Untidy brown curls stuck out at all angles from underneath a red ski-hat, and a large body seemed all the larger for being crammed into an unsexy brown duffel coat. Green and silver moon-boots and baggy-kneed leggings completed the ensemble – a far cry from Binnie's beloved Nicole Farhi. As for Jim, he trudged mutinously in Binnie's wake, his normally-cheeky grin distinctly strained around the edges.

'Taz,' he muttered, taking the case from her hand and giving her a desultory peck her frozen cheek. She beamed at him, confident she could cheer him up.

'Hi Jim, it's lovely to see you again, how are you?'

'Oh, you know. Can't grumble,' said Jim with a shrug.

'But he does anyway,' sniffed Binnie; and it was obvious she wasn't joking. 'Come here Taz, and let's get a proper look at you.' She placed her hands flat on Taz's magnificent bump. 'My God, is it triplets?'

'It'd better not be!' giggled Taz, engulfing as much of Binnie as she could reach in a big bear-hug. It occurred to her that the two of them must present a comical picture, their arms stretched to breaking point and their bellies squashed together like Tweedledum and Tweedledee. 'You're looking well.'

Binnie stuck out her tongue.

'Fat, you mean. Be honest, I look like Compo's granny.'

'Well I think you look wonderful,' insisted Taz, looking to Jim to back her up. Hadn't he always found Binnie's voluptuousness a major turn-on? And now there was just a bit more of it for him to lust after. But Jim was glancing indifferently at his watch.

'We'd better call in at the sawmill on the way back, and get some more logs for the stove.'

'We will not!' Binnie snapped. 'We'll get straight back to Amy, you can go and get your stupid logs later.'

'It's a wood-burning stove, Binnie,' growled Jim. 'No logs, no central heating. Surely even you can work that one out.'

Taz stared at Binnie, then Jim, then Binnie again. She'd never seen them like this before, practically at each other's throats over something and nothing.

'Oh? And whose fault is it we've nearly run out again?' demanded Binnie between clenched teeth. 'Don't tell me – you're expecting me to chop wood at the same time as breastfeeding the baby . . .'

'For crying out loud, Binnie! Why do you always have to over-react?' Jim marched out through the ticket office to the Range Rover, Taz's suitcase banging angrily against his hip.

'Sure, great idea. And while I'm at it, why don't I build us a nice conservatory at the same time? For pity's sake Jim, all I'm asking is to be with my baby . . .'

'Calm down Binnie, Amy's fine, she's with her granny.'

'Yeah, that's what's bothering me.'

'What the hell is that supposed to mean?'

'Whatever you want it to mean,' sniffed Binnie, wrenching open the back door with a kind of miserable resentment.

'My mother's quite capable of looking after her own granddaughter for a couple of hours. She brought me up, for God's sake. And my four sisters.'

'I rest my case.'

'Oh, right. So now I'm some kind of freak am I?'

Jaws clenched, they glared at each other across the

bonnet, flinging silent insults at each other. Taz took this as the right moment to get a word in edgeways.

'Er ... shall I get in?' she asked quietly. 'Only it's a rather big step up.'

Binnie and Jim turned slowly towards Taz, all three of them red-faced and mortified with crippling embarrassment.

'Oh Christ, I'm sorry,' muttered Jim. 'We're a bit stressed out right now. Here, let me help you up.'

'No it's all right, let me,' cut in Binnie, taking charge and helping Taz up into the back seat. 'Take no notice Taz, we're not usually like this.'

Taz could have sworn she heard Jim mutter, 'Oh yes we are' under his breath, but she could have been mistaken.

Binnie sat down and took two long, deep breaths.

'It's just what with the christening ... and all these relatives coming, and so much to organise ...'

Taz patted Binnie's hand, calming her down, remembering all the times it had been the other way round.

'There's no need to apologise,' she said, as reassuringly as she could. 'Really there isn't.'

'You won't say that when you've met Jim's relatives,' observed Binnie, gazing out of the side window.

Taz waited for Jim to rise to the bait, but he just kept on driving, steering the Range Rover past a huddle of depressed-looking Highland cattle. Taz knew just how they felt. She was beginning to have a dreadful sense of foreboding.

'I'm really looking forward to seeing your house,' said Taz brightly. 'And I can't wait to see little Amy.'

Was anything the way it seemed? Jim and Binnie's 'little cottage' turned out to be an eighteenth-century stone-built farmstead on the edge of a tiny village, the main building added to over the years to form a dwelling of almost mansion proportions.

'You said it was a cottage!' exclaimed Taz as they walked up to the front door. 'It's huge!'

'The wages of sin,' explained Jim with a wink, a slightly more relaxed Jim Lethbridge emerging from the stressed-out cocoon. 'At least with my new job we can afford a really nice family home.'

'I just wish you were in it a bit more often,' said Binnie, not so much waspishly as with limp resignation.

'I will be,' said Jim. 'Just give me time to settle into the job, you know I need to prove myself.'

He was still talking about 'wonderful opportunities' and 'making quality time' as they walked into the house. The warm, delicious fug of a slow-cooked roast hit Taz full in the face, making her mouth water with anticipation. She forced herself to think of something besides food.

'What a wonderful house!' Taz meant it. She could see now why Binnie had been won over by the place the very first time she saw it, despite being a confirmed 'townie'. Craigview House was old and beautiful in a profoundly cosy, family kind of way, the stone-flagged floors worn smooth by generations of Scottish feet, the exposed beams so low that even Taz had to stoop slightly to avoid banging her head.

'It *is* – lovely,' sighed Binnie. 'But . . .'

'Mum – Auntie Shula, we're back,' called Jim. 'Give me your coat Taz, I'll go and hang it up.'

As Jim went off to hang up Taz's coat, a diminutive crone in a tartan hat and sheepskin boots emerged from the kitchen, a shopping bag in her gloved hand. You could feel the temperature drop ten degrees when she and Binnie looked at each other.

'This is Jim's Great Aunt Shula,' said Binnie with a valiant attempt at enthusiasm. 'Auntie Shula, this is . . . er . . .'

She didn't finish the sentence. She didn't need to. Great Aunt Shula' eyes glinted like cold blue pebbles in her corrugated face.

'So this is *her*, is it?' Taz mentally added the words 'the barefaced hussy'.

'That's right, Auntie, this is Taz. She's going to be Amy's godmother.'

Great Aunt Shula shook her head slowly as she prepared to leave.

'Right. I'll be off then. The cake's iced and there's one of my special trifles in the fridge.'

'That's very kind,' said Binnie, not sounding as if she meant it. 'But really, there was no need . . .'

'Well we have to make an effort sometimes, don't we dear? And I know you're not much of a cook,' replied Great Aunt Shula sweetly. 'Goodbye dear, I'll let myself out the back way.'

'Bitch,' mouthed Binnie silently behind her retreating back. Then, 'Come on Taz, let's go and rescue Amy.'

Four-month-old Amy was fast asleep on her back on the sofa, her soft mouth open and dribble drying on her chin, her chubby limbs cosy in a white sleepsuit with pink rabbit ears. Lorinda Lethbridge, Jim's mother, was sitting at the other end of the sofa, knitting something interminable and beige. She smiled and placed a finger to her lips.

'Shush Binnie dear, I've only just got her down and we don't want to wake her.'

Binnie's face registered instant concern.

'You shouldn't leave her lying near the edge like that, she might roll off and hurt herself!'

'Nonsense dear, not while Granny's here to take care of her wee darling girl.' Lorinda pushed her half-moon spectacles up her nose and smiled indulgently at the baby, staking a proprietorial claim.

Binnie retaliated by gently gathering Amy into her arms and lowering herself onto the sofa. Amy didn't wake, but squirmed dozily and let out a quiet gurgle before settling back to sleep.

'Lorinda, this is Taz. I told you about her.'

'So you did.' The tone spoke volumes. 'Pleased to meet you, I'm sure.' And if you believe that, you'll believe anything, thought Taz. The blue eyes peered hard. 'Should you be travelling all this way in your condition?'

'I'm fine, thanks.' Taz sat down selfconsciously in the nearest armchair.

Binnie stroked Amy's sleeping cheek, asking, 'She's been all right?'

'Right as rain, dear, you've not been worrying have you?'

'She must be due a feed . . .'

'I gave her some of that leftover porridge . . .'

'But you'll make her ill! She's only just starting on solids.'

'Nonsense, my Jim was on mashed banana at three months and it never did him any harm. Now, dear, she had a wet botty so I changed her – you do know terries are far better than these disposables, don't you?'

'I find disposables just fine,' said Binnie through gritted teeth.

'Oh, they're very convenient, I'll grant you, but terries are much more economical. That's what I used on all my babies. Of course, there was no choice in those days and mothers stayed at home to look after their children properly.' Lorinda turned to look at Taz, who had hoped she might be allowed to be invisible. 'You'll not be going back to work after the baby, dear?'

'Not much choice, I'm afraid. I'll need all the money I can earn.' She chickened out of adding that actually she *wanted* to go back to work, and couldn't think of anything worse than being imprisoned twenty-four hours a day with only a four-month-old baby for company.

'No.' Lorinda dropped her voice to a solicitous whisper. 'No, of course not, I was forgetting. Such a pity for you Tasmin dear, you're very brave to go through with it. Now, Jim, everything's organised for tomorrow?'

'Everything's fine. Binnie's mum's staying with Dan at the Inverdowrie Arms, Cousin Rob and Jennie are driving up in the morning.'

'Excellent.' Lorinda beamed and cast off her finished knitting. 'Oh, and I've reminded Jennie to bring the christening gown, like we agreed. She's had it professionally laundered, of course.'

The colour drained from Jim's face and he clapped his hand to his forehead. Binnie stared at him, realisation slowly dawning.

'Like we *what*? What christening gown?'

'The Lethbridge family gown, didn't Jim tell you, dear?

That was naughty of him. But of course we'll be using the family gown, it's been used for every child since Jim's great-great grandfather.'

'Actually,' said Binnie quietly, 'My mother has just spent rather a lot of money having a brand-new gown made. You might have told me,' she added with a gimlet stare at Jim. He turned a shade of deepest beetroot.

'Erm.' Taz gave a small cough. 'I was wondering . . . if my room's ready . . .'

'Of course,' said Binnie. 'Jim'll show you up, *won't you Jim*?'

Jim couldn't get out of the room fast enough. He took the stairs two at a time, Taz's suitcase in his hand, then waited on the landing for Taz to drag herself up.

'We've put you in here.' He opened the door into a pretty room with a sloping ceiling and a Victorian brass bedstead. 'Hope it's OK.'

'It's lovely, thanks.'

'The bed's more comfy than it looks. Bathroom's just down the end on the left.' Jim hesitated. 'About Binnie . . .'

'Yes?' Taz wondered if Jim was about to come out with some kind of big apology.

'The way she's behaving. She can't help it. It's her hormones I expect – she's just not herself at the moment.'

I'm not flipping surprised, thought Taz as she closed the door on Jim and collapsed gratefully onto the bed. Its springs twanged protestingly under her sudden weight. And, patting her stomach thoughtfully, she wondered if all babies turned nice, normal, childless people into grouchy, paranoid parents.

If so, she was in for a bumpy ride.

By some miracle, the snow stopped overnight; and the day of the christening dawned blue-skied and bright as a kingfisher's eye.

The frosted hillsides might look romantic and pictur-esque, but in Binnie and Jim's house it was pandemonium. Carloads of distant relatives (virtually all Jim's) seemed to arrive on the hour every hour, the kitchen was full of Scottish aunties baking shortbread, and Binnie and Jim

127

managed to keep their tempers only by avoiding each other like the plague.

Only little Amy, the centre of all the attention and the cause of all this disharmony, seemed oblivious to it all; sleeping serenely through the most ludicrous arguments, a pink-white bundle, moist and fresh from the bath. Taz stroked the tiny curled fingers and felt an enormous surge of admiration. This kid would go far.

No one but Amy got any lunch that day, because they were all 'saving themselves' for the après-baptism bun-fight, whether they wanted to or not. So it was with a growling stomach that Taz arrived at the church for the service.

It was probably inevitable that she would find herself gravitating towards the other two 'outsiders': Binnie's twice-divorced mother Irene (once a Bluebell Girl and still gorgeous at fifty-seven), and her flamboyant younger brother Dan, a trainee opera singer and gay as a paper hat. They made a curious trio as they walked down the central aisle towards the front row of pews.

Dan dug Taz in the ribs and whispered in her ear: 'Just look at 'em. The Addams Family at prayer.'

Taz had to put her hand to her mouth to stifle an unholy laugh – which would be sure to echo all round the church and confirm everybody's suspicion that she was no better than she ought to be.

'Don't!'

'It's true. Look at Uncle Fester over there, he's got no neck!'

It was fair to say that the assorted Lethbridges did not make an especially pretty sight. The males in particular seemed to share a unique family expression, somewhere between leering and gurning. The women spent all the time eyeing each other up, evaluating the relative merits of their hats. Amy alone took the whole thing in her stride. It was as if she knew she was the star of the show.

When the moment came for the godparents to step forward, Taz could not have felt more conspicuous. Amy's other godparents – one of Jim's university friends and the local minister's daughter – were squeaky clean, a religious studies teacher and a policewoman. Why on earth had Binnie chosen *her*? What could she possibly have to offer Amy in the way of moral guidance?

The minister, a kindly man with crinkly eyes, lit a candle and passed it to each of the godparents in turn.

'Do you turn to God?'

'I turn to God.'

'Do you renounce evil?'

Taz felt her knees start to tremble. She knew it was silly, but her mouth was really dry, and she could almost feel the eyes of two dozen Lethbridges, firmly fixed on her large and unsanctified stomach. But Binnie looked as proud as punch; and for her sake Taz held up her head and spoke out clearly: 'I renounce evil.'

'I give you this candle as the symbol of the passage from darkness into light.'

Strange how touching, uplifting even, it was when the minister took Amy in his arms and cradled her gently over the font. It was just silly sentimentality, Taz knew that, after all she was hardly what you could call a proper Christian; but even so she couldn't prevent the pricking of tears beneath her eyelids and had to blink them swiftly away.

Unfortunately not everything went with perfect smoothness. Someone had forgotten to warm the water in the font and – it being January – an ice-cold shower wasn't on Amy's list of favourite things. At the very first drop of water on her forehead she let out a full-throated yell of protest.

'Amy Margaret Shula Lethbridge ...'

'Wah!'

'I baptise you in the name of the Father ...'

'Aaah!'

'And of the Son ...'

'Baaah!'

'And of the Holy Spirit ...'

The noise was deafening. Nothing the minister did seemed to calm Amy down. Before Binnie could take her, Jim's mother stepped forward and scooped her up, leaning her bonneted head against her shoulder.

'Here, vicar, let me take her, she loves her granny, don't you my wee pet?'

It seemed to work. The shrill cries turned to muted wails, then sotto voce grumblings. Amy raised her head to look over her granny's shoulder, and Taz could have sworn she winked at her. Then she burped.

And brought up mashed banana, all down the back of Lorinda Lethbridge's brand-new suit.

Chapter 9

'Six thousand eight hundred,' mused Binnie, steering the Range Rover out onto the slushy road to Dungallow Station.

'What?' Taz turned back from the retreating village, to look at Binnie.

'Six thousand eight hundred *nappies*. That's the number your average baby gets through before it's potty-trained.'

'You're kidding!' said Taz, aghast.

'Cross my heart, it's the truth. You try adding it up. Six thousand eight hundred . . . and do you know how many Jim's changed so far?'

'Go on,' said Taz, suspecting she might already know.

'Three. And only one of *them* was a smelly one.'

Taz chuckled softly.

'I thought he said he was going to muck in and be a real New Dad.'

Binnie pulled a face.

'Oh he *did*. He read all the books, he could tell me all the symptoms of placenta praevia by the time I was three months gone. In fact he'd have breastfed Amy given half a chance . . . and if I'd known about the cracked nipples I'd have let him.'

'So what happened?'

'Amy was born and Jim found out what babies are really like. Noisy, smelly, demanding, infuriating, exhausting, incontinent insomniacs . . . shall I go on?'

'You've forgotten gorgeous, irresistible and totally loveable.'

Binnie smiled. The smile of someone who has discovered a secret and is hugging it all to herself.

'Well OK. She's just a bit loveable.'

'Binnie, you're besotted!' laughed Taz.

To Taz, Amy Lethbridge might look pretty much like any other four-month-old baby, but she was beginning to realise that all mums were endowed with perfect rose-tinted vision. And in a couple of months' time she, Taz Norton, would have her own noisy pink blob, which would also be the prettiest, most talented and super-intelligent baby the world had ever known.

'Have they told you what you're having yet?' asked Binnie out of the blue, leaning forward in the driver's seat and peering between the swishing windscreen wipers.

Taz stroked her bump. The baby within had just calmed down after one of its mad half-hours, and she imagined it curled up inside her tummy, placidly sucking its thumb as it slept.

'I haven't asked.'

'If it's a boy he can be Amy's toyboy.' Binnie drove on slowly, the snow turning sticky and wet as it hit the windscreen, obscuring her view of the road ahead. 'Thanks for coming, Taz,' she said suddenly. 'I know it wasn't easy . . .'

'Oh Binnie, of course I wanted to come – I may be pregnant, but I'm not so fat I can't get on a train!'

'I didn't mean that.'

'What then?'

The Range Rover drew slowly into the station car park. This early in the morning there were few people around, and the station windows glowed dingy orange in the half light. With the melting icicles hanging off the pitched slate roof, the discarded bobble-hat and the lopsided snowman in the car park, the scene looked faintly unreal and not quite perfect, something off a budget-priced Christmas card.

'I know Jim and I . . . we haven't been very easy to live with, have we? At each other's throats all the time, scoring points off each other.'

Taz felt caught between loyalty and honesty; though she knew Binnie had always preferred the latter.

'You've just had a baby, it takes time to adjust.'

'I guess when you're thirty-eight it just takes a bit longer, huh?'

'Bound to. And Jim's nearly forty-two, suddenly being a father's bound to come as a shock. But you'll bounce back.'

Binnie gave her breasts a disdainful poke. A fathomless acreage of chest undulated beneath her vast Arran sweater.

'Listen kid, these two are never *ever* going to bounce again. Dangling's about the limit of their ambitions these days.'

'Binnie, don't! If you make me laugh I'll wet myself!'

They laughed about it anyhow, with flakes of soggy snow forming wet dollops on the bonnet of the Range Rover. The silence seemed unnaturally dense and sluggish, like a drunkard slowly surfacing towards consciousness after a very long night on the tiles.

'I wish I was coming back with you,' said Binnie. 'Even the china and glass spring stocktake seems exciting now.'

'You don't mean that.'

'No. No, you're right.'

'But you *must* come and see me, all three of you. When the baby's born.'

'OK, I promise. But you'll be busy, you won't want me and Jim around to mess up your routine.'

'Don't talk rubbish. What I need is somebody who can talk a bit of sense and keep me sane!'

'What about that girl you told me about . . . Mandy was it?'

Taz chuckled.

'Mandy's a real character. I don't know about sane, though. She's got this rebel streak, she can't resist winding people up. Did I tell you her latest scam? She comes into S&G and moves the stock around. You know, waits till she's sure every security guard in the store is watching her then picks up something expensive and wanders about

133

with it. Last week it was a pair of Calvin Klein underpants.'

'What would she want with underpants?'

'That's just it, she didn't want them. They ended up with the frozen peas in the food hall. She just has this really bent sense of humour. Of course, every time she does it the security guards and store detectives all follow her round the store and it ends up like some kind of ridiculous conga line. I've told her they'll ban her from the store if she keeps on doing it, but she says she doesn't care.'

'She sounds a bit of a head case.'

Taz laughed and shook her head.

'Believe it or not she's nice, you'd like her. *And* she reads Gabriel Garcia Marquez.'

'You're having me on. What does your mum make of her?'

'So far I've kept them apart.'

'Sounds wise. I can't imagine your mum approving of anyone with green hair.'

'No.' Taz couldn't imagine her mum approving of any friend who wasn't rich, respectable and a *Daily Telegraph* reader. Never mind Mandy, that put Taz herself pretty low down the list. 'Did I tell you I've asked Mum to be with me at the birth? I thought I ought to, now she and I are on speaking terms again.'

This provoked the first genuine belly-laugh Taz had heard from Binnie over the whole weekend.

'Your mother!'

'Why not?'

'Let's just say rather you than me.' Binnie looked at Taz's face and relented. 'Don't worry, she'll be fine, of course you'll want your mum with you. It's just that I'm remembering the language I came out with in the delivery room.' She glanced at her watch. 'Best get you onto the platform, the train's due in ten minutes and there isn't another until teatime.'

Taz and Binnie unloaded Taz's luggage from the Range Rover and they hugged in front of the open train door.

'You *will* come?'

'I promised didn't I? And you'd better promise to take care of yourself.'

'I've got no choice. Mandy keeps shoving iron tablets down me.'

'Quite right too. And don't forget to do your exercises, or you'll end up looking like me.' Binnie fiddled with something under her jumper. 'Damn, my breast pads are leaking, I knew I should have used the pump before I came. Now listen, Taz, I don't want to hear that you've been overdoing it with that American thingie.'

'I'll do my best. And Binnie . . .'

Binnie turned round from putting Taz's bags onto the train. Taz noticed how tired and defeated she looked. It was quite upsetting, like suddenly noticing that your parents are turning into old people.

'I've got a spare bedroom, you know. If it ever gets too much for you and you need somewhere to stay . . .'

Binnie laughed.

'Don't! I might just take you up on it.'

Back at Seuss & Goldman, Taz threw herself into her work with renewed vigour. Department of the Year was all very well, but that was *last* year; and Brendan had everything still to prove. She wasn't naive enough think he'd just roll over and play dead.

The Tuesday morning meeting was meant to be a general pep-talk, a bomb up the backside for the menswear sales team, who were starting to wilt a bit after the fortnight-long January sale. But after the compulsory chat about sales figures, the stern reprimand about disappearing stock, and the outline of the week's new gameplan, the meeting was virtually hijacked by questions about Binnie and the new baby.

Taz waved away the barrage, painfully aware that the male members of staff were exchanging grimaces and rolling their eyes heavenwards.

'Now isn't a good time,' she told Kate, who had come visiting from her new job as assistant DSM in women's accessories. 'But yes, I did take a few photos . . .' A few,

135

she thought with a suppressed smile. Only about three dozen.

'When . . .?' began Pauline, bristling with a degree of enthusiasm she seldom if ever showed in her job.

'Later. I'll pin them up in the canteen, then everybody can see how gorgeous Binnie's baby is. OK? I think that's all for this morning's meeting. Now Marion . . .'

She swung round, expecting Marion still to be standing at her elbow, looking sour, bored, irritated or all three. But Marion had stalked off to the other side of the department and was tearing open a carton of men's white shirts with savage slashes of a craft knife.

'Marion – Marion, what are you *doing*?' Taz made a beeline for the stooping figure in the grey skirt and cardigan. 'Marion, will you listen to me?'

Taz seized Marion by the shoulders but she was shaken off. Marion stood up slowly, pushing a straggling curl of greying hair off her forehead. It was only now that Taz saw Marion's eyes. They were very bright, pink-rimmed, moist wells sunk deep in a lined white face, whose only other colour was a thin double stripe of unfashionable orangey lipstick.

'I've got to get this stock out,' snapped Marion, dropping the knife onto the ground. 'Can't you just leave me alone?'

Taz's voice dropped to a shocked whisper. A heart-to-heart with Marion was long overdue, but the timing was lousy. The last thing Taz wanted to do was start some kind of scene, less than half an hour before opening time.

'What's the matter, Marion? I've never seen you like this before. If you have problems I need to know. I want to help you.'

'Help me? *Help* me? Oh, you think you're so bloody perfect don't you?' Marion's voice rose to an angry shout, her whole body shaking. 'You think you know everything, with your friends and your babies and your nice lives. Well you know nothing, nothing, so why don't you all just get off my back and leave me alone?'

Marion stumbled away across the sales floor, half running towards the personal shopping suite and slamming the door shut behind her. Taz stood and gaped. Soft footsteps behind her announced the arrival of Leroy.

'Do you want me to get someone? Personnel?'

Taz shook her head.

'I'll sort this out.'

The door into the personal shopping suite was shut but not locked. She pushed it open and stepped into the reception area. A quiet sobbing was coming from one of the curtained cubicles.

'Marion.'

No answer. Just a brief pause, then sobbing again.

'Marion, we have to talk.'

The sound was coming from cubicle two. Taz drew aside the curtain. Marion was crouched on the bench, her head in her hands, her face buried in her skirt. Taz hesitated, then sat down on the bench opposite Marion.

'Mind if I sit here?'

No response.

'Is it something personal, Marion? A family problem?'

Marion lifted her head slightly. Her eyes were angry red and brimming with tears.

'Family!'

'You can tell me, it doesn't matter what it is.' She tried a long shot. 'Is it something I said? Something about Binnie and the baby?'

She was horrified to see Marion dissolve into sobs before her eyes.

'Nothing ... you don't know ... I've got nothing. It's all a waste of time, all of it, all of it!'

Taz slid with difficulty to her knees on the carpet, in front of Marion. She took Marion's hands in hers.

'What's a waste of time? Tell me, I only want to help.' She rummaged in her jacket pocket and took out a tissue. Clean, thank goodness. 'Here, take this. Have a good blow and tell me what's wrong.'

'It's ... my ... mother,' she said after a minute, between gulps of air.

'Is she ill?' Taz had a vague idea that she knew Marion looked after her elderly mother. She cursed herself for not bothering to find out more.

'I . . . gave up everything . . . for her.' Taz realised to her surprise that there was no love in Marion's voice, no warmth even. If anything, she spoke about her mother with hostility. 'Everything. I was pretty, you know.' The pink eyes challenged Taz to disbelieve what Marion was saying. 'I had a boyfriend, Stanley, I was twenty and he was a soldier. She said . . .' Marion swallowed.

'Go on,' said Taz gently, trying to ignore the awful ache in her knees and the fact that the clock was ticking relentlessly on towards nine o'clock.

'Mother said . . . she was ill and I'd have to give him up. He was so handsome . . . I said if we could just wait till Mother was better . . . but he couldn't wait, he thought . . . I didn't love him.'

Understanding was dawning slowly.

'You wanted to marry Stanley but your mother said no?'

'She said she was ill but she wasn't. She was just jealous. Dad left us when I was six, she was afraid . . . of being alone.' Marion dabbed, her eyes again, took a deep breath that made her chest shudder with the effort of keeping in control. 'He married someone else. And I . . .'

'You stayed home to take care of your mother.'

'I gave everything up for her, everything!' There was a blaze of fury and pain in Marion's eyes, Taz wondered how she could possibly not have seen it before. 'Thirty-two years. I could have had a baby of my own . . . a nice house . . .'

'A slave, that's what I've been. She said she was ill but she wasn't. And now . . .' The tears trickled unhindered down Marion's face.

'What's happened?' asked Taz gently.

'She was so good at play-acting . . . I never realised . . . I thought it was all put on. How was I to know she really was ill?'

Taz felt a sympathetic chill creeping round her heart like a closing hand.

'Sh-she . . . started losing her memory . . . forgetting things . . . Then it got worse. Th-the doctor said it was

Alzheimer's. Just before Christmas they took her away . . . to a home.'

'And now . . .' Marion's voice faded to a dry, quavering croak. 'She doesn't even recognise me any more. My own mother. After everything I've done for her . . .' Her voice tailed off. She wiped the back of her hand across her swollen eyes.

'I'm sure she does know, Marion.'

But Marion snatched away her hand, suddenly angry again.

'You don't understand, do you? Not one word of what I've said. I threw it all away and it's all for nothing. No babies, no husband.'

'Stan's gone and Mum's gone . . . and I'm going to be on my own for ever.'

Personnel sent Marion home in a taxi, one of the part-timers came in at short notice, and on the face of it, menswear got quickly back to normal.

But it wasn't quite so easy to banish Marion from Taz's mind. The image of that stark red and white, almost clownish face would stay with her for a long, long time. And she couldn't help blaming herself.

Absolutely the last thing she felt like doing was sorting through the entries for the children's poster competition (first prize: a family holiday in Los Angeles and VIP tickets to the grand opening of S&G). But she'd said she'd do it and do it she would.

Brendan, Ted and Cara were already in the committee room when she got there, surrounded by mounds of paper marked 'seven and under', 'ten and under' and 'eleven to sixteen'.

'Hard at work I see.' Taz slung her pager and handbag onto the table and surveyed the multicoloured jumble. 'Good God, what's that supposed to be?'

' "My Mummy opening the shop in America" by Emma Cartwright, aged eight,' Cara read with difficulty. 'I wonder which way up it's supposed to be.'

'And does Mummy realise her face is purple with

139

orange spots?' enquired Ted. 'Oh no, that's her frock, silly me.'

Taz picked up one of the smaller piles.

'These the short-listed entries then?'

'Ten in each age-group, like we agreed,' confirmed Ted.

'And we've lined up an independent panel of judges?'

'Of course. There's Nina from Frontline Travel, Henry Goldman from head office . . .'

'Hardly independent,' pointed out Cara.

'Yeah, well, we had to have someone from S&G to present the prize . . . then there's some bloke with a beard off kids' TV – oh, and Uncle Smiley from the *Evening Courier*.'

'Not Uncle Smiley,' groaned Cara. 'You'll have to keep him off the vodka, or you won't get a word of sense out of him.'

'Sounds like the perfect art critic,' said Brendan archly. 'Anyhow, I've done my bit. I'm off.'

Taz shot him a glance which warned 'don't move a muscle'. To her surprise and pleasure, it worked.

'Once through the short-list first,' she said. 'Just to make sure we're all agreed.'

Taz sorted through the pile marked 'seven and under.' For once, it was a relief to find that Ted had everything in hand. There was enough to think about without having to evaluate the relative merits of different shaped blobs of coloured paint.

'Hey, this one's *good*!' she exclaimed in spite of herself, suddenly coming upon the last painting in the pile. Quite simply, it stood head and shoulders above all the other entries in its class. For a start, you could tell what it was.

As she looked up, she caught Ted and Brendan looking at each other. She knew that look. It reminded her of naughty schoolboys in the back row of the class.

'Something wrong?' she enquired.

'Nothing,' said Ted.

'It's a great picture', said Brendan. 'Shows real talent, should win by a mile.'

'Go on, tell her,' Cara sighed.

'Tell me what?'

'Tell her, Ted, or I will.'

Taz looked down at the picture. It really was excellent, she couldn't have done that well herself – maybe the kid was older than seven, and Ted knew and was trying to cover up for some stupid reason best known to himself. She turned the painting over. The name, age and address were clearly pencilled on the back, in large block capitals:

RUPERT CORNFORTH aged 6½
HIGHTOWER STUD FARM
Nr CHELTENHAM

Suddenly everything became clear. Cornforth. Rupert Cornforth. Hightower Stud Farm . . .

'You idiot, Ted. You surely weren't going to let this go through to the final! This boy's the grandson of Angus Cornforth, isn't he?'

'So?' Ted shifted from one foot to the other, hands in his pockets.

'*So*, the grandson of the Goldman family lawyer isn't eligible to enter the competition!'

'It really is a great picture,' said Cara softly. 'It deserves to win. And I don't suppose anyone would notice . . .'

'Of course they'd notice! And in any case, the rules are clear: no employees of S&G, nobody connected with the firm, no families or friends.'

'Angus Cornforth won't be pleased,' pointed out Brendan.

He didn't need to point that out. Taz had already imagined Angus Cornforth's scowling face, not to mention little Rupert's tears as he sobbed into his Coco Pops.

'I'm not breaking the rules just to please one of Henry Goldman's drinking buddies,' replied Taz. Especially not one who once pinched my bottom, she added silently.

Even as she made the decision, she was wondering if she might live to regret it.

It had been a funny old day.

When Taz got home it was dark, and the lights were on in all the flats except hers. Cosy little units where people lived two by two; or three by three, but at any rate not on their own. That's if you didn't count Al, and he had Elvis for company.

There was a good weepie on the telly, pizza in the fridge and a cupboard full of Maltesers. But Taz didn't settle down in front of the TV for a quiet night in. Nor did she ring her mum, or Dee, or Steffi Parkes. She wasn't in the mood for other people's good advice. The episode with Marion had shown her how useless advice could be.

On a whim she changed into her maternity jeans and a sweatshirt which had once been absurdly baggy, and crossed the drive to her garage. It was one of six, the last one in a purpose-built block. Unlocking the side door, she clicked on the light and stepped inside.

The BSA Gold Star was sitting in splendid isolation, leaking almost imperceptibly into the oily patch of sawdust on the floor. It looked lonely, and all at once Taz felt guilty.

'I've been ignoring you, haven't I?' she whispered, running her hand over the cold leather seat, forcing herself to accept all the scents and sensations which reminded her that, after all was said and done, this had been her dad's bike. He'd given it to her to look after, not to ignore. And definitely not to sell either, no matter how short money might be. 'I wonder if I'll ever ride you again.'

'Course you will', chirped a voice behind her. It was Mandy, clad head to toe in Belisha Beacon orange with Doc Martens and a single gigantic earring. 'Nice little sidecar, strap the kid in and off you go . . .'

'Mandy, you wouldn't!'

'You can get it little goggles and a helmet. Can I come in?' Without waiting for a reply, Mandy closed the door behind her and leaned against it, arms folded. She whistled. 'Mean wheels. Can I take it for a burn-up sometime?'

'You've got a licence?' asked Taz dubiously.

'OK, OK, I'll ride pillion. Dave said he'd teach me, then he got banged up didn't he? This the clutch is it? I know someone who could fix that oil leak for you.'

'It's OK. I'll fix it myself.' Taz stretched her aching back muscles. 'Sometime. How are you, anyhow?'

142

'All right.' Mandy clammed up, as though considering whether to say anything more or not. 'Went to see Dave last week, didn't I?'

'How is he?'

'Pissed off. And that place . . .' Mandy shivered, hugging her bump protectively. 'God I hate those places, they're like cages for animals.' She shook herself like a wet dog, banishing the bad thoughts. 'Where's my haggis then?'

'What haggis?'

'I could go one with chips and curry sauce. Your friend all right was she?'

'Fine,' lied Taz. There seemed little point in going into the more depressing details of Binnie and Jim's domestic life. 'So what's the latest gossip?'

'Steffi took her bloke back but they had another row and he's out on his ear again. And Dee's got a new job. Down the art school.' Mandy grinned.

'Art school? I didn't know she could paint.'

'She can't.' Mandy winked. 'But that boyfriend of hers can. It's modellin'. *Nude* modellin'. For the life class.'

'No!' Taz dropped the oily rag she was using to buff up the engine. 'You're having me on!'

'I never am. You ask her. She says a pregnant woman is the Mother Goddess's most wonderful work of art, so it's off with her pants and she couldn't care less who knows it. Course, Chloë nearly choked on her hot chocolate when Dee told her . . .'

'I'm not surprised.' Taz conjured up a mental picture of Dee's ample curves in all their naked glory. Ken's deli counter sprang irresistibly to mind.

'You know Chloë's acting funny again, don't you? She won't talk about the baby, won't even buy anything for it. Clive's all excited but it's like she doesn't want to know. Could be scared I s'pose,' she reflected.

'We're *all* scared. Giving birth's a scary thing.' Taz looked up. 'I still can't quite believe it's happening. I can't *start* to think about names . . .'

'I have,' said Mandy promptly. 'I'm havin' a boy and I'm goin' to call him Dylan.'

143

'Dylan? What – like the rabbit in *The Magic Roundabout?*'

Mandy's face turned to a picture of righteous indignation.

'*Dylan after Dylan Thomas, you prat! You have heard* of Dylan Thomas?'

Taz went red. Another misconception about Mandy flew out the window.

'Well . . . yeah. I did him at school.'

'Yeah? I didn't go to school much. Kept gettin' excluded for giving cheek. But I got these books of poems from a stall on the market. 'The Waste Land'. T. S. Eliot, totally cool. William Blake – acidhead or what? Course, my mum and dad thought I was crazy . . . the only thing my dad's ever read is a bettin' slip.'

'You didn't think of naming the baby after him then?'

'What, "Arsehole"? Mandy laughed drily. I'm not calling my kid that.' She fiddled with the chipped orange varnish on her nails. 'Taz . . .'

'Mmm?'

'You asked your mum to be with you when you have the baby, right?'

'Well, I thought I ought to . . . she'd be upset if I didn't. How about you?'

'My mum says if it's too late for an abortion I've to have it adopted, an' it'd be better off dead. I told her to go to hell. She's the last person on God's earth I'd want with me. And Dave's not much use locked up in a cell, is he?'

Mandy took to staring down very intently at the scuffed toes of her DMs.

'I wondered . . . I mean, you can say no and it doesn't matter or anythin' 'cause I don't really care one way or the other . . . But . . .' Mandy looked up at Taz. 'Will you be with me? When I have the kid?'

Taz gaped. Be Mandy's birthing partner? But there were only three weeks between their due dates! And she knew nothing at all about what to do, nothing about having a baby. What possible use could she be?

But she was so astonished and delighted that the next thing she knew, she'd gone and said yes.

144

Chapter 10

It was a typical late-February afternoon: dark, drizzly, bone-cold and depressing.

Taz stood near the back of a very long queue, waiting for the bus driver to turn up. She gazed longingly at the empty Metro bus, parked ten yards short of the bus stop, driverless and tantalising, its lights switched on. Oh to park her aching coccyx on one of those itchy moquette seats. Oh to drag herself home and flop, comatose, in front of *Brookside*.

Finally – and not without a fight – Taz had been forced to give up driving, since she could no longer squeeze herself behind the wheel. How many years was it since she'd been a pedestrian? More than she cared to remember. And the last thing she needed after a long day at S&G was a half-hour stand in the drizzle.

Setting down the carrier bag containing her Haddock Dinner for One, Taz resigned herself to waiting a bit longer. Gingerly she rested the very edge of her bottom on one of the plastic flip-up shelves that passed as seats; leaning back to balance the weight of her bump, the twin cones of her maternity bra tilting expectantly upwards like gundogs' noses.

Taz was a realist. Her glamour days were long gone and she knew she looked a sight. The expensive perm she'd treated herself to in defiance of her mother's advice had turned to shapeless frizz at the first hint of dampness. Rainwater had seeped under her coat collar and was wrinkling the back of her navy-blue maternity smock. Her voluminous raincoat seemed tailored for a midget, its buttons straining fit to pop with every breath she took in. Her ankles, once enticingly slender, had turned into plump, water-filled balloons, overhanging flat and sensible shoes. She wasn't a woman any more, she was a blob.

So much for Dee and Steffi, who'd warned her she'd probably feel 'exceptionally sensual' during the latter stages of her pregnancy, and want to have sex with everyone and everything. Right now, Taz would gladly have traded a night of passion with Keanu Reeves for any pile remedy that actually *worked*.

The sooner you arrive, kiddo, the better, she told her listening stomach. And she thought about Dee, who'd given birth to beautiful twins – Dodie and Kai – only three days before and was already back at the café, dispensing Aqua Libra and taking it all in her stride; Chloë, in hospital waiting for a caesarian and telling everyone she didn't want any visitors . . . and of course, Mandy. Mandy who was due to pop any day and was expecting her, Taz Norton, to hold her hand while it happened.

'Course, the buses haven't been the same since this lot took over,' said a disgruntled pensioner at Taz's elbow.

'Nobody cares about us,' sniffed her friend. 'We could all die of hypothermia and they wouldn't give a toss.'

'My faggots are defrosting while he's off having his tea break,' grunted a man in a sheepskin car-coat.

'Mummy,' piped up a small voice somewhere round Taz's ankles. She looked down. A girl of three or four in a red velvet coat and furry mittens was tugging at her mother's sleeve, her eyes all the time fixed on Taz.

'Yes dear?' replied Mummy automatically, not even looking down.

'Mummy, why is that lady so fat?'

Good question, thought Taz. A titter of embarrassed laughter ran along the bus queue.

Mummy glanced at Taz.

'Sorry love, she's at that age, it's why why why all the flaming time. The lady's having a baby, and stop staring Kayleigh, it's rude.'

'Mummy . . . is the baby inside her tummy?'

'Yes.'

146

'How did it get there?'

Go on, answer that one, thought Taz. Mummy looked like she wanted to strangle Kayleigh with her bobble-ended scarf.

'Did she *eat* it?'

Taz looked away, the only way she could stop herself bursting out laughing. Oh the joys of parenthood. And she was about to discover them all for herself.

'Taz? Taz Norton? It is you isn't it?'

She swung round. A tall, golden-haired man in a fleece zipper jacket was grinning at her from underneath a golfing umbrella. Her hugeness suddenly forgotten, Taz's flirtatious heart skipped a beat.

'Adam!'

'Here, you can't push in like that,' growled the woman in the tea-cosy hat. 'The back of the queue's over there.'

'It's all right, I'm not stopping.' Adam stepped a little closer, his umbrella catching the water-drips from the edge of the bus shelter. 'How *are* you?'

'Oh you know, fine.' This hardly seemed the place to give Adam the lowdown on her stress incontinence. 'I haven't seen you in ages,' she added, hoping he wouldn't notice the slight edge of accusation in her voice. Every visit she'd made to Dee's café, she'd secretly hoped for another chance to ogle Adam from afar.

'I've been doing some extra evening drop-in sessions at the law centre.'

'I don't know how you do it.' You gorgeous, selfless hunk of manhood, she added silently. She patted her tummy. 'It's all I can do to manage nine-to-five at the moment.'

'Of course. You must be worn out.' He looked, bless him, as if he really cared one way or the other. Not like Gareth. No, not one bit like Gareth. 'Look, it's late-night opening – why don't I take you for a cappuccino? Warm you up a bit.'

'Well . . .' Taz gazed despairingly at the bus, still empty, still no driver anywhere in sight. 'If I miss my bus . . .'

'I'll run you home.'

'But it's miles out of your way!'

'No problem. I've got nothing else planned for this evening.'

Me neither, thought Taz. And if I had, I'd cancel it right now.

They ended up not at the Green Café, but the theatre bar in Regent Street, where Adam managed to force a way through the teeming crowd of theatregoers and found them a table for two in the corner.

Huddled over a giant mug of hot chocolate with marshmallows, Taz felt her toes beginning to defrost. Adam stirred brown sugar into his cappuccino and took a sip.

'Mmm, not bad. I always come here when I need a hit of caffeine – Dee won't have anything but decaffeinated in her place.'

'How is she?' asked Taz.

'Oh, flourishing – and so are the twins. She's breastfeeding, of course.'

'Of *course*.' Taz appreciated the gentle irony in Adam's tone. 'Anyone else would go mad, trying to cope with five children *and* a café to run!'

'Not Dee,' laughed Adam. 'And don't forget the latest toyboy.'

'She's amazing.'

'No more amazing than you,' replied Adam. If anyone else had said it, it would have sounded like empty flattery; but coming from Adam it seemed entirely sincere.

'Amazing? *Me*?'

'Yes, you. I don't know how you keep going, I had a cousin who used to work at S&G, and he said it was hell on earth.'

'Not hell,' protested Taz good-humouredly. 'Just purgatory. The worst thing is this American Event I've got landed with organising. It's a huge honour to be asked, but if I'd known it'd be this complicated and I'd be this exhausted . . . Still, you don't want to hear all my woes.'

'Oh but I do,' he said softly. 'I want to hear all about you.'

Taz blushed crimson, the way she hadn't blushed since she'd had a crush on her music teacher at fourteen. She covered up her confusion by dunking her chocolate flake and biting the end off.

'I'm sure Dee's told you all about me already. But I don't know anything about you.'

'What's there to know?'

Taz licked melted chocolate off her lips and looked Adam in the eye. She shivered pleasurably. God, this was ridiculous. She was about as pregnant as it was possible to be without exploding, her wet hair was plastered to her head, she had brown patches on her face and she was at least a stone heavier than she ought to be. And she was *flirting*. It was all she could do to stop herself kicking off her shoes and playing footsie under the table.

'Everything. Your darkest secrets.'

'I haven't got any dark secrets.' Could he really be flirting back? Don't be stupid, of course he couldn't. But it was an enjoyable game, all the same. 'Not unless you count the divorce. And that's hardly a secret.'

A tiny thrill of triumphant excitement shivered across Taz's skin. Adam was divorced.

'You're ... on your own then?' she ventured. Adam nodded. And a wistful sadness seemed to flood into him, making Taz wish she hadn't said anything.

'Liz and I split up three years ago.'

'I'm sorry, I didn't mean to ...'

He waved aside her embarrassment.

'It's OK, I don't mind talking about it. Liz got the chance to go to South Africa ... we hadn't been getting on for a long time.' He looked down into his coffee. 'I haven't seen her since and I'm fine about that. It's just ... I miss my kids sometimes. No, all the time.'

'You have children?'

'Perry's five now, Olivia was born after we split up, I've never even seen her, just photographs.'

'Oh Adam.' Taz gazed at him, horrified at the change she'd produced in him. This wasn't what she'd intended at all. Oh poor Adam, poor, poor Adam.

'Not much of a dad, am I?'

'It doesn't sound like you had much of a chance to be.'

149

'No. No, I suppose you're right. I . . . didn't mean to bore you with my problems.'

'You haven't.' Taz meant it. Adam drained the last of his coffee and set down the cup.

'Buy you another?'

'It's getting a bit late . . .' said Taz, glancing at her watch.

'Go on. One more and then I'll run you home.' The warmth from his eyes melted her apprehension like spring sun on snow. 'Cross my heart.'

'That's it!' exclaimed Taz, throwing down her handbag and subsiding into an armchair. It fitted round her hips as snugly as a corset. 'No more. I've had enough.'

'You can't give up now!' scolded Mandy, hands on hips, bump thrust forward. 'If you don't sort it out now you'll never get a childminder. Well, not one worth havin', anyway.'

'I know, I know.' Taz groaned and wriggled in her chair. Whoever Braxton-Hicks was, she hated him. His fake contractions were giving her the most annoying stomach-ache, and to make matters worse, Norton Junior was firmly lodged against her spine, provoking spectacularly awful backache. 'But that last one . . .'

'That last one ought to be locked up,' declared Mandy.

'Locked up? Why? She wasn't that bad.'

Mandy laughed and waddled off into the kitchen. She looked like Big Bird, thought Taz, her tightly-upholstered stomach very taut and round above thin legs clad in red and white hooped leggings and lace-up boots.

'You want a cuppa or what?'

'Go on then.' Taz made a half-hearted attempt to get up, then gave up the struggle. She could do with a wee – even though she'd only had one half an hour previously – but she was too worn out to move. 'So what was wrong with that childminder then?'

'You did *see* those pot plants on her windowsill?'

'What about them?'

'That was exactly what they were. *Pot* plants. Get it?'

'No!' Taz stared at Mandy. Cannabis plants? In a nice, suburban semi in Leckhampton? 'You're joking.' But she could see Mandy wasn't. 'And that woman's been looking after people's babies . . .?'

'So you're going to cross Julie off the list, right?'

'Too right.' This time Taz managed to haul herself to her feet. She struggled into the toilet, leaving the door ajar so she could still talk to Mandy. 'But I've been through the entire list, and I couldn't leave my baby with any of them!'

'Then you'll have to try harder,' replied Mandy firmly. The loo door opened wider and Taz was presented with a mug of tea. 'Here, get this down you.'

'There was that one in Prestbury.'

'She sticks them in front of the TV all day. And did you see the filth under her fingernails?'

'I suppose I could think about a nanny-share . . .'

'Don't talk crap.' Mandy teased her fingers through her spiked hair, now mousy at the roots, green in the middle and vibrant purple at the ends. 'You can only just afford the childminder.'

'I know.' Taz sighed and stared down at her knickers. It was hard enough managing on her salary at the moment; what was it going to be like with a baby to support and no one to share the mortgage with? 'Perhaps I could advertise . . .'

'Well just you make sure you get somebody registered, that's all.'

Taz wondered how Social Services could possibly have any doubts about Mandy's aptitude for motherhood, no matter how horrendous her home circumstances might be. And she felt a twinge of guilt at having a nice flat and a good job to go back to, not like Mandy who had – by her own admission – sod all.

She was about to suggest giving the second childminder a second try when Taz's mobile rang.

'I'll get it,' said Mandy, and disappeared, returning a moment later. 'It's Steffi, she says she's found you a child-minder.'

'What! That's fantastic!' Taz seized the phone. 'Steffi, hi! What's all this about a childminder?'

'Melinda's wonderful Taz, you're so lucky. Normally she's booked up a year in advance, but a last-minute

151

vacancy's come up and I've persuaded her to talk to you. If she likes you – and I'm sure she will – I think there's a good chance she'll agree to take you on.'

Hang on, thought Taz; isn't it supposed to be the mum who interviews the childminder, not the other way round? But she dismissed the thought as sheer ingratitude.

'You're a marvel, Steffi. Tell me more!'

Melinda Thompson was everything Steffi had said she would be: educated, middle-class, full of wonderful ideas for stimulating child development, and above all, quintessentially *nice*. She and her architect husband lived in a big house surrounded by half an arboretum, and she 'kept her brain alive' by illustrating exquisite children's picture-books. Exactly the sort of person Mum would approve of, thought Taz, reminding herself that this was not necessarily a disadvantage.

Best of all, Melinda was just – though only just – affordable. And she liked Taz. Taz thought that she probably quite liked Melinda too, despite Mandy's muttered comment of 'snooty bitch'. Which meant that, thank goodness, childcare arrangements were finally sorted out and that was one less thing to worry about.

And Taz had plenty to worry about.

Like the American Event, for example. Friday night found her at the cricket ground, running through a dress rehearsal for the grand parade down the Promenade. It was hardly the ideal venue, but where else could you cram in a couple of hundred majorettes, two marching bands, a dozen cheerleaders and assorted cartoon characters, without an awful lot of people noticing?

'I've just heard half of the baseball team have gone down with suspected mumps,' announced Cara in the middle of a chaotic routine. 'And somebody's nicked the baton-twirler's baton.'

Taz groaned and silently pleaded with heaven to give her a break. To add to her stress, Diana Latchford had brought Henry Goldman along for a sneak preview, plus a couple of American bigwigs and – horror of horrors –

Angus Cornforth. She decided the best thing she could do was try and pretend they weren't there.

'OK, OK, let's run through that last bit again,' she instructed Cara, who was armed with a walkie-talkie and a clipboard. 'And this time can we get them all to play the *same* tune?'

'The thing is, they can't see their music. The floodlights aren't working properly.'

'So I noticed.' Taz squinted into the gloom, illuminated just well enough to expose all the inadequacies in the choreography. 'Do your best, eh?'

Cara took a step away, then turned back and out of the blue patted Taz on the arm.

'I was a bit of a bitch, wasn't I? To start off with?'

'Well, I wouldn't say . . . not exactly . . .' muttered Taz, taken aback.

'I'm sorry Taz. You're doing a great job, take no notice of Ted, it's what comes of having a microscopic dick.'

Taz didn't have the leisure to wonder how Cara knew. Somehow, in the next fortnight, they had to get this show on the road.

'Positions everyone. One, two, one-two-three-four . . .' floated up from the pitch.

Boom, boom, boom-boom-boom.

'I'm a Yankee-Doodle Dandy . . .'

Music started, stopped, started again, this time almost in tune. Just when things were looking good, someone took a wrong turn, the Seven Dwarfs cannoned into each other and three of their heads fell off. Then Uncle Sam stepped in the big bass drum, and the whole caboodle crashed and jingled to a halt.

'All right everyone, take five.'

Taz was so busy sorting out arms, legs and musical instruments from the muddy tangle that it was ages before she became aware of Angus Cornforth, standing right behind her. It was Cornforth's distinctive growl that made the hairs stand up on the back of Taz's neck.

'I want a word with you, young lady.'

She straightened up and turned round. Cornforth's eyes widened first in surprise and then in disgust at the sight of her immensely pregnant belly. One point to me, thought Taz with sadistic satisfaction.

'Good God, you've changed,' Cornforth remarked.

'Mr Cornforth, how nice to see you again,' Lied Taz, smiling.

'Oh really? Miss Norton, do you realise that my six-year-old grandson has been crying his eyes out because of you?'

'Let me guess,' said Taz quietly. 'The painting competition.'

'I've seen the so-called winner, *Miss* Norton. And you and I both know it can't hold a candle to my boy's painting.'

'It was a very good painting, yes, but rules are rules . . .'

'What *is* this? Some misguided attempt at positive discrimination?'

Taz recalled the winning entry: a jolly collage of paint and sequins, painted by a little Asian girl.

'We couldn't accept Rupert's entry because of the competition rules, Mr Cornforth. You know that. No one associated with Seuss & Goldman was eligible to enter . . .'

Diana caught up with Angus Cornforth, the two Americans in her wake. It took her only a couple of seconds to read the situation.

'I see you two have met. Tasmin, you're doing a very good job – isn't she Angus?'

'Looks like a bloody shambles to me,' replied Cornforth with measured malice, then he returned to his argument like a dog to a well-chewed bone. 'Associated! He's a six-year-old boy, for Christ's sake!'

'And you're the Goldman family's solicitor,' pointed out Taz, mentally counting to ten. How could a grown man – and a multi-millionaire at that – get himself into such a state over a colouring competition? 'What would it look like in the media if your grandson walked off with the top prize?'

'If this is about the painting competition,' said Diana wearily, 'we've been through this before, Angus. Tasmin's quite right. Rules are rules.'

'And after all,' Taz pointed out sweetly, as the two

Americans strolled across to join them. 'You'd want everything to be above board and done properly, wouldn't you Mr Cornforth? The Seuss & Goldman way?'

'Mum, this is Mandy. Mandy, this is . . .'

'Don't tell me, I've already guessed.'

Mandy and Isobel stood on either side of Taz's mother's Metro, looking each other up and down. It was hard to tell who was the more disgusted.

'So this is her is it?' Isobel sounded just like Jim's Great Aunt Shula.

'I'm going to be with Mandy when she has her baby,' said Taz firmly. 'So I thought we should all go and take a look at the hospital together.'

Bloody stupid idea, she admitted to herself in retrospect. It had been inevitable that Mum and Mandy would loathe each other on sight. Still, they'd have to make the best of it now. The midwife was expecting them.

With considerable difficulty, Taz and Mandy squeezed themselves into the back of the two-door Metro.

'God, me waters'd better not break in here,' commented Mandy cheerfully. 'I'd never get me leggings off.'

'Heaven forbid,' muttered Isobel as they set off for the General. Taz caught sight of her face in the mirror; Isobel looked, as Bill was wont to say in his coarser moments, as if she knew the far end of a fart. Taz could imagine her scrubbing down the Metro with Jeyes Fluid the minute she got the car back to Painswick.

Miraculously they managed not to argue between Charlton Kings and the hospital, mainly by not saying anything at all; and even more miraculously there was an empty space in the car park.

'Who does your hair?' demanded Mandy as Isobel reluctantly helped her out of the back of the car.

'Ronald at Salon Classics. Why?'

'It's not straight at the back.'

And with that parting shot Mandy was off towards the double doors which led to the maternity unit. Isobel hung back, clutching her daughter's forearm.

'Tasmin, you simply cannot do it. You absolutely *cannot* be with that girl when she gives birth!'

'Of course I can, I've promised.'

'Tasmin, no! The next thing, she'll be expecting you to be her friend . . . and then she'll want her baby to be friends with your baby . . . and she'll introduce it to her dreadful family, and it'll learn the most appalling habits – it'll never end!'

'But Mummy, we already *are* friends,' Taz laughed, delighted by this ludicrous snobbery.

Isobel was still warning her that she was 'making a rod for her own back' when the midwife welcomed them into the maternity unit.

'Hi, I'm Christine. I'll just give you a quick tour,' she explained, 'So you have a better idea what to expect. I take it you've drawn up a birthing plan?'

Taz nodded and took hers, neatly folded, out of her handbag.

'I'm hiring a TENS machine. I'm not sure about painkillers . . . I'd rather not have them, but what if the pain gets too much?'

'We can always adjust pain relief on the spot,' Christine assured her. 'You don't have to make up your mind now, the plan's just there to give us a better idea of what you want from your birth. After all, it is *your* birth. You want to take away happy memories, not bad ones.'

'I can't imagine anyone having happy memories of giving birth,' said Isobel with dramatic emphasis. 'Thirty-six hours I was in labour with Tasmin, thirty-six hours of unimaginable agony . . .'

Christine smiled nervously.

'Things have changed a bit since your time,' she said. 'These days there's really no need for anyone to be afraid of childbirth. Now, shall we go through to the delivery suite?'

The delivery suite was nothing like Taz had expected. It had chintzy curtains, pretty wallpaper and a CD player 'so you can play some of your favourite music while you're waiting for Baby to arrive.' Taz wondered what Mandy would bring along – Anthrax? Sex Pistols? The Prodigy?

The way things were shaping up, she'd probably want John Taverner or one of Bach's really difficult violin concertos.

It was afterwards, when the three of them were wandering back towards the car park, that Mandy had her brainwave.

'I bet Chloë's still here! Why don't we go and see her?'

'Chloë?' enquired Isobel.

'Married, loads of money, speaks posh,' said Mandy. 'You'll love her.'

'But she said she didn't want any visitors,' pointed out Taz. 'Besides, we haven't got her a bunch of flowers or anything.'

'She won't care about that. Bet she's sick to death of flowers.'

Taz went along with the idea, though she had faint and inexplicable misgivings. In all honesty, she'd been feeling uneasy about Chloë for weeks now – they all had. There was something unnatural about a young, pregnant wife who adored her husband but didn't want to talk about their baby. Still, pregnancy could do funny things to your hormones. Yes, that would be it. Hormones. They'd go and cheer Chloë up, and it would do her the world of good.

'Chloë Baxendale? She's in the private room at the end,' the nurse informed them. 'Yes, she's quite well enough for visitors.'

Taz knocked on the door of Chloë's room and turned the handle. She and Mandy stuck their heads inside almost simultaneously.

'Surprise!'

Frankly, it was difficult to work out who was more stunned: Chloë and Clive, or Mandy and Taz.

Chloë was sitting up in bed, looking fragile and pink in a white lacy nightdress, her big blue eyes red-rimmed and her cheeks puffy and wet from crying. Clive was sitting on the edge of the bed, his hands raised, his mouth open. It was obvious they were in the middle of some kind of argument.

And when Taz looked into the cradle at the end of the bed, it wasn't difficult to see why.

Because Chloë Baxendale's baby was black.

Chapter 11

Cara's voice came across on the walkie-talkie.

'Taz, the people from the *Guinness Book of Records* have just arrived.'

'Great, can you ask someone to take them down to Ken?'

'Done it already. What next?'

Taz ticked one more item off the list on her clipboard. It was happening, really happening; the American Event she'd been planning for the best part of six months – and so far, not one major disaster. OK, so they were down to six Dwarfs and there were only three brides for the seven brothers, but nobody seemed to have noticed. And it wasn't even raining! It was almost too good to be true.

'Make sure the local media people get some really good shots of the World's Biggest Hot Dog.'

If it *is* the world's biggest, she reminded herself; there had been a last-minute panic when someone had started a rumour that the frankfurter was six inches short of its target.

'The *Courier*'s there already, and Mercia TV should be here in the next ten minutes.'

'Oh, and don't forget the stars and stripes hats. Nail Ken's to his head if you have to.'

'It'll be a pleasure. Oh yeah, the fireworks are scheduled for five minutes to midnight, we've got the safety officers in position.'

Taz clicked off the two-way radio and took a deep breath. Midnight. Only another hour to go ... From her second-floor vantage point she could see the good-natured swarm of humanity queueing up for free food and a go on the anti-gravity ride, their upturned faces ghostly orange in the light from the sodium street-lamps. Hot dogs with tomato relish and mustard. Ugh. Taz felt queasy just thinking about it. In fact she hadn't felt hungry all day, just hyperactive and on edge. Stage-fright always did this to her.

'Tasmin.' Just when Taz was allowing herself a moment's relaxation, Diana Latchford emerged onto the balcony, perfectly chic in a black YSL dress, velvet jacket and Daniel Swarovsky crystal necklace. 'I've been looking everywhere for you.'

'Why?' said Taz, her spirits plummeting instantly.

'My office, now. Come on.' Diana prised the two-way radio from Taz's fingers, clicked it on and spoke into it. 'Cara, it's Diana Latchford here. Take charge for ten minutes. Out.'

She pushed Taz back inside the building. Taz hung back.

'*Now*, Tasmin, not in five years' time.'

It was barely twenty yards from the balcony to Diana's office, but it felt like walking down Death Row. Diana held the door open and Taz walked reluctantly inside. The door closed behind her with slow, almost silent restraint.

'What's wrong?' demanded Taz.

Diana shook her head and smiled.

'Somebody's got to make you sit down for five minutes, Taz, how many hours is it since you took a break?'

'I'm fine,' protested Taz. 'Honestly. And there's so much to do.'

'Let somebody else do it for a few minutes. Relax. Here. You're not going anywhere till you've had this.' She poured a coffee and added two chocolate biscuits from the tin in her desk drawer. 'And these.'

'I'm not really that hungry.'

'Eat them. Or I'll get Ken to feed you some of his giant hot dog.'

Taz pulled a face but drank her coffee. It was funny, she didn't feel tired at all, just incredibly restless and full of nervous energy; like she wanted to empty out the whole world's kitchen cupboards and scrub them down. Still, a coffee was welcome; and a quick sit-down would give her a chance to clear her head.

'Thanks. It's very kind of you.'

'I've been called a few things in my time, but kind isn't one of them.' Diana folded her arms, gazing over Taz's shoulder towards the celebrations. 'It makes good economic sense to take care of your staff. And besides, sometimes I look at you and I tell myself, don't let that girl make the same mistakes you made, Diana.'

Taz looked up, surprised. Whimsy wasn't one of Diana's specialities. Maybe it was something to do with the menopause, though it was hard to imagine Diana Latchford having any truck with hormones.

'Mistakes? You mean . . . the baby?' Instinctively Taz's hand moved to her bump, curling round the unborn child, protecting it, defending it from a cold, hard world that dared to suggest it ought not to exist.

'No, no. That's not what I mean at all.' Diana went on talking, still gazing over the top of Taz's head to the street beyond. 'When I was your age, Taz, twenty years ago, things were very different.' If you were a woman and you wanted a career on the same terms as a man, you had to make certain . . . sacrifices.

'Harry and I, we got married straight out of college – too young really, but you don't listen to anyone when you're in love, do you? Anyhow, I always thought I'd have kids one day but the time never seemed right. I wanted to get to the top – how could I cope if I had a board meeting and my child was sick?'

'So you decided not to have a family?'

'Nothing so deliberate as deciding.' Diana shrugged. 'I just let it happen – next week, next month, next year I'd have a baby, there was always time for that later. Only later catches up with you in the end and suddenly there isn't a choice any more . . .'

Diana straightened up, brushing the creases from her jacket. Taz wiped her chocolatey fingers on a tissue; any excuse to avoid saying anything. What *could* she say? She'd never thought of Diana Latchford as forty-five, divorced and lonely before. Maybe success wasn't everything after all.

'I . . . never knew. I'm sorry.'

'It's not regret exactly. Let's just say I wonder sometimes. When I look at you, I ask myself if maybe I was wrong, maybe I could have had it all, if I'd fought a bit harder for what I wanted.'

'But I haven't got it all,' Taz pointed out. 'Far from it.'

'True. But you've got all the bits that really matter.'

The walkie-talkie on the desk crackled. Diana picked it up and handed it to Taz.

'Taz, Cara here. It's official – we've got the world record.'

'Fantastic.'

'Promotions have fixed up something with local radio for tomorrow morning – they want to know if you're up for it, or do you want Ted to do it? He says he doesn't mind.'

'I'll do it,' said Taz, exchanging looks with Diana.

'Can you come down asap? Only the fashion show's about to start, and we want a picture of you with Deputy Dawg before he slices the hot dog.'

'Fame at last,' grinned Taz. And she and Diana went to rejoin the fray.

Taz and Diana arrived just in time to squeeze into a photo of the World's Longest Hot Dog, which was lying on top of about fifty trestle tables, laid end to end along the lower end of the Promenade in all its aromatic glory. Behind a makeshift rope barrier, several hundred locals slavered with their plastic forks and paper plates. This most genteel of Cheltenham's avenues had never seen anything quite like it.

The photographer darted about, arranging arms and legs, sticking an American flag into Ken's hat and a squeezy bottle of ketchup into Ted's hand.

'Big smiles, that's right – if the lady in the green could just sit on the dog's lap . . .' Flash, flash, flash. 'Lovely. Now if you could all go and stand *behind* the hot dog and pretend to take a bite out of it . . .'

'If I were you I'd hold the fashion show for ten minutes,' commented Diana as she surveyed the surge towards the refreshments. 'Better let them finish eating first.'

Taz radioed across to Brendan, and he waved an acknowledgement back at her from the outdoor stage.

'What on earth is he wearing?' giggled Taz in disbelief at the sight of Brendan's hideous suit: a broad-shouldered two-piece in gold lamé, with matching gold-sprayed shoes.

'It's the suit that bloke out of ABC used to wear,' whispered Cara. 'Don't say anything, he paid a fortune for it. Doesn't Kate look gorgeous in that Donna Karan suit though? She's got a fantastic figure.'

'Gorgeous,' agreed Taz with an envious sigh. It'd be a long time before anyone called her gorgeous again. She took her eyes off the preparations for the fashion show, and the giant video screen bringing live pictures from LA, and focused on Ted, who had somehow managed to monopolise Henry Goldman and was steering him towards the VIP marquee.

'Oh yes, Mr Goldman, it was my idea to offer the holiday as a prize. Naturally, with my contacts in the travel industry . . .'

Brendan might have temporarily taken leave of his fashion sense, thought Taz, but Ted was the same devious little toad he always was. Why, the treacherous blob of slime was even trying to take credit for the basketball international that Cara had arranged! Right, Ted Williams, she muttered under her breath. It's about time somebody burst your bubble.

At that moment however Cara directed her attention to a minor commotion in the queue for the fashion show.

'Taz – there's something going on over there, I'd better get security.'

Taz shook her head. It didn't look like a fight or anything serious, just a few people pushing and shoving, and waving their arms about as if arguing the toss about something.

'Don't jump the gun, it's probably nothing. Let's take a look.'

As they got nearer, Taz caught some of the conversation; irritated, slightly panicky voices snapping at each other over the background chatter.

'Get back and give her some air, you stupid woman, can't you see she's ill?'

'Don't you "stupid woman" me!'

'Somebody ought to get an ambulance or a doctor or something.'

'Well I'm not losing my place in the queue, I've been here two hours and I'm not going to the back.'

And then another voice made itself heard. A voice which, even at screaming pitch, was instantly recognisable to Taz.

'Will you stop fuckin' arguing, and fuckin' *help* me!'

Taz stopped short. *Mandy*? Surely even Mandy wouldn't be stupid enough to get herself mixed up in a seething crowd, two days before she was due to give birth! But the top of a spiky head was just visible between the milling arms and legs . . . and there couldn't be two people in the whole of Cheltenham with green and purple hair.

'Mandy, is that you? Excuse me, could you make way please? Let me through, thank you . . . excuse *me*.' Taz elbowed her way through. And there, crouched on her knees on the cold, hard tarmac, was Mandy.

She was completely white-faced, her thick black eye-liner and dark lipstick making her look like a fancy-dress ghoul. And she was clutching her stomach and shaking all over.

'Taz – it's started Taz, I'm havin' it!'

Horrible realisation washed over Taz like a cold shower. There was to be no reprieve.

'You're . . .?' She swallowed hard, unable to get the words out.

'I'm having the baby, don't leave me, you promised! Taz, please don't leave me!'

'You can't leave her,' said Diana, helping Taz to lead Mandy to a chair and sit her down.

'But she's got to go to hospital,' insisted Taz. 'Right now!'

'Then you'll have to go with her.'

'In the middle of all *this*?' Taz gazed around her despairingly, taking in the fashion show, the jiving competition, the remains of the world-beating hot dog, the shoppers milling in and out of the still-open doors of Seuss & Goldman.

'You promised!' wailed Mandy, her eyes panda-like with melting mascara.

Oh God, thought Taz, drowning in guilt. Please don't make me choose! I can't bear the thought of letting *anybody* down. But Diana was already taking charge.

'Cara?'

Get Ted Williams here right away. Tell him it's urgent.'

'Ted?' enquired Taz, puzzled. 'What's Ted got to do with any of this?'

'Ted's going to drive you and Mandy to the hospital. It's no use waiting for an ambulance, it'd take too long to get it through the crowds. Ted's car's just round the corner and besides, right now he's expendable.'

'It . . . hurts. Oh Taz, it hurts!' waited Mandy.

'I know.' Taz stroked Mandy's hair. It felt like Mandy's personality, dry and brittle, ready to snap at any moment; fragile too, and infinitely vulnerable. 'Hang on Mandy, everything'll be all right. Take deep breaths.' She looked at Diana. 'You're sure you can spare me? What about the fashion show?'

'I'll take charge of it, Taz. Just get on with helping this kid have her baby, OK? Oh here's Ted, you took your time Ted.'

Ted glowered, not happy to be dragged away from his conquest of Henry Goldman.

'What's up? You said it was urgent.'

'This young lady – Mandy is it?'

'M-mandy R-robson,' confirmed Mandy, wincing.

'Mandy's having a baby. I want you to drive her and Tasmin to the maternity unit.'

Colour seemed to drain from Ted's smooth cheeks.

'The maternity unit? In *my* car?'

'Just do it, Ted,' snapped Taz. 'And get a move on. Unless you fancy yourself as a midwife.'

Ted was not pleased. As if it wasn't bad enough to be missing out on a one-to-one propaganda session with Henry Goldman, he was being forced to expose the beautiful leather upholstery of his beloved Jaguar XJS to *two* hugely pregnant women.

'You're not going to have it right now are you?' he demanded, darting nervous glances in the rearview mirror as they headed out towards the General. 'She's not is she?'

'How should I know?' Taz put her arm round Mandy's shoulders. 'Come on, remember your breathing – do you want a paper bag, I've got one somewhere . . .'

'A paper bag? To be sick in?' Ted's voice rose a full octave as unease turned to near-hysteria.

'To breathe into, dickhead. She needs calming down. In, out, that's it, really deep, in, out. Here, lean forward and let me rub your back.'

As Mandy bent forward, a very loud, very unladylike noise resonated off the leather seat.

'Sorry.' Mandy managed an embarrassed smile. 'It just slipped out.'

'Strewth.' Ted coughed, his eyes watering, and wound down the window. 'What's she been eating?'

'Are you all right?' enquired Taz solicitously.

'Actually,' said Mandy slowly, 'I'm feelin' a lot better.'

The midwife at the General was very nice about it. Apparently they got a lot of false alarms in the last few weeks of pregnancy, and Mandy had done absolutely the right thing in coming straight to the hospital. But she was perfectly fine, the baby probably wouldn't come for days yet, and she was to go straight home and have a nice rest.

'Get in,' snarled Ted, flinging open the rear passenger door. 'Go on, I haven't got all night.'

'Is he always like this?' asked Mandy.

'Oh no,' replied Taz witheringly. 'Sometimes he can be quite rude.'

'Dry up Taz, it's a quarter-to already. If we don't get back by midnight it won't be worth bothering.'

'Don't you ever think about anything but yourself?

Honestly Ted, you'd think the poor girl did it deliberately. It wasn't Mandy's fault she had wind.'

He turned disapprovingly out of the hospital car park, swung the Jag onto the main road and put his foot right down. The car lurched forward, and Taz was almost thrown off her seat.

'Slow down, Ted!'

But Ted wasn't listening. It was obvious he cared about one thing and one thing alone: getting there by midnight, so he could make sure of having his picture in the paper.

How pathetic, thought Taz as she held on for grim death. What a sad little life you must lead . . . But she was feeling tired now, surrendering to an ache in her back and a distinct queasiness which came and went in bilious waves. She wished to goodness that he wouldn't take the corners quite so fast.

What Ted hadn't bargained for was the thin, invisible sheet of black ice which had formed on the surface of the road; or the traffic lights which changed to red with a suddenness that caught him completely unawares.

'Ted, look *out*!' squealed Taz, completely losing her cool as the brakes locked and the Jag spun across the road in what seemed like slow motion, though it must all have happened in the blink of an eye.

Everything spun dizzily. Car headlights panned through the side window, a horn sounded, somebody swore loudly . . . and then there was an awful, sickening lurch and a kind of soggy crunching noise as everything was flung abruptly sideways.

In the silence, lying sprawled half across Mandy, Taz stared up at the domed interior of the Jag. By some quirk of physics, Ted's sports jacket was still dangling from its hook in front of the rear passenger door. Mandy squirmed and grunted. Ted cursed under his breath. Slowly the realisation crept over Taz that they weren't dead.

Ted slid out onto the frozen pavement. The Jag was half off the roadway, the left indicator lamp neatly scrunched up against the trunk of a horse chestnut tree. Head bowed, Ted stroked its wounded bonnet like a cowboy comforting his injured palomino.

'Oh God,' he whispered. He was shaking uncontrollably. 'Oh shit oh shit oh shit, five hundred quid at least this is going to cost me . . .'

'You moron, you fuckin' bloody useless tosser!' screamed Mandy, suddenly springing up and leaping out onto the pavement, fists flying. 'You nearly killed us and all you can think about is your car!'

Ted parried the blows with an air of baffled disgust.

'Will you calm down, you stupid woman? Haven't you caused enough trouble for one night?'

'*Me*? You're accusin' *me* of causin' trouble?' In her righteous fury, Mandy's diminutive body seemed to tower over Ted. 'You're the one who can't drive in a straight line . . .'

'And you're hysterical,' he snapped back, pushing her lightly so that she almost slipped over on the ice.

'Are you pushin' me? Like pushin' defenceless pregnant women around, do you?'

'Oh shut up and get back in the car.'

Taz lay curled up on the back seat of the Jag, her arms wrapped round herself in a hug of reassurance. She felt cold, shivery, sick, not well at all. Perhaps when tonight was over she'd take a day or two off, just to have a bit of a rest. That would put her right.

It was only then that she realised she was soaking wet. There was a funny liquid sensation all down her legs and underneath her on the seat, and her horrible maternity suit was stuck to her. Her stomach turned a somersault – not blood! She touched the wetness with her fingers and peered at them. But in the light from the street-lamp overhead she saw no redness, only a glistening like water . . .

'Aah!'

The sound of her own voice surprised her as much as it did Mandy and Ted, who stopped in mid-altercation to turn and stare into the car.

'Taz?'

'You all right in there? Not hurt are you?'

Arms squeezed tight around her belly, Taz felt her entire being contract as the most dreadful spasm of pain took hold of her and squeezed out all her breath. When at last it let go of her, she crumpled down onto the seat like an empty crisp bag. Mandy had stuck her head in through the back door and was gazing down at her, round-eyed.

'Mandy . . . Mandy, I think I'm . . .'

'Taz! Taz, what's up – oh my God Ted, her waters've broken!'

'What! On my upholstery? Get out the way and let me see.'

'Never mind your soddin' upholstery, does this car still go or what?'

'Yes, but . . .'

'Get in, shut up, an' drive.'

To say that the midwife was surprised to see them again so soon was a bit of an understatement.

'What – you again?'

Mandy took charge, commandeering a wheelchair and bundling Taz into it. Ted hung back at the entrance, wondering if he could scarper off back to S&G without anyone noticing.

'Not me, her', said Mandy. 'It's me friend, she's in labour.'

'I can't be!' wailed Taz. 'It's not due.' But another contraction, stronger than the last, caught her by surprise and she let out a bellow of pain that would have done credit to a bull-elephant. Ted turned pale and took another step towards the door. 'I . . . I haven't even bought any nappies yet . . .'

'Babies love surprises,' smiled the midwife, tucking a blanket around Taz's legs. 'Now, let's get you up to the labour ward. What's your name dear?'

'T-tasmin. Tasmin Norton.'

'Had I better go now then?' said Mandy, suddenly diffident. 'You won't want me around . . . when your mum gets here.'

Taz reached out and grabbed her hand, almost crushing it.

'Don't you dare go, don't you *dare*!' Taz's eyes pleaded

169

with the midwife to be wrong. 'Couldn't it be a false alarm?'

'No dear, you're definitely in labour.' A pat on the hand did nothing to reassure. 'But don't worry, you're in good hands now.' She smiled coaxingly at Ted, who recoiled at the touch of her fingers on his arm. 'Now Mr Norton, we'd better get you gowned up if you're going to be with your wife at the birth.'

Despite everything Taz managed to find the breath to laugh. Ted? Her *husband*?

'Mr Williams isn't the father,' she gasped. Ah well, her skirt was already soaked through. If she lost control and wet herself now, nobody would be any the wiser.

'Thank God,' muttered Mandy, winking at Taz.

'He's ... a business colleague.' Panic clutched at Taz, as suddenly as an unexpected contraction. 'I've got to get back to work ... the fashion show ...'

'I'll take care of everything,' said Ted promptly, with more eagerness than Taz would have liked. 'Don't you worry about a thing – I'll be off now then, shall I? And tell Diana you'll not be there for the grand finale?' If she hadn't been doubled up, Taz could have smacked his smug face for him.

'Hang on a minute,' said Mandy, catching up with Ted's rapidly-retreating figure. 'What about Taz's mum? She's Taz's birthing partner, you'll have to get her here before she has the baby.'

'*What*?' Hands on hips, Ted pulled his face into a picture of total exasperation. 'Look, I've got a major fashion show to sort out, right?'

'Diana's got the number,' panted Taz, heartily wishing she had the strength left to strangle him. 'Just tell her ... she'll do the rest. Oh ... and there's my cat, Minky ...'

'Honest to God Taz, you really pick your moment, don't you?' Ted glanced irritably at his watch. 'But I suppose I could sort something out if I set off right now.'

'Don't strain yourself,' Mandy called after Ted as he made a beeline for the car park and his distinctively squashed Jag. 'Prat.'

'Right Tasmin,' beamed the midwife, taking charge of

the wheelchair and heading for the nearest lift. 'Now that's sorted out, let's get you up to the ward. You've got some hard work to do tonight.'

Just how hard, Taz could never have dreamed.

This wasn't anything like she'd imagined it would be. There was no TENS machine (she hadn't collected it from Boots yet), no tasteful classical music (the tape was still lying on the kitchen table, next to a half-eaten can of pilchards), and no doting partner to give soothing back massages and read her inspirational poetry. No Isobel yet, either; mind you that was more of a relief than anything.

'Bloody. Hell. Bloody *Hell*!'

'Get a move on Taz, push, what are you, bone idle or somethin'?'

'Shut up Mandy, I hate you!' She squeezed Mandy's hand even tighter, so hard that the ends of her fingers went white. 'I hate everybody!'

'God Taz, you tryin' to break 'em or what? Come on, push!'

'Push your bloody self. Have you any idea what this feels like? Just you wait till it's your turn . . .'

Eileen the midwife's hands fiddled around between Taz's legs. She couldn't tell what she was doing and frankly, didn't much care. Any thoughts of dignity had flown out the window the first time she had an internal, and the doctor had left off halfway through to ring the garage about his Bentley. All she wanted was for this to be over, for this medicine ball which was trying to force itself out through a hole no bigger than an orange to get the hell out of her and leave her poor, exhausted body alone.

'You're crowning, Tasmin dear. A couple more good pushes and you'll be there.'

Mandy sneaked a look.

'It's got hair! Loads of it!'

'I don't care if it's King Kong, just get it *out* of me – ow, ow, aaaaagh! Gareth, you bastard . . .'

'She's not usually like this,' smiled Mandy. 'She's all refined.' Eileen winked.

'You'd be surprised the things I hear. Now Tasmin, the head's delivered, one more really good push . . .'

It happened in an incredible rush, like the four-man bobsleigh hurtling down the Cresta Run. One minute Taz was heaving and straining, swearing and panting on the bed; the next, she felt a sudden urge to push with every ounce of strength left in her body, and it seemed as if the whole of her had turned inside out, leaving her hollow and drained and spent.

The faraway, high-pitched cry seemed to come from a distant planet.

'It's a boy – Taz, it's a *boy*!'

Dizzy and overwhelmed, Taz struggled to raise her head and look at the tiny, squalling bundle in the midwife's arms. It was a baby boy, covered in blood and grey-green slime, twitching and wriggling and wrinkled; and not at all beautiful.

Taz loved him instantly.

'Is he . . . all right?'

'Right as rain, all his bits and bobs in working order. Want to hold him? There we are, little feller. Let's introduce you to your mum.'

Washed and weighed, he was gently handed to Taz. His eyes were a dark and fathomless blue beneath a mop of dark brown hair, and he was making little wet whimpering sounds.

'Hello baby.'

'That's right dear, lay him on your tummy. You can put him to the breast if you like.'

'What you goin' to call him then?' whispered Mandy, gazing in awe at the perfect miniature human being lying cradled in Taz's arm.

'Jack.' Taz took his tiny right hand and put it to her parched lips, kissing them with more tenderness than she had ever felt in her whole life before. 'Hello Jack.'

And even though she knew she was imagining it, Taz could have sworn she saw Jack smile.

Taz woke up, several hours later, still in a side room off the labour ward. Mandy was slumped across the end of

172

her bed, sound asleep and snoring softly. It was light outside, and weak sunshine was filtering into the room, the leaves of the trees outside the window sending shifting patterns across the plain pink coverlet.

A tiny flutter of panic stopped her heart for a micro-second. Where was Jack?

Jack was asleep too, safe in his cot beside the bed. Worn out yet curiously elated, Taz rolled onto her side with a rustle of starched linen, leaned over and peeped at the baby. Her baby. Her son. He was lying on his back in what looked for all the world like a plastic fish tank, his tiny fists clenched as though ready to ward off any unseen threat, his toothless mouth hanging open, pink and wet, beneath a button nose. His grandad's nose.

Taz felt tears prick her eyes. So much emotion was flooding into her that she scarcely knew how she felt: happy or sad, desperate or exultant, it was all so very confused and confusing. She wondered if the American Event had gone all right, but she didn't wonder about it for more than a few seconds. This new and completely fascinating life seemed to have filled every tiny space in her existence, squeezing out everything else, making it seem trivial and irrelevant.

She was a mother. A mother! And this small, red-faced life was her responsibility. For ever. She longed to reach out and pick Jack up, but was afraid of waking him, terri-fied of not knowing what to do. So she just lay there and adored him silently, searching his face for something that would remind her of Gareth; and rejoicing when she found none.

The door opened softly, and one of the junior nurses asked, 'Ready for visitors, Tasmin?'

Taz struggled to sit up, still groggy and dazed. My but her stitches hurt; now she knew what Binnie had meant about sitting on razor blades. Just as well she'd decided to give up sex for ever.

The nurse straightened the bedspread and sharpened up its mitred corners. She beamed down at Jack, his mouth quivering in sleep as though he was trying to say something.

173

'Ah, isn't he lovely? There. All ready. I'll send them in, shall I? And some tea and toast.'

But Taz wasn't really ready. Not for the two people who walked in through the open door. Isobel came in first, bright-eyed, pale-faced; and three paces behind . . . Bill.

Mandy stirred and woke up just as Isobel, Bill and Taz were staring at each other, each one willing the others to say something.

'Well bugger me,' commented Mandy. You could always count on Mandy to come up with the *mot juste*.

'Hello Mummy.' Taz met her mother's gaze.

'Oh Tasmin. I'm so sorry I couldn't be here. Some stupid man from Seuss & Goldman called the wrong number . . .'

'That's all right, don't worry. We're fine, aren't we Jack?'

Jack had woken up and was beginning to make small, fretful noises. Not at all sure that she was doing it right, Taz scooped him up and cuddled him in the crook of her arm. His blue eyes peered sleepily up at her, wondering, exploring. Taz looked up and saw her father watching her, his face frozen into an expressionless mask. Her heart thumped in her chest; but she told herself that she'd stopped being afraid of Bill Norton. She wasn't just his daughter any more; now she was somebody's mum.

'Hello,' she whispered, her voice quavering slightly. Her eyes sought out her father's. 'Hello Grandad.' And tears suddenly spilled in silent cascades down her cheeks.

'Oh sweetheart,' he murmured, and she noticed how bright his eyes seemed as he raised them to meet her gaze. 'Oh Tasmin . . .'

'There's no fool like an old fool,' observed Isobel acidly. But she was sniffing tears away; and a moment later, Bill was crying too.

Chapter 12

Isobel had set her sights on a private room for Taz, but Taz was more than happy to spend the rest of her hospital stay on the postnatal ward. Apart from anything else, she liked having the company of the other new mums and their babies. It helped to reassure her that there were other people who were just as incompetent, just as neurotic, just as excited – and just as determined to get things right in the end.

There were four beds in Taz's bay, though only three were occupied. The fourth was crisply made up with white sheets and a cream bedspread; awaiting the arrival of 'poor Mrs Paterson', who was discussed in hushed whispers because the umbilical cord had got wrapped round her baby's neck and he had been whisked off to intensive care. Taz looked at Jack, plump and placid in his cot, and knew that she had an awful lot to be thankful for.

There wasn't much time to think; there was so much to learn, things that had to be done even if you hadn't a clue how to do them. One of the nursery nurses showed her how to change Jack's nappy and give him a bath; then Nancy from the next bed showed her how to do it all over again, because she was so tired she'd hardly taken any of it in.

Lola, who was Argentinian and had four children under six, assured Taz that everything was much easier the second time around, and laughed when Taz assured her that no way was there ever going to be a second time, not if she had anything to do with it.

She slept when she could, did her best to breastfeed

Jack and joined him in a bit of a weep when neither of them could quite get the hang of it. Everyone told her to persevere, and that she was doing absolutely the right thing. Dee sent a big jar of Peruvian honey, with a short note: 'Put some on your maternity pad, it really takes the sting away.'

Isobel shook her head in disbelief, and shut the jar of honey out of sight in the bedside locker. She tut-tutted reprovingly when Taz told her she was being kept in for a couple of days longer.

'You should have gone private, I told you I'd pay.'

'I didn't want to go private!' Aware of several pairs of eyes watching her with interest from across the ward, Taz lowered her voice to a stage whisper. 'Besides, it's only a little infection, I could have caught it anywhere.' She shifted painfully on her rubber ring, fervently dreading the first postnatal bowel movement. Lola had described it to her in eye-watering detail. Trust Taz to be the one with the infected perineum. 'The midwife says it'll soon clear up.'

Isobel observed Taz's attempts to breastfeed with a critical eye, Jack fidgeting tetchily as Taz stroked his cheek and tried to get him to latch onto the nipple.

'You'll never produce a lot of milk with breasts that shape,' Isobel lamented. 'Besides, if you absolutely insist on going back to work . . .'

'You know I am,' interjected Taz defensively.

' . . . then you'll have to put him on the bottle, won't you? It's such a pity. You were breastfed till you were nine months old – I had the teeth marks to prove it.'

Bill Norton appeared round the corner and stuck his head into the bay. Taz could have wept with relief to see his silly grin, and the elephant-shaped rattle sticking out of his jacket pocket.

'Now then Isobel, not interfering again are you?'

'Don't be silly dear, I'm just giving Tasmin the benefit of some sound advice.'

'Best leave it to the experts, eh?' Bill winked at Taz. 'Take no notice of your mother, she means well.'

Everybody meant well, that was the trouble. In this

place you couldn't move for well-meant advice, most of it conflicting. Sometimes Taz found herself ungratefully longing to be back in her flat with Jack; just the two of them, learning to cope on their own.

On the fourth day, Chloë turned up, out of the blue.

'Can we talk?' Her eyes darted round her nervously, as though imagining that she had instantly become the focus for the entire ward. She was in her dressing gown and nightie, her pale hair wispy and unkempt and her eyes circled with shadows so dark and bluish that they were almost bruises. There was no sign of Clive. Or the baby . . .

'Yes . . . of course.' Taz rearranged Jack's cot blanket for the umpteenth time. 'It's lovely to see you. You haven't seen Jack yet, have you?'

Chloë took the most cursory of peeps at the gurgling baby in the cot, then looked away. It was almost as if she couldn't bear the sight of him.

'He's . . . nice,' she said, awkwardly. 'Very nice.' She subsided into silence, supporting herself on the bed-rail, slightly bowed forward by the stitches from her Caesarian. Taz could feel the desperation inside her, sensed that there was something she wanted and needed to say but couldn't quite bring herself to blurt out. Hardly surprising really, Taz thought.

'You're well?' she said brightly.

'Fine.' Chloë didn't sound it.

'Why don't you sit down? You'd be more comfortable.' Taz eased Chloë onto a chair and perched herself, very gingerly, on the edge of the bed. Never in all her life had she been so acutely aware of her buttocks. 'This is Lola,' she said, indicating the occupant of the bed opposite.

'Hi,' said Lola, summing up the situation in an instant and slipping on a bed-jacket. 'Actually, I was just going to the day room to watch Richard and Judy. I'll bring you back a couple of coffees, shall I?'

Lola shuffled off down the ward, leaving Taz alone with Chloë. Taz willed Chloë to make the first move, but she just kept on staring down at the toes of her furry slippers.

'How's the baby?' Taz began finally. Chloë's head

snapped up, and Taz was instantly certain she'd said the wrong thing.

'About ... about the other day. I owe you an explanation.'

Taz touched Chloë gently on the arm. Her skin felt cold and shivery under the thin dressing gown, even though the ward was ridiculously overheated.

'Don't be silly, you don't owe me a thing. You don't have to tell me anything you don't want to.'

'But I do want to.'

This time Chloë's voice was firmer, less quavery. Taz had the definite impression that she'd psyched herself up to say something, and that she wasn't going to leave until it was said.

Taz sat back and held her breath. Admittedly she was more than a little curious. That two-second glimpse of Chloë's baby, and the awful embarrassed silence that had preceded the tactical retreat, had left a lot of big questions unanswered.

'The baby ... Clive wants to call it Ayesha, but I can't see the point.'

'The point? I don't understand, it's a lovely name.'

Chloë's eyes were as blank and unresponsive as blue glass pebbles in a china face. But the words came out, fast and frantic now that the dam had been breached.

'What's the point of giving it a name when I'm not going to keep it? Clive says he doesn't care that it's not his, but *I* care and I had to give birth to it! I want it adopted Taz, you've got to help me make Clive see sense.'

This bombshell hit Taz for six. For a few moments she couldn't find any words to reply. Her eyes kept drifting to Jack, gurgling sleepily in his cot. Could she ever want to get rid of him? Have him adopted? Think of him as an 'it'? No, no, it was unimaginable, no matter how terrible the circumstances might be.

'Chloë, steady on! Why? *Why* do you want Ayesha adopted?'

Chloë turned to look at Taz. Her expression was stony, unnatural, as if the only way to lock out the bad emotions

178

was to lock out all emotions. Yet behind the facade Taz was certain she could sense the most terrible pain.

'Because it's not Clive's.' She shuddered. 'Because it reminds me of what I did.'

'Do you want to talk about this?'

Chloë nodded. She looked down at her feet again, very small and white in the huge pink slippers. She swallowed.

'Clive and I . . . we've been together for years, we'd always planned to get married, once we'd bought a nice house and got everything organised. I don't know why it happened. It's not as if I don't love Clive, I do. And everybody said we were made for each other. But I suppose I got . . . bored. Does that make sense? Bored with Clive, bored with my life. You see . . . I met this taxi driver.'

'You and he . . .?'

'Yes. We had an affair. It's finished now, it only lasted a couple of weeks.'

Taz tried hard not to look stunned. But the thought of Chloë Baxendale, old girl of Cheltenham Ladies' College, having anything in common with a taxi driver, was hard to swallow.

'It just sort of happened. I had a skiing accident last year when Clive and I were in Kitzbühel, broke my ankle and couldn't drive for a couple of months. Clive insisted on getting me a regular driver.

'I told Clive everything afterwards, said I wanted an abortion, but oh no, typical Clive. He said we'd get married straight away, and everything would be fine. We'd bring the baby up as if it was his.'

'That was good of him.'

'Oh, it was good of him all right. Good old Clive. Only it isn't fine, is it Taz? You've seen the baby . . . And he still says everything's going to be all right. Even his *mother* says it's going to be just fine, they're all crazy!'

'But Chloë, if Clive's all right about it . . .'

'I thought you'd understand,' said Chloë bitterly, getting unsteadily to her feet. 'I thought you of all people . . .'

'Chloë, I'm sorry, I didn't mean to upset you, what did I say?' Damn, thought Taz. And as if to confirm the fauxpas, Jack began a series of throaty whimpers which turned into a high-pitched wail as she gathered him up in her arms. 'Chloë, please don't go.'

But she already had, leaving the curtain swishing behind her and Taz marvelling at the dreadful mess Ayesha Baxendale had got herself born into.

On Wednesday morning, Taz got the all-clear from the doctor to go home. She was just packing up her things, waiting for her parents to come and drive her and Jack back to the flat, when Diana Latchford arrived in a cloud of Chanel perfume; quite a contrast to the overwhelming ambience of sterilising fluid and warm milk.

'Tasmin, I'm so sorry I couldn't get here sooner! Bit of a panic on in men's casualwear . . .'

Taz's blood froze; instinct was hard to unlearn.

'Men's casualwear? What's happened, do you need me to come in?'

'Don't be silly Tasmin,' laughed Diana, 'you're on maternity leave! Besides, Ted's managing perfectly well on his own – did I tell you we've appointed him acting departmental manager while you're away?'

'No.' Taz didn't even try to hide her disgust. Ted! Ted Williams in charge of her beloved menswear! Why couldn't it have been Justin, or Leroy?

Diana sat down and helped herself to a grape.

'I know you two aren't the best of friends, but we had to think on our feet. It's only for a few months anyway, until you come back to work. You *are* still planning to come back aren't you?'

'Of course I am!' Taz indignantly.

'You haven't changed your mind?'

'You know I wouldn't. My career means a great deal to me.'

Diana smiled at Jack, all snuggled up ready for his trip out into the big wide world. You could hardly see his face, just a pink nose peeping out between blankets and a white woolly hat.

'I know. But he *is* cute . . .'

'Yes.' Taz bent down and kissed Jack on his nose. 'And

right now, he's the centre of my world. But that doesn't mean I'm not committed to Seuss & Goldman.'

'So you're still planning an early return?'

'Of course.' Taz hoped that she sounded more enthusiastic than she really felt. She'd been so sure she'd be desperate to get back to work the minute the baby was born, hungry to escape the world of nappy rash and cradle cap, and pick up the threads of her life. But that was before. Before Jack. She forced herself to be positive. 'I've lined up an excellent childminder, there shouldn't be any problem.'

'Good.' Diana stood up, laying a gift-wrapped package on the bedside locker. 'Just some cK One cologne, I know you like it. Keep me informed won't you? And take care of yourself. Must rush now, I'll be in touch.'

'Who was that?' demanded Isobel as she and Bill arrived on the scene, just in time to catch the businesslike click of Diana's heels disappearing out of the ward.

'Diana. You know, my manager at S&G.'

'I hope she wasn't putting pressure on you. You've got enough to think about right now, you shouldn't be thinking about work.'

'No harm in keeping in touch,' said Bill. 'Got to think ahead, isn't that right little feller?' He scooped Jack out of his cot and tickled him under the chin, provoking howls of protest from Isobel.

'Put that child down this minute! Breathing your germs all over him, the poor mite . . .'

Isobel took charge. After a moment's thought of rebellion, Taz let her. She'd be on her own soon enough, and it would hardly do to have a row with her parents when she'd only just got back on speaking terms with them.

'Come along Tasmin, and give me Jack, you shouldn't be carrying anything heavy,' said Isobel firmly.

This was one point Taz wasn't going to concede. She held Jack firmly against her, his small face pressed to the warmth of her breast.

'I can manage, Mum. I'm not an invalid. Jack and I are going to get along just fine.'

Spring had arrived in Cheltenham at last! Over the few days that Taz had been in hospital, the world seemed to have made up its mind that winter was well and truly over. There was a touch of real warmth in the late-March sunshine, and tender sprigs of brilliant green dotted the branches of the trees.

Bill drove his big old Rover as though he were chauffeuring the Queen in a vintage Rolls, pleased as punch to be showing off his brand new grandson to the people of Charlton Kings. Taz could hardly believe he had changed so much. And there was so much happiness in her heart that there was no room left for recriminations. Nothing in the past mattered any more.

The Rover swung left and drew into the driveway of Shepcote House.

'Careful, Bill – mind the ruts in the drive . . .'

'I'm going as slowly as I can.'

'We don't want to wake Jack, he's only just got off to sleep.' The stopped with the gentlest of lurches. 'Give me your door key Tasmin, I'll unlock the front door for you.'

The familiar smell enveloped her as she stepped through the main entrance door into the hallway. Floor polish, tinged with the slightly herby scent of the big potted ferns at the foot of the stairs. Taz paused for a moment, breathing it in, getting used to being home.

'This is where we live, Jack,' she whispered into the tiny screwed-up face. 'This is home.'

Isobel bustled past, followed rather more slowly by Bill, weighed down like a belated Father Christmas with presents, cases, changing bags, a carry cot and an assortment of plastic carriers. She slid the key in the lock, pushed open the recaltricant front door and headed to the kitchen.

'Come along Tasmin, let's get you and baby settled and put the kettle on. Do close that front door Bill, you'll let in a draught. Now Tasmin, where do you keep the . . . good God! What on earth do you think *you're* doing here?'

Taz arrived at the door of the kitchen and almost dropped Jack in astonishment. Mandy was standing in the middle of the kitchen floor, a duster in one hand, spray-can of polish in the other, and Minky draped around her shoulders. In her tightly-stretched Dayglo tee-shirt and leggings, she looked like a grounded hot-air balloon.

'Oh bugger,' said Mandy cheerfully. 'It was supposed to be a surprise.'

Well, it was that all right. Isobel drew in an outraged breath which made her demure bust swell a good two inches.

'Tasmin, you've been burgled. Call the police, Bill.'

'Burgled?' Taz laughed. 'But it's Mandy.'

'Precisely.' Isobel gave Mandy the kind of look normally reserved for cockroaches. 'God only knows how she got in . . .'

'With a key,' replied Mandy with perfect serenity. 'I got your spare off those gay blokes upstairs – you don't mind do you Taz?'

'Well no . . .' began Taz, thinking how sweet it was of Mandy to have wanted to make the flat nice for her and Jack, even if her idea of tidying up did seem to be to pile everything up in the sink and leave it there.

'Mind? Of course you mind!' snapped Isobel. 'This . . . this *girl* lets herself into your flat without a by-your-leave, and . . . and . . .'

'And *cleans* it?' suggested Bill with heavy irony. 'Face it, Isobel, she's a cut above your average burglar. Now, why don't you go and sit down with Tasmin and Jack, and I'll make us *all* a nice cup of tea?'

Two days later, Taz closed the door on her mother with a sigh of relief.

'I'm sure she has the best of intentions,' said the district midwife later, as she and Taz had coffee in Taz's front room.

'Why does everyone keep saying that?' groaned Taz. 'I *know* she does. I just wish she'd stop telling me everything I do for Jack is wrong!'

'Look. If it's right for you and right for Jack, what does it matter what anyone else says? Just nod and smile, and when she's gone home go back to doing it your way.'

'Sounds like you've dealt with a few meddlesome grannies in your time,' chuckled Taz.

'Oh thousands, believe me. And at least you've only got the one to handle. I've seen some new mums reduced to tears by their mothers-in-law.'

'I hadn't thought of it that way before,' confessed Taz. 'You've got a point.'

'Good. Now Taz, I want you to tell me how you're getting on with the breastfeeding.'

Taz thought of her sore and protesting nipples, then of Jack's little pink mouth, sucking away at her breast; and allowed herself a small feeling of triumph.

'Better.'

'But you're still having some difficulties?'

'Sometimes I find it so hard to relax. Especially when it's the middle of the night and I'm worn out – or when I've had ten visitors in a row and Jack hardly knows if he's coming or going.'

'The night thing gets better. Really it does. But you're going to have to be firm with visitors. Put a notice on the front door, saying you're resting. Or give them something constructive to do when they get here – like the ironing, or hanging out the washing.'

'I couldn't!' Taz clapped her hand to her mouth, vastly amused by the thought of Diana Latchford cleaning the loo, or burping Jack onto the shoulder of her latest designer suit.

'Of course you could. They'll feel better because they're doing something to help you, and you'll feel better because you're not worn out all the time. Think about it.'

Taz was doing just that when the telephone rang.

'Ms Tasmin Norton? Sister Tomlinson from the maternity unit here.'

The hospital! But she'd only just got out of that place. What now?

'Is there a problem?'

'Nothing to worry about. It's one of our patients – a Miss Mandy Robson. She asked us to get in touch and tell you she's just gone into labour.'

Chapter 13

With each day that passed, Jack became less like a blob and more like a baby. No, a real-life person.

The way he changed and grew was really quite miraculous. Every time Taz looked at him she seemed to notice something different, some new and exciting development she simply had to tell the whole world about. By the time he was six weeks old, she was convinced he was the cleverest, most advanced baby ever, in the entire history of babies. It didn't matter that Binnie assured her all mums felt that way about their newborns. Or that Isobel said that Jack only pulled faces because he had wind. Taz knew, as only a mother could know, that he was smiling.

Bill wasn't posing too many problems. He was still basking in the glow of being a brand-new grandad, and spent whole hours lost in dreams of Scalextric and the football matches he'd have an excuse to go to when Jack got bigger. By night, his shed resounded the sounds of sawing as he recreated the home-made wooden toys Taz had so loved when she was a little girl.

No, it was Isobel who was the real fly in the ointment. She had discovered a new mission in life: grandmotherhood. And now that she'd retired from her job at the surgery, she had all the time in the world to devote to it.

Between unannounced visits from Isobel, Chloë and Dee, Taz scarcely knew whether she was coming or going.

Six weeks of broken nights, spent walking up and down with Jack crying in her arms, seemed to have turned her brain to jelly. No more watching BBC2; inane quiz shows were all she could cope with these days. She'd ditched the

Independent for the *Daily Mirror*, and some days didn't even manage to get through that. Whole days passed by in a blur of washing, ironing, feeding, trying not to lose her temper with Isobel, more washing, nappy changing, and a bit more washing before falling asleep in the middle of a breastfeed.

If it hadn't been for Mandy, she'd probably have gone round the bend.

Much to both their delight, Mandy had given birth to six-pound Dylan after a positively graceful labour, marred only by the arrival of Mandy's social worker, with the news that Dave had been refused permission to be present at the birth.

'I'm very sorry, Mandy.' Irene was making a real effort, thought Taz, even managing a weakly sympathetic smile. Not that it would cut much ice with Mandy – this relationship was firmly based on mutual loathing. 'The thing is, he didn't do himself any favours with the governor, trying to escape on his way back from the last bail hearing.'

'Bastard,' Mandy sniffed into her pillow, pretending not to care.

'Who – Dave or the social worker?' enquired Taz.

'All of them.'

Since Mandy had taken Dylan home from the hospital, she and the baby had spent more time at Taz's than at her parents' flat. Taz had never seen inside number 382, Bluebell House, but from what Mandy had let slip life there was not exactly one long tea-party.

'Can't you move out?' suggested Taz one day, as they flopped down in Taz's front room with mugs of orange squash.

'Social Services have put me on a list, and you know what that means.'

'No? What does it mean?'

'God, Taz, you're so . . .' Mandy let out a little sigh of exasperation.

'So what?'

'So *nice*. Your lot have never had the coppers round three times in one night, have you? Your mam doesn't scream at you and call you a dirty whore. An' I bet your little brother wasn't taken into care for muggin' old ladies either.'

'Well . . . no,' admitted Taz, beginning to feel like some kind of over-privileged social inadequate. 'So tell me, what does it mean?'

'There's no decent housing round here, not for the likes of me. If they find me somethin' it'll be some disgustin' B&B, won't it? Then Dylan'll catch somethin' and they'll take him off me. Well I'm not havin' that!' She cuddled Dylan close, rosy-cheeked and snug in his blue Babygro. Mandy had a real eye for a charity-shop bargain. 'He's his mummy's boy, and he's stayin' that way.'

'But surely – the social workers want what's best for you and Dylan, they wouldn't take him from his mum . . .'

'Believe me, Taz, I'm best off at me mam's till I can save up an' get somewhere decent. That's if she doesn't chuck me out first.'

'You really think she might? Her own daughter?'

'God knows. It's not so bad when she's half-pissed, she ignores me and the baby then. But like I said, soon as I've saved up enough I'm off.'

'But how? You've got hardly any money coming in!'

'I'll just have to get another cleanin' job, won't I? I'll sort it out for me an' Dylan, you wait an' see.'

Taz found herself wondering how an eighteen-year-old kid could plumb such depths and still believe in a better tomorrow.

On Thursday afternoon it was half-day closing at the Green Café, and time for a long-overdue Old Girls' Reunion.

Old Mums to be more accurate. The whole of Steffi Parkes' childbirth class was here, some with partners in tow. There was a chaotic, carnival atmosphere in the café, babies chuckling, babbling, crying, wailing; mums chattering, coaxing, shushing and soothing. Paradise or purgatory, depending on your point of view.

Chatter and decaffeinated cappuccino soon steamed up the windows, giving the gathering a kind of intimacy reinforced by the hand-painted 'closed' sign on the front door.

'Well we're all here,' commented Dee, sitting on the counter with her legs dangling down and a carry cot on either side. All but Chloë and Clive, thought Taz. No one had heard a word from either of them in a fortnight, and Taz had almost picked up the phone a dozen times to call Chloë. She often found herself wondering ... had Chloë changed her mind? Had she persuaded Clive to go ahead with her crazy plan to have Ayesha adopted?

Dee raised a glass of freshly-pressed apple juice to her lips.

'Here's to us!'

'To us!' came the response, echoed immediately by an indignant wail as Priti's small daughter demanded to be fed.

'Have a sandwich,' said Wendy, handing round the plate. She smiled at Kevin, beaming in his identical blue sweatshirt, baby Wynona strapped to his chest. 'Kev made them, he's such a sweetie.'

'Oh, you know,' said Kevin, blushing. 'Anything to help Wendy, she has so much work to do with the baby, and ...'

' ... and we like to share *everything*,' echoed Wendy, generously finishing his sentence for him and slipping her arm through his. 'Oh Taz, we're so *happy*!'

Taz caught sight of Mandy out of the corner of her eye, pulling a face. It was all she could do not to burst out laughing.

'And the baby?' she managed to ask.

'Wynona? Oh, she's a perfect darling. Sleeps right through the night, has done since she was born ...'

' ... and we actually have to wake her for her feeds!'

Typical, thought Taz. A perfect baby for a perfect couple. In a couple of years' time she'd have a perfect brother, and the whole family would be decked out in identical leisure suits. She couldn't suppress a small silent cheer as Kevin put his hands up to undo Wynona's baby-sling, only to discover that she'd filled her nappy and the contents were oozing onto his chest.

Kevin and Wendy retreated to Dee's living room to

change Wynona, pursued with fascinated fixation by Dee's daughter Petula, and her sister Emma-Louise, at six already the image of her mum and cradling a life-size baby doll in her arms.

Mandy came across and slid into the seat next to Taz.

'Have you seen the state of Steffi? She looks like somethin' out of *The Avengers*.'

Steffi's outfit was a distinct contrast to her usual Jaeger and Country Casuals. She was in head-to-toe black leather, from high-heeled boots and squeaky trousers to a fitted jerkin by Dolce & Gabbana, unzipped to just below the breasts to reveal a good portion of see-through crimson lace. Her elegantly body-waved hair had been cut short and spiky on top, her make-up was bold and her very ordinary mouth had been transformed into a plum-coloured pout.

'What's *that* in aid of?' Taz asked after she'd blinked and whistled.

Mandy leaned closer, baby Dylan kicking happily on her lap.

'Sebastian. You know, her bloke. They had another big bust-up and he said she was dowdy, so she's changed her image.'

'You can say that again. Is he worth it?'

'See for yourself. That's him, over there by the window.'

Taz cast an eye in his direction, and felt profound disappointment. Sebastian Parkes was Mr Average in Marks & Spencer casuals, the back of his dung-brown hair thinning to reveal a circle of gleaming scalp.

'Yuk.' Taz downed her fruit juice. 'Why does she bother?'

'Can't stand being on her own. That's what she told Dee.'

Taz sat back and reflected, gently rocking Jack in his pram.

'I don't mind being on my own,' she said. 'Well I'm not really. I've got Jack.'

'Bet you wish you had a bloke though,' ventured Mandy through the bubbles of a glass of lemonade.

A gale of dirty laughter, coming from just by the

189

espresso machine, announced that Dee was talking about sex again. Taz wondered if she would ever get her sex-drive back again. Would her body ever get back to normal? How long before she felt brave enough to peel off in front of a bloke and reveal her wobbly stomach and cellulite-ridden thighs? If, of course, there was a decent bloke out there and Jack didn't take an instant dislike to him.

'Not really,' she decided. 'Except when it's cold in bed. I'd rather have a Mars Bar. How about you?'

'I've got my Dave, haven't I?' She didn't sound terribly convinced.

'Yeah. Course you have. I expect he'll be out soon. When's the trial?'

'Dunno. His brother was on remand for almost a year. It's not right, he never done nothin', not this time.'

'No.' Taz dithered, torn between loyalty to Mandy and the sneaking feeling that, like Sebastian Parkes, Dave Clayford definitely wasn't worth it. 'You know what you need don't you?'

'What?' The purple tips of Mandy's rainbow hair jiggled in muted expectation.

'Cheering up. Tell you what, why don't I take Dylan one day next week, and you can have a day out?'

'What – on me own?'

'Of course! It's just what you need.' Taz racked her brains for the sort of things Mandy might want to do. Shopping? No money. A rock gig? No money. A nice meal out? ' . . . and you can do whatever you feel like doing,' she finished lamely. 'How about it?'

'There's nothin' I want to do.'

'There must be!'

'An' I hate being on my own.'

'It's only for one day, and I'll take good care of Dylan for you. You trust me, don't you?'

'Course I do!' Mandy's gaze darted around the cafe, lighting on Priti and Raj, completely wrapped up their little daughter even though Raj had sworn he wanted a boy. 'Well . . . I suppose there is one thing. There's a travelling exhibition comin' to Gloucester museum.'

'The *museum*?' Taz's eyebrows shot up.

'I'm not a total airhead you know!'

'I know, I know. I'm sorry.' Taz scolded herself for being so narrow-minded. 'I just never thought . . .'

'It's them Burne-Jones tapestries from Birmingham, I've always wanted to see them, only it don't cost so much to go to Gloucester.'

Literature, art, whatever next? Taz had a feeling there were still more lessons to be learned about Mandy Robson.

It was while Taz was looking after Dylan that Diana Latchford came calling.

'Diana!' Taz stepped back to let her in, and she edged along the un-Hoovered hallway on slender-heeled shoes, past the economy pack of Peaudouce and the basket full of smelly washing. 'I'm sorry about the mess, if I'd known you were coming I'd have tidied up a bit . . .'

'Don't apologise, Tasmin, you must be rushed off your feet. I'd have rung first, only a spare half-hour cropped up and I thought I'd make the most of it. You know how it is.' She popped her head into the spare bedroom. '*Two* babies? Isn't one enough?'

'More than enough,' laughed Taz, suddenly aware of how awful she must look, her hair unwashed and greasy, her ancient tee-shirt blotched with stains. Sartorial standards had definitely slipped in these last couple of months. 'I'm just babysitting for a friend. It's lovely of you to pop in, can I get you a coffee?'

'Thanks. Black, no sugar.' Diana hovered while Taz put the kettle on. 'Missing work yet?'

Taz spooned Nescafé into two cups. She'd long since consigned the gleaming coffee-machine to the back of the kitchen cupboard.

'Oh yes,' she nodded. Funnily enough, she'd scarcely thought about work until Diana arrived, but now she was here Taz suddenly missed S&G with a painful passion. For the first time since Jack's birth, she began to feel really torn. 'How is everything?'

'Fine. Well, more or less fine. Actually, I didn't just come to see how you were, I wanted to ask you a favour.'

'Right. Yes.' One ear cocked for the first baby whimper, Taz poured boiling water into the cups, added a dash of milk for herself and led the way into the living room. 'Sorry, no biscuits, I haven't managed to get out to the shops today.'

'Not to worry.' Diana made a space for herself on the sofa, closing the giant baby book and laying it on the floor at her feet. 'Now, this favour. It's about Marion Grey.'

'What's she done now?' asked Taz, groaning slightly.

'Nothing specific. But she's in such an emotional state that she's just not performing. To be frank, I think it's as much a personality clash with Ted Williams as anything.'

'Ted!' I might have known, Taz thought, fuming inwardly.

'It's not that he isn't doing a good job of keeping the department ticking over. But let's just say inter-personal skills aren't his forte.'

'You can say that again,' muttered Taz.

'So I thought perhaps you wouldn't mind having a chat with Marion, calming her down.'

'But why me? Surely Leroy . . .'

Diana's smile slipped a fraction.

'Actually, Tasmin, Leroy's not with Menswear any more. We moved him to the Food Hall last week, to stand in for Ted as ADSM.'

'What! But . . . you can't! I can't do without him – we *need* Leroy, he's the mainstay of the whole department! And you could at least have consulted me, surely.'

'I'm sorry Tasmin, there was no time. Ken's been on sick leave, and we had to get someone competent into the food hall.'

'But what about menswear? What are you doing to my department? Ted's going to run it into the ground, it'll be a shambles by the time I get back.'

'Look, Tasmin. Don't worry about menswear, OK?' said Diana, looking uneasy.

'But . . .' Taz didn't like the way Diana was avoiding

looking her full in the face. 'Is there something you're not telling me?'

'No, of course there isn't. I just don't want you worrying yourself silly about things that'll have been sorted out long before you get back to work. And do you really think I'd sanction anything that would harm the department?'

'I suppose not.' Taz ran her fingers through her uncombed hair. She was a mess. And she'd let her hormones get the better of her, which was unforgiveable. What would Diana think of her? 'Sorry, I think I overreacted a bit there. Now, what exactly was it that you wanted me to do with Marion?'

'Hello Tasmin dear, you didn't mind me letting myself in, did you? Now, where's my lovely grandson?'

Isobel breezed through the flat like a miniature tornado, heading straight for the spare bedroom and the unsuspecting Jack. Taz set off in hot pursuit, and just managed to get there first, blocking off the doorway.

'Actually Mum, I'd rather you didn't wake Jack up, I've only just got him down and you know how fretful he gets . . .'

'Are you sure you're all right, dear? Tell you what, I'll look after Jack for a couple of hours while you get on with a bit of cooking and cleaning. The flat looks like it could do with a good tidy.'

'The thing is, Mum . . .' Taz recalled what the district midwife and health visitor had both told her, and decided to go for it. She couldn't stand much more of this. 'I'd rather take care of Jack while you do a bit of tidying up, if that's all right by you. I am his mum, after all. I think it's important for us to spend as much time together as we can.'

To her credit, Isobel took it quite well, at least on the face of it. There was only the faintest hint of a scowl, and it lasted only a couple of seconds before being replaced by a businesslike smile.

'If that's what you want, dear.' There was, however, a definite hint of acid in the voice.

'Oh Mum, don't be like that. It's just that I'll be back

at work before I know it, and I don't want to miss out on any time with Jack. You do understand, don't you?'

'Yes dear.' The face relaxed into a genuine smile. 'I understand. Now, why don't I start by doing out your kitchen cupboards?'

Taz counted to ten, telling herself that at least her mother couldn't get up to much mischief emptying out a cupboard. But it couldn't have been more than two minutes before Isobel came marching into the nursery, rubber-gloved to the elbow and a brandishing a large tin of baked beans in either hand.

'What are these?'

'Baked beans.'

'I can see that, Tasmin dear. But *twenty* tins of baked beans?'

'I like beans.' And they're cheap, she thought, but she didn't say so. She wasn't about to admit her growing financial crisis to her mother – the next thing she knew, she'd be getting daily food parcels and visits from Meals On Wheels.

'But I've looked in your fridge, there's nothing in there but a bit of stale cheese and half a pint of milk.'

'I haven't managed to get to the shops today. Anyhow, beans are very nutritious.'

'But you have to look after yourself, Tasmin!' Isobel waggled the cans of beans to emphasise the point. 'You can't breastfeed that poor child properly if you eat nothing but baked beans. What about green vegetables . . . you need your iron – and your calcium . . .'

'I'm fine.' Taz straightened up and brazened it out. 'Absolutely fine.' And even if you might be ever so slightly right, she thought to herself, there's no way I'm going to admit it to you. She made a mental note to have a proper salad and some chicken for tea.

'I could go out to the shops now for you if you like.'

'It's all right Mum, I'll go later.'

Jack chose that moment to wake up, and started wriggling in his cot, his pink fingers jabbing up at the overhanging mobile of fluffy zebras.

'Hello little man,' smiled Taz. 'Did you have a lovely sleep?'

'He seems to like that nice new mobile, dear,' commented Isobel, examining the dangling zebras. 'Where did you buy it?'

'I didn't.' Taz savoured the moment. 'It was a thank-you present from Mandy, for looking after Dylan. I'll tell her you liked it, shall I?'

It was obvious from the look on Isobel's face that she'd rather have died than admit she liked something chosen by Mandy Robson.

'It's Mother,' sighed Marion, cutting a slice of shop-bought Madeira cake and handing it to Taz.

'She's worse?'

'I'm afraid so.' Marion gave a dismal nod.

'Oh. I'm sorry to hear that.' It sounded so empty and inadequate; she didn't mean it to sound that way, but frankly, Taz and Marion had never had much to say to each other.

Taz sat awkwardly on the edge of Marion's very old Chesterfield sofa, Jack on her lap. At a rough guess, all the furniture in Marion's large Prestbury semi dated from the days when her parents had first married. The moquette was worn thin on the arms of the chairs, and the colours in the carpet had turned to indistinct shades of beige, orange and brown. Even the wallpaper had a distinctly Fifties look to it, with its design of floor-to-ceiling bamboo canes. The whole place was a time-capsule, a shrine to a past that could never return.

Marion sat down opposite Taz, and picked at her slice of cake, pulling it into sticky crumbs.

'He's a beautiful baby.'

'Thank you.' That at least broke the ice a little. Taz never tired of talking about Jack, or listening to compliments about how gorgeous he was – all of them richly deserved. She wiped his nose. 'He's a little bit sniffly today, hope you don't mind me bringing him with me. We go everywhere together, don't we Jack?'

As if he understood every word, Jack burbled and snuffled, kicking out his legs and arms. A shaft of dust-dancing sunlight touched Jack's face and made him look like the pot of gold at the end of the rainbow.

'Mother used to love babies,' said Marion. 'She wanted lots, but after me she had to have it all – you know – taken away.' She blinked and sat up very straight and stiff, as though determined not to cry. 'It's her mind, Miss Norton. Physically she's quite strong, the doctors say she could last another ten years. But mentally . . .'

Marion stared into the middle distance.

'She's just like a baby,' Miss Norton. Only she won't ever grow up. 'I go up to the nursing home, every day I can spare, but she keeps refusing to see me. Says she's never seen me before in her life. Can you imagine? I try to keep going, really I do, but it's not easy. And then, as if that's not enough to bear, everything's going from bad to worse at work . . .'

Taz sat forward, her ears pricking up.

'It's that *man*. He's nothing but a horrible, slimy, lazy toad. And a bully with it. When I asked him to change my day off so I could see Mother, he practically laughed in my face.'

'I take it we're talking about Ted Williams?'

'Oh Miss Norton.' Marion's face had never looked more earnest, more open, more girlishly vulnerable. 'I wish you'd hurry and come back.'

Taz slipped her little finger into the corner of Jack's mouth and he began sucking at it. Oh little one, she thought, I don't want to leave you, not ever; her heart ached at the very idea of it. But if I don't, I'll turn into a mindless vegetable and we'll have nothing but baked beans to eat for ever and ever, until we both explode.

'I will,' she reassured Marion. 'Just as soon as I can.'

'There's something else,' ventured Marion uncertainly. 'A favour . . . I was wondering . . .' 'Would you come with me – the next time I visit Mother?'

'Well, yes. If you think it would help.'

'Oh it would, really it would. Thank you Miss Norton, I'm ever so grateful.'

'No need for that,' Taz assured her. 'I don't mind at all.'

196

But she couldn't help wondering just what she'd let herself in for – and what else Ted Williams was doing to the menswear department.

Her department.

Chapter 14

'. . . and this little piggy went "wee, wee, wee", all the way home!'

Bill Norton tickled the soles of his grandson's feet, and Jack rewarded him with a series of hiccups and giggles. Jack lay across his lap on a sheepskin, staring up in fascination at the light glinting off Grandad's balding head.

'Who's going to play for Everton when he grows up then?' Bill didn't wait for an answer, but bent and gave Jack a noisy kiss right on his bare belly-button.

'He might not want to!' protested Taz.

'Of course he will – look at those chubby knees. He's got footballer's legs, just like his grandad.' Bill took a reluctant glance at his watch. 'Better get back home I suppose.' Taz noticed that he didn't sound too keen. It wasn't often that Isobel let Bill out on his own.

'Mum's expecting you?'

'She's got a roast in the oven, there'll be hell to pay if it dries out. Ah well fella, best give you back to your mum.' Bill got up slowly, cradling Jack with the semi-confidence of someone who'd been a parent a very long time ago.

Taz retrieved Jack and snuggled him close. As the flat of her hand made contact with the seat of his nappy, he started to squirm and grizzle – and there was no mistaking that tell-tale pong.

'Uh-oh, who's got a soggy bottom then? Let's make you nice and dry, shall we?' She tut-tutted affectionately. '*More* washing! I don't know where it all comes from.'

'At least your machine should hold out a bit longer. I think I've sorted out that problem with the drum.'

'Thanks ever so much, dad. What would I do without you? Jack and I are getting through two full loads a day!'

Bill collected his shapeless old sports jacket from the hall. He'd had that jacket so long that it had actually distorted to fit every lump and bump of his ageing body. Isobel made periodic attempts to give it to a jumble sale, but Bill always foiled her at the last minute. He adored it as much as she detested it.

'It'd make more sense to buy a new machine,' commented Bill, opening his briefcase and dropping an adjustable spanner into the bottom of it. 'You can get good discounts if you pay cash. Or there's always HP if things are a bit tight.'

Taz covered up her embarrassment by snuggling her face into Jack's baby-soft brown curls and gently kissing his ear. Buy a new washing machine? On credit? No one in their right mind would give credit to a single mum on half-pay, who'd had to live on baked beans for weeks just to meet last month's mortgage payment.

'I'll think about it, Dad,' she promised him – which wasn't a lie, since she'd actually been thinking about it for weeks; it was just that she didn't have the money to do more than think.

'Mind you do. And if you're a bit short of cash . . .'

'No Dad, I'm fine, really.'

A prickle of panic raised the hairs on the back of her neck. Had Bill somehow guessed just how tightly stretched her finances were at the moment?

There was no way she'd take money off her mum and dad. It would be the thin end of the wedge. The next thing, Isobel would be pointing out how lonely Taz must feel, living on her own; and how much more 'sensible' it would be for Taz to sell up and move in with them. No way!

'Listen, love. If there's anything you need, you know where to ask. And you will ask? Promise?'

'Promise.' It didn't really count though, since Taz had

her fingers crossed behind her back. 'Oh, and thanks for the wooden train – Jack'll love it when he's a bit older.'

The painted train was snaking across the front room, enormous and bright and completely unsuitable for a baby who was too small even to sit up on his own. But its wobbly wheels and multicoloured paintwork exuded love, and Taz felt quite emotional just looking at it.

'I'll just take a last look at that machine before I go – make sure it's not leaking.'

Taz got out the changing mat, for the umpteenth time that day, and laid Jack down on it on the living room floor.

'Come on, big boy, let's get you out of this wet Babygro.' She kissed his tiny fingers as she undid the poppers and eased his arms out of the stretchy suit. 'That's a good boy, stay still for Mummy . . .'

The cordless phone rang, under a heap of laundry on the bathroom floor, and Bill called out, 'I'll get it shall I?'

'If you can find it. It's probably Dee, she said she might ring. Can you take a message?'

A few moments later, as Taz was unfastening Jack's nappy, Bill stuck his head round the living room door, his hand over the telephone mouthpiece.

'It's that Mrs Latchford. Shall I get her to ring back later?'

'Better tell her I'll call – no, hang on.' The reflex tensing of her stomach muscles at the sound of Diana's name was every bit as instinctive as the milk which leaked from her nipples whenever Jack started crying. 'I'd better speak to her now. Hold the phone to my ear.' She cleared her throat and tried to sound business like. 'Ms Latchford? Taz Norton here.'

'Taz, lovely to talk to you. Is this a bad time?'

'No. Not at all,' lied Taz, easing the nappy from under Jack and arming herself with a good handful of baby wipes. 'It's OK, I'm just changing Jack.' She hoped Diana would be suitably impressed by her multi-tasking skills. 'What can I do for you?'

'I just wanted to thank you for what you did with Marion Grey.'

'Really? But I didn't do anything . . . that's a good boy Jack, nearly done now . . . just went with her to the nursing home, and let her cry on my shoulder.'

'Well it obviously meant a lot to her, there's a definite improvement in her attitude. You're good with people, Tasmin, it's a quality I value in my managers.'

Praise indeed, thought Taz, a warm glow of self-righteous pleasure adding to her pleasure at Jack's toothless smile. She dried Jack's bottom and sprinkled it with a small snowstorm of baby powder.

'Thank you. It's nice to be appreciated.'

There was something about the short pause which followed that made Taz sense that Diana hadn't rung up just to lavish praise on her.

'So – you're well then? You and the baby?'

'Absolutely fine.' Flabby, frumpy and falling-over tired might be more accurate, but 'fine' would do for the time being.

'Have you fixed a date for coming back to work?'

Taz looked into Jack's innocent, trusting eyes and felt a twinge of real pain. Something told her that even a date five years from now would be too soon. But that would be allowing emotional weakness to get the better of a perfectly good brain, and she wasn't about to let herself be blackmailed, not even by the most gorgeous baby in the whole wide world.

'Not yet. But I've got the childcare arrangements sorted out – a really super lady, I was lucky she had a vacancy.'

'Exellent. Well, you won't forget that we need three weeks' notice of the date you're planning to return? Oh – and there was one other thing. Did I mention that Gerry Rothwell's been seconded to the Los Angeles store for a couple of months?'

'No? Really?'

'Just in an advisory capacity, he has a lot of experience in setting up new operations. The thing is, I'm feeling the lack of experienced managerial support myself, and you did mention that you wanted to keep fully in touch with developments at S&G . . . So what I'm proposing is that you could do some fairly routine administrative tasks from home. You know, analysing figures, working on spread-sheets, generally providing me with management information to make basic day-to-day decisions.'

'Oh. I see.' Taz looked at Jack, then at Bill, then at Jack again. Beyond Bill's shoulder she had caught sight of the open bathroom door, and the giant pile of dirty washing on the floor.

'Naturally, you can say no if you feel it would be too much to cope with . . .'

That time, Diana hit the magic button. If there was one thing Taz couldn't stand, it was the suggestion that she might not be able to cope.

'No, no, of course I'll do it. It'll be,' she swallowed, 'a good way of getting back into the swing of things.'

'Fine, excellent.' Diana sounded relieved. 'I knew you wouldn't let me down. I'll get my secretary to bike you over a laptop PC and some printouts this afternoon.'

Diana rang off, and Bill pushed down the aerial on the phone.

'What was that all about?' His expression told Taz that he'd overheard enough of the conversation to work it out for himself.

'It's Diana – she wants me to do some work from home. Dad . . . don't tell Mum, eh? You know she'll only worry.'

'Oh yes love, I know your mother all right. But if it all gets too much for you . . .'

She patted his hand, glad that they had got back some of their old intimacy and trust.

'I know, Dad. Don't worry. Everything's under control.'

Jack wriggled in her grasp as she took out a fresh nappy, lifted him up by the ankles and slid it under his bottom.

'There, sweetheart, we'll soon get this fastened then you can have a lovely sleep.'

A second later, and quite without warning, Jack retaliated with his very own protest vote: a graceful arc of pee which hit Taz full in the middle of her nice clean sweater.

That Sunday evening, with Jack snoozing in his cot, Taz made her mind up to get on with the work Diana had sent over. Every time she switched on the PC or picked

202

up a sheaf of computer printouts, the phone was sure to ring, or Jack would decide that it was dinner time.

But this time there weren't any interruptions. She managed almost three quarters of an hour on the last six months' sales figures, and very interesting reading they made, too. One fact that intrigued and pleased her was that whichever department Kate was working in at any given time seemed to flourish. Right now electrical were getting the benefit of her golden touch, and Taz wondered vaguely if there might be a chance of poaching her for her own department, maybe doing some kind of swap for Justin, who loathed menswear and all its works.

The story was very different in the food hall. Sales down, profits down, turnover down, problems with stock levels, promotions that just weren't paying off; it was starting to look as if Ken was really losing the plot. Poor Leroy, Taz found herself thinking. And then she couldn't help laughing to herself, at the thought of tall, aristocratic Leroy condemned to wet fish and the bacon counter.

'Minky . . . Minky, don't do that!' she giggled as Minky sprang onto her lap and started patting the tracker ball on the PC. 'You'll erase all my files . . .'

She tucked a hand under Minky's soft, round belly and lifted her onto the arm of the chair, out of harm's way. But Minky wanted to be queen of the castle, and promptly hopped onto Taz's shoulder, purring triumphantly.

Just then the phone rang and she had to dig it out from underneath one of the seat cushions, so outraging Minky that she slid off Taz's shoulder, leaving long scratches down her arm. Ah well, it had been that kind of day – this was probably Diana, ringing to find out why Taz hadn't finished the figures.

'Oh Taz, you *are* in, thank God!'

It was Binnie's voice, tired, emotional, almost hysterical; not much like Binnie at all.

'Binnie – is something wrong?'

A muffled sob on the other end of the line was strangled instantly, and Binnie's voice came back stronger, harder, as though steadied by an act of will.

'It's Jim.'

'Jim! What's happened?' Taz's mind filled with terrible imaginings – an explosion on an oil rig, a car accident, some incurable disease.

'Me and Amy – we've left him.'

Binnie let the bombshell hit home, explode, and the dust settle.

'I had to do it, Taz, I couldn't take any more.'

'Steady on Binnie, calm down. Where are you?'

Binnie launched her second missile; the really big one.

'In the street outside your flat.'

Binnie trudged wearily over the threshold, Amy sleepy and bewildered in her baby buggy, Binnie festooned with bags and overnight cases. A much-chewed bunny rabbit drooped long ears out of her jacket pocket.

'I feel terrible about this,' she said, pushing her tired fringe out of her eyes.

'Don't be silly, you know you're welcome. Come in, sit down, you look worn out.' Taz made space on the sofa. 'Have you been driving all day?'

Binnie nodded, unbuckling Amy from her buggy and easing her out of her coat.

'And half the night. We set off before Jim got home. I couldn't face him, I just had to get away. Oh Taz, I'm sorry to impose, but I just couldn't think of anywhere else to go . . .'

'Not even your mum's?'

Binnie shook her head, sinking down onto the sofa.

'You're kidding. She'd do her nut, she thinks the sun shines out of Jim's backside. I'm not going to see her until I've got something sorted out for me and Amy. The thing is . . ., that time when you came up for the christening. You mentioned that if things got bad, the two of us could come and stay with you for a while. You did mean it, didn't you?'

Taz's mouth was dry. She couldn't decide if she was more pleased to see Binnie, or worried about the way things were heading.

'You know I did. Stay as long as you like.'

'Thanks Taz, you're a real friend. Not like that bunch

of Scottish harpies,' she added under her breath. 'You've not had Jack christened yet then?'

'To be honest, I haven't really thought about it. Mum makes noises, you know . . .'

'Yeah,' chuckled Binnie drily. 'And she'll go on and on making noises until you give in.' She picked up her daughter and sat her on her knee. 'I don't suppose you've got any baby juice?'

'Sorry. Jack's still on milk, milk and more milk.'

'I'll make her up a bottle then, you don't mind if I sort it out in the kitchen?'

'Of course not.' Taz's head whirled. On the outside, Binnie seemed unnaturally controlled, cold even. But underneath, Taz sensed that things were very different. She followed Binnie and Amy into the kitchen. 'She's grown a bit since I last saw her!'

Binnie stroked the hair back from Amy's face.

'Hasn't she just. Could you hold her for me a minute?' She handed Amy over to Taz, who marvelled at the amount of weight one baby could put on in nine short months.

'Heavens, she's huge! She'll be walking soon.'

'She's already crawling all over the place,' laughed Binnie, 'you have to have eyes in the back of her head. Only the other day, Jim was saying . . .' Binnie stopped short and started taking a very minute interest in ladling baby formula into Amy's bottle.

'Binnie . . . do you want to talk about it?'

'He's a bastard, Taz,' said Binnie, her hands shaking, but her voice steady.

'But you love Jim, you've always been devoted to each other.'

'Oh yeah, the perfect couple. Until I get pregnant and he decides we're heading off to Scotland.'

With her free arm, Taz led Binnie to the kitchen table.

'Sit down.' She joined Binnie at the table, sitting Amy on her knee. Her ears strained for whimpering from the nursery, but for once Jack was good as gold. 'Now, what's wrong?'

Binnie let out a long, loud explosion of breath.

'In a word, Jim. First he gets me to give up my job and move to Scotland, then he promises he'll be working shorter hours so he'll be able to do his share with Amy – and what does he do? He pisses off to some oil rig for Christmas, he works seven days a week and sometimes seven nights too, he's never at home and when he is, he's on his sodding PC in the attic. I tell you, Taz, I doubt he's even noticed yet that I'm not there.'

'Oh Binnie, I'm sure that's not true!'

'And just to make things worse, he tells all the poisonous old crones in the district to pop in whenever they damn well feel like it. Which of course they do. And the one time we get a chance to be together and actually go out for the evening . . . the *one time*, Taz, is that so much to ask?'

'You had something special planned?'

'It was our anniversary yesterday. Our tenth. Jim promised faithfully he'd make a special effort to be home by seven. By some miracle I actually managed to get a babysitter – one who wasn't related to Jim. I got dressed up, I had my hair done, I was really looking forward to it, the first time I'd been out since Amy was born. And then . . .'

'He didn't turn up?'

'It was almost eight thirty before he bothered to ring up. "Hi darling, bit of a problem at work, I'll have to work late." And that was it, no apology, no nothing.'

'Oh poor Binnie,' sighed Taz, remembering the terrible pain of rejection she had felt over Gareth. And Gareth had scarcely been more than a series of one-night stands.

'So anyhow, I sent the babysitter home, then I sat in the kitchen for a couple of hours, just drinking coffee and thinking of slow, painful ways of murdering Jim. About two a.m. it came to me: why sit here waiting for him to come home, when you know all he wants is a shag and a clean pair of underpants? Why not get your own life back?'

'And that's when you decided to leave?'

Binnie reached out and took Amy from Taz, hugging her very close as though she was the one truly precious thing in her universe.

'I'm sick of being an appendage, Taz. Sick of being Jim's English wife, the one who doesn't really fit in. I want to be *somebody* again, and I don't need Jim to do it.'

When Mandy arrived, at breakfast time on Monday, Taz's flat was in perfect chaos. A laptop computer sat perched on top of a pile of papers, dumped into the armchair by the window. Amy was crawling around on the carpet, playing with the wooden train Bill had brought for Jack. Taz was feeding Jack, who was far more interested in what Amy was doing, and Binnie was busy burning toast in the kitchen.

It was Binnie who ran to open the door and found Mandy on the doorstep, Dylan tied into a shawl on her back, like a papoose.

'Taz, I need to . . . oh.' Mandy's face fell, a single beaded strand of tricoloured hair swinging down across her eyes. She pushed it back. 'Where's Taz?'

'She's feeding Jack.' Binnie beamed a welcome; she was feeling a lot better after a decent night's sleep and an entire day spent many hundreds of miles away from Jim. 'You must be Mandy.'

Mandy looked faintly suspicious, but nodded.

'Yeah. Right. Can I come in then?'

'Who's that?' Taz called out.

'Mandy. Come on, she's in the living room, do you want a cup of tea or some breakfast or something?'

'Er . . . no.' Mandy's gaze dwelled for a long second on the curled-up, perfectly blackened slice of toast. 'No, I'm all right. I just wanted a word . . .'

But Binnie wasn't listening, she had already bounded back into the kitchen and out again, with a tray of cereal, juice and bread in varying stages of carbonisation.

'Taz—' began Mandy. Taz carried Jack into the nursery, with Mandy in pursuit. 'Taz, there's somethin' I need to ask you . . .'

'Mmm?' Taz busied herself with Jack, settling him on his back in his cot. 'Oh Mandy, hi. I'll be right with you.' But Binnie called from the living room:

'Do you remember that time – on the survival course?

207

When I had to cook the dinner and all those ants got into the baked beans?'

Taz remembered all right. They'd laughed about it for weeks, especially about the pain in the arse from HQ who'd got food poisoning. She tiptoed out of the nursery, ushering Mandy out, and closed the door behind them.

'Yeah, I reckon you did it deliberately.'

'I did *not*!' Binnie was red-faced with a mixture of mirth and indignation. 'I wouldn't!'

'Taz.' Mandy grabbed Taz's arm and spun her round. 'Please Taz, it's important.'

'Oh, sorry.' Taz fought the urge to laugh, but of course the more she tried not to laugh, the more she wanted to. 'Mandy, I'm sorry, it's just so nice to see Binnie again.'

'Yeah. I can see that.'

Taz wasn't so thick-skinned that she couldn't detect the note of bitterness in Mandy's voice, or read the signs of jealousy in her eyes. Immediately she felt terribly guilty, torn between the urge to share memories and companionship with Binnie, and listen to whatever Mandy had to say.

'The thing is, Binnie's going through a rough patch, she's staying here for a few days.'

Mandy took a deep breath, considering what she was going to say.

'It's . . . about Dave. When I went up to the prison . . .'

But just as she was about to open her heart, the phone rang.

'Just a mo, Mandy, let me get that.' Taz snatched it up. 'Hello?'

'Taz, thank God. Is Binnie there?'

Taz lowered the phone and looked across at Binnie. She didn't need to say anything. The smile slowly slipped from Binnie's face.

'Tell him to go to hell,' she snapped.

'I've got to talk to her,' insisted the voice on the other end of the phone. For God's sake, Taz, you're supposed to be a friend!'

'I think you should talk to Jim,' said Taz, forcing the receiver into Binnie's hand. 'You have to sort this out.'

Binnie stared at the phone for a few seconds, then raised it slowly to her ear.

'Jim? Jim, why don't you just drop dead? I hate you, I hope I never see you again.'

She crashed the receiver onto its hook and burst into tears.

'Oh Taz, I do love him, I do! And he's Amy's dad, she needs her dad. Why does he have to be such a bastard?'

And then of course Taz ran over to her and comforted her, getting down on her knees and hugging her reassuringly as the two of them sobbed along together. Which naturally set off Amy and filled the flat with the sounds of lamenting sisterhood.

Completely ignored by everyone but Minky, who was angling for a second can of Whiskas, Mandy stood in the doorway and looked at Binnie and Taz. Friends. Two self-contained people who didn't need anybody but each other. There seemed little point in sticking around.

Mandy walked unnoticed to the front door, and let herself out; her head down and her tatty top-knot wilting like the leaves of a dejected palm-tree.

Frankly, Taz would never have cast herself in the role of marriage guidance counsellor; but then again, perhaps Diana Latchford had a point and she really was 'good with people'.

In any case, bringing Binnie and Jim back together proved to be the kind of thing that needed very little outside help. Driving flat out, Jim reached Cheltenham by supper time and pounded hell out of Taz's front door, demanding to see his wife and daughter. Taz peeped at him through the spy-hole. He looked a complete fright: unbrushed hair sticking out Ken Dodd-style, stubbly chin, stains on his shirt, bloodshot eyes. He was taking this even worse than Binnie.

'Binnie, it's Jim.'

'Tell him to fuck off.'

Jim's voice filtered through the door, slightly muffled. Taz wondered what the other residents of the flats must be thinking.

'Taz – Taz, are you going to let me in and talk to Binnie?'

'Don't let him in, Taz.'

'I'm sorry, Binnie. But I really think you two need to talk.' Taz released the latch, not without some trepidation, and stood back to let Jim in. He stumbled in like the living dead, haggard and clumsy.

'Where are they?'

'In the living room. But Jim – be careful.'

'For God's sake, Taz, I only want to tell her I'm sorry.'

Naturally, Binnie insisted that she didn't want to see him, in fact never ever wanted to set eyes on him again. But five minutes later they were having a good shout at each other in Taz's front room, and by the time Binnie had slapped Jim's face and he had wept all over her blouse and Amy's dress, it was obvious that he had learned his lesson. Well, this time anyhow.

'I'll leave you to it then,' said Taz as she placed Jack in his car carry-seat and put on her coat. Not that Binnie and Jim were listening. They were kissing passionately on the sofa, oblivious to everything except the rediscovery of each other's bodies. As an afterthought, Taz scribbled a quick Post-It note and stuck it to the side of the kettle. They were bound to want a cup of tea. Eventually. 'I'll . . . er . . . see you later then.'

Much later, she told herself; just to be on the safe side.

Dee seemed pleased to see her, even though Lorenzo – her new boyfriend – was smouldering provocatively in the background and looked like he had other things on his mind besides Barleycup and wholegrain digestives.

They sat together in the sitting room of Dee's first-floor flat, Dee cradling the twins while the other children played happily around her feet. Taz felt a distinct twinge of envy. OK, so the flat wasn't exactly the tidiest place, but then neither was Taz's – and she didn't have five small children to look after, and a busy café to run, plus a gorgeous and insatiable Italian boyfriend.

'I don't know how you do it,' she commented. 'What's your secret?'

'What – the kids you mean?' Dee laughed. 'There's no secret.'

'But you've got the café . . .' Taz waited until Lorenzo had gone out to the loo, then nudged Dee in the ribs. 'And . . . you know . . .'

'Sex? Oh, I don't think I could cope if I didn't get plenty of regular sex. Good sex, too. It helps to keep me sane. And besides, if you relax and enjoy them, kids bring you nothing but pleasure.'

'Pleasure – and worries.' Taz sighed.

Dee shuffled her chair a bit closer.

'Something's bothering you?'

'Oh you know, just the usual.' Taz sipped her drink and let her eyes roam over the gurgling figure in the carry cot; adoring the button which was slowly developing into a nose, and the cute kiss-curl on his forehead, that made him look like Bill Hailey. 'The thing is, Dee, I'm just not managing. I've tried cutting back on everything I can, but no matter what I do the sums don't add up. I don't know how I'm going to find the money for the mortgage this month.'

'You'll be going back to work in a couple of months,' pointed out Dee. Taz knew that ought to make her feel better but it didn't. She dreaded that first day without Jack as though it were the beginning of a life sentence. 'Won't that help?'

'Some. But it'll still be incredibly difficult to make ends meet, a departmental manager doesn't earn a huge amount and I can't see them promoting someone like me – can you?'

'Why not? You can do anything you want to.' Dee said, shrugging.

'Oh yeah?' I wish it was that easy, thought Taz.

'You just have to believe you can do it – and then make them believe it too.' It sounded easy when Dee said it. She bit into a biscuit, then carried on serenely talking through a fine spray of crumbs. 'So – you need to get some more money coming in. Why don't you take in a lodger?'

Taz stopped, a digestive halfway to her mouth, the

211

portion she had just dunked in her drink wilting dangerously over her lap.

'A lodger? Can I do that?'

'As long as your building society doesn't mind – and they never do. The last thing they want to do is repossess your flat.'

'But I can't!' It's impossible, thought Taz, though she couldn't think precisely why. 'I've only got the two bedrooms, and I'm using the spare one as a nursery.'

'Jack could sleep with you, and you could turn the nursery back into a bedroom. It's not as if it'd be for ever, just until you got on your feet. And it just so happens that I've got the perfect lodger for you.'

Taz blinked.

'*You* have? Who?'

Dee grinned broadly and wriggled her toes in her comfy sheepskin moccasins.

'Adam.'

'Adam Rolfe?' Taz's head spun, she couldn't quite take this in. 'But – he's a bloke!'

'I noticed.'

'Why on earth would Adam Rolfe want to be my lodger?'

'Because Lorenzo's moving in with me here, and what with the kids growing up and now the twins, I've decided I need some extra space. So it just so happens Adam's looking for a nice place to live. Talk to him, he's perfect. He's completely trustworthy, he loves kids . . .'

'That's true I suppose,' admitted Taz, recalling her conversation with Adam, and how much he was missing his own kids. 'But that still doesn't mean I'd want to share my flat with him.'

Dee topped up her mug with a dash of milk.

'Think it through, Taz. You need money, he needs a place to stay. And if you have to have a lodger, then you may as well have a really nice one – and he *is* nice, Taz, I can vouch for that. Besides,' she smiled as Lorenzo came back into the room, all designer-tousled and sleek in his Italian separates. 'I can't think of anything worse than living on my own.'

'We're not talking about sex here,' protested Taz, half-amused. 'We're talking about a business arrangement!'

Dee put up her hands in apology.

'OK, OK . . . but you might as well have a lodger you get on with. And you do, don't you?'

'He seemed quite nice . . .' was as far as Taz was prepared to commit herself.

'And he likes you too,' added Dee, offering Taz another biscuit then feeding the last one to Lorenzo.

'He does? How do you know?' asked Taz eagerly.

Too late, she realised that she had betrayed her latent interest in Adam Rolfe. And it was perhaps a little more than your average business interest.

'Because he said so.' Dee hauled herself up out of her chair, smoothing down her tee-shirt over her ample hips. She looked, thought Taz, the very picture of contented motherhood. 'He's in most evenings, shall we go up and see if you two can have a friendly little chat?'

Chapter 15

Adam Rolfe ran a sinewy hand through his ruffled hair.

'Sorry I haven't shaved,' he yawned as he led the way into his cluttered living room. Piles of books rose like miniature skyscrapers between a rattan armchair and a coffee-table which was scarcely visible beneath the workings of a disembowelled alarm clock. 'I was at the police station half last night.'

'Your wicked ways caught up with you, have they?' enquired Dee teasingly, grabbing Taz by the shoulders and giving her a shove forward.

'Oh you know, one of those things,' Adam smiled sleepily, scratching his stubbly chin and stifling another yawn. 'People will get themselves arrested at all hours of the day and night. Can I get you a coffee?'

'I . . . well . . . you're sure this isn't a bad time?'

Taz edged uneasily towards the door, certain that Dee had timed this badly. The poor bloke looked half dead. He looked so vulnerable, thought Taz, noticing the undarned hole in the toe of his stockinged foot, and the way his rugby shirt was buttoned up all wrong.

Adam's crinkly smile made his face lopsided.

'Course not. It's not often I get visited by *two* gorgeous ladies.'

'Flattery will get you everywhere,' winked Dee. 'If you play your cards right.' She set up a folding chair and flopped down onto it, her bulk making the canvas squeak against the wooden struts. 'Sit down, Adam, Taz has a proposition to make.'

Taz burst out laughing as Adam's eyebrows shot up

almost to his hairline. His hazel eyes twinkled mischievously under the straggly sand-coloured curls.

'A proposition? This is my lucky day.' Adam removed a heap of hillwalking magazines from the rattan chair, dusted it down with his hand and offered it to Taz; then squatted down on the rug at her feet. 'Fire away.'

'Dee,' protested Taz, feeling very hot under the collar. She darted a 'shut up and butt out' look at Dee, but Dee didn't know the meaning of the word tact.

'Taz wants you to move in with her,' said Dee, enunciating the words with lascivious emphasis. Taz felt her cheeks flame. 'Don't you, Taz?'

'Shut up Dee, it's nothing of the sort!' Taz looked down at Adam, appealing to the better nature she felt sure lay behind those mischievous hazel eyes. 'Dee's got this crazy idea... that I should clear out my spare bedroom and find myself a lodger.'

'Doesn't sound crazy to me,' said Adam slowly. 'But where do I come in?'

Dee raised her eyes to the heavens, as though trying to be incredibly patient in impossible circumstances.

'What Taz is avoiding saying, Adam, is that she wants to offer you the room.'

'Really!' Adam's eyes were on Taz; they seemed to be searching her face to discover the truth. 'Is this a wind-up Taz?'

Taz shook her head apologetically.

'Take no notice of Dee, she's just got this bee in her bonnet. You see, I happened to mention finances are a bit tight now that I've got Jack to look after and not much money coming in – and Dee's taken it on herself to sort me out.'

'I'm just suggesting something that makes good sense. You need money, Adam needs somewhere to live.'

'Look', Taz smiled encouragingly at Dee, trying to find a way of saying no nicely. 'It's not that I don't appreciate what you're trying to do...'

'But you'd rather I didn't stick my nose in where it's not wanted? It's OK, tell me to sod off if I'm being an interfering old cow. But think about it, yeah?' She got to her feet. 'Tell you what, I'll leave you two to talk about it.'

Taz opened her mouth to protest, but Dee had a surprising turn of speed and was already halfway out of the door. It closed behind her with an emphatic thud. Taz and Adam looked at each other and both opened their mouths simultaneously.

'Sorry.'

'You first.'

'No, you.'

They laughed, suddenly transformed into tongue-tied adolescents. It was Adam who eventually broke the deadlock.

'How about that cup of coffee? Don't tell me – white, no sugar.'

'You have a good memory.'

'Only for things I want to remember.' Adam opened the door to the kitchenette and talked as he reached down jars from the cupboard over the stove. 'So, what do you reckon to the flat then?'

Taz took it in in a single sweep. It was a mess, true, but a clean, likeable kind of mess. Books and magazines covered most of the floor that wasn't already occupied by sports equipment, board games and tied-up bundles of documents. Even the fold-down formica table sported a pile of *National Geographics*. She breathed in, slow and deep. The air smelt blokish, a scent she recalled from her college days – that indefinable blend of muscle-rub, old socks and Jaffa Cakes. She grinned.

'It's . . . a typical man's flat.'

Adam popped his head round the door.

'I stand condemned. It *is* a bit of a pit, isn't it? I'd have tidied up if I'd known.'

'No need,' confessed Taz. 'I'm just as bad. When my mother comes round I hide all the ironing behind the bathroom door.'

'Ah, but you've got an excuse – you're a harassed mum.' Adam stirred milk into the coffee. 'I'm just an unreconstructed slob.'

That was hard to believe, thought Taz as they sat and

216

chatted in Adam's living room. Surely slobs were louts who drank lager and farted under the bedclothes. They didn't subscribe to *Liberal Democrat News* or wear corduroy trousers that had gone baggy at the knees. She was just daydreaming when Adam's voice called her out of her reverie.

'Penny for 'em.'

'Oh. Oh, sorry, I was miles away.' Her eyes drifted back to the photo in the papier mâché frame, sitting on the window-ledge. The flickering neon sign above the door of the café below cast red and green shadows across the three faces: a young woman, one arm around a young boy, the other cradling a small baby. 'Are those . . .?'

Adam followed her gaze. His smile clouded slightly.

'My ex-wife and kids? Yeah. I don't know why I keep the photo, really. It's not as if they're a part of my life any more.'

'But surely . . . your kids . . .'

'They're on the other side of the world, Taz. They've got a new dad now. What would they want with me?'

She wanted to think of a good reply, but she couldn't. So she covered up the awkwardness by turning her mug round and round in her hands.

'This lodger idea of Dee's . . .' she began.

'I guess it wouldn't work.' Adam sipped his coffee reflectively.

'No. It's crazy. I don't even *want* a lodger.'

'But you do need the money?'

Their eyes met. Taz held the look for a few seconds, then looked away.

'I wish I didn't. My parents think I should sell up and move in with them. Which of course makes perfect financial sense . . .'

'Only you'd rather die first?'

'Well . . . almost,' laughed Taz. 'You'd understand why if you'd met my mother. She thinks she's the only person in the world who knows how to bring up a baby.'

'Aren't all mothers like that? I bet you'll be like that with your grandchildren.'

'I will not!'

217

'Bet I'm right.' Adam drank that last of his coffee, his throat stretched back and undulating gently as the hot liquid slid down. Then he wiped his mouth on the back of his hand. 'So basically you're turning me down?'

Taz almost choked on her drink.

'You're not telling me you'd actually *want* to be my lodger?'

'I don't know. I might. I mean, Dee's great but she's made it pretty clear she can't wait to see the back of me.'

Taz was puzzled. Something didn't quite add up.

'Adam – you're a solicitor. Why don't you buy a place of your own? I thought you lot were all on forty grand a year.'

'Not solicitors who work in legal aid centres! And in any case, until the decree absolute comes through my finances are in a mess. I'm just looking for somewhere to stay for a month or two . . .'

Taz had to admit that made a difference. It wasn't as if Adam would want to move in for ever and she'd never get rid of him. Just long enough to sort out her money worries but not long enough for them to get on each other's nerves. But no. No, it was a thoroughly bad idea.

'The thing is, Adam – it just wouldn't work. Jack's not four months old yet, he's noisy and he's going to get noisier . . .'

'That's no problem, I like kids.'

'Even at three a.m., when they're screaming their heads off?'

'Even then. But listen Taz.' Adam looked her straight in the eye. 'This isn't about Jack, is it? It's about you and me – could we share the same flat without driving each other crazy?'

A treacherous little voice inside Taz was whispering, 'Well, I'm game if you are,' but it was no good letting hormonal attraction call all the shots. She had to be level-headed.

'God knows,' she shrugged. 'The last flatmate I had ran off with my boyfriend.'

'Well, I think I could promise not to do that.' Adam

218

drew a finger across his chest in mock solemnity. 'Cross my heart and hope to die.'

The next morning, even as she was waving goodbye to Binnie and Jim, Taz was still fretting about whether or not to offer Adam the spare room.

'Just be careful,' Binnie told her with a final hug and a peck on the cheek. 'You don't want to land yourself with another Gareth, do you?'

'But I'm thinking about getting a lodger, not a boyfriend!' Taz protested, secretly wondering whether she was being entirely honest with herself.

'All the same, I've seen that twinkle in your eye, Taz Norton! Just watch you don't end up with more than you can handle.'

'Why do people always think if two people of the opposite sex share a flat they have to be having an affair?'

Why indeed. And besides, she hadn't even made up her mind yet. Right now, she had other things to think about – like getting the latest bundle of work back to Diana Latchford. She could have rung and asked for a courier to pick it up; but it was a beautiful spring day, she might as well deliver it in person. Afterwards, she could take Jack to Pittville Park and they could feed the ducks.

She drove into town just before lunchtime and parked round the corner from S&G. With Jack firmly strapped into his brand-new buggy, she made for the main entrance facing Imperial Gardens, and leading into the grand glass atrium.

'Good morning, Ms Norton.'

Taz was quite taken aback to be greeted with cap-touching reverence by the doorman. After all, she didn't look much like a departmental manager in her comfy jacket and baggy jeans.

'Hello Sidney, how are you?'

'Right as rain, Ms Norton. See you've brought the nipper with you, fine little lad he is too, aren't you sonny?'

Jack seemed unperturbed to be chucked under the chin by a whiskery man in a red uniform. In fact, he reached out, fascinated by the highly-polished brass buttons, and it was all Taz could do to distract his attention long enough to wheel him away.

She crossed straight to the lift, deliberately avoiding eye contact and telling herself that she wouldn't, positively *wouldn't*, call in at menswear to check up on Ted. All the same, she couldn't help noting all the little changes as she walked through perfumerie and women's accessories – the coloured lighting, the subtle relocation of the hat display, the new-style wooden shelving for the coordinating silk scarves.

Switching off was next to impossible. Everywhere she went, Taz saw things she'd have done differently, things that she'd change instantly if she was in charge.

The buggy rattled its way towards the lifts, Jack lulled by the continuous gentle motion. That was one thing to be grateful for, at any rate. It would be kind of embarrassing if he started yelling at the top of his voice. She waved and smiled vaguely at a couple of assistants she knew.

Then, quite without warning, Kate leapt out at Taz from behind the glove display.

'Ms Norton! How lovely to see you – oh, you've brought the baby, isn't he *gorgeous*?'

Taz chuckled at Kate's sheer energy. She might be an ADSM now, but underneath that sober suit she was still a kid.

'Gorgeous, but hard work. How are you?'

'Fine. Wonderful! Did you know I'd got ADSM in women's accessories?'

'Diana told me. Congratulations. Don't suppose I can persuade you to defect to menswear?'

'Not if Ted Williams is still there!'

'Don't worry, he'll be heading straight back where he came from the minute I get back to work.'

They had a brief chat, then Kate rushed off to sell someone something, and Taz struggled to manoeuvre the buggy into the old, brass-gated lift. Getting out and about with a baby was a revelation. Before, she'd always muttered irritably behind harassed mums who were blocking the way with their shopping and their buggies and their fractious toddlers. As she cursed and wrestled her way out onto the administration floor, Taz promised herself that she would never, ever mutter again.

Nikki Fraser, Diana's PA, broke off typing to greet Taz with a beaming smile.

'Oh Taz, what a lovely surprise. I didn't think you were coming back to work just yet.'

'I'm not.' Taz extracted the bundle of papers from the shopping tray under Jack's buggy, and dumped them on Nikki's desk. 'I just thought I'd bring in these for Diana – the analysis she wanted is in the brown envelope.'

Nikki finished tapping a string of figures into her PC, swivelled her chair round and peered at Jack over the desk. Jack opened his eyes and returned her gaze with a quizzical frown. Nikki laughed and tut-tutted benignly.

'I don't know how you do it, Taz. When I had my two I was brain-dead for the first six months. I once left the baby in the butcher's, and didn't even realise till I was halfway down the road. Did you want to see Diana? Only she's at lunch.'

'No need. I just wanted to drop these in. Jack and I have got a bit of shopping to do, haven't we Jack? Then we're going to feed the ducks.'

Nikki sighed and stretched her aching neck muscles, swivelling her head from side to side.

'Wish I could come with you. I've got this lot to finish by two o'clock, then I'm taking minutes for the Wednesday managers' meeting. Don't suppose I'll get off till after six. Still, you're never off-duty with a baby, are you?'

'Don't remind me! This little monster woke me up three times last night.'

Taz was just turning the buggy round when the door opened and she collided with Diana Latchford, who was conducting a conversation over her shoulder as she walked into the office.

'That's right Cara, get on to them right away and don't take any nonsense, I . . . ouch! Tasmin!'

Diana rubbed her bruised ankle, Taz wrestled the buggy back into the office and wished the ground would swallow her up.

221

'Oh Mrs Latchford – I am *so* sorry, I really am. Did I hurt you?'

Diana waved away her concerns.

'It was my fault, I wasn't looking where I was going.' Her eyes dropped downwards and took in Jack's pink and rather dribbly face. 'Oh. You've brought the baby with you.' She didn't sound all that delighted; in fact, she didn't sound pleased at all. 'Did you come in through the staff entrance?'

'Well – no. I walked through the store. You don't mind, do you? Only I wanted to make sure you had those figures in good time, and I couldn't get a babysitter at such short notice.'

'No. No, of course.' Diana's voice softened, but she seemed thoughtful. She patted Taz's shoulder. 'Still, best leave him at home next time you come. I know you'll want to present a professional image, and he'll need to get used to being without you when you come back to work . . .'

This rather took the wind out of Taz's sails. Diana had been so supportive throughout her pregnancy, had encouraged her to fight for her rights, had backed her against people who had argued that being a good mother meant being a lousy manager – but now, all of a sudden, the situation seemed to have changed.

'Come into my office, Taz, let's have a little chat. Nikki will look after Jack for a few minutes, won't you Nikki?'

'Of course. Don't you worry, he'll be fine with me.'

Reluctantly, Taz followed Diana into her office and sat down, facing her across the desk.

'I'm sorry. I didn't realise I wasn't supposed to bring Jack to the store.' She tried, but she couldn't keep the resentment out of her voice.

'Don't get me wrong Taz, please.' Diana fiddled with the fountain pen on her blotter. 'Jack's a lovely baby, and I know how important he is to you. And of course, while you're on maternity leave and doing extra work out of the goodness of your heart . . .'

'Quite,' muttered Taz sulkily.

'But Jack's part of your personal life, and you know as

well as I do that to succeed in this job you have to keep your personal life and working life rigorously separate. Which brings me to the question of when you're planning to come back to work.'

It was the question Taz had been dreading. The question she'd avoided asking herself, let alone answering, ever since the moment Jack had yelled his way into her life.

'I . . . haven't finalised a date.'

'I know. So let's do it now, shall we?'

Taz stared blankly at the diary which Diana pushed at her across the desk.

'Pick a date that suits you. It doesn't have to be tomorrow, or next Monday, but I have to know. You understand that, don't you?'

Taz nodded. How could she not understand? This was a make-or-break moment for her. Either she could wimp out, resign, sell up, move back with her mum and dad and wave goodbye to any independent life of her own; or she could face up to the fact that from now on, her life would be filled with irreconcilable tensions, insurmountable challenges, guilt and frustration . . . and the chance to make something for herself and Jack. A better life. A proper future.

She steadied her hands and forced herself to flick through the pages.

'OK then.' Even as she was saying the words she was regretting them, but she made the supreme effort to look Diana straight in the eye. 'Let's say three weeks today, shall we?'

'You're sure about that?' asked Diana, surprised.

'Positive. Just let me check with my childminder, and I'll ring you to confirm tomorrow.'

Taz rushed home in a whirl, completely forgetting about the pint of milk and economy pack of nappies she'd planned to buy on the way back.

'It'll be all right Jack,' she told the baby, twisting her head round to smile reassuringly at him as they sat in a queue of traffic. 'Everything'll be all right, just you wait and see.'

She wondered exactly who she was trying to convince. Jack seemed perfectly, heartrendingly serene, strapped snugly into his car seat and blowing bubbles as he gazed, wide-eyed, at the world around him. It wasn't Jack who was worrying about fitting size sixteen love-handles into a size twelve suit; it wasn't Jack who was frantic about being entrusted to a complete stranger; and it wasn't Jack whose heart was breaking at the prospect of an imminent separation.

When Taz got home the sun-warmed air hit her with the full, sweet scents of spring flowers. You couldn't help but feel optimistic when the air was as fragrant and intoxicating as Chanel No. 5.

'Here we are, Jack, back home. Oh damn, I've forgotten the milk, never mind we can get some later. Let's get you inside and give you some dinner, shall we?' She hauled Jack out onto her hip and fetched his buggy out of the back, rather pleased that she was becoming so good at all these baby-related gymnastics. She snatched a quick glance at her watch. 'Quarter to three already! And it's Wednesday! What do you think Mandy will bring us today, Jack?'

Jack didn't offer his opinion, but his slobbery smile seemed to know that Taz was secretly hoping for cream buns.

Pushing the buggy in through the side door, she allowed herself to experience a small pang of guilt. Really she shouldn't have ignored Mandy like that, the other day when Binnie was there. No wonder she'd gone off in a huff, without saying goodbye. Still, today was Wednesday and Mandy always turned up on a Wednesday, bringing some gloriously unhealthy afternoon snack for them to share. There'd be plenty of opportunity to apologise. They'd have fun together, just like they always did. Taz knew she was really going to miss these afternoons when she started back at S&G.

The buggy trundled smoothly along towards the door of Taz's flat. Mandy would probably be there already, she'd have let herself in with the key Taz had had cut for her, and would be lolling in front of the TV with one leg cocked over the arm of the chair and Dylan gurgling on her lap. As if anticipating fun and frolics, Jack let out a loud yell and started wriggling.

'Nearly there, Jack. Just let me find my key.'

As she neared the front door, Taz spotted something on the floor outside. A plastic carrier bag, the handles knotted together like rabbit-ears.

She bent down, prodded the bag. As she poked it it fell over, with a kind of liquid thud. Intrigued, Taz untied the handles of the bag and peered into it. Inside sat two jam doughnuts, squashed messily flat by a large bottle of Tizer. A jammy note was scrawled on the paper bag, in black felt pen.

'Suppose you must be out with your friend. You might as well have these. M.'

'Oh Mandy . . .' groaned Taz. Now she thought about it, she knew she'd seen a glimmer of resentment in Mandy's eyes at the sight of Binnie Lethbridge. 'Oh Mandy, we really have to sort this out.'

But not right now, said a little voice in her head. Right now you have to ring Melinda Ross and sort out this childcare once and for all.

The business card with Melinda's number on was on the hall table. Taz grabbed it as she went past, parking Jack in his buggy while she went hunting for the phone.

'Just you stay there for two minutes, little man. Just two minutes, I promise. Mummy has to make this call . . .'

It was only then that she noticed the buttermilk-yellow envelope sticking out from underneath the doormat. Post was always sliding under there, she wondered how long it had been there. Still, at least it wasn't a brown envelope – she already had a nice collection of those in a shoebox marked 'unpaid bills'.

Taz picked it up. She ripped it open, and unfolded a single sheet of lightly-scented notepaper.

Dear Tasmin

I tried contacting you by telephone but you were out. Something rather urgent has cropped up.

Did I mention Rena, a really close friend of mine

from college? Her firm has transferred her back to Cheltenham early after a placement in Australia, and she desperately needs a childminder for her little girl. Naturally I don't feel I can let a friend down, and the local authority regulations won't allow me to look after more than three under-fives at any one time . . .'

Taz read on with a creeping sense of horror.

'Oh no, Jack. No, please let this be a horrible dream.' She forced herself to read on, and immediately wished she hadn't.

I really am very sorry, but I'm afraid I won't have a vacancy for Jack after all. Still, I'm sure you won't have any difficulty in finding another childminder.

Best wishes
Melinda Ross

Chapter 16

'The thing is . . .' Adam fiddled with his hair, the way he always did when he was embarrassed. Taz was getting to know his mannerisms, and this was only the fourth time she'd met him. 'I don't want to put pressure on you, only . . .'

Taz nodded.

'I know, Adam, I'm sorry. I know you need a decision about the flat.'

'It's Dee, you see. But if you definitely don't want me to move in . . .'

'No, no, I didn't say that.' She wished she could shake the black cloud of panic out of her head, so she could think clearly for two minutes at a time. 'But I can't think straight, not with Jack's childcare falling through at the last minute. Right now I'm not sure *what* I want.'

Adam smiled, and got up from his chair.

'I am,' he said enigmatically.

'You are what?'

'Sure what you want. You want the best for this young gentleman, isn't that right, your lordship?' He bent over Jack's baby-bouncer and pulled such a comical face that Jack's eyes grew huge and round with fascination. 'Right now your mummy's whole world revolves around you, and quite right too.'

'He likes you,' commented Taz, feeling a sudden urge to giggle despite Melinda Ross's appalling eleventh-hour betrayal.

'Of course he does. He knows I'm the same mental age as he is.' Adam slipped his arms into his jacket, a Gap taupe denim number which had probably been quite fashionable about five years previously. 'Look, I'm sorry I bothered you about the flat, it's the last thing you want right now.'

'You weren't to know. And I know how awful it is, knowing if you don't find somewhere quickly you'll end up with nowhere to live.'

Adam shook his head good-naturedly. She caught the faint scent of some rather nice cologne, quite spicy-smelling. Distinctly appetising, like its owner. For a split second, she almost forgot that she had a baby, no child-minder, and less than three weeks to find one.

'Take as long as you like, Taz. It won't kill me to put up with the sound of Dee's bedsprings a few weeks longer.'

He strolled out into the hall, Taz following him. Taz very nearly begged him not to go. But she knew it would be a mistake to say yes just because right now she was feeling at a low ebb. On impulse, she said the first thing that came into her head.

'Do you like pizza?'

'I like anything that's bad for me. Why?' Adam looked at her.

'My mum's babysitting for me tonight. I was going to the pictures, but I thought . . . maybe we could go for a pizza and thrash this thing out once and for all?'

'Sounds fine by me. Shall I call for you?'

'No need. I'll come round your place about eight. And I promise I'll give you a decision tonight.'

As the morning went on, Taz's mood slipped gradually from pessimism to depression and finally utter dejection.

She sat on the floor of the living room, surrounded by telephone directories, Social Services lists, even the small ads from the local free newspaper. Surely somewhere in the whole of Cheltenham there must be a nice, normal, reliable childminder with a vacancy for one small baby?

'You know what you are Jack, don't you? You're a whole load of trouble, that's what you are!' She went across to him and planted a big soppy kiss on his forehead, lifting him out and cuddling him close. 'And you're also the best thing that's ever happened to me, and if I can't find somebody we both *really* like to take care of you properly, I'm going to resign.'

Right on cue, Jack stared back at her, as though he understood the sheer enormity of what she had just said.

'Oh, so you don't believe me, huh? Well look here little man, you're the most important thing in the world to me, and if I have to sacrifice everything else I have, I'll do it to make you happy.'

It was a strange moment, warm and close and cathartic; the huge surge of love stunning her with its compulsive power. All these years she'd laughed at people who'd warned her about the 'maternal instinct', and now she was beginning to understand what crazy things it could make you do. Even give up the career you'd longed for all your life, abandon your independence and move in with your mum.

Not that it would come to that. She was a manager, a good one; now all she had to learn to do was manage her own life.

'Come on Jack, we're going back to the council offices. We're going to find you a childminder if it's the last thing I do.'

Just as she was getting ready to carry Jack to the car, there was a click of a key turning in the front door. Naturally it was Isobel, freshly permed and bearing gifts. Taz counted to ten under her breath and forced herself not to scowl.

'Mummy – what are you doing here?' She accepted the obligatory peck on the cheek, then resigned herself to being ignored as Isobel homed in on Jack. 'I'm not expecting you till seven o'clock.'

'I thought I'd come a bit early . . . who's Granny's best boy then, yes he is, yes he is!'

'A bit? It's not three o'clock yet!'

' . . . and help you with your ironing. I know you've been hiding it behind the bathroom door – don't look at me like that, Taz, – but it's no use ignoring it, it won't go away.' Isobel straightened up and took a long, hard look at Taz. Her voice softened. 'Whatever's the matter, dear?'

'Nothing, Mum. Everything's fine.' If Isobel got an inkling of the childcare crisis, she'd be so delighted that she'd probably write Taz's letter of resignation for her.

'Well remember what your granny used to say. If your face wants to smile, let it. If it doesn't, make it. Now, where do you keep your ironing board?'

'It's in the pantry, but the leg's a bit wobbly . . . Mum, where are you going?' Taz followed Isobel's determined progress towards the bathroom.

'You can help me sort out these smalls, dear. My word, how long have you had these knickers?' As if by instinct, Isobel homed in on Taz's most revolting pair of pants, the ones she only resorted to wearing when she'd worn everything else in the drawer. The ones with the holes in the seat. 'You'd better not get run over wearing those!'

'I wasn't planning to . . .'

'Well we'll wash them and you can use them for dusters. Not that you do much dusting, as far as I can see.'

Taz held her breath. If she'd dared open her mouth a stream of invective would have forced its way out, and there would have been no way she could control it.

'Now, why don't you go and put the kettle on, Tasmin. And cut up some slices of banana while you're in there – at Jack's age, you should be trying him on solids.'

'Actually Mum, Jack's just had his feed, and I was about to take him into town.'

'Well, if you must go, leave Jack with me.'

It wasn't the solution Taz was looking for, but she had to admit it made sense. Jack was tired, he didn't want dragging all over Cheltenham twice in one day.

'You're sure you don't mind?'

'Mind?' Isobel's face cracked into a huge and indulgent smile, and for the first time in a while Taz felt guilty for resenting her interference. 'Of course I don't mind, I'm his granny!' She bent over Jack, cooing and fussing. 'And we're going to have *such* fun together, aren't we, sweetheart.'

'Oh. Well. I'll be off then, I shouldn't be too long. There are clean nappies in the spare bedroom, and there are three bottles of breast milk in the fridge . . .'

'Don't you worry dear.' Isobel wasn't even looking at Taz. It was Jack who was occupying every spare cubic millimetre of her consciousness. 'Take as long as you need to, Jack and I will be fine. Oh – and Tasmin dear . . . you will have him christened John, won't you? Jack is ever so slightly vulgar, don't you think?'

'I haven't really thought about it yet.'

'Well don't leave it too long, or we'll never find a christening gown to fit him. He's such a lovely big boy, aren't you darling?'

Taz wrenched open the door and fled into the spring afternoon.

It was a waste of time. She'd hoped against hope that somebody at the council offices would be able to produce another list of childminders like a rabbit out of a hat, but all she'd come away with was sympathy. Everyone half decent was booked up months in advance. The best offer she'd had was, 'Try me again in October, I might have a vacancy then.' Which, of course, was absolutely no use at all.

She'd even tried a nanny agency; but all that had done was confirm her worst fears. On the money she could afford, she couldn't even employ a quarter of a nanny, let alone a whole one. Some of them earned even more than she did! Maybe it was time to think about making a career change.

In desperation, she found a phone box with a telephone directory, looked up the number of Mandy's parents and called it. It was a big mistake.

'Hello – Mrs Robson? I wonder, could I speak to Mandy please?'

'Why? Who are you?'

'Taz, Taz Norton. I'm a friend of hers.'

'Oh you are, are you? Well I've never heard of you. Anyhow she's not here. Darren, will you fuckin' put that down before I tan your fuckin' backside!'

'Could you tell her . . .?'

'Look. She's not here, OK? I don't know where she fuckin' well is, an' I don't care.'

Crash. The line went dead.

'Oh Jack,' Taz sighed to herself, trailing back along the Promenade. 'What on earth is your mummy going to do? There has to be a way . . .'

She was so lost in her own morose thoughts that she almost collided head-on with Chloë Baxendale, who was striding along, head down, as though there was something she wanted to get to – or away from – as quickly as possible. Clive was four or five paces behind, Ayesha strapped to his back in a baby sling. Taz would never have guessed they were together, if she hadn't known they were husband and wife.

'Chloë! I haven't seen you for ages.'

Taz grabbed Chloë by the shoulder and she spun round. It was only then that Taz realised she hadn't even seen her.

'How are you, Chloë? How are you feeling?'

She looked gaunt, thought Taz. Gaunt but puffy-faced, with the kind of unhealthy pallor you might get from living underground.

'What?' It was as though Chloë had only just switched on, and it was taking time and effort for her to tune in to the same channel.

'How are you?'

Chloë looked at Taz, her gaze beginning at her feet and moving slowly upwards.

'Where is it?'

'What?'

'The baby. Where is it? Have you got rid of it?' She sounded almost eager, pleading.

'No, of course not! Jack's with his granny.'

'Oh.' At this, Chloë seemed to lose interest. She looked vaguely in Clive's direction. 'I'm going now, I want to look at hats.'

Clive's facial muscles fought a losing battle against panic. His eyes appealed to Chloë's to make contact, but they drifted away, scanning the passers-by without really seeming to see them.

'I think Ayesha's wet, shall we take her somewhere and change her?' he asked gently. 'Chloë . . .?'

But Chloë had switched off completely now.

'I'm going. I'll see you later.' And she strode away, into the crowd heading towards Boots Corner.

Taz gaped at her retreating figure. Was this really the same Chloë Baxendale, the timid little mouse, the perfect public schoolgirl who had wanted nothing more than to be the perfect wife?

'Oh Clive . . .' she began, not knowing what to say or how to say it.

A kind of desperate eagerness filled Clive's face. He seized Taz's hand, so hard that she winced.

'She's better,' he said. 'Much better, since the doctor prescribed her the anti-depressants.'

'Better? You really think so?'

'Oh yes, she's improving every day. Everything'll be fine soon – and we're getting an au pair, so Chloë has more time and space to herself.'

Taz said nothing. But inwardly she was thinking that being on her own was just about the last thing Chloë needed.

'Wine?' Adam waggled the bottle in front of Taz's tired eyes. She focused on it, smiled weakly.

'Go on then. Just one glass.'

They were sitting in Pizza Paradise, eating Quattro staggione and chips under fake Tiffany lamps; and frankly, it was the best thing that had happened to her all day.

'Bad day?' enquired Adam sympathetically.

'You would *not* believe . . .' Taz looked up. 'Actually, you probably would. At least I don't have people calling me out to police stations in the middle of the night.'

'No, just a baby who likes his dinner at three a.m. So – no luck with the childminders then?'

Taz shook her head, turning the stem of her wine glass round and round in her fingers.

'Nope. And you would not believe the price of nannies. Short of a miracle, I don't know what I'm going to do. I don't suppose you know anyone . . .?'

'Sorry. But I'll ask around, you never know.'

Taz sighed into her wine. But when all was said and done, she hadn't come here just to feel sorry for herself.

'I've made a decision,' she said. 'About the flat. The room's yours if you want it.'

'Really?' Adam looked perfectly amazed as he sat back in his plastic seat. 'No kidding?'

'Really. So, what do you think?' Taz suddenly realised that she was holding her breath.

'Fantastic! Let's drink to it. Ugh, this house red's a bit rough. So – when can I move in?'

'As soon as you like. No, hang on though, can you wait a couple of days? I'd like to warn my mother first.'

'Very wise. Otherwise she'll probably chase me down the road with her broomstick.'

They laughed, and Taz felt some of her tension begin to lift a little. But, beyond his affable exterior, Adam looked weary and borne down under the cares of the world. The creases at the corners of his eyes and mouth, deepened by the lamplight, took on the aspect of age-old crevasses.

'Something wrong?' she asked tentatively. 'Only you look ... you know ... a bit tired.'

Adam swallowed a morsel of pizza crust.

'Nothing really. It's just a heavy time at work for me, and I can't help getting personally involved with every case I take on. Which, of course, makes me completely unprofessional and a hopeless solicitor.'

'I don't believe that for a moment.'

'It's nice of you to say so. Anyhow, yesterday, I was asked to take on a really tough case at very short notice. It's coming to trial next week.'

Taz nibbled the end of a chip, dunked it in ketchup and took another bite.

'Why the short notice?'

'This lad's solicitor was taken ill and they had to get someone else in. And God knows, this lad needs all the help he can get. You name it, he's done it: housebreaking, car theft, handling stolen goods, he's got a record as long as your arm. And as for attitude problems ...'

'Sounds tough.'

'Oh it is. And defending him is just about impossible. He knows there's enough evidence against him to write a book, but will he plead guilty and make it easier on himself? Oh no, not Dave . . .'

'Dave?' Taz's ears pricked up, though she knew it had to be a coincidence. There must be thousands of petty criminals called Dave.

'Yeah.' Adam toyed with the food on his plate, pushing a lettuce leaf round and round the rim with his fork. 'The thing is, I think you know this lad's girlfriend. Mouthy kid, multicoloured hair, no fashion sense . . . came to Dee's with you a few times?'

'Mandy!' Taz clapped her hand to her mouth to stifle the sound. She looked around and lowered her voice. 'You're representing Mandy Robson's boyfriend?'

'Uh-huh.' Adam chewed reflectively, as though considering his next words very carefully indeed. 'And between you and me, Taz, I'm beginning to wish I wasn't.'

Mandy thumped Taz's front door down just after nine the following morning, her hair braided into two aggressive bunches which stuck out from her head like Viking horns.

Taz, head aching from one glass of very rough red wine, edged gingerly to the door and eased it open as smoothly as possible. She needn't have bothered trying – Mandy wasn't in the mood for peace and quiet.

'What the hell do you think you're playin' at?' she demanded, stomping into the hall with Dylan on her hip. 'What did you think you were doin', ringin' me at me mum's?'

'I didn't know how else to get in touch,' said Taz lamely. 'And the number was in the book.'

'Don't you ever, *ever* do that again. You hear?'

'If you say so. I'm . . . sorry.' It was only as Mandy's face tilted a few degrees to the left that Taz noticed the faint shadow of a new bruise, just visible under her thick make-up. 'Have you hurt yourself?'

'What?' Mandy's hand leapt reflexively to her face.

'Your cheek. Have you hurt it?'

'What's it to you, I'm all right, OK?'

235

'OK.' It was a long time since Taz had seen Mandy so aggressive, and she didn't feel good about being the cause of it. Or – she suspected – the cause of Mandy's bruise. Inanely, stuck for anything else to say, she added, 'Thanks for the doughnuts, I missed you.'

'She's gone then?'

'Binnie, yeah. Like I told you, she was only here because she'd fallen out with Jim. They've gone back to Scotland now. Do you want a coffee?'

'S'pose. I could use a sit down, I'm knackered.' She sank down onto the settee and sat Dylan on her knee, lifting up her tee-shirt to give him a feed. 'It's these early mornings. Cleanin' offices, did I tell you?'

'No.' Taz looked at Mandy; she had the hard, sinewy, worn-out look of someone ten years older. Life hadn't been kind to Mandy so far, and it wasn't getting any kinder. 'Mandy – why didn't you tell me? About Dave?'

'What about him?'

'About the trial . . . Adam Rolfe told me.'

'Oh he did did he?' Mandy didn't look pleased, in fact she looked positively suspicious. 'Anyhow, I tried. Remember? But you were too busy playing Siamese twins with your mate Binnie.' She waited a few seconds for the knife to go in, then twisted it. 'But I'm supposed to come runnin' when you whistle, aren't I?'

'Of course not! I just thought . . .'

'You just thought, I've got a problem, Binnie's pissed off home so I'll ring Mandy, she'll bail me out.'

'No! It wasn't like that. Well, not really.'

'So what was it this time?' Mandy seemed furious, yet poised on the verge of tears.

'It's just, Melinda's let me down, and I'm committed to going back to work the week after next.'

'And that's it, is it? One pathetic little problem and you want the world to come runnin'? God Taz, you can be a selfish bitch! All you ever think about is your own problems – what about me, eh? What about me an' Dylan? What are we goin' to do when Dave gets put away for somethin' he didn't do?'

'Oh Mandy.' Guilt and remorse flooded through Taz.

Perching on the arm of the settee, she tried to put an arm round Mandy's shoulders, but she shrugged it off.

'Leave me alone.'

'Mandy, listen. I'm sorry, really I am. I should have listened, but you see, I was all wrapped up in myself – and I had no idea about Dave until Adam told me last night.'

'Last night?' The suspicion in Mandy's eyes deepened. They narrowed, like a cat's, uncertain whether or not to pounce. 'What were you doin' with Adam Rolfe last night?'

'Just . . . talking.'

Taz swallowed hard. It was obvious that Adam and Mandy had hardly made a favourable impression on each other. She wondered how on earth she was going to break it to Mandy that Adam was moving into her spare room in three days' time.

Chapter 17

Taz locked the back doors of Adam's old Morris van, and ran back up the stairs to his flat. She arrived at the top panting but full of enthusiasm.

'How about these?' Taz held up a cardboard box full of back issues of *Viz*. 'Shall I take them down to the van?'

Adam looked up from wrapping cups and saucers into little newspaper bundles.

'No need. Dee said she'd store them in her loft until I get my own place.' He put on the sternest expression he could manage, which wasn't very. 'And put those down this minute, you shouldn't be lugging heavy weights around. Jack wouldn't thank me if I let his mum put her back out helping me, now would he?'

Taz thought fondly of Jack's wonderfully simple, ego-centric world, and chuckled to herself.

'As long as he got his dinner on time, I shouldn't think he could care less!'

'Tell you what, why don't we have a glass of wine? There's a bottle of Tesco's finest in that coolbag.'

'I'd love to – but you're driving,' Taz reminded him.

'Good point. Tea then?'

'OK, fine. Where's the kettle?'

'Ah. You don't suppose I've packed it?' **???** Adam, peering around ineffectually.

'God but you're hopeless, Adam.'

'I know,' he grinned. 'Declan at the office reckons I need a good woman to take me in hand.'

'Dream on sunshine, I'll accept nothing less than a handsome millionaire.'

Nevertheless, Taz took pity on him; it was difficult not to, he looked so charmingly bewildered standing there, not at all capable of managing on his own. Besides, she'd forgotten how much fun a bit of harmless flirtation could be. A real boost to flagging self-esteem. She was almost beginning to feel feminine again. A short search revealed the kettle and a packet of teabags in a box of coats and jumpers.

'Got it! Big mug or dainty teacup?'

'Big mug please, all this dust gets in your throat.'

As Taz picked her way through the jumble to the kitchenette, Adam got on with his packing.

'There.' He packed the last ball of newspaper into the corner of the box, taped down the flaps and wrote 'crockery' in black capitals across the top. 'That's the last of it.' He stood back to survey the emptiness of his front room. 'This place looks a bit roomier without all my stuff in it, don't you reckon?'

'Thank goodness you're leaving half of it here, we'd never fit it all in my spare room.'

Adam ate a biscuit from a packet Taz had produced in one enormous bite, chewed and swallowed in a couple of seconds.

'You know, it's ages since I last slept in a room with Beatrix Potter wallpaper,' he remarked. 'I'm looking forward to it.'

'You don't think it might dent your macho image a bit, having Jemima Puddleduck stickers on your wardrobe door?'

Adam threw back his head and roared with laughter, a warm and comfortable sound, like the growl of a favourite teddy bear.

'What macho image? You can't be macho *and* vote Liberal Democrat.'

Taz made the tea then helped Adam carry down the last of his things. By the time they'd finished, the Morris was sitting very low on its tyres, its suspension squeaking under the weight of suitcases, boxes, bags, books, a guitar, squash rackets and a pair of Wellingtons. It took several minutes just to jam the back doors together and lock them shut.

'Hey!'

A familiar voice hailed them from somewhere above. Taz looked up. Dee's head was sticking out of a first-floor window.

'Hi, Dee. Didn't see you there.'

'If you get back to Charlton Kings without the back end going, my name's Barry Manilow.'

'You've got the nose for it anyway,' ventured Adam cheekily.

'Hit him for me, Taz. I'm coming right down.'

Dee arrived with a Peacock's carrier bag, and held it out to Taz.

'Adam's underpants. I found them mixed up with my smalls.' She winked broadly at Adam, who cleared his throat, snatched the bag and stuffed it into his jacket pocket. Dee promptly gave him the benefit of her best Mae West impression. 'Naturally, I'm hanging on to the silk boxer shorts – for old times' sake . . .'

'Dee . . .' Adam gave Taz a despairing look. 'Don't believe a word she says, it's wishful thinking.'

'He should be so lucky,' replied Dee archly. 'Lorenzo could eat ten of him for breakfast. Now, Taz.' She fixed Taz with a schoolmarmish look. 'I've got a bone to pick with you. Come inside, and let's talk. Adam can fiddle about with his spark plugs or something for ten minutes, can't you Adam?'

Taz allowed herself to be steered through the café and up the stairs to Dee's living room.

'Sit down, Taz.'

'What's this all about?' Taz was beginning to feel uneasy. Was there something she'd forgotten to do? Something that had annoyed Dee so much she wanted to have it out, face-to-face?

'You might have told me, Taz, about your childcare falling through.'

The mist cleared.

'About . . .? But why?'

Dee dropped heavily into the chair opposite Taz's, shaking her head in exasperated disbelief.

'Why? Because we're supposed to be friends. Because maybe I might like to help.'

Taz's heart turned a small somersault. Dee? Help? She'd been so busy trying elsewhere that it had never occurred to her to ask.

'I never thought . . . I mean, you've got a lot on your plate.'

'Not so much that I can't help out a friend,' said Dee, more gently now. She leaned forward in her chair. 'Adam says you're still looking for a childminder for Jack.'

Taz nodded wearily.

'I'm supposed to be going back to work the week after next, and I can't find a vacancy anywhere. A nanny's out of the question; and all the day nurseries are full up. Besides, their hours are all wrong. I don't know what I'm going to do.'

'Do? It's simple.' Dee spread her hands wide. 'I'll look after Jack for you.'

'You?' For a few seconds the significance of Dee's words didn't quite sink in. 'Did I just hear you say that, or am I hallucinating?'

'I said, I'll take care of Jack for you.'

'But . . . how could you? You've got the café, and the twins, and everything else.'

'Look. The café's no problem, Lorenzo does his share and I've got a girl serving part-time now too. Petula and Emma-Louise are at school, and Denny goes to nursery three afternoons a week. Now I've got the twins into a routine, I can easily take on one more little one. Like I told you, the more the merrier!'

Taz's heart soared, defying all the doubts thrown up by reason. Dee! Kind, practical, eminently earth-motherish Dee – could there be a better childminder for Jack? She made a determined effort to think sensibly.

'Dee . . . you really think it could work?'

'No, I'm *sure* it could work.'

'And what about Lorenzo?'

'He gets on great with all the kids. You know what Italians are like, they adore their bambinos.'

'But you know I work long hours at S&G. I might not be able to pick up Jack before seven – later some nights.'

'That's OK. No problem.'

Taz began to allow herself a twinge of guarded optimism. Maybe this could work, after all.

'If we did this ... I'd want to pay you the full rate.'

'That's fine by me, the extra money would come in handy.'

'And we'd draw up a proper contract?'

Dee shrugged, but she was smiling.

'Whatever you're happy with. Aha, Adam,' she waved to the lanky figure framed in the doorway. 'What do you think? Would I make a good childminder? I think Taz needs a little persuading.'

'Not about you,' Taz said hastily. 'It's me. I can't believe this is happening, I keep trying to think of the catch.'

'I'd stop trying if I were you,' said Adam promptly, 'and bite her hand off before she changes her mind.' He took his doorkey out of his jacket pocket and tossed it across to Dee, who caught it one-handed. 'All done upstairs, Dee. Everything's packed and ready to go.'

'So this is goodbye then?'

'Just au revoir. After all, you've still got custody of my underpants.'

Adam and Taz were still laughing as Taz unlocked the door of the flat, shutting up promptly at the sight of her mother with her finger to her lips.

'Hush dear, Jack's only just got off, you don't want to wake him.'

'Sorry Mum.' Taz felt the insane urge to giggle uncontrollably, like a mini-skirted fifth-former, but managed to bite her lip. She lowered her voice to a whisper. 'You've moved him into my bedroom?'

'Yes, of course.'

'And he's been all right? Only he was a bit sniffly this morning, and I did think he might be running a temperature ...'

'He's been good as gold. And he took all his bottle, *and* half a slice of avocado.'

'Really? That's clever of you. When I tried, most of it ended up in his hair.'

Without switching on the light, Taz peeped inside her bedroom door. The sight of Jack, deeply and innocently asleep in his cot, brought her instantly back to her responsibilities. It was strange; as though the last couple of hours had been a kind of holiday from her new self, but the holiday was now over and life must begin again.

She closed the door and tiptoed away.

'Mum, Dad, this is Adam. My new flatmate.'

'So I gathered,' said Bill drily, pausing in his reading to take a good, hard look at Adam. Taz knew that look only too well. It was her father's 'bank manager face', as Isobel called it. Her heart sank.

'Pleased to meet you Mrs Norton, Mr Norton.' Adam offered a firm but not bone-crunching handshake. Isobel simpered and melted like an adolescent girl. Bill accepted the gesture with a curt nod, and went back to reading his magazine.

'Adam's a solicitor,' ventured Taz. This revelation had the desired effect on Isobel, who rewarded Adam with a dazzling smile.

'A solicitor! How lovely, your mother must be so proud.'

Adam's lips twitched into a disarming smile.

'Actually, I think I'm a bit of a disappointment. My late father was a QC.'

'A QC!' Isobel's pleasure rocketed towards stratospheric ecstasy. Add a bishop and a gynaecologist to the Rolfe family tree, thought Taz, and her contentment would be complete.

'I expect you'd like to get settled in your room?' suggested Taz. Adam looked relieved.

Taz ushered Adam into his room and closed the door.

'Sorry,' she said.

'What for?'

'My parents. They're ... how can I put it? ... an acquired taste.'

Adam unzipped a holdall and started lifting out shirts.

Taz watched in fascination as he managed to heap five of them onto one groaning plastic hanger.

'They're fine. Really. It's just like being at home. In fact,' he hooked the hanger onto the wardrobe rail and turned round to pick up another shirt, 'I think I'm going to be really happy here.'

The twinkle in his eyes made Taz suspect that she was going to be rather happy, too.

At three fifteen on Thursday afternoon, Taz and Mandy were sitting in Adam's office at the law centre. Two half-empty teacups sat on the desk in front of them. Dylan slept the sleep of the innocent, slumped in his buggy. Two miles away, Jack was being introduced to kiwi fruit by his grandma.

There was only one thing missing. Adam.

'He said he'd be here by three,' said Mandy, scraping back her chair and pacing the room like a caged animal. 'I knew I should've gone with him.'

'I expect he got caught in traffic.' Taz sympathised with Mandy's anxiety, but wished she would sit down and grit her teeth and wait. 'He'll be here soon.'

'You really think so?'

'I know so.' Taz's fingers closed on Mandy's wrist as she walked past, and eased her back down onto her chair. 'He's doing his best for Dave, you know he is.'

'Then why wouldn't he let me go to the prison with him? He knows I can't afford the train fare.'

Taz hesitated for a moment before answering. What Adam had actually done was beg Taz to stop Mandy going up to the prison: 'Find some way – please. Tie her up and gag her if you have to. I need to talk to him alone, it's the only way I'll ever get through to him. If Mandy's there, she'll interfere. You know she will. She just can't resist.'

She'd had to agree that Adam had a point. Which was why she'd persuaded Mandy to come shopping with her, promising that they'd come straight to the law centre at three o'clock to find out what news Adam had of Dave.

'Well?' demanded Mandy. The red and yellow parrot

earrings Taz had bought her jiggled against her face, making it look as if the parrots were pecking at her earlobes.

'I . . . I expect he needed to have a heart-to-heart with Dave. His trial's tomorrow, it's important for Adam to prepare the case properly if he's going to help Dave.'

'You think he'll get Dave off? You really think there's a chance they'll believe him?'

Taz felt the weight of Mandy's hope descending on her shoulders. But she couldn't lie, not even for the sake of their friendship.

'All I know is that Adam will do his best for Dave. You can't ask more than that.'

Mandy was up and on her feet again, picking up leaflets from the displays around the office and discarding them without even looking at them. They'd been here for three quarters of an hour; by now even Taz knew them all off by heart.

Footsteps sounded on the stairs outside. Mandy was at the door and wrenching it open before Adam had even reached the landing.

'Well? What happened? I want to know what happened.'

Adam was beaming all over his face. Mandy was breathless with expectation, the suspense almost killing her.

'What happened, tell me for fuck's sake!'

'Steady on.' Gently, Adam detached Mandy's metallic yellow nails from his jumper and sat down. 'It's good news, Mandy. I did it.'

Taz didn't comprehend. 'Did what?'

'It took some doing, but I finally persuaded Dave to change his plea to guilty.'

The last vestiges of colour drained from Mandy's pallid face. For a couple of seconds she just gaped at Adam, open-mouthed and still as a statue. Then she found her voice, a hoarse and incredulous whisper.

'You. Fuckin'. Did. What?'

'I explained that the evidence was overwhelming, so the best thing all round was for him to admit that he was guilty. With a guilty plea he won't have to give evidence, and he'll get a much shorter sentence . . .'

'You BASTARD!' Mandy's screech of rage and pain came so suddenly that Taz almost fell off her chair. It was difficult to believe that a small, frail figure like Mandy's could produce such an alarmingly savage burst of sound. 'You cheating, lying, useless bastard! That's why you wouldn't let me go with you! Isn't it! Isn't it! You wanted to bully Dave into pleadin' guilty, when you know he's fuckin' innocent!'

'Mandy . . .' began Taz, but Mandy paid her no attention.

'Well – isn't it?'

Adam stayed very calm.

'Look, Mandy,' he said slowly. 'All I care about is doing the best for Dave.'

'You expect me to believe that?'

'Whether you believe it or not, it's true. And there's little point in Dave proclaiming his innocence when there's enough evidence to convict him ten times over.'

Mandy's screaming rage moderated to something much more dangerous: a bitter, glacier-cold fury.

'If Dave says he's innocent he's innocent.'

'I'm sorry, Mandy, I can't believe that. No jury would acquit him. And by pleading guilty, he'll get a much lighter sentence, surely you can see that . . .'

'All I can *see* is that you get paid whether he gets put away or not.'

It was at that moment that Taz made her big mistake. Torn between sympathy for Adam and loyalty to Mandy, she fell into the trap of making a choice.

'Mandy . . . Mandy, Adam's right. You've got to try and understand . . .'

'*What*?' Mandy swung round and stared at her. 'Oh, that's it, is it? You think because I'm a single parent from a bug-infested council flat, I'm too thick to understand what's good for my own boyfriend?'

'I don't think that Mandy, you know I don't . Please, be reasonable.'

'Reasonable! My God, Taz, and I thought you were my

friend. And all the time you were looking down your nose at me.'

'I *am* your friend, I'm only trying to help.'

'Yeah. Like he's tryin' to help Dave. By puttin' him away for a ten-stretch an' throwin' away the key.'

Taz saw that Mandy's eyes were sparkling with tears, tears she was far too proud and too stubborn to shed in their presence.

'Come on Dylan, we're goin'.'

She wrenched open the door. Taz and Adam leapt to their feet simultaneously, trying to stop her, but already she was straining to lift the buggy down the stairs, the tears running freely down her cheeks now, all pretence at hope long gone. Suddenly, Mandy Robson looked like exactly what she was: the half-grown outcast of a world that didn't care.

Taz felt a dreadful emptiness clutching at her heart.

'Mandy, Mandy – please come back.'

But Mandy's only response was a final, venomous retort over her shoulder as the street door swung shut behind her.

'Fuck off. Both of you. Why don't you just fuck off an' die?'

Mandy's words haunted Taz all through that night. She lay for hours in the darkness, listening to Jack's snuffly breathing and the sound of gentle snoring coming through the partition wall from Adam's room.

How did he manage to sleep? How could this affect him so little? Yet in her heart she knew she was being naive. How many cases like Dave's must Adam have to battle with, every working day of his life? How many more no-hope petty criminals with a past they'd rather forget and no future worth mentioning? One thing was for certain: it was a job Taz could never cope with.

Adam went off early to court, and Taz was grateful for that. It gave her time to think, to wonder what she was going to say when next she saw Mandy. In a mad moment she'd almost made up her mind to go to the trial, to see if there was anything she could do, but no; that was a ridiculous idea.

'Come on Jack, come on sweetie, just one mouthful.'

Off his guard for a couple of seconds, he let his mouth slacken slightly and she sneaked in half a spoonful of anaemic mush; but most of it came straight out again, and he promptly smeared it all over his face.

Ah well. Deep breath. And start again.

She was just warming up the apricot and rice dessert (more pale-grey mush), when the doorbell went. To her complete amazement, Clive Baxendale was standing outside, his shirt steaming gently in the warmth after a sunshower.

'Er – Taz. I'm sorry to bother you.' Clive took in the plastic spoon, the handful of soggy kitchen towel, the apron. 'Is this a bad time?'

'No. No, of course not. Come in. Mind the kitchen floor, it's a bit slippy.'

'I hope you don't mind my mentioning it, but there's some grey stuff on your forehead.'

Taz peered into the kitchen mirror and wiped away a blob of Jack's dinner.

'Oh, so there is. Jack's at that messy stage – I expect you and Chloë are having the same problem with Ayesha. Come on Jack, lovely apricot rice. How is Chloë, by the way?'

'Actually.' Clive cleared his throat and sat awkwardly on one of Taz's kitchen stools. 'It's Chloë I've come to see you about.'

'Oh?'

'She was really excited you know, about meeting you in town the other day.'

'Excited?' Taz found that hard to believe. Chloë had seemed scarcely conscious.

'Oh yes, she's talked about hardly anything since. And the thing is . . . she's been so down lately . . . well, you're the first person she's shown any real interest in since Ayesha was born.'

Taz wiped Jack's mouth and lifted him out of his high chair to burp him.

'Oh surely, that can't be true.' She saw from Clive's face that it was.

'You see, Taz, our GP's been very good, but he can't spend very much time with Chloë, and with me being at work most days, she spends a lot of time with nobody to talk to. Not that she shows much interest in other people. Except you. In fact, I was wondering . . .'

'I don't know Chloë very well,' Taz cut in, hoping to forestall Clive. 'I don't know what possible help I could be.'

'Oh but you could,' Clive insisted, and Taz knew she would never be able to refuse that look of desperate pleading. 'If you could just come and see Chloë some time, have a little chat . . . it would mean an awful lot to her. And me.'

Chapter 18

Still not knowing why she'd given in to Clive, Taz drove over to Dee's the following afternoon. Jack gurgled as she unstrapped him from his car seat and carried him inside.

'You're sure you don't mind looking after Jack for a couple of hours?'

'As if! I'll be looking after him full-time from next week, remember,' said Dee, beaming.

How could I forget, thought Taz.

'I didn't think it'd be a good idea, taking Jack to Chloë's. She seemed a bit . . . well . . . unpredictable last time I saw her.'

'Really? That bad? I thought she just had a touch of the baby blues. Still, you never know – seeing Jack might just perk her up – why don't you take him with you next time?'

'What next time? I'm only doing this because Clive twisted my arm. And I got the distinct impression the last thing Chloë wants to talk about is babies.'

'Oh, but Jack's *such* a lovely baby. Come here, gorgeous, and give your Auntie Dee a big hug.'

Dee curled strong arms around Jack and snuggled him close to her not-inconsiderable bosom. Jack promptly reacted by rooting around in her T-shirt, much to Taz's embarrassment.

'Oh Dee, I'm sorry, he must be hungry again. Here, let me have him, I'll give him a feed before I go to Chloë's.'

Dee shook her head wisely.

'You're going back to work next week, and you won't

be able to nip out and breastfeed him between meetings, will you?'

'No . . .' Taz looked longingly at Jack. His gurgles were turning to little whimpers of impatience, and she could feel her nipples tingling, ready to feed. This was dreadful. How was it going to be when she had to leave him for whole days at a time? 'I suppose I could give him his bottle before I go.'

'Believe me, Taz. He'll take it better from a stranger. The minute he smells you he'll want the breast and start playing you up.'

'You're right,' Taz sighed. He always takes his bottle from Granny, even his baby rice, but whenever I try it's hopeless.' She bent over and gave Jack a big slobbery kiss. 'Be good for Auntie Dee.'

'He will. He's a little cherub, aren't you love? Come on, let's settle him upstairs before you go.' Dee led the way through the side door of the café, past the distant cacophony of clinking cups and the high-powered hiss of boiling water pounding onto herbal teabags.

'Sounds like you're busy in there,' commented Taz.

'Oh, business is booming, never better. And this new girl's a godsend, the customers love her. Only eighteen, but she's got her life well sorted out.' Dee paused on the landing, and turned to look at Taz. 'How's Mandy? I haven't seen her in ages.' She pushed open the door of the kitchen. The twins were in a playpen in the centre of the room, rolling about on a sheepskin. 'Wasn't it Dave's trial the other day?'

'Yesterday.' Taz thought of Mandy's tear-soaked, furious face; that last, venomous look of betrayal. 'He got five years.'

'*Five years*! I knew Dave was a bit dodgy, but five years!'

'With the time he's spent on remand, Adam reckons he'll be out in two. But . . .'

'But two years is a long time.' Dee handed Taz one of Jack's bottles. 'You couldn't warm it up could you?' She shook her head slowly, reflectively. 'I knew he should have pleaded guilty.'

Taz swallowed.

'He did.' Taz put on the kettle to boil some water. 'Adam persuaded him to change his plea at the last minute. But it didn't do much good, the judge said he had to make an example of anyone who'd committed a serious crime. The thing is, Mandy swears he's innocent.'

Dee sat herself down at the kitchen table, and unzipped Jack from his little outdoor jacket.

'Yeah, well, she would. But she's better off without him, Taz. He's a nasty little thug, all his family are. You want to tell her so, talk some sense into her.'

'I wish I could,' said Taz. 'But first I have to find a way of making her speak to me.'

Taz wasn't sure what to expect as she drove up the driveway to Clive and Chloë's house.

It was a very nice house, in a very nice suburb; that much was predictable enough, with Clive's father's money firmly behind the young couple – but what about Chloë? The way Chloë had seemed last time they'd met, Taz wondered what kind of reception she was going to get.

She rang the bell and waited. As she stood on the doorstep her eyes automatically scanned her surroundings. A gravelled drive, sweeping in a broad curve from the gateposts, each topped with a life-sized stone pineapple. Well-stocked flower-beds, a pond with a statue beside it, koi carp and water-lilies blossoming under a July sun. And right in the middle of it all a bijou Georgian villa, a more than generous tax-deduction from Daddy's thriving company. Very nice. Very . . . upper middle-class.

The door opened. Taz almost expected to be greeted by a liveried footman. But it was Chloë herself who appeared on the doorstep, whippet-thin in a short-sleeved jersey dress that clung to every jutting bone in her body; her blonde hair elaborately styled in some kind of complicated French pleat, and her make-up so salon-perfect that Taz secretly wondered if she would whisk off the mask and reveal a real face underneath.

But the strangest, most unexpected and most disturbing thing about Chloë Baxendale was the spark of unnatural brightness in blue eyes which, only days before, had seemed to have lost every glimmer of recognition.

'Taz, Taz darling, you *came*!' Chloë's fingers clutched so eagerly at Taz's hand that they left white indentations which might well turn to bruises.

'Yes, of course. Chloë, it's good to see you. Are you well?'

'Clive said you were coming, but I was afraid you might not, he was so rude to you in the street the other day . . . he didn't upset you did he Taz?'

'Rude?' Taz gaped. 'No, no, not at all. You and Ayesha, you're all right?'

Taz felt stupidly nervous as Chloë dragged her into the hallway and shut the door behind them. It felt cold inside after the warmth of the summer sunshine, and she gave an involuntary shiver as she drew her thin jacket around her more closely. Chloë didn't seem to notice the chill; she was so hyperactive that she generated her own nervous electricity.

'I'm fine, I'm fine.' Taz couldn't help noticing the way Chloë avoided including Ayesha in the bulletin. 'Come into the conservatory, I've got a lovely cake and some Lapsang Souchong, you do like Lapsang Souchong don't you?'

Taz smiled. Chloë didn't appear to require any other response; besides, Chloë wouldn't want to be told that Lapsang Souchong tasted like roadmenders' underpants.

'Come in, sit down, do you like the conservatory? Mummy thinks it's out of keeping with the house, but I don't see why you can't have a Victorian conservatory on a Georgian house, what do you think?'

This flood of words almost left Taz floundering in its wake. She looked around the conservatory; it was an opulent, arching structure of white-painted wrought-iron pillars entwined with creepers and vines. Lloyd Loom chairs with soft green cushions clustered casually around a rattan table decorated with a white lace cloth and topped by a silver tray loaded with tea and cakes.

'I think . . . it's . . . lovely.'

The look of relief and pleasure on Chloë's face only

lasted a second or two; then she was fretting and fussing again, patting cushions, making sure that Taz wasn't facing the sun, finding imaginary specks of dirt on immaculate china cups.

'You *do* like the cake, don't you?'

This time, at least, Taz could be completely truthful.

'I *always* love cake, especially fresh cream gateau.' She licked a blob of cream off her upper lip and patted her spare tyre. Even in this most forgiving of summer dresses, there was no disguising it. 'But you *are* naughty, feeding me all these wonderful cakes – I'm supposed to be on a diet!'

Chloë stared at her as though she were mad.

'On a diet? Why? You look fabulous.' She pushed away her plate of cake, virtually untouched.

'Aren't you hungry?'

'No. No, I mustn't have any more, I have to get my figure back.'

Taz almost dropped her cake fork at this. If there was anyone who could afford to stuff herself with gateau, it was Chloë Baxendale. Mandy's youthful figure had snapped back into shape days after the birth, Dee's had taken on an extra layer of plumpness, Taz's had developed all the elasticity of boiled Lycra – but Chloë's wasn't so much a figure any more, as an arrangements of bones overlaid by pale, translucent skin.

'Chloë – what on earth do you want to diet for? You're as thin as a rake!'

Chloë looked unconvinced. Getting slowly to her feet, she placed one hand on her belly, the other on her bottom, breathed in, then turned round and round like an electric mannequin, her eyes fixed on her reflection in the glazed windows.

'Clive says I've got my figure back, he says you'd never know I'd had a baby . . . but I don't know if I can believe him.'

'Of course you can. You have a lovely figure. And Clive loves you, he only wants what's best for you.'

'You really think so?' The blue eyes searched Taz's face for any hint of insincerity.

'I know so. He wants you to be a happy family, all three of you.' Taz took her courage in both hands. 'How's Ayesha?'

For a moment, Chloë seemed not to comprehend. Then she waved her hand dismissively.

'I don't know. How should I know? Clive takes care of that, he has this girl – an Australian – she deals with it.' Chloë passed a hand over her brow. There was a fine mist of perspiration on the white skin. 'I think I'll just have a little sit down.'

'That's a good idea.'

Taz took Chloë's hands and drew her back down onto her chair. Outwardly, Taz tried to be as calm and reassuring as she could be, though inside she was reeling. How could a mother talk this way about her baby? She recalled her first impressions as she'd stepped into the hallway of the house. How startled she'd been to find that the air carried no scents of babyhood – no warm milk, no baby powder, no Milton – only the artificial sweetnesses of beeswax polish and pot pourri.

'Here, have some Lapsang, you'll feel better.' She topped up Chloë's cup, making sure to put only the merest dab into her own.

'But I *am* better!' protested Chloë, her head springing up like a jack-in-the-box's, the alarming spark of brightness re-illuminated in her round eyes. 'That's why I stopped taking the pills.'

A warning bell tolled deep in the recesses of Taz's mind.

'You've ... stopped taking the anti-depressants?' she said slowly.

'Of course I have! What do I need them for, I'm not depressed am I?'

'And Clive?'

Chloë giggled, laying her hand conspiratorially on Taz's arm.

'He thinks I'm taking them, but I'm flushing them down the loo. He keeps on telling me how much good they must be doing, because I'm getting so much better – isn't that funny!' She put her finger to her lips. 'You won't tell Clive, will you? It'll be our little secret.'

Taz promised, but not until her fingers were crossed behind her back. She hated lying to Chloë, but this was something that Clive had a right to know – whether he wanted to or not.

'I just don't know *what* to do,' declared Taz, watching Adam change Jack's nappy, with such good-humoured adeptness that Jack completely forgot about wriggling, wetting himself or shrieking.

Adam left off wiping Jack's bottom and looked at her over his shoulder.

'What you have to do is stop taking on everybody else's problems. And anyhow, you've sorted out Chloë, haven't you?'

Taz plonked herself down on the floor next to Jack, relishing the chance to let someone else change him for once, but wondering what black magic forces Adam was employing to keep Jack from rolling off the changing mat.

'Have I? All I did was tell Clive that Chloë's not been taking her pills.'

'And what did Clive say?'

'He said he'd make her take them. But I don't know if he will, he really does seem to think she's getting better.'

'Perhaps she is. Pass me the Johnson's would you? Yes, Jack, this *is* a lovely game isn't it?'

Taz handed over the baby powder.

'You're a little monster, Jack. Why don't you lie still for Mummy, huh? Come on Adam, tell me your secret.'

'I've got him in a Vulcan death-grip. He's powerless to resist me, aren't you Jack my boy?'

Taz smiled ruefully, recalling how very delicious Adam's veggie casserole had been, and how Isobel had rhap-sodised over the quality of his ironing.

'Are you perfect at *everything*?'

Adam wiggled his eyebrows suggestively.

'Well, I haven't had any complaints!' His ridiculous leer subsided as he saw that Taz wasn't laughing. 'What's wrong? Are you still worrying about Mandy?'

'Of course I am!'

'You tried ringing her . . .'

'Yeah, and her father told me to piss off. I even tried the company she used to clean for, but she's left. So what do I do next?'

Adam sealed the tapes on Jack's nappy and swung him up onto his shoulder.

'You could try waiting for her to cool down and get in touch with you,' he suggested.

'You don't like Mandy, do you?'

Adam let out a 'hmm' of deliberation.

'Let's just say, we haven't got off to a good start. And remember, *you* haven't done anything wrong.'

'But Adam!'

'You haven't,' he repeated with emphasis. 'And you've got enough problems of your own to worry about, with going back to work next week and your Dad being so suspicious of my intentions . . .'

'He isn't! It's just his way, he's a bit old-fashioned. He'll come round,' protested Taz, colouring up.

Adam shrugged.

'If he does, he does. In any case, it's you I'm concerned about. It's about time you had a bit of fun. Which is why I'm taking you out tonight. The Reduced Shakespeare Company are on at the Everyman.'

'Out? I can't go out! I've not washed my hair, and there's nobody to babysit Jack . . .'

Adam checked his watch, and put his ear to Jack's mouth, pretending to listen.

'What's that – the show doesn't start till eight, so she's got a whole hour to get ready? And you're really looking forward to your granny coming round and babysitting you?'

'You've persuaded my mum to give up her bridge class to babysit Jack?'

'It was easy as pie. I just fluttered my eyelashes.'

'Shame on you.'

'I know.' Adam's warm hazel eyes crinkled at the corners. 'But once I know what I want, Taz, I don't give up until I've got it!'

A night out at the theatre did wonders for Taz's morale.

Adam made witty company, and she was still chuckling over the thirty-second version of *Hamlet* on Friday morning, as she got ready to go and see Diana Latchford. On Monday she would be walking back into the store as manager of menswear, and this meeting would be her only chance to reacclimatise before being thrown in at the deep end.

'For goodness' sake have some breakfast,' tutted Isobel, who had come over early to babysit Jack 'just this once' because Dee had the VAT inspectors in, even though Isobel thoroughly disapproved of Taz going back to S&G and Taz knew she'd dearly love to sling a spanner in the works. 'You can't think straight on an empty stomach.'

Taz took one large bite from the slice of toast which Adam jammed into her mouth, and chewed on it as she struggled to do up the zipper on her skirt.

'And I can't turn up in Diana Latchford's office looking like a bag lady. It's no good, I'll never do this up, I'm *gross*!' she wailed.

'Rubbish,' snorted Isobel. 'You should just accept you'll never be a size twelve again, not after Jack. I waved goodbye to my hourglass figure the minute I had you.'

Taz flung her a thunderbolt, but it bounced right off.

'I *will* be slim again,' she muttered. 'Once I get back into the swing of things . . .'

'Is that a ladder in the back of your tights?' enquired Adam. Taz swung round, craning her neck to see; sure enough, a fine white line was snaking up the back of her right leg.

'Damn and blast! And I haven't got a spare pair.'

'Don't worry.' Adam was up and out of his chair, checking his watch. 'I don't have to be at work for another hour, I'll just drive down to the corner shop and get you some.'

'Such a nice young man,' Isobel reflected, gazing adoringly after Adam.

'Yes, Mum.' Taz was getting used to this; which wasn't to say that she liked it.

'Jack thinks he's wonderful.' Right on cue, Jack started crying; and as Taz turned to pick him up Isobel got there first, scooping him up and half-smothering him with kisses. 'Does Jackie want a nice new daddy then, does he, does he?'

Taz winced as she managed, at last, to tug her skirt zipper up that last, crucial half-inch.

'Ow!' She sucked the tip of her finger, tasting blood where the teeth of the zipper had taken a bite out of it. 'Look Mum, I don't have time for this now, I've got to find my briefcase ... and those figures, where did I put those figures?'

Saying goodbye to Jack was dreadful, even with fresh tights and a brand-new pair of breast pads, so thick and absorbent that they added an extra cup-size to her already-generous bust. She kissed him, handed him to his granny and forced a smile as she walked out to her car and Isobel waved Jack's arm in a bewildered goodbye.

She could hear him start to cry as she got in and switched on the engine. The temptation to run back inside was almost unbearable. But she wasn't going to give in, she wasn't going to cry, she wasn't going to be the female stereotype her mother longed for her to be.

Taz Norton had always been in control. And she didn't see why today should be any exception.

It felt strange to be parking in the staff car park again, in one of the spaces designated for departmental managers. Of course, technically speaking she wasn't one until next Monday, but she wanted to get back into the right frame of mind and she was certain Diana Latchford would approve.

As she walked towards the atrium of S&G, Taz admired her reflection in the row of freshly-washed display windows. OK, so her skirt was too tight, but she looked good. The longline, fitted jacket of her peacock-blue suit disguised the bulge around her waistline, and her legs and hair were as good as ever. Jack, she told herself, I'm going to make sure you have a mummy you can be proud of.

And I'll start by changing *that*, she thought as she passed one of Menswear's display windows, containing a cluttered mess of half-dressed mannequins and a binbag full of rubbish.

Resisting the urge to go straight up to menswear and find out what a pig's ear Ted had made of it, Taz forced herself to respect etiquette. After all, Ted was still technically in charge until Monday; it wouldn't be right to barge in. First, she must go and see Diana for her briefing.

Nikki was in the outer office, supervising a junior who was stuffing envelopes for a mailshot.

'Ms Norton! How lovely to see you. You're looking wonderful!'

'You think so?' Taz felt a warm surge of gratification; it *had* been worth spending the extra money to get a really good suit, after all.

'Absolutely. I'll just ring through to Mrs Latchford and tell her you're here.'

It was like being the new girl on the very first term at secondary school as she pushed open the heavy oak door of Diana's office and stepped into the warm fug of freshly-brewed coffee. A steaming cup was already waiting for her on her side of the desk, Diana standing by the window, gazing out across Imperial Gardens.

'Ah. Tasmin.' She turned and smiled, extended her arm in a firm handshake. 'Welcome back to S&G.'

'Thank you, it's good to be back.'

'Sit down, we've a lot to talk about.'

There was something in Diana's tone of voice that set Taz's antennae quivering.

'Your childcare arrangements are all sorted out now?'

'Yes. There shouldn't be any problems there.' And, thought Taz through her smile, I'm not going to let on that I'm missing my little son like crazy. Not even if I'm weeping buckets on the inside.

'Good.' Unusually, Diana seemed uneasy, her ringed fingers toying with the blotting paper in front of her. She looked tired, thought Taz. Tired and demotivated.

'I'm looking forward to getting back to my department.'

Diana cleared her throat. She looked up, fixing Taz with a square-on gaze.

'There's no easy way of saying this, Taz. There's been a change of plan.'

'What change? What plan?'

Diana let out a long, controlled explosion of breath, as though it was the only way of releasing the pressure of steam-hot anger inside her.

'You know that Ken Harris has been on sick leave for some weeks?'

'I'd heard something of the sort, yes. Why?'

'It seems that Ken has been less than honest with us. All the time he was absent from S&G, he was busy setting up a restaurant in Bourton on the Water.'

Diana's crimson-glossed lips managed an ironic smile. 'A gourmet sausage restaurant. I received his resignation on Wednesday. He's not coming back. Which leaves S& G in a difficult position.'

'I'm sure ... but how does this affect me?'

Diana stood up, walked round the desk and sat down on it facing Taz.

'The board of directors has decided that Ted Williams should be appointed departmental sales manager of menswear. Permanently.'

Ice-cold horror flooded Taz's consciousness, raising the hairs on her scalp, sending icy shivers down the back of her neck.

'No ... no, you can't do that! That's *my* department! The work I've put into it ... the success I made of it ...'

Diana nodded, but her expression didn't soften.

'I know. I know how much it means to you, but you know the rules at S&G. You can be moved at any time, anywhere. It happened to me twice when I was your age, and I hated it. But I picked myself up, told myself it was a challenge, and got on with making a success of it.'

'A challenge! Diana, this is crazy – you can't just give my department to Ted Williams!'

'It wasn't my decision.' You could tell that Diana was choosing her words with the utmost care. 'It came from higher authority. Henry Goldman was particularly keen for Ted to be given a chance to prove himself.'

'Oh. Right. Now I see.' Cold rage turned to bitterness, as Taz recalled the night of the American Event, the sight of Ted walking practically arm in arm with Henry Goldman, filling his head with countless lies about how wonderful he was, taking credit for everybody else's work. 'So Henry Goldman leans on you and you dump me, right?'

'Wrong, Tasmin.'

'Oh really? Then explain to me what this is if it's not the sack! And what about my maternity rights? My job's supposed to be waiting for me when I come back . . .'

'Correction.' Diana put up her hand. 'Your job, or a job of equivalent status. Which is what we're offering you.'

Taz leaned forward. Her pulse was racing, her palms were cold and slimy with sweat.

'Meaning?'

'Well . . . the menswear department at York S&G will need a new DSM in a fortnight's time. It's a big new department, it needs a strong hand on the tiller.'

'York!' Taz forgot moderation as her voice rose to a shout. 'How on earth am I supposed to up sticks and move to York, I've just had a baby . . .'

'Of course. Or you can become DSM in the food hall, here at S&G Cheltenham.'

Taz blinked. Diana waited, arms folded.

'With Ken gone and Leroy having so little supervisory experience, it desperately needs someone with excellent management skills.'

'But I don't know anything about the food hall!'

'Of course you do, you've worked in every department in this store.'

'Oh yes. I did a three-week placement there, four years ago, that'll stand me in really good stead won't it?' Taz laughed sarcastically.

'I'm sorry, Tasmin, I know it's not what you wanted, but think about what I said. It's a challenge. And you'd be working with Leroy again, I know how badly you felt about him being transferred out of menswear.'

Taz stared at her feet.

'So that's that then? York or the food hall? No room for negotiation?'

'I'm afraid not.'

'Then I supposed it'll have to be the food hall.'

'Excellent!' Diana looked positively jubilant. 'I knew

you'd see it my way. Come along then, let's go and meet your new team.'

The Food Hall was just the way Taz remembered it; only worse.

It was here that Old George (seventy if he was a day) presided over the saddest collection of wet fish Taz had ever seen. Where Mo and Gloria chewed gum and chatted about boyfriends as they worked the tills. Where spotty Ian and lank-haired Mark trailed around looking like they wished they'd never heard of Seuss & Goldman. Where Delilah blew her nose over a rack of cream cakes whose appearance was considerably less enticing than her name.

And – worst of all – where customers wandered around aimlessly with empty baskets, forlornly searching for things that Seuss & Goldman didn't sell.

The only glimmer of light was Leroy; and he wasn't exactly on top of the world.

'I thought once you got back they might transfer me back to menswear,' he admitted forlornly as they walked past the Bonbon Box and the cheese counter.

'Quite. Me too. I certainly didn't expect to end up in Ken's wonderful world of sausages.'

'I was looking forward to working with you again.'

'I'm flattered.'

Leroy gave Taz one of his dry looks.

'Well face it, if it's a straight choice between you, Ted Williams and Ken . . .'

'Ah. I get your point.' Taz took a long, hard, sweeping look at her new domain. It was going to take more than a wet mop and a bagel stand to bring this graveyard to life. 'Now, why don't you fill me in on the food hall? I have a feeling I've a great deal to learn before Monday morning.'

Mandy struggled along in the rain, her wet hair plastered to her scalp, her small body shivering under its thin, sodden tee-shirt and worn-out leggings.

Rainwater dripped off the end of her nose, streamed down her face like a cascade of tears; but Mandy wasn't crying. What was the point? She'd long since stopped thinking that the things that happened to her weren't fair. Fair was for other people. Nice people. Not her.

It was hard to believe that this could be July. Only the day before the sun had been cracking the pavements, turning the diesel fumes to poisonous smog; but today the whole world was taking a shower, standing under the cold tap and turning it on full. If it hadn't been for Dylan, Mandy would have wished it could wash the whole world away, and her with it.

Dylan wept inconsolably beneath the torn plastic canopy of his buggy. She'd tried to mend it, but there was only so much you could do with Sellotape.

'Nearly there, soon have you nice an' dry.' Somehow she'd make this all right for them both, she'd sworn it to herself and Mandy never broke a promise. What's more, she'd do it on her own. If you waited long enough, other people always let you down. School. The Social. Adam. Mam and Dad. Even Taz.

And now Dave was gone, banged up on a trumped-up charge for God knows how many years, she had nobody anyway. She wasn't blind. She'd always known that, deep down, Dave was shite. But he was *her* shite. 'Me an' you against the world, Mandy love. We won't let the bastards grind us down.'

Ha fucking ha.

Along the main road they trailed, buses and lorries spattering them with muddy water as they ploughed past. The suitcase banged against Mandy's hip, its base scraping the wet pavement, the combined weight of the rucksack and the duffel bag on her shoulder bending her to the ground like a sapling in a storm. The soaked arm of Dylan's favourite teddy protruded forlornly from the top of the duffel bag. Underneath, the weight of the few precious books Mandy had salvaged from her father's sadistic rage weighed heavier than despair against her bag.

She stopped for a moment, turned and squinted back along the road. The bus stop was a long way behind. So was Cheltenham, the only place she'd ever lived in all her eighteen years – no, nineteen. It had been her birthday a week ago, not that anyone had bothered remembering. Not even Mandy. The bruises on her arms and the black eye had been her Dad's present to her. Well, it was a family tradition.

And now she was in Gloucester, or at least, some foetid outgrowth of it, with an abandoned factory filling the horizon and decrepit houses feeding like maggots on the corpse. She hadn't wanted to come here, to find some stinking hole of a bedsit, the only thing she could afford. But she'd had no choice.

Everybody blamed Mandy. First, Dave's family had blamed her for not giving him an alibi. Why couldn't they understand that she couldn't lie to save him, even though she knew he hadn't done what he was accused of?

Then the harassment had started, not just against Mandy but her whole family. The threatening phone calls, the abuse, the broken windows, the dog-shit through the letter box. That had been the last straw for Mam and Dad. They already thought she was a cheap slapper, a filthy whore; the minute they felt the sting of blame touch their own hide, they'd done the only decent thing. Chucked her out on the street. Which was how come she'd ended up in Gloucester: cheap enough to live, far enough away from Dave's mates.

A parade of six dismal shops stretched out along the pavement: a chippy, a bookie's, Asian grocery store, video hire, iffy junk shop and the boarded-up remains of a burnt-out sub-post office.

'This is home, Dylan.'

She felt in her pocket for the key, trying to make herself feel excited, positive. This was her home and Dylan's, she'd paid for it with the money she'd saved, this was their new start.

But when she'd unlocked the door and dragged the buggy all the way up two flights of stairs to the bedsit above the chippy, all Mandy felt like doing was crying. She would have done, too, only Dylan was cold, damp and hungry, and she needed to get busy and find fifty pence for the meter.

It was only afterwards that she sat down on the edge

of the solitary single bed, and really began to appreciate her new home for what it was. A pit.

On the wall over the fireplace, water had got in down the chimney, and the paper was hanging off in billowing tatters, like strips of peeling skin. It was cold, damp, disgusting, the stench of mould surpassed only by the all-pervading odour of frying grease.

Mandy opened up her suitcase. There, among the assortment of incongruously bright clothes and cheap jewellery, lay a plastic bag full of cleaning materials. No one was going to do anything for her; now that she was sure of this, in a funny way she felt better. She pulled on the rubber gloves and filled the washing-up bowl with water from the kettle.

'It's just you an' me now, Dylan,' she whispered, kissing each one of his tiny fingers in turn. 'You an' me, an' bugger the rest of the world.'

Chapter 19

'Taz.'

'Hmm?'

With a huge effort of will, Taz dragged herself back to the uninspiring world of the staff canteen. It was eleven thirty on Monday morning, she'd been apart from Jack for all of four hours, and already it felt like forty years.

'You're missing him, aren't you?'

Taz realised with a start that she was staring blankly at a yellowing poster featuring two winsome tots in S&G designer kids'-wear. For some reason, she felt a tremendous urge to confide in Leroy, though she couldn't think why. It was hard to imagine Leroy with baby formula down the back of his perfectly-fitting grey suit, or a gummy infant using his cufflinks for teething practice.

'He'll be having his dinner now,' she sighed, disconsolately stirring her cup of low-cal chicken soup. 'Lamb casserole with pureed parsnips.'

Leroy grimaced in the way that only Leroy could, his eyebrows lifting half an inch towards his hairline then returning to their habitual arch of faint disdain.

'Pureed parsnips? I thought you *liked* him.'

They looked at each other, Leroy perfectly poker-faced Taz's nerve gave out first and she laughed silently, achingly, her stomach straining the waistband of her skirt. Thank God for Lycra.

'What must you think of me?'

'The same as I always have,' replied Leroy enigmatically. 'You know, my sister was the same when she went back to work.'

'You've got a sister?' Somehow, she'd never imagined Leroy as part of a family unit; he was so cool and independent. ???

'Two. One's in insurance, and the other's a ??? on the Stock Exchange. They've both got families, so ... I guess I have some idea what you're going through.' He considered for a moment. 'Does that sound pompous? It wasn't meant to.'

'No. No, it doesn't.'

Intrigued, Taz longed to probe deeper. In point of fact, she had to admit with more than a touch of guilt, she knew hardly anything about him at all. Subconsciously she had thought of him as existing only between the hours of eight and six, a kind of hologram which would disappear if it tried walking out of the doors of Seuss & Goldman.

'Game plan,' she said firmly, taking her notebook out of her pocket. If she didn't get down to doing some serious work, she'd spend all day fretting about Jack and her problems would never get sorted out. 'I daren't leave the food hall to its own devices for more than half an hour, Old George will probably have a coronary over the red snapper.'

'Fire away.' Leroy leaned back in his seat and folded his arms.

'Well, I've got my own ideas, but before I do anything about them I want to hear yours. After all, you've been there a hell of a lot longer than I have.'

'You're sure you *want* to hear what I think? It's not good.'

'Give it to me. Right between the eyes.'

'OK. Mainly I think we're dealing with a people problem. In short, the people who work in the food hall are ... in general ...'

'Crap?'

Leroy managed a quarter-smile.

'I was going to say "underskilled", but "crap" is a good place to start. There's Old George, he's a nice old boy but he's not up to the job any longer.'

'You think we should retire George?' Taz jotted notes on her pad.

'Not necessarily. From what I've seen he's a bit of an old charmer, and the customers like him. I thought we could put him on lighter duties – maybe packing bags, or some kind of customer service job. Then there are the checkout girls, who basically couldn't give a damn about whether they're working at S&G or Kwiksave, and that woman with all the make-up who runs Grape Harvest . . .'

'The wines and spirits concession?'

'Right. Oh, and the two lads of course.'

'Mark and Ian?' Taz added them to her doomsday list; it was getting longer by the second. 'I noticed they didn't seem to be pulling their weight.'

'They're demotivated, poorly trained, and their product knowledge is practically zero. The other day I heard a customer asking Ian for porcini, and he sent him to the sausage counter.'

'So you're saying they have potential, but they're not getting a chance to use it properly?'

'They're not up to much, any of them. The quality of the staff is far lower than anywhere else in S&G, and as for some of the people who work on the concessions . . .'

Taz recalled Delilah sneezing over the bun counter, and had to agree.

'Agreed. But you still think there's room for improvement?'

'Definitely – but not without a lot of support from upstairs. I've been getting somewhere with the younger members of staff in the last month or so, but it's been an uphill struggle, having to do their work, my work and Ken's as well. Which brings us back to the same old question, time and time again.'

Taz looked down at her notebook. In the middle of the page she had drawn a great big pound sign. She drew three circles round it.

'Where's the money coming from?'

'Exactly.' Leroy lowered his voice, checking that no one else in the canteen was listening in. 'The fact is, Taz, as far as I can see nobody at head office gives a damn about the food hall.'

Taz nodded.

'That's the impression I get. As far as they're concerned it can just run itself into the ground until they've got a good excuse to close it down and use it for something else.'

It wasn't difficult to figure out what that something else might be. Everyone in S&G knew that Ted Williams was big buddies with Henry Goldman, and doubtless was bending Henry's ear to create more and bigger opportunities for the wonderful new Ted Williams menswear empire. Hadn't the original Goldman's Stores been based on menswear? Wasn't Ted's department the most profitable in the entire Cheltenham store? Wouldn't it be a good idea to expand it, at the expense of some of the smaller, less profitable departments?

'I'll have to talk to Diana Latchford,' she decided.

'But can she do anything?'

Good question, thought Taz. Rumours abounded there had been blazing rows between Diana and Henry Goldman and in a contest between a mere store manager and S&G's chairman, it wasn't too difficult to work out who was likely to come out on top.

'She'll have to,' replied Taz firmly. 'And I'll be counting on you to back me up.'

Leroy opened his mouth to reply, but at that moment a voice behind Taz made her squirm with displeasure. A cheerful, unctuous, calculatingly insincere voice that made her stomach tighten with rage.

'Taz, hi, how are you? I've been looking for you everywhere.'

Instinctively, Taz flicked shut her notepad. There was nothing on it that would be of any interest to Ted Williams, but she wouldn't even have trusted him with her shopping list.

'Hello Ted.' She greeted him with the frostiest and most professional of smiles. 'How are you? Enjoying menswear?'

'Wonderful, wonderful.' Ted exuded false bonhomie. He

stuck out his hand but Taz pretended not to notice it and he slid it back into his jacket pocket. 'I really wanted to see you, Taz, to wish you luck with your new . . . challenge.'

'Oh really?'

'Definitely. And to thank you for leaving me such a good platform to work from.'

'My pleasure,' replied Taz between clenched teeth. Out of the corner of her eye she could see Leroy's jaw-muscles tensing to steel-hard strings; but somehow he managed not to say anything at all.

'And in any case,' Ted went on, 'I'm sure you'll be much happier in the food hall. It's much more . . . you.'

Ted eased up the sleeve of his crisp new shirt, so recently removed from its packaging that there was a still a knife-sharp crease across the cuff. Underneath, his smooth and hairless wrist was bisected by a very new, very shiny, very hideous Rolex. He glanced at it, but it was fairly obvious he was only flashing it for Taz's benefit.

'Nice watch,' she commented. 'These Far-Eastern copies are so good, aren't they? You can hardly tell them from the real thing.'

Ted's lizard smile faded momentarily, then widened again, uncovering his over-sufficiency of teeth.

'Well, must dash. I'd love to stay chatting to you, of course, but if I don't go now I'll be late for lunch with Henry Goldman. And that'd never do, would it?'

'Scum,' muttered Leroy with admirable restraint as Ted slunk off.

Taz raised her fingers in the shape of a gun, pointed them at Ted's back and pulled the trigger.

'Ted Williams,' she growled, 'You're dead.'

Life in the food hall might be unremittingly horrible, but at least Taz felt she was gradually getting back control of her own life. She got herself and Jack into a routine more quickly than she could have hoped; Adam had such a magical effect on Isobel that she forgot to interfere and acted like a flirtatious adolescent; Bill reserved his comments to restrained monosyllables; and of course, there was Adam himself . . .

271

When Taz panicked that Jack might have a squint, who was it who reassured her and arranged for Jack to see an orthoptist, just in case? Adam of course. And it was Adam – kind, sensible, sensitive Adam – who explained that lots of babies had difficulties adapting to solids, that projectile vomiting was perfectly normal, that just because Jack was a little sleepy and grouchy when Taz got home in the evening, that didn't mean he resented her for leaving him.

In short, Taz was beginning to depend upon Adam. At first, she'd resisted it with all her strength, feeling that it wasn't right to rely on someone who was at worst a lodger, at best no more than a friend. But little by little, she was relaxing her guard, accepting that Adam could and should be trusted, that the experience he'd had with his own children was something valuable.

And yet, no matter how exhausted she might be, Taz still cherished Jack's night feed, dragging herself out of bed to sit with him at her breast in the darkness, listening to the soft, snuffly sounds of his contentment. These were the precious moments when Taz knew that Adam was right. Dee might be Jack's childminder, Isobel his granny, Adam his occasional babysitter; but Taz was, and always would be, his mum.

Whatever else might happen in her life, whatever dreadful turn events might take at Seuss & Goldman, Taz knew that this was the centre of her world; and somehow, that made her able to face anything. Even a late-afternoon summons from Diana Latchford.

'Ah, Tasmin. Not dragging you away from anything too important, I hope? I asked you to come and see me because I value your advice.'

'Oh?'

Taz felt vaguely flattered, but she wasn't under any illusions. Right now, life at S&G was about survival, the law of the jungle, and scavenging whatever you could get for yourself.

'There's no need to look so surprised, Tasmin, you know you're one of the most skilful and experienced managers at S&G. That's why I've every confidence in your ability to turn the food hall round. But that's not why I've asked you here – I wanted to talk to you about menswear.'

Taz did her best not to look pissed-off, but she knew there was an edge in her voice as she replied, 'I hardly think it's my place to comment . . . menswear's not my province any more, is it? You made that very clear.'

'You're a professional, Tasmin. I think you have the objectivity not to take things personally – or at least, I hope you have. What I want is your opinion on this.' Diana opened her desk drawer, took out a large sketch pad and pushed it across the desktop. 'Take a look.'

Taz flipped through the drawings. There were ten of them in all, every one a view of the menswear department, seen from a different angle, proposing a different theme. Not that it was easy to recognise as menswear, mind you; this was menswear as it might be if some power-crazed shop-fitter was given his head.

'What exactly . . .?'

'We're discussing designs for a complete refit of menswear. The one on page two is the current front-runner.'

Taz flicked back to the second drawing. A twenty-foot-high fibreglass swordfish was leaping out of the main sales floor, right at the top of the listed 1920s' escalator, snapping its jaws at the ceiling.

'You're not serious?'

'It's not my idea. But there are certain people at head office . . .'

'Henry Goldman, for instance?'

'I can't name names, Tasmin, you know that.' But the look on Diana's face spoke for itself. 'Let's just say there are people with a lot of influence, who are keen to redevelop and expand menswear into . . .'

Taz eyed the blue swordfish, and the giant mock-up of a tea-clipper filling one side of the drawing.

'Into a Ted Williams theme park? Look, can I say what I really think?'

'I wouldn't have asked you here if I didn't want you to speak your mind.'

'I think this is hideous. It destroys the whole character of the department – it's supposed to be listed, for God's sake! And where's sports and leisurewear on this drawing?'

'The idea is to incorporate it into the new, expanded menswear department.'

'Meaning Cara loses her job and Ted's empire gets a bit bigger? Oh Mrs Latchford, you can't let them do this! I mean, apart from anything else, how much would it cost?'

Diana sank down onto her chair, pushing back her hair with a weary hand.

'Off the record, more than this store can realistically afford. This kind of thing is a drain on resources, it makes no verifiable commercial sense and it's taking money which could be more profitably spent on bringing other departments up to standard.'

'Tell me about it,' muttered Taz, dropping the sketch pad onto the desk with a snort of disgust. Diana's eyes narrowed. She leaned her elbows on the desk top, rested her chin on her hands.

'No, Tasmin. You tell me about it. Something is obviously bugging you.'

This was the moment Taz had been waiting for; her big chance to make her sales pitch.

'If that's what you want.' She took a deep breath. 'The food hall is dying on its feet. I know it, you know it, everybody knows it – so why is head office allowing it to happen?'

The question hung in the air, but no answer was forthcoming. Diana pursed her smoothly-outlined lips.

'Tell me what's wrong with the food hall. *Exactly* what's wrong. In detail.'

'OK.' Taz martialled the jumble of thoughts into some kind of order. 'As I see it, there are three main problems. One, our suppliers. They're not getting paid for months, and consequently nobody wants to supply us with fresh goods. In fact, the only way we can be sure of getting them is to sign long-term contracts with mediocre firms who pocket the money and then run a substandard concession.

'Two, overstocking. Have you seen the state of the

stockroom lately? There are cases of stuff in there that have been there for the last ten years, for God's sake! And they'll be there another ten if we don't do something about it.

'Three, staff.' She brought down her fist on the desktop, making the silver lids jiggle on the inkwells. 'They're apathetic, unambitious, slovenly, complacent, developmentally subnormal . . .'

'And on the down-side?' enquired Diana wryly.

Taz looked at Diana and wondered if she was being laughed at.

'I'm serious! You said you wanted it straight, and that's how I'm giving it to you.'

'I'm sorry, Tasmin, I'm not taking a rise out of you. It's just your energy – whenever you work yourself into a frenzy about something I remember how much everything *matters* when you're twenty-six.'

'When you're twenty-six, single and have a baby son to provide for, they matter even more,' replied Taz pointedly. Her pulse was racing, she felt angry as hell, though she wasn't sure exactly who she was angry with.

Diana nodded.

'Fair point. So – now you've told me what's wrong, tell me what you want to do about it. And since this is off the record, you needn't pull any punches.'

'First, we have to ditch our current suppliers as soon as possible. I'm thinking in particular of fish, meat, fruit and veg and confectionery. Maybe wines and spirits too. We need to update our accounting procedures, and play on our reputation for quality to bring in new, varied, reliable suppliers.

'Next, there must be tens of thousands of pounds worth of old stock which we're never going to sell at full price. We may be able to discount some of it, but most of it will have to be written off.

'And last but not least, staff. We have to get rid of the dead wood, bring in new blood, and train existing staff members to S&G quality standards. Luckily most of the worst offenders work for the concessionaires, so they would go in time . . . but I'm still talking about getting rid of a substantial proportion of our current workforce, one way or another.'

She held her breath, waiting for Diana's verdict. It didn't come immediately. Diana tapped the end of her fountain pen on the desk, marking out a rhythmic beat. Outside the window, in a different world, two pigeons were necking and cooing on the sunny balcony rail.

Finally Taz could take it no longer.

'Well? What do you think?'

'I think you should write me a report. A detailed one.'

Taz felt her heart sink to her boots. After all that, she was being fobbed off like some junior sales assistant with a 'brilliant' idea that had been tried twenty times before.

'A report. That's that, is it? I write a report, you file it and forget about it?'

'I didn't say that.' Diana got up from her seat. 'What I said was, write me a report for the board – and make it a good one. It's bound to take you a while to put it together. But in the meantime, don't let it stop you taking . . . appropriate steps.'

Wednesday evenings with Mandy and a box of chocolates had somehow given way to Thursday evenings with Chloë and a fresh cream gateau.

For once, as she drove across Cheltenham to Chloë's house, Taz felt almost inclined to curse Adam Rolfe. If it hadn't been for his serene willingness to babysit Jack, she'd have had an excuse not to pay yet another visit to Chloë. A thought which instantly made her feel ashamed of herself, partly for looking a gift-horse in the mouth and partly for resenting Chloë when – finally, after all this time – she really felt as if they were getting somewhere.

It was a mint-chocolate torte this evening, death to the waistline and served with double cream for good measure. Not that Chloë was eating much herself; she seemed more than content to sit and watch Taz down a guilt-laden second helping, her round, attentive eyes following every movement of the silver cake fork as it repeated its journey to Taz's mouth.

'Tell me what you did today,' she urged, sitting forward

on her chair with her hands wrapped daintily round her slender knees. You could see every vein in those hands, thought Taz; like the veins in white marble, or delicately-painted blue lines on translucent wax.

'Nothing special. I hired a new girl for the bacon counter. Oh, and we had a bit of a problem with a difficult customer . . .'

'But you sorted it out?' Chloë was hanging on her every word, childlike and breathless with anticipation.

'In the end, yes.' Not that it had been easy, mused Taz. People who had been accidentally doused with red wine seldom took it very well.

'You're so clever. And you have a wonderful life, I wish I was clever, then I could be like you . . .'

The thought that she might be living a wonderfully glamorous life hadn't really occurred to Taz before. There was nothing very glamorous about Old George and his wet fish counter. She decided it was time to change the subject.

'This is great cake, did you make it?'

'It's nothing really, in fact it's a bit heavy, don't you think? I'm so clumsy aren't I?' Chloë blushed.

'You're not clumsy at all! And I bet Clive doesn't think so either.'

This was Taz's cue to launch into her usual character-building spiel about 'taking charge of your life' and 'believing in yourself and what you want from your future'. At times she felt more like a lecturer on an assert-iveness course than a friend, but it was nice to feel as if Chloë was beginning to take notice. Nice, too, to have such a loyal, attentive and uncritical audience, though occasionally Taz found Chloë's hero-worship a little oppressive. It was almost as if Minky had learned to talk and serve cake.

'I really do appreciate everything you've done for me,' said Chloë, sliding Taz's empty plate underneath her almost full one and laying the two cake forks exactly parallel across it.

'I haven't done anything,' protested Taz.

'Oh but you have. You're sure you've had enough to eat?'

'Absolutely. Any more and I'll burst.'

Chloë busied herself topping up the teacups.

'You see, you've really made me think about my life. It's like you said, I have to take control and decide what I want . . . plan for the future. Think about what I want for me and Clive.'

'That's good,' smiled Taz, certain now that her words had struck a chord. Maybe, if she was careful, she could even get her to talk about Ayesha.

'I did what you said. I sat down and made a list of what I want, and it really helped. In fact,' she announced proudly, raising her eyes to meet Taz's, 'I've actually come to a decision. And I couldn't have done it without your help.'

'I'm so glad,' said Taz. 'What is it?'

'It's about the baby. I've had enough of it.'

Taz felt a cold tide of horror swamp her.

'Steady on, Chloë . . . you . . .?'

'I've given Clive an ultimatum, Taz. Me or the baby. One of us has to go.'

Chapter 20

The following Monday morning, just before the flash meeting, Taz drew Leroy into the departmental office and shut the door. He looked at her quizzically.

'Is something wrong?'

'I've been looking in the stockroom,' Taz announced. 'And you're right, we *aren't* as overstocked as we're supposed to be.'

'I was hoping I'd got it wrong,' he sighed. 'I should've noticed earlier . . .'

Taz stopped him before he got into full self-immolation mode. If Leroy had a fault, it was that he tended to blame himself for everything that went wrong in the department, whether it was his fault or not.

'Maybe, maybe not,' she said. 'But the fact is, when I went to check over the crates of stock we're planning to write off, I found half of them were empty. And what's even more interesting . . .'

She unlocked her filing cabinet and took out a small tin of red caviare.

'I found this. Or to be precise, three boxes full of top-grade luxury goods, unlabelled and tucked away at the back of a cupboard where nobody would think of looking for them. Caviare, Stilton with port wine, tinned whisky cake . . .'

Leroy picked up the tin, turned it over in his hand and replaced it on the desk. He whistled softly.

'It's a scam,' he said, looking up. 'It has to be.'

'Or the remains of one,' nodded Taz. 'The question is, how long has it been going on, and who's behind it?'

'You don't think . . .' Leroy's composure slipped for the very briefest of moments. 'You don't think it's me, do you?'

If she had doubted his innocence for a second, those doubts would have evaporated instantly at the injured expression written all over Leroy's face.

'No, I don't. For one thing, if you were going to rip off S&G you'd do it with a bit more style. For another, I've a feeling this is something that's been going on for ages – the food hall's been on the skids for as long as I can remember.'

'I should have realised . . . this is all down to me, isn't it?'

'Dry up, Leroy. What's done is done and all that matters right now is putting a stop to it.'

'So what do we do about it? How do we find out who's responsible? Should we refer it to Diana Latchford and let her deal with it?'

Leroy, almost back to his normal self now, was adjusting the knot on his silk tie. No one but Leroy would have worn a handpainted tie to the food hall, where it was bound to end up like a mottled dishrag by the end of the day, but even in the deep degradation of wet fish and condiments, Leroy McIntosh had a shred of dignity to uphold.

'Leave this to me, Leroy.' Taz tossed the tin of caviare back into the filing cabinet and locked it away. 'I think I've come up with a way of smoking them out.'

Flash meetings in the food hall weren't like flash meetings in menswear. For a start, they had to begin half an hour early because the tills opened for business at eight forty-five. Besides which, Taz had come to regard it as an achievement if she could get everybody to turn up on time and look as if they were listening.

But today, she had promised herself, they would be hanging on her every word.

'Right.' Taz perched herself on the wines and spirits sales counter, to give herself a few inches of extra height. Spotty Ian was picking his blackheads, Old George was playing with his false teeth and Delilah was examining the contents of her handkerchief. It was enough to make you weep on this fine August morning. Unless of course you were a salmonella bug. 'I hope you're all listening. *Carefully*. Because time is short, and we're here to sell people food, not pick our spots and stare into space.'

Somebody at the back muttered, and Spotty Ian suddenly thrust his hands into his trouser pockets, but so far she'd avoided open mutiny. Things were going better than she'd expected.

'First of all, food hygiene regulations.' Moans and groans ran around the huddle of staff.

'But we've all bin on a course,' sniffed Mo, tossing her non-regulation spiral perm. 'I'm certified,' she added proudly.

Ian tittered, Delilah blew her nose. Taz suppressed a smile.

'Then you'll know how vital it is to follow the regulations properly whenever you're in contact with food. Do you want to poison somebody? Do you want to get us closed down by the environmental health people?' No answer came, but there was a muted shuffling of feet and staring at the floor. 'Well?'

'No,' came the doubtful and almost inaudible response.

'I'm glad to hear it.' She held up a sheaf of photocopied pages. 'I want everyone to take one of these, read it, commit every word to memory, and *act on it*.' Her eyes moved across the sea of slouching figures. 'That means you as well, Mark, I don't want to see that shirt again until you've washed it.'

'But I have!'

'Then get a new shirt, do you think customers like seeing egg-stains down the front of it? And Delilah, if I see you wipe your nose on your apron one more time you'll be docked half a day's pay.' Delilah's jaw squared into an angry mask of protest, but Taz wasn't about to let her get a word in edgeways. 'And while we're here, a word or two about attitude.'

People were looking in a dozen different directions, doing anything to avoid her gaze, but Taz knew they were listening; praying that they wouldn't be singled out for special humiliation.

'There have been customer complaints about the level of service in this department, and it's not good enough. I won't tolerate rudeness, inefficiency, bad product knowledge, unhelpfulness ... in fact I won't tolerate anything less than *the best*. In-store NVQ training programmes are available, and I expect you to make use of them. Now, Mr McIntosh will take us through last week's sales figures.'

She nodded to Leroy, and he stood up, picking up his clipboard from the counter.

'Right. The overall picture is a gradual decline, down three per cent on the same week last year. Last week sales of fruit and veg were minus five, confectionery minus one, and static on canned goods, fish and meat. In other words,' he put down the clipboard. 'Not good, and getting worse.'

'What Mr McIntosh is saying,' explained Taz slowly, 'is that this department is under-performing in every section. Unless we do something about that – and I mean we, I don't intend doing this all on my own – pretty soon there may not be a food hall. And how ever much you may hate your job, it pays your rent.'

'I don't see what we can do about it,' whined Gloria, her checkout overall gaping open at the bust to reveal something sparkly and purple underneath. 'I wouldn't be seen dead shoppin' in this place.'

'Yeah,' nodded Mo, eager now to put the knife in. 'It's a dump.'

Heads nodded in assent. Taz secretly agreed with the consensus of opinion, but she wasn't here to concede defeat. She was here to kick ass.

'OK, I know there are problems, and I'm working to solve them. I know sometimes it feels like you're trying to sell snowboots in the Sahara. But that doesn't mean giving in – it means trying harder. Which is why,' she announced, 'I've decided to raise the monthly sales targets by five per cent.'

This revelation was greeted with complete amazement.

If they hadn't been listening properly before, they sure were now.

'*Raise* them? Don't you mean lower them?'

'You heard me right first time,' Taz confirmed.

'But . . .' spluttered Old George. 'Nobody ever makes the sales target, not in the food hall!'

'Exactly. So I'm also raising bonuses – by fifty per cent. As an incentive.'

'Fifty per cent!' Even Mo was impressed by this, her mind swiftly calculating the precise implications of a fifty per cent larger bonus. 'Fuckin' Ada.'

'Not much use though, is it?' pointed out Gloria. 'Not if you never get it.'

'True. But if we all work a bit harder, sell more, put ourselves out to be more helpful to the customers, then we will earn it, won't we? And I know I could do with the extra cash, couldn't you?'

'Look,' cut in Leroy. 'If everyone who came into the food hall bought something, even if it was just a loaf of bread, we'd soon be meeting our targets. Think about it, eh?'

'Can we go now?' piped up Ian. 'I've got a delivery of carrots waiting in goods inward.'

'In a minute. Just one more thing.' Taz treated them all to a dazzling smile. 'Harvest hampers.'

'What?' Faces turned from grumpiness to bafflement. 'What hampers? We only do hampers at Christmas.'

'Ah, but these are hampers with a difference. This year, S&G will be donating free harvest hampers for the needy to local churches and charities. We'll be making them up using the overstocks of tinned and packaged food in the stockroom. Wonderful idea, isn't it?'

She didn't bother waiting for an enthusiastic reply. This was Monday, everybody hated her on principle, and there was at least one person present who had something to hide.

'So what I'm asking for are volunteers to do the packing. When is it exactly, Leroy?'

'A week on Sunday. It should only take a couple of hours.'

'Sunday? What? No way!' Moans and groans ran around the assembled throng.

'I knew you'd be right behind the idea. Sign up on the list in the office. Oh – and if I don't get any volunteers, I may have to make it compulsory.'

'You can't do that!' protested Gloria. 'It's not in my contract.'

'Don't worry Gloria,' smiled Taz. 'I'll find a way round it.'

On the way up to administration for the afternoon management meeting, Taz made a point of seeking out Patros Nikephoros.

She found him with one of his juniors in the attic studios, fussing over a bolt of shop-soiled white tulle and some tatty silk roses.

'I can't use this rubbish, Tracey, you'll have to take it back to haberdashery.'

Taz hovered on the threshold, then knocked tentatively on the wall.

'Sorry to bother you Patros . . . is this a bad time?'

Patros swivelled round on his axis. In his red jumper and black ski-pants, topped off by slicked-back black hair and a pencil moustache, he looked like a tin soldier.

'What? Oh, it's you. Can't you come back later?'

'Well, it's about a display.' Taz tried her best to look fluffy and appealing, recalling that this was how Binnie had always managed to twist Patros round her little finger.

'What's wrong, something need rearranging? Tracey'll deal with it.'

'Actually I need to ask you a favour.' Taz had never fluttered her eyelashes in her life, but it was never too late to learn. 'I was hoping you might be able to help me out, it's something rather special you see . . .'

'Special?' Patros's ears pricked up. Taz knew she had spoken the magic word. 'What do you mean, special?'

'You know I'm in charge of the food hall now?'

'Poor child, no one deserves that.' Patros shuddered. 'Not even people who wear French navy,' he added archly with a glance at Taz's practical but very uninteresting suit.

'The thing is, you've probably heard that we're not doing very well. It doesn't help that we've hardly got any display window-space, and half the people who come into S&G don't even notice the entrance to the food hall. What we need is a radical facelift.'

'How radical?' asked Patros doubtfully.

'As radical as you can get without spending any money, basically.'

Patros snipped temperamentally at a length of white net.

'Always on the cheap . . . never any money to spend on doing anything properly . . . what do they think I am?'

'They think you're a star,' Taz gushed. 'And so do I. They only ask the impossible of you because they're so sure you can do it.'

'Well . . .' Patros paused in mid-snip. 'I couldn't start on it until next week. And I can't work miracles, there's not much *anybody* could do with that ghastly dark hole.'

'Next week would be fine; as long as it's ready for the pre-Christmas rush. Oh please, Patros, I don't know what I'm going to do if you can't help me out.'

Her girlish angst must have paid dividends, because Patros rewarded her with a peremptory nod and what passed for a smile.

'Well, all right. I'll see what I can do. But I'm not promising anything.'

He almost fell over with astonishment when Taz planted a kiss of gratitude on his cheek.

It was Wednesday, Taz's afternoon off. She knew she ought to go and see how Chloë was, but she just couldn't face her, not after what she'd said last time. Not after the tears and recriminations, and Clive's desperate pleas to Taz to 'do something'.

Do what? It wasn't that she didn't care, but what could she do, other than leave Chloë and Clive to sort out their lives and hope that they came to the right conclusion?

In any case, there was someone else on her mind today. Mandy. It had been weeks since she'd seen her, she'd tried ringing but every time she did, whoever answered slammed the phone down on her. But she couldn't let this go on, she had to explain to Mandy that she was sorry, that the last thing she'd wanted to do was hurt her.

There was nothing else for it. Taz would have to go to the Hollybush Estate, find Mandy and have a heart-to-heart.

Oh God. The creeping chill of horror started at her toes and worked its way right up to the top of Taz's head. The estate looked worse, much much worse, in daylight; and even in the dark it had looked like a bombsite.

The deeper she drove into the estate, the more she felt like a war correspondent, dodging the landmines and the gun-emplacements that might be hidden on every corner. A gang of children were hanging around the wire-meshed window of a newsagent's shop, furtively giggling over something in a brown paper bag. How old were they – eight, nine? Why weren't they at school? Silly question.

She drove past the ends of bleak streets with laughably florid names – Honeysuckle Walk, Primrose Way, Crocus Avenue – and the rough triangle of grass where stray dogs sniffed among discarded Coke cans, chip wrappers and worse. Taz remembered what Mandy had said, about grazing sheep on it. They'd probably laugh about it together, when they'd talked things through and made it up.

There it was: Bluebell House, the tallest of the three tower blocks, looming malevolently over the estate. Taz felt her stomach contract with nameless dread. Absolutely the very last thing she ever wanted to do was walk through that graffiti-scrawled lobby.

She got out, locking the car under the eye of three grinning youths who gestured obscenely and whistled at her knees. She knew she should have worn a longer skirt.

'Want a bit, darlin'?'

'Course she does, she's gaggin' for a bit of rough.'

'Show us yer knickers then.'

She walked past in silent fury, her face burning, forcing her way between them as they closed ranks and tried to rub themselves against her.

The entrance to Bluebell House was dank, dismal,

covered with graffiti – but mercifully empty. It must be
her lucky day. Even the lift worked, though its grey steel
cage stank of Harpic where some well-meaning janitor
had tried to mask the smell of stale pee. Poor Mandy,
thought Taz; poor, poor Mandy, and poor Dylan too: how
could they bear to live here? Another stupid question.
Nobody lived in a place like this if they could live somewhere else.

As the lift doors squeaked shrilly open, revealing a long
landing, it occurred to Taz that she could just head back
down the ground floor, turn tail and drive to Chloë's for
cake and middle-class woe. But something directed her
feet onto the landing, her stomach turning over as she
heard the lift doors scythe shut behind her. Well, this
was it.

She counted the numbers on the doors! Some of the
doors had dents in them, some were singed round the
edges, one or two had been covered with thick metal
shutters. She rounded the corner.

The sound of children's laughter stopped her in her
tracks. Two boys, aged perhaps eleven or twelve, were
spray-painting something across the door of number 382.
Mandy's door. Even from five doors away, it wasn't difficult to read what the wet red letters spelled out: SLAG.

The boys turned and caught sight of Taz at exactly the
same moment as the door sprang inwards.

'C'mon Gaz, leg it!'

A great red fist caught the side of Gaz's head, but the
boys were already off, speeding down the landing towards
the stairs, Gaz throwing a stone through the Robsons'
front window as a parting shot.

'Fat cow, your Mandy's a dirty slag!'

'You little bastards, wait till I fuckin' get my 'ands on
you Gary Middleton . . .'

The woman was immense, a great red-faced ball of
muscle with mud-brown, grey-streaked hair pinned back
from her square-jowled face with a single metal grip. Taz
approached with a mixture of horror, fear and fascination.

'I . . . Mrs Robson?'

The woman's beady black eyes darted suspiciously in

287

Taz's direction, taking in the smart skirt, the clean blouse, the polished shoes. The only emotion those eyes held was pure hatred.

'Did you see them do that? Did you?' The face was two inches from Taz's, and she could feel herself starting to shake.

'Well . . . no, sort of . . . I'm sorry.'

'Fuckin' do-gooders, you're all the bleedin' same aren't you? See all, hear all, do nothin'. Fuckin' social workers.'

'I'm not . . .' protested Taz, but there was no halting the flood of bile.

'Lookin' for 'er are you? Mandy? Well she's not here, right? We got rid of the dirty little tart, slung 'er out weeks ago. So you can just fuck off an' leave us alone. You an' all the rest.'

The door slammed in Taz's face just as she was opening her mouth to ask where Mandy had gone. She tried knocking, ringing, shouting, but there was no response from inside the flat. Just the distant sound of children's mocking laughter.

And, she could have sworn, the ominous screech of a key being dragged along the side of a car.

'Taz! Taz, what on earth is the matter? Is it Jack? He's not ill is he?'

Adam dropped his briefcase on the living-room floor and ran across to Taz, who was slumped on the sofa, Jack tightly cradled in her arms and tears streaming silently down her face.

She looked up at his shocked expression, barely able to focus through tear-blurred eyes. Her head moved mechanically from side to side.

'It's . . . nothing. Nothing. I'm fine.'

'You don't look fine to me. Look, give Jack to me, you're almost squashing the life out of him.'

Reluctantly Taz released her grip on Jack, still blissfully asleep and his sleepsuit only a little dampened by his mother's tears, and watched Adam carry him gently across to his cot.

'There, little chap. Just you keep on snoozing, OK?

288

Your mum and I have got things to sort out. Now Taz.'
He sat down on the sofa and took her hand, the fingers
wound round a sodden tissue. 'What's this all about?'

'It's ... M-m-mandy. Sh-sh-e's gone.'

'Gone? Where?' Adam looked at her, puzzled. He
reached into his pocket, took out a big hanky and
unfolded it. 'Here, have a good blow and start again.'

'M-mandy. Her Mum and Dad have thrown her out,
her and Dylan. They won't tell me where she's gone,
Adam – oh Adam, I'm so worried ...'

Very slowly and unthreateningly, Adam slid an arm
round Taz's shoulders, calming the convulsive sobs which
were shaking her whole body.

'Steady on, don't upset yourself. She'll be OK, you
know she will, you said yourself she's a survivor.'

'I was wrong, she can't look after herself, she's got
nowhere to go – and there's the baby. Oh Adam, what
am I going to do?'

'Hush. Hush, it'll be all right, we'll work something out.'

The warmth and strength of Adam's arm about her
shoulders was so comforting that Taz snuggled into the
angle of his chest, feeling the beat of his heart through
his shirt. Gently he began to stroke her hair with long,
slow, smooth caresses.

'It'll be all right, I promise. Everything will be all right.'

Taz raised her face to his. He was smiling at her; his
whole face smiling, his eyes steady and warm and sincere.

'Oh Taz. Taz, don't be sad, I can't bear it.'

Her lips moved to meet his, yearning for the taste and
feel of his mouth on hers, the warm crush of his strong
embrace.

It was even better than she'd expected. Her head was
in a whirl, her body taking control and leaving her senses
panting in its wake. All she could do was abandon herself
to the sheer physical and emotional pleasure of wanting
and being wanted. It had been so long that she had almost
forgotten what it felt like.

Right at the moment when she really thought she was
beginning to get the hang of it, the telephone rang and
naturally, Jack woke up and started crying.

'I'll see to him,' said Adam, as they slid smoothly and lingerly apart.

'You don't mind?'

'Of course I don't mind.' He kissed her on the forehead.

Adam gathered up Jack and carted him off to his changing mat in the bathroom. Taz took a couple of moments to compose herself before picking up the phone.

'Hello?'

'Taz, thank goodness, look it's Binnie here . . .'

'Binnie!' Taz curled her legs under her on the sofa, preparing herself for a long and cosy chat. 'I haven't heard from you in ages, how are you? How's Amy? How's Jim's job . . .?'

'Oh Taz, I'd love to talk but I'm in a terrible rush.' Odd, thought Taz. It wasn't like Binnie to turn down the chance of a long chat.

'Is everything OK?'

'OK? Fine, it's fine. I just wanted to check that you're coming up for Amy's first birthday party on the thirtieth – you *are* coming, aren't you?'

'Yes, yes I've booked that weekend as annual leave.'

'Good, just checking. Look, got to go, ring you soon, 'bye.'

Taz was still staring in puzzlement at the receiver when Adam reappeared with Jack on his hip.

'Anything important?'

'No. No, it was just Binnie, that's all.' She tried to look Adam in the face, but bottled out at the last moment and looked away, her face hot with embarrassment. 'Jack's . . . all right, is he?'

'Fine. He wasn't wet at all, he was just fooling, weren't you Jackie-boy?'

If it was any consolation, Adam seemed to be every bit as embarrassed as she was.

'I'll put the kettle on, shall I?'

'Er . . . yeah. Good idea.'

It was a relief to get into the kitchen and busy herself with mundane tasks, while on the other side of the wall she could hear Adam neurotically rearranging all the china cats on the mantelpiece. Minky came into the kitchen and wound herself around Taz's legs, whining for attention, but Taz's mind was elsewhere. And she knew that Adam's mind was there too.

Something significant had just happened between them, that much was obvious. The question was, what – if anything – were they going to do next?

Chapter 21

As if getting carried away with Adam wasn't enough to worry about, there was the question of what had happened to Mandy; not forgetting the food hall, looming large and horrible over every aspect of Taz's life.

And then, just to make things really complicated, there was Chloë.

It wasn't as if Chloë was even a close friend; they had hardly anything in common, despite what Clive might say. And if it hadn't been for Clive's tearful pleading, she definitely wouldn't have volunteered to get any more involved.

'Please Taz.' She couldn't get his distraught face out of her mind. 'You're the only one who can help.'

'But Clive,' she'd protested, 'I don't know anything . . . I don't even know Chloë that well. She needs help, proper help, not me.'

His fingers grasped the sleeve of her blouse with a drowning man's last, convulsive strength. Taz remembered thinking that that honest, open, friendly face wasn't made for grief; it was made for sincere smiles and affable good humour.

Baby Ayesha sucked her thumb and gazed wonderingly into that very same face, the face of the man she would soon learn to call 'Daddy'. It almost broke Taz's heart to see the love in Clive's eyes, the way he cherished the baby with the caramel skin and chocolate-drop eyes. The baby who had cost him his wife, and whose existence he ought – at the very least – to resent bitterly. Whatever the reason for it, Taz was powerless in the face of such unquestioning devotion.

'I really don't see what I can do,' she ventured lamely.

'You can talk to her, persuade her to come back to me. I've tried again and again, but her mother won't let me anywhere near Chloë. She's got this hold over her . . .'

'She can't be that bad,' began Taz. But then again, maybe she could. 'Look, what about Chloë's doctor . . . or a priest? Relate counsellors can be really helpful, I'm sure Adam could get you a number to ring.'

But Clive's face had set in emphatic denial.

'If anyone can make her see sense, you can.'

Taz wished she could be so sure. Hadn't Chloë made it more than plain that she had no intention of coming back to Clive, unless he agreed to put Ayesha up for adoption? And Hell would freeze over before Clive ever agreed to do that; he was Chloë's husband, his name was on Ayesha's birth certificate, he adored her and as far as he was concerned he was her father. Fathers didn't give their daughters away to total strangers.

Stalemate.

'She might not want to come back, Clive,' said Taz, preparing him for the worst as gently as she could.

'I know.' Clive hugged Ayesha. She giggled and blew raspberries in his face. 'I love her, Taz.' She noticed the worry-lines, deepening around his eyes. 'I love them both. Make her come home.'

Taz made no promises; sooner or later she was bound to fail and then Clive would be even more heartbroken than he already was.

She had to give up a precious Sunday morning with Jack to drive to the other side of Cheltenham. It was a dank, misty September morning, cold enough for a jumper and miserable enough to set your nose running and make you long for spring.

Bracken House was quite a culture shock. Chloë's nice Georgian villa had been impressive enough, but this place was big enough to have its own postcode. Chloë was in a short-sleeved blouse and skirt, barelegged and throwing sticks for two lolloping red setters. She came bounding across the lawn, her blonde hair escaping from an untidy ponytail. Taz had to remind herself that this bony school-girl with the scrubbed face was actually seven years older than she was.

'Taz, Taz, it's been ages.' She called towards the open kitchen door. 'Mummy, it's Taz, isn't that lovely?'

Gwen Barstowe emerged from the kitchen in full make-up, a broderie anglaise apron arranged over her Country Casuals two-piece. She didn't look like the sort of person who would cook anything less elaborate than pan-fried guinea-fowl with truffles. And then, only under protest. Her nails were mathematically perfect, complementing the huge and lustrous diamond cluster of her engagement ring,

'Tasmin, how nice. Chloë has told me so much about you.' Gwen extended a rather limp handshake; her fingers felt cold and dry. 'You'll take a cup of coffee with us?'

'Thank you, that'd be lovely.'

Taz trailed behind Gwen and Chloë, through the entire length of an immense Shaker-style kitchen hung with copper pans and herbs that were only there for show, and into an antiseptically cosy parlour. This was decorated with stencils, and a malevolent white Persian cat which looked as though it was stapled to its cushion and wouldn't have dared moult on the upholstery.

'I . . . can't stay long,' hazarded Taz, preparing an escape route even before she'd balanced herself on the astonish-ingly uncomfortable sofa. 'I have to go into work this afternoon, we're packing hampers for the old folk.'

This seemed to go down well with Gwen Barstowe, who looked like the sort of woman who might fill her days with charitable works.

'You're at Seuss & Goldman, I understand.'

'That's right. In the Food Hall.'

'Ah.' Gwen gazed thoughtfully into her black coffee. An undisturbed arrangement of six ratafia biscuits sat, ridiculously, in the middle of the painted coffee-table. Taz stifled a terrible urge to disturb their maddening symmetry by eating one. 'They used to be rather good, but not any more. The staff are quite slovenly, don't you think?'

Taz refrained from saying exactly what she did think. She smiled non-committally.

'What Seuss & Goldman needs,' Gwen went on, 'is more nice young ladies like Chloë. She'd be such a credit to you, wouldn't you dear? And she has such a wealth of experience.'

'Mummy, don't!' Her cheeks dimpled with embarrassment. 'I've only worked part-time in a china shop . . .'

'A very *exclusive* china shop, dear, you mustn't run yourself down. And now you're independent again, you'll need to find ways of occupying your time.'

Taz took this as her cue.

'I . . . called on Clive yesterday.'

Chloë flinched. Gwen's fingers tightened round the handle of her coffee-cup.

'Oh,' said Chloë, very quietly.

'He's missing you, you know. He keeps asking when you're going to come home.'

This was just too much for Mrs Barstowe, who promptly thrust the plate of ratafias under Taz's nose.

'Biscuit, Tasmin? I brought them back from Tuscany. Did Chloë tell you we have a villa in Tuscany?'

'Thank you.' Taz took a biscuit and balanced it on her saucer, completely ignoring Gwen. If she could have contrived some way to get rid of her for five minutes, she was almost certain she could begin to get through to Chloë, who was twitching and quivering under her gaze like a roe-deer caught in car headlights. 'He really does miss you, Chloë.' She paused, then played her ace. 'And so does Ayesha.'

Chloë turned paler than ever, leaving red dots in the centre of hollow, white cheeks.

'No,' she whispered.

'Yes, Chloë. Ayesha misses you, she loves Clive but she needs her mum.'

'This is Clive's doing, isn't it?' snapped Gwen, slamming the plate of biscuits down on the table. 'Why won't he just leave my daughter alone, hasn't she suffered enough?'

'Mrs Barstowe,' said Taz, 'Chloë's his wife, he cares about her.'

'If her cared about her,' replied Gwen with energy, 'he would carry out her wishes, not flaunt the one mistake she has ever made, and torture her with it!'

Chloë let out a curious sound, a kind of dry sob. When Taz looked at her her eyes were very wide but tearless, staring unblinkingly into space as though seeing something that no one else could see. Something terrible.

Taz tried appealing to reason.

'Mrs Barstowe, please. Ayesha is Chloë's daughter – your granddaughter. Surely you wouldn't want to lose her?'

'Lose her!' Gwen Barstowe gaped at Taz as though she were quite insane. 'Miss Norton, not only is this . . . child . . . illegitimate, the result of some beast taking advantage of my poor daughter, but she is also . . .' She halted in mid-spate and swallowed. 'Not like us.'

'You mean she's black?'

So that was it. Gwen Barstowe couldn't even bring herself to speak the word, it was so hateful to her. Taz felt nausea tightening her stomach, and her hand shook as she replaced her cup on her saucer. Suddenly Gwen's West Indian Blend tasted intolerably bitter. She searched for words that would express how she felt without resorting to abuse.

'But Clive has accepted her as his own, his family have welcomed Ayesha as their first granddaughter – they love her, Mrs Barstowe!'

'What they choose to do is none of my concern. And what Chloë chooses to do is none of your business.'

'If she makes that choice freely.' Taz looked towards Chloë for some telltale sign, but Chloë was plucking fretfully at a stray strand of hair.

'Chloë has made her choice, and she has my full support.' I bet she has, thought Taz. A black granddaughter would really put the cat among the pigeons down at the tennis club. 'And frankly, Miss Norton,' went on Chloë's mother, 'since you yourself are an unmarried mother, I scarcely think you are in a position to lecture me on morality!'

Taz felt her right hand clench into a fist. She would

dearly have loved to smash it straight into the middle of Mrs Barstowe's pious face, but she contented herself with standing and picking up her handbag.

'I think I'd better go,' she said coldly.

'Yes. I'm sure you have plenty to do.' Gwen Barstowe's frigid smile reflected the twin bluish ice cubes of her eyes. 'I'll show you to the door.'

'Don't bother.' Taz threw Chloë a final, despairing glance, but she was miles away, lost in a world of her own. 'I can find my own way out.'

The atmosphere in the food hall stockroom was only slightly warmer than the atmosphere in the parlour at Bracken House.

'Do you think this'll work?' wondered Leroy, rolling up the sleeves of a 'casual' shirt which anyone else could have worn to a wedding. 'They *all* look guilty to me.'

Taz left off unpacking bottled grenadines and surveyed the scene: a dozen or more dejected stooping figures, blowing the dust off packets and jars before stuffing them into a production line of cardboard boxes. They looked like fugitives from a chain-gang, all except Old George, who was regaling everyone with endless anecdotes about the 'good old days' at S&G.

'Who knows? But I have a hunch. Whoever's behind this, they're sure to want to deflect suspicion from themselves.'

Leroy stretched up to the top shelf and started reaching down dusty jumbo-sized cans.

'Good grief, what's this?'

'Jugged hare with apricots. Hmm. Did we ever *sell* any of these?'

'Doesn't look like it, there are another thirty of them up here.'

Old George was now managing to whistle and tap-dance as he juggled with cans of spicy chestnut puree.

'Put a sock in it, George,' moaned Delilah, cobwebs in her hair and dirt-smears up the front of her nylon overall.

'Just trying to cheer us all up, you know, bit of the Blitz

spirit. How about a sing-song? Come on, "Roll out the barrel..."'

'Shut up, George, and get on with it. The sooner we're done the sooner I can get home and watch the match.'

Old George sniffed disdainfully, flipped a can over his shoulder and caught it behind his back.

'Kids. When I was your age...'

'Yeah, yeah, you lived in a cardboard box and ate nothing but black pudding...'

'Cheek! When I was your age, we used to do hampers every year for the kids in the children's home. Course, in those days I'd never seen a banana...'

The stockroom door opened and two more figures squeezed inside. Taz wiped her hands on her jeans.

'Patros, it's good of you to come.'

Patros was accompanied by a young, small, intense young man dressed head to toe in black.

'Taz, I'd like you to meet Sushil Gupta. He's just joined us after getting a First from St Martin's.'

'Really? I'm impressed.' Taz shook hands. Sushil swept his shoulder-length black locks back from his fine-featured face, and she noticed that he was wearing silver eyeliner. Mmm. Artistic. 'Pleased to meet you, Sushil.'

'Hi.' Sushil wasn't looking at Taz. He was chewing his lower lip, and squinting up at the neglected plasterwork of the stockroom ceiling from behind a pencil.

'Sushil specialised in gallery design for his final-year project,' explained Patros, regarding his protégé with fatherly pride. 'I thought I might ask him to work on some designs for the food hall. He's already got some pretty happening ideas...'

Taz was about to ask exactly *how* happening when a voice piped up from behind a pile of boxes.

'Miss Norton?'

Taz turned towards the voice. A head popped up, the heavily-made-up face topped off with a riot of henna-red curls, and a hand held up a small tin of red caviare, accompanied by an expression of enquiring innocence.

'Miss Norton, I've just found these. Are you sure they go in the hampers?'

Well, well, thought Taz. Theresa from the wines and spirits concession. How very interesting.

Life and work were so hectic over the next few days that it was the following Friday before Taz could give herself a day off and make her next move.

Leaving Jack at Dee's, she headed off towards Bourton on the Water, making sure to ring Ken Harris first, to be sure of a table for lunch. Apparently, La Saucisse Dorée was already making quite a name for itself in the world of sausage cuisine, with a mention on *Food and Drink* and half a page in *BBC Good Food*. Not bad going for someone who'd made a complete mess of running the food hall at S&G.

The appetising aroma of Ted's special Cotswold honey marinade engulfed Taz as she stepped into the lobby of the converted mill cottage. It was just as she'd expected it to be, all low beams and exposed stonework, with here and there a dangle of horse-brasses or a local watercolour. Not the epitome of chic, perhaps, but very English and very appealing.

Ken's wife, Vi, was on the desk, and welcomed Taz with hug and a kiss on the cheek.

'Taz, it's lovely to see you.' She gazed around her pride and joy. 'What do you think of the place then?'

'It's great.' She breathed in very deeply. 'And it smells *fantastic*!'

'Ah,' giggled Vi delightedly, 'Nobody knows sausages like my Ken. You're looking well, Taz. How long is it since I saw you? It must be months – how's the baby? Jack isn't it?'

'Growing fast! He's six months old, I can hardly keep up with him, he changes from day to day.'

'Our boys went to prep school last month, and oh, I do miss them. I suppose the corgis are our babies now, but it's not really the same as having your own kids around, is it?'

Taz nodded and sympathised, and agreed that perhaps it wasn't, although Reeves and Mortimer were good company if you didn't mind having your ankles bitten from time to time.

'I was wondering . . . is Ken around?'

'Of course, he's in the kitchen. Why don't I get Tracey to show you to your table and take your order, and I'll tell him you're here?'

One large plate of honey-glazed Cumberland sausage later, Ken made his grand entrance from the kitchen, his white chef's blouse and check trousers liberally smeared with selections from the menu. He was doing something Taz hadn't seen him do in years. He was smiling.

'Taz, great to see you.' He shook her hand with an enthusiasm which almost broke her fingers, twirled a chair back to front and sat astride it. 'Enjoy your meal?'

'It was perfect.' Taz looked wistfully at her empty plate. The diet had been going so well . . . up to now.

'How about some tarte au citron, Tony does a wonderful one.'

'Better not, you know what they say – enough's as good as a feast.' She dabbed the corners of her mouth with her napkin. 'The thing is, Ken, I wanted to ask you a few things . . . about the food hall.'

Ken's enthusiasm slipped a notch or two.

'Ah. Yeah, I heard you had it dumped on you.' He shrugged. 'I guess that's my fault. Sorry.'

Taz secretly thought that he ought to be sorry – very sorry – but what was done was done.

'Look. Ken. I need to pick your brains. I think you and I both know it's in a bad way, and I need to know why. Because until I do, I can't start putting things right.'

Ken took a swig from Taz's water-glass.

'I wouldn't get too fired up if I were you,' he sighed. 'That place has been in a bad way for longer than I can remember.' His watery eyes met hers briefly then flitted away, embarrassedly. 'I know you think it's all down to me . . .'

'I didn't say that, Ken.'

' . . . and maybe some of it is, but when I first got the job – a couple of years ago – I *really* tried to get it back on its feet. It was useless. Everything was against me –

location, staff, lack of money, terrible suppliers, archaic procedures. I got nowhere. Which is when I started digging my escape tunnel.' He glanced around him, his pride and relief obvious. 'I'm bloody glad I did too, if I'd stayed there much longer I'd have gone mad or got the sack – probably both.'

Wonderful, thought Taz. I come all this way looking for advice, and all I get are sausages. But there was still one thing she needed to get straight.

'I don't know how to put this,' she began.

'Try.'

'OK.' She cleared her throat. 'I think – no, I'm certain – that somebody's been on the fiddle. Can you think who that might be?'

Ken shook his head, shrugged, took another sip of water.

'God knows. But it doesn't surprise me. For all I know, they're all at it, they're not up to much you know.'

'Yes I do know.' Taz fetched her handbag from under the table. 'Anyhow, thanks for lunch. I guess I'd better pay and get back to pick up my son from his childminder.'

Ken laid his hand on her arm.

'This one's on the house. There is just one thing . . .' he added slowly. I was a bit surprised when I found out they'd given you the food hall job.'

'Oh – why?'

'I was pretty sure Theresa would get it – you know, Theresa Carvell from the Grape Harvest concession.'

Taz sat down, rested her handbag on her knees, and tuned in. Now, at last, they might just be getting somewhere.

'What made you think that?'

'Well, she's Ted Williams's girlfriend, isn't she? You'd have thought he'd put in a word or two with the people at head office, now he's on the way up at S&G.'

Taz checked the time as she drove into Cheltenham and headed for the Lower High Street. She'd arranged to pick Jack up at four o'clock, but she didn't suppose Dee would mind her picking him up a little early.

301

The front door of the Green Café was open, and there were four or five customer inside, but there was no sign of Dee – only the teenage part-timer, trying to stop Dee's little son Denny from getting his fingers caught in the till while she served an old man with a mug of Horlicks.

'Where's Dee?' enquired Taz. 'I've come to pick up Jack.'

The girl looked a bit taken aback. 'Er . . . she's up in the flat, I think. But . . .'

'Right, I'll just go straight on up then.'

It didn't occur to Taz to ask but what. If she could collect Jack now and hurry back home, there would just be time to call Leroy and discuss what Ken had said, before Leroy went off somewhere exotic for the weekend. Lucky old Leroy. Then there was Adam. Sometime this weekend, they really must sit down and say all the things they'd both been avoiding saying.

She squeezed past a group of tea-swilling market stallholders, and pushed open the door marked 'Private'. Dee's hallway was much as it always was, strewn with toys. But as Taz walked towards the stairs, she saw that the toddler gate was unlocked and swinging open. There were toys littering the stairs too, treacherous in the semi-darkness. That wasn't like Dee, leaving stuff lying all over the place. What if Denny or Petula fell down the stairs? It didn't bear thinking about.

Fumbling for the light switch, she pushed it on. It was one of those slow-release ones that stayed on just long enough to let you get to the next landing and Dee's front room. Just as Taz set foot on the bottom step, she heard a furious commotion from somewhere upstairs. A child's voice, full of anger and hurt. Then another. And suddenly a second sound, forming a horrible counterpoint to the first: a dreadful, fretful crying. She knew that cry, she couldn't have mistaken it even if it was lost among a thousand other children's voices. It was Jack!

'Jack, Jack, oh my God, what's the matter?'

Taz hurtled up the stairs. She knew she was overreacting, that children cried and shouted and made a fuss all the time, that Jack was probably just tired and playing

Dee up. But she was his mum; the sound of his distress was like a magic button, switching on a million half-forgotten neuroses. He'd swallowed something . . . he'd fallen out of his cot and done himself some dreadful injury . . . she should never have left him . . .

Then the crying stopped.

'Dee – Dee, are you there? It's Taz. Is everything OK?'

On the landing, she paused to get her breath back. Taz, calm down, she told herself. You trust Dee, she's a great mother, nothing's wrong with Jack.

But Jack started wailing again, and this time other shrill voices joined in; and Taz leapt for Dee's kitchen door, practically punching it open.

The first thing that struck – or rather enveloped – Taz was the steam. It was everywhere, in great billowing clouds tinged with something more acrid, the stench of burning milk. A pan was rattling on the hob, blackened and boiled almost dry, completely forgotten in the chaos.

The twins were in their playpen, sobbing quietly and disconsolately in nappies that sagged with wetness. That was bad enough. But the sight of Jack, screaming his head off as Emma-Louise tried to force-feed him spoonsful of cold baked beans, turned Taz's blood to ice.

'No, Emma-Louise, you mustn't!'

She grabbed the spoon and the can of beans, shoved the pan off the hob, turned off the gas and flung open a window. Her heart was pounding like a bass drum in a military band.

The safety-strap on his high chair wasn't even done up properly; he could have fallen out at any moment, hit his head on the floor, done himself some terrible damage. She grabbed him out of the chair, covered him with kisses and cuddles that turned his wails and screams to mournful sobs.

'Emma-Louise . . .'

The little girl looked up at her, her eyes puffy from crying.

'Jack was hungry,' she said, wiping her runny nose on the sleeve of her dress.

'I know.' Taking a deep breath, Taz smoothed down

Emma-Louise's unbrushed hair. The last thing she should do was take this out on a seven-year-old girl. 'Where's your mummy, Emma-Louise?'

'Upstairs in bed,' she replied promptly. 'Having a lie down.'

'Is she ill?'

'I don't know, Mummy never said.'

Taz hardly knew what to think as she headed for the stairs which led up to the second floor. There might be a perfectly reasonable explanation for all this. Dee could have been taken ill . . . but then again . . .

She couldn't have been more than halfway up the stairs before any charitable doubts evaporated. There could be no mistaking the sounds wafting forth from Dee's bedroom. The oohs, the aahs, the moans and groans that had nothing whatever to do with pain.

'Oh. Oh yes, yes, YES!'

Taz wondered afterwards how she had ever summoned up the sheer nerve to walk right in. She supposed it must have been anger that drove her on, the protective anger of a mother whose trust had been betrayed.

The door opened almost silently. In any case, the couple on the bed probably wouldn't have noticed if an earthquake had erupted underneath them. Dee was completely naked, her flesh greased with sweat and quivering violently as she bounced up and down on top of her equally naked lover. With every creak of the bedsprings, Taz felt her anger mount. But when at last she did find the strength to speak, the voice that came out was strangely quiet and controlled.

'Dee Wiechula. How could you. How could you *do* this to me?'

At the sound of Taz's voice, the two bodies on the bed froze in mid-coupling. She heard Dee let out a soft gasp.

'Oh hell. Taz . . .'

Dee rolled off, grabbing a sheet and wrapping it round her. Her body wobbled unappetisingly under the poly-cotton; it didn't look sexy and bountiful any more, just cheap and deceitful.

'Taz . . . I'm sorry . . .'

304

'You'd better be. You should be ashamed of yourself, Dee. I trusted you to take care of my baby.'

'It's not as bad as it looks . . .'

Oh but it is, thought Taz bitterly. It's worse. Her gaze lighted on the bloke on the bed, the one trying desperately to cover his embarrassment with a pillowcase.

And it wasn't even Lorenzo.

Chapter 22

Things didn't look any better the following morning. If anything, they looked worse.

'No luck then dear?' Isobel enquired.

Taz, after making numerous unsuccessful phone calls, raised her head and shook it almost imperceptibly, too defeated to do any more than that. Adam sighed. Bill's *Daily Mail* sagged in the middle. Jack, strapped into his high chair with Isobel wiping egg-yolk off his chin, seemed to wonder what all the fuss was about.

'That's it then.' Taz fingered the crumpled list of child-minders on the table in front of her. Every single name had been crossed off, not once but three times over. 'No one can take on Jack at such short notice, I'll have to give up my job.'

She threw her pen onto the table-top, watched with much fascination by Jack. His trusting innocence almost broke her heart; thank God he didn't realise how close he'd come to disaster with Dee Wiechula. Taz didn't look in her mother's direction; she couldn't bear to see the look of triumph in her eyes.

'Surely not,' ventured Adam. 'It's early days . . .'

'It's Saturday, Leroy's on annual leave till Tuesday, I'm supposed to be in early on Monday – and there's no way I'm letting Dee Wiechula anywhere near Jack, however desperate I might be. It's impossible. I should have known this would happen in the end, it was too good to be true.'

'I blame myself,' said Adam. 'I was living in the same house, I should have realised.'

'Don't be silly dear,' cut in Isobel. 'You couldn't possibly know what that woman was getting up to when everyone's back was turned.' She sniffed. 'Though I did think Tasmin might have asked a few pertinent questions . . .'

Taz blazed. Why couldn't her mother resist the cheap dig? She was only too aware of her shortcomings, she didn't need Isobel to point them out to everybody.

'For God's sake Mum! You've got what you wanted, why can't you just leave it?'

Isobel looked slightly taken aback, but shut up and went on wiping Jack's eggy fingers with a damp flannel.

'I'm sorry,' sighed Taz, leaning back in her chair and stretching out her stiff and aching back. 'I didn't mean to snap, it's just . . . oh why does it all have to be so difficult?'

Adam looked at Isobel, who looked at Bill. Bill scraped back his chair and coughed.

'I'm just off for a breath of fresh air then.'

Taz watched her father rubbing the side of his neck. He only did that when he particularly wanted to get out of the way. Taz quizzed Isobel and Adam with a searching look, but they weren't giving anything away.

'Is there something I should know?'

The door closed behind Bill, and Taz heard his heavy, uneven footsteps clumping away down the passageway. She wished she could have jumped ship with him.

'Right – what's all this about?' demanded Taz, turning back to the table. 'And don't say "nothing", I'm not stupid.'

Isobel unstrapped Jack and sat down with him on her lap.

'Go on then, Adam. You tell her.'

'While you were phoning round the childminders,' began Adam, 'Your mum and I were having a little chat.'

'Oh yes?' The seed of suspicion in Taz's mind was sprouting roots and leaves. 'And what was this cosy chat about? Or aren't I supposed to know?'

'It was about Jack. We think we may have come up with a solution. Well, a temporary one anyway.'

'What do you mean, a solution?' Taz longed to seize Jack from his granny's lap and cover him with pro-prietorial kisses, but he looked so happy sitting there, giggling as Isobel made his fluffy rabbit do bunny-hops along the edge of the table.

Adam fiddled pensively with a stray cornflake, crushing it to powder with the back of his spoon.

'You trust your mum with Jack, don't you?'

'Of course I do, she's my mum.'

'And what about me? Do you think you could trust me too?'

Taz's brow knitted.

'Adam – what has this got to do with anything?'

'Please, Taz,' insisted Adam, 'answer the question, it's important. Do you trust me with Jack?'

'Yes, I think so. Why?'

'Because your mum and I reckon we could take on Jack's childcare between us ... but only if you're happy with the idea.'

'I don't understand!' Taz stared at Adam, then Isobel, then Jack. But none of them did anything but smile back at her. 'You – look after Jack?'

'You said yourself that you trust Adam,' pointed out Isobel. Adam does have experience of looking after his own children, after all – and he's so good with Jack. Jack adores him, don't you little man?'

Right on cue, Jack giggled and stretched out his arms to Adam. So Jack was in on this conspiracy too.

'Even if I thought this was a serious idea,' said Taz slowly, 'and I don't – how could you possibly take care of Jack when you're working all day at the law centre? What'd you do with him, stick him in the filing cabinet?'

Adam laughed, but in a serious and responsible kind of way.

'You remember I mentioned that Declan had plans to introduce more flexible working practices? Well, I'm ninety-nine per cent certain I can persuade him to let me alter my hours, so that I spend two or three days a week working from home.'

'And of course,' cut in Isobel, 'I'd be able to take Jack when Adam was at the law centre.'

Taz really *was* astounded now, this was unthinkable. How many times had Isobel told her how busy she was, how she couldn't possibly babysit Jack on a particular day because of her watercolour class, or her *cercle français*? 'Mum, you don't have the time . . .'

'Of course I have the time,' replied Isobel with a kind of injured solemnity. Her still-elegant hands tightened a little about Jack's round tummy. 'I'm Jack's granny, I'll *make* time.'

Adam reached across and touched Taz, who was sitting staring ahead of her in a kind of hypnotic daze. She started at the touch of his fingers.

'Oh!'

'Taz, what do you think? It's the perfect solution, isn't it?'

'Well, I . . .'

Taz got up, rather dazedly, from her chair. She knew she ought to feel profoundly grateful, and in a way she did; but she couldn't help feeling that she and Jack had been hijacked. Her head was starting to ache. She knew now why her father had been so keen to get out of the way.

'Would you excuse me, just for a minute? I need to think about this.'

She went outside and walked across to her garage. The side door was unlocked and ajar; somehow she'd suspected it might be. Inside, the BSA Gold Star sat on its stand with Bill astride it, his old-fashioned motorcycle helmed perched on top of his head with its leather straps dangling down. His right hand was resting on the throttle, as though at any moment he might kick-start the engine and hurtle through the up-and-over door at ninety miles an hour.

'Hello Dad.'

He nodded a greeting without actually looking at her.

'Feeling like your life's not your own any more, Kitten?'

Kitten. He'd coined that nickname for her when she was five years old, with a white furry hat that had triangular ears like a cat's. She'd grown out of the hat, but not the name.

'You knew, didn't you? You might have warned me.'

'You know what your mum's like, once she gets an idea

309

in her head.' He turned and looked at Taz. 'And it is a sensible idea,' he added kindly.

'I know.'

'Your mum's a good-hearted woman really. She mea . . .'

'Don't.' Taz put her hand over her father's mouth. 'If anyone else tells me she means well, I swear I'll scream.' She took her hand away and stroked the bike's gleaming chrome. 'She needs a bit of a polish, doesn't she? And the plugs need cleaning.'

'She's fine. You've done a good job on her. Remember when you were little and you wanted me to take you out in the sidecar?'

'And Mum said over her dead body, but you sneaked me out anyway. And she was waiting on the doorstep when we got back . . .'

They laughed together.

'She gave me hell that night,' mused Bill, wincing slightly as he eased his damaged leg over the petrol tank. 'I tell you, some of the names she called me would make a sailor blush.' He patted Taz on the shoulder. 'You make your own mind up, Kitten. Don't let her force something on you if you're not happy with it. But . . . It does make sense, doesn't it?' He didn't exactly look enthusiastic, and Taz didn't exactly feel enthusiastic, but they both knew what he meant.

'So you think I should do it then? After all, it'd only be temporary, until I get something better fixed up. And it'd make them happy, wouldn't it, thinking that they were helping me out?'

Bill smiled and drew his daughter towards him in a big hug.

'Good girl. Now why don't we go and find your mum before she sends out a search party?'

By way of a thank-you, Taz took Adam out for a meal that night. To be more precise, Adam took her out and she paid, since it was Adam who booked the table, Adam who did the driving – and Taz who got properly tipsy for the first time since she'd had Jack.

They giggled over the cannelloni, exchanged terrible

310

jokes over the tiramisu, and lingered so long over the grappa that Luigi enquired if they'd be wanting a room for the night.

'Let's go back the long way,' suggested Adam out of the blue.

'What long way?'

'You know, over the top of the hill. You can see right over the whole of Cheltenham.'

'That's a *very* long way round,' commented Taz, collapsing gratefully onto the front passenger seat as the chill night air sent alcohol coursing to her brain. She struggled to focus on her watch. 'What time is it?'

'Not midnight yet – don't worry, I'll get you back home before your mum turns into a pumpkin.'

The elderly Morris van bumped and twisted along country lanes that wound upwards in tortuous spirals towards the crest of the escarpment. Adam was right, you *could* see right over the whole of the town, though in the darkness it was nothing but a random arrangement of sulphur-orange dots.

They parked up high on the ridge, where it was quiet and dark and really rather snug inside the van. Adam switched off the engine.

'See that? That must be the racecourse. And just over there, to the right, that's Pittville.'

'How can you tell? It all looks the same to me.'

Adam leaned a little closer, and Taz snuggled into his warm, strong embrace.

'Jack's all right isn't he? With Mum?'

'Right as rain, he'll be stuffed full of banana and dreaming of Rupert Bear.'

Taz smiled, a warm langour making her tingle rather pleasurably as Adam stroked her shoulder. Her mouth was dry with the sheer enormity of what she was doing as she spoke the words that meant something and nothing . . . and everything.

'Let's not go back. Not just yet.'

The moonlight caught Adam's eyes as he turned to look at her, and planted a kiss on the end of her nose.

'You're sure that's what you want?'

'I'm sure.'

She heard herself moan very softly as Adam kissed her, his tongue parting her lips and the slightly stubbly texture of his chin rubbing across her cheek. It was so long since she'd done this, anything like this, that her lips could hardly remember how to respond.

Other parts of her seemed guided by a surer instinct. With sudden embarrassment and a huge surge of guilty excitement, she realised that her hand was resting on Adam's thigh, her fingers stroking closer and closer to the danger-zone, the point of no return.

'Oh Taz, do you know how much I've wanted this?' murmured Adam between kisses, his strong hand sliding oh-so-gently down to cup her breast, somehow managing at the same time to flick open the top two buttons of her blouse.

'Adam . . .'

Even Taz wasn't sure if it was a sigh of shameless lust or a last-minute second thought. Maybe it was both. In any case, there was no room for second thoughts right now. At this very moment Adam's lips were closing round her right nipple, the nipple that for months had been Jack's sole property; and now her own fingers were impetuously unzipping Adam's trousers, desperate to rediscover the simple oblivion of casual sex. Now was not a good time to play the timorous virgin.

She wanted to want this *so* much. Having Adam as her lover would complete the last piece of the jigsaw puzzle. It felt so right, so perfect, the natural next step in her life.

And yet, in a tiny corner of her mind, she half-wondered if she wasn't doing this not just because she wanted to, but because she felt as if she should. As if, because Adam had almost taken on the role of Jack's father, he must become her lover too.

It was Tuesday morning in the food hall at Seuss & Goldman. As yet, nobody seemed to have been poisoned by a harvest hamper, Gloria was being almost polite to the customers, and Old George was packing carrier bags with a gung-ho zeal that made Taz wonder if he was heading for a stroke.

So far, so good – although Taz kept expecting Adam to page her at any moment and tell her that something dreadful had happened to Jack. Not that it would; as Isobel kept reminding her, Jack couldn't have a more conscientious childminder than Adam Rolfe.

She yawned as she put the finishing touches to a page of figures, part of her forthcoming report. This was no use, she was going to have to get some sleep. A wicked smile twitched the corners of her mouth. How many years since she'd shared a night of passion in a single bed? Not since university, and in those days she hadn't had a baby and a bad back.

'Leroy?' She stuck her head out of the office door. 'Could I have a word? There's one or two things we need to discuss.'

'Any new developments?'

'Not since I phoned you. But we ought to go over the facts and decide what to do next. I want to be sure we're both on the same wavelength before I go off to Scotland on Friday.'

Leroy pulled up a chair, wiped the seat and sat down.

'So, Ken Harris wasn't much help?'

'To be honest, I didn't really expect him to be. You know what he's like. But he did say one interesting thing. Theresa Carvell is Ted Williams' girlfriend.'

'Really?' One eyebrow arched. 'I wondered why we didn't see eye to eye. And you think Theresa . . .?'

'To be honest I don't know what to think.' admitted Taz, tapping her pencil on the notepad in front of her. 'And one thing we mustn't do is jump to conclusions?

'So, let's look at the facts. May I?' Leroy spun the notepad round to face him. He took out a pen out and started making notes. 'OK, point one: somebody is – or was – hiding large quantities of high-value merchandise in the stockroom.' He drew a figure two and circled it. 'Point two: why is this happening? To make us overstock expensive items?'

'Maybe,' nodded Taz. 'But more likely, to make it easier to steal from the food hall.'

'Well, whoever's doing it has nerves of steel,' observed Leroy. 'I mean, we're not talking petty cash here, are we? This looks like a real money-spinner.'

'So, bearing in mind the large quantities involved, we're looking at somebody who has regular, easy access to the stockrooms?'

'Right.' Leroy doodled for a moment, then looked up. 'And, the way I see it, that means somebody in a supervisory position. Ken, Ted, their predecessors, or maybe someone in charge of one of the concessions.'

'Which brings us back to Theresa,' said Taz thoughtfully.

'Or . . .' Leroy cleared his throat. 'Me.'

He looked so comical that Taz could have laughed in his face.

'You! If it turns out to be you, Leroy, I really will lose my faith in human nature. But one thing is bothering me.'
'Why aren't these stolen goods showing up in the quarterly stocktake?'

It wasn't the best time to be taking a holiday from the food hall, but Taz trusted Leroy to keep things under control, and besides, she'd promised Binnie that she and Jack would be there for Amy's first birthday party.

And what a party it was. The wildest teenage rave could hardly have competed with the din produced by fifteen squealing, giggling, screaming, screeching tots and their assorted siblings; gathered around a giant ladybird sponge cake to watch Amy's mum blow out the single pink birthday candle. The significance was definitely lost on Jack, who was sick all over his new red dungarees and then slept the rest of the afternoon away.

'Thank God that's over,' gasped Binnie as she and Taz flopped in the sitting room with a post-party drink.

'Only another seventeen years and she'll be off your hands,' grinned Taz. 'That's if she doesn't elope with that little red-haired boy first.'

Binnie chuckled.

'Oh, you mean wee Angus? The one she was trying to

kiss all over? I don't mind if Amy runs off with him, his daddy's got five hundred acres and a castle.' She kicked off her shoes and wriggled her constricted toes. 'I'll swing for Great Aunt Shula, did you see her, trying to feed them peanut-butter sandwiches? That silly woman's got no sense. Still, the little ones seemed to enjoy themselves.'

'It's a pity Jim couldn't be here,' ventured Taz.

'Yeah . . . well . . . another crisis on another oil rig, you know how it is.' Binnie's fingers plucked at the chintzy settee cover. 'It couldn't be helped.'

'I thought he was going to try and spend more time at home?'

'Oh, he *is*. Trying that is. It's just that it doesn't always work out.' Binnie reached out for the bottle. 'Another glass of wine?'

'Thanks. You two are getting on all right now though, aren't you?'

'Fine.' Binnie was facing away from Taz, but her voice sounded bright enough. 'Thanks for coming, Taz, it means a lot to me.'

'I wouldn't have missed it for anything. The question is, when are you going to come and see me again?'

'Next time I walk out on Jim?' suggested Binnie wryly.

'Binnie, don't!'

'It's OK, just a joke. I wouldn't want to go through all that again. Anyhow, from what I hear you haven't got room for any visitors – what's all this about you and your gorgeous young solicitor?'

'Adam's just a lodger!' protested Taz.

'Oh yeah?'

'Well . . . a friend, you know. And he takes care of Jack. That's all.'

'There's no more to it than that? Not a hint of rumpy-pumpy?'

'Binnie!' squealed Taz, red-faced with embarrassment.

'Look me in the face Taz Norton, you were always a useless liar.'

Taz exploded with laughter.

'Just make sure I get an invite to the wedding, OK?' Binnie settled herself more comfortably on the sofa. 'So

315

– when do I get to be a godmother then? You still haven't told me when Jack's christening's going to be.'

Taz closed her eyes to shut out the horrible spectre of Isobel in powder-blue Berketex.

'Don't talk to me about christenings. Mum's threatening to organise it herself if I don't do something about it.'

'But you're still not keen?'

'About as keen as you were. The trouble is, Mum's got me in a kind of emotional headlock, what with offering to look after Jack for me while I'm at work. And she really knows how to pile the pressure on.'

'Well, if you want my advice, hold out for what you want. If you give in on this one, you'll never hear the last of it, it's the thin end of the wedge.' Binnie picked up the wine bottle, tilted it over her glass then, at the last moment, put it down again. 'I shouldn't be drinking this, you know.'

'Why not?' Taz sniffed her drink. 'What's wrong with it?'

'Not it. Me.' Binnie sighed, her exhausted body sagging forward like a deflating balloon. 'Haven't you guessed, Taz? I'm pregnant again.'

Taz almost dropped her glass in astonishment. She searched Binnie's face for some clue as to how she ought to react.

'No! Are you ... pleased?'

'Ecstatic.'

'You don't look it.' Which was an understatement. Sick as a parrot would have been nearer the mark.

'How would you feel? I was just starting to feel like a human being again, Jim was even starting to *fancy* me ... Now he's sulking and I feel like a blimp. I'm only six weeks gone and I've put on nearly a stone! Mind you, Granny Jean's over the moon, she's already started knitting blue bootees.'

'Blue?'

'It's going to be a boy, she's decided. A son and heir for Jim. Nothing to do with me, naturally, I'm just its mother.'

316

'Oh poor Binnie,' sighed Taz. 'Still,' she brightened, 'you did always plan to have another one, didn't you?'

'Did I?' said Binnie dully. 'I must've wanted my head examining.'

Just before noon on Sunday, Gareth Scott parked his silver-blue Mercedes outside Shepcote House, got out and smoothed creases from his cashmere-blend raincoat. Well, well. It was quite some time since he'd been back to Cheltenham, fifteen months as he recalled. And in those fifteen months it hadn't changed much; it still stank of provincial second-raters and retired colonels who lived on the dregs of yesterday's dreams. Not his kind of people at all.

Naturally, he'd only come back to Taz's place to collect a few of Melanie's things. Well, that was what he told himself, anyway. It absolutely, definitely had nothing to do with the fact that he was a dyed-in-the-wool philanderer, with an itch that needed regular scratching. Melanie was a nice girl, reasonably enthusiastic between the sheets; she made a perfectly serviceable wife – but you couldn't expect a man's appetites to be satisfied by one woman, no matter how appealing. That would be like living on smoked salmon for the rest of your life.

Checking the time, he walked swiftly up the path towards the side door which led to Taz's flat. He mustn't linger too long, he had lunch with Henry Goldman to think about, and if he was going to allow Henry to head-hunt him back to S&G, he wanted to be well prepared to screw a king's ransom out of him for the privilege.

He rang the bell and stood back, remembering Sundays past when he'd stood exactly here, waiting for Taz to come to the door, freshly showered and perfumed, and completely naked underneath the satin negligée he'd brought her back from Paris. Even now, the memory awoke the faint stirrings of something pleasantly primeval.

Gareth liked to think he was the sort of man who was prepared for anything. But he wasn't prepared to be greeted by a young man in an apron, a Hoover in one hand and a feather duster in the other.

'Yes?' enquired the young man, who – despite first appearances – didn't look entirely homosexual.

'Oh.' Gareth adjusted his tie. 'I was looking for Tasmin Norton.'

'Taz? I'm afraid she's not here right now, she's away for a few days. Can I help you?'

'I don't know. That rather depends on who you are,' replied Gareth smoothly.

'I'm Adam, Adam Rolfe.' The young man switched the feather duster to the back pocket of his jeans, wiped his hand and offered it. 'I live here.'

'Really?' Gareth's mind worked overtime. Lodger or lover, that was the question. Probably both, though Adam Rolfe hardly seemed Taz's type. Too insipid, though muscular enough under that ridiculous pinny.

'Really. And you are?'

'Gareth Scott. My wife used to flat-share with Taz. Actually I called by to pick up a few things she left behind when she moved out . . . but if this is a bad time . . .'

The crinkly eyes registered a flicker of indecision, a quality which Gareth had always despised in any adversary. And he felt instinctively, viscerally, that Adam was destined to become exactly that. Finally the eyes came to a decision – of sorts.

'Why don't you come in for a coffee or something? No point in hanging around on the doorstep.'

Adam led the way into the flat. Gareth breathed in old, remembered scents; but there were new aromas mixed up with the perfumes of washing powder and cologne and drinking chocolate. Like warmed-up milk; talcum powder; gripe water . . .

And what on earth? A plastic duck squeaked under his foot as he stepped right on its head.

'Sorry,' smiled Adam, stooping to pick it up. 'That's one of Jack's.'

'Jack?'

'Taz's son, didn't you know?'

Gareth pursued Adam into the living room, striding over the detritus of discarded toys and dodging the baby-bath propped up against the wallpaper that he had chosen, now scuffed and dented near the bottom from the constant to-ing and fro-ing of buggies and high chairs.

'No. No, as a matter of fact I didn't. We've not been in touch for a while.'

'Oh. I see.'

On the mantelpiece, next to the Deco dancer and the lava lamp, sat a photograph in a silver frame. A photograph of a wrinkly-faced newborn baby, red and unappealing, and completely indistinguishable from any other newborn baby. Next to it, in a smaller frame, was another photograph of a baby, perhaps the same one, this time bigger and chubbier, with blue eyes and curly brown hair.

Something tensed inside Gareth.

'So . . . you and Taz . . .?' He nodded towards the photographs. Adam smiled and shook his head.

'No, no, Jack's not my son. He's Taz's from . . . you know . . . a previous relationship.' He spoke the words with the ghastly, politically correct tactfulness of a social worker, thought Gareth with infinite distaste.

'So . . . how old is he?'

Gareth wasn't quite sure why he bothered asking. He stretched out his fingers and ran them along the top of the silver frame. Not a trace of dust. Well, well, Taz had got her little houseboy nicely trained.

'Jack? Oh, about six months. Lovely little chap, isn't he? The image of his mum. Look, I'm being terribly rude, aren't I? Can I get you a coffee or something?'

'Mmm?' At first Gareth didn't hear. He was staring distractedly at the photograph of the chubby, smiling baby, trying to do a simple sum in his head; and every time he did the sum, he ended up with the same answer.

'Coffee. Can I get you one?'

'Er . . . no. No, thanks but I'd better be going. When did you say she'd be back?'

'On Monday. Can I give her a message?'

Gareth shook his head, trying to rearrange the jumble of his racing thoughts.

'A message? No. Just tell her I called, will you? I'll be in touch.'

It wasn't until he was outside in the crisp September air, with the door safely closed behind him, that Gareth allowed the full weight of realisation to come crashing down on him.

Six months plus nine months, that came to fifteen months. And it was fifteen months, give or take the odd week or two, since Gareth Scott had enjoyed his last horizontal tango with Taz Norton. It didn't take a genius to work out what that meant.

Good God, he thought as he slid into the driver's seat and waited for the cold shivers to subside. Gareth Scott, you randy old goat, forty-six years old and you've finally gone and done it.

You're a father.

And a not entirely pleasant smile began to spread like a razor-slash across Gareth's disbelieving face.

Chapter 23

'It's past eleven, George, this lot should've been on display hours ago,' protested Ian as he and Old George struggled across from goods inward to the food hall with a gross of mini Cheddar cheeses.

'It would've been,' replied George, placidly removing one hand from the base of the box to rub a dewdrop off the end of his nose, 'If I hadn't had to wipe up all that damson jam – jam an' glass all over the bloody place there was.'

'Come on,' urged Ian, nudging open the door which led into the main escalator area. 'If we get a move on and cut across here we'll have it all sorted out before she gets back from her meeting.'

'What? Oh, all right then, my back's giving me gyp.'

Not without a pang of reluctance, George allowed himself to be persuaded to take the quickest route to the food hall – not the permitted route, admittedly, but Taz was in a meeting with Patros Nikephoros and what she didn't know wouldn't bother her.

As luck would have it, the arrival of the box of cheeses coincided exactly with a commotion at the top of the 'down' escalator.

'Stop her, she's a shoplifter!'

'Somebody get security . . . madam, will you come back please madam, if you walk out of the store with that shirt . . .'

A hand lunged. A blonde-haired woman, nicely dressed but rather wide-eyed and dishevelled, pushed her way onto the crowded down escalator. She swung round and yelled cultured abuse at her pursuers, Pauline from menswear and Cara Mondini.

'Get off me, get off me, I've done nothing! Get OFF.'

There didn't seem much likelihood of that happening. Every alarm in menswear was squealing at the top of its electronic voice and as Pauline made a grab for the woman's shoulder, the sleeve of a man's rugby shirt escaped from underneath her suspiciously over-stuffed jacket, swinging guiltily around her skirted legs.

'Do something!' Pauline called out to George and Ian, but they simply stood there, the box of cheeses suspended between them, rooted to the spot. Shoppers huddled, frozen where they stood, entranced by this impromptu free entertainment.

Reaching the bottom of the escalator, she swung this way and that, as though looking for the one person who could give her what she wanted.

'I want Taz. I want to speak to Taz Norton. Now!'

She pulled the rugby shirt out from under her jacket, ripped off the collar, threw it on the ground and ran out through the swing doors towards the statue of Jacob Seuss. Pauline made a dive for her; Kevin winced and grabbed what was left of the shirt. It was a Ralph Lauren Polo Original.

Two security guards were closing in on the shoplifter. She was standing on the plinth of the statue, brandishing second prize, a plum-coloured 'Friday shirt', ninety-five pounds a time with a lovingly hand-sewn collar.

'Taz Norton, where is she? I want Taz Norton.'

Before Pauline and one of the security guards could seize her, she had ripped it right down the middle.

'It's OK, I've got her,' panted Pauline.

George and Ian were still staring imbecilically as the woman was escorted back into the store, shreds of purple shirt trailing defiantly from her clenched fingers. But her expression wasn't triumphant, it was restless and desperate.

'I want *Taz*,' she kept on repeating endlessly. 'Aren't you listening? I want Taz, where's Taz?'

Old George put down his end of the box and rubbed

his back, gazing thoughtfully at the wriggling figure disappearing up the escalator towards menswear.

'Better go and find Miss Norton,' he concluded. 'Sounds like this has got somethin' to do with her.'

Taz wasn't surprised to be paged in the middle of her ad hoc meeting with Patros and Sushil. The staff of the food hall seemed less capable than most of sorting things out for themselves.

What did surprise her was the response when she phoned through to the switchboard.

'Ms Norton? You're wanted in menswear.'

'Menswear? Don't you mean the food hall?'

'No, menswear. There's been an incident – some woman's been caught shoplifting. Asked for you by name, apparently, won't talk to anybody else.'

There was one word passing through Taz's head as she put down the receiver and made her apologies to Sushil: Mandy. Presumably this was Mandy's idea of just retribution. Or was Mandy in desperate straits, and only stealing from S&G because she thought Taz could save her from the consequences of getting caught? Either way, they had some very stiff talking to do.

When Taz reached menswear, she was directed straight to Ted's office. For weeks she'd avoided coming anywhere near her old department. My God, she thought as she took in the new mahogany-veneered fittings, the leather sofas outside the revamped fitting rooms, the expanded personal shopping suite; Ted really does have friends in high places. This little lot must've cost thousands.

And that wasn't even counting the new stock – vast quantities of exorbitantly priced high-fashion merchandise from the top designer houses. She clocked some of the labels as she passed – those brocade waistcoats must retail at five hundred plus and those silk shirts were so incredibly fragile that she'd never have dared sell them, let alone display them casually folded in open-fronted cubes. She wondered how Ted managed to get away with it. The slimy toad.

When she reached Ted's office she realised the surprises

weren't over. Pauline was sitting on a stool in the corner, looking like she wished she could be somewhere else. Ted was leaning against the filing cabinet, arms folded, looming menacingly over the collapsed figure of a young woman, sobbing as she clutched a torn purple shirt.

'Chloë!'

The blonde head snapped up. The eyes were blue pools sunk deep in circles of puffy red.

'T-t-taz!' She tried to stand up, but Ted pushed her back onto her chair.

'Stay right where you are,' growled Ted. 'Where I can see what you're up to.' He sniffed in Taz's direction. 'So – she's not *completely* barmy then, you *do* know her?'

'Yes.' Taz had to fight a terrible, guilty urge to say she didn't. She squatted down in front of Chloë, prised the fingers from the shirt and took them in her hands. 'Chloë, whatever is the matter?'

Chloë's sobs subdued to a kind of snuffling, shuddering distress; a child's distress.

'I w-w-was looking for you. I c-came to m-menswear but y-y-you weren't there.' The eyes, agonised in their searching, roamed all over Taz's face as though scrutinising it for a key to understanding.

'I don't work in menswear any more,' said Taz gently. 'I told you, don't you remember?'

'N-no. D-don't r-remember anything about that.' She raked her fingers through her hair, the blonde curls grown frizzy from the drizzle and the central heating. 'I h-had to s-see you, you understand don't you? N-n-nobody else understands.'

'But why on earth did you steal from the shop?' asked Taz. 'Why didn't you just ask somebody where I was?'

'I . . . I don't know, I w-was f-frightened. I though if I stole the sh-shirts you'd c-come and find me . . .'

'Oh for Christ's sake!' muttered Ted, shuffling restlessly in the corner. 'Do we have to listen to all this crap?' He glanced at his watch. 'Ten past, they should be here by now.'

Taz ignored Ted and went on talking to Chloë. It was obvious that nobody else was going to bother trying.

324

'Why did you need to see me?'

'B-because of C-c-clive. He . . . k-keeps trying to r-ring me up.'

'And you don't want to talk to him? It might help to talk things through, you know.'

'M-m-mummy says I m-mustn't speak to him. H-h-he's b-bad . . .'

Interfering, poisonous old bag, thought Taz; but she kept her thoughts to herself.

'Bad? Clive? He's not bad, Chloë, he loves you.'

'I don't know what to do . . . I th-thought maybe you could t-tell me.'

Taz felt a silent sigh of depression pass right through her, like tumbleweed rolling down the main street of a ghost town.

'I can't tell you what to do,' she said softly. 'And neither should your mother. You have to make up your own mind.'

They might have got a little further, but there was a knock on the door, and Marion Grey stuck her head into the office.

'Excuse me, sorry to disturb you, only the police have arrived.'

'The p-police?' Utter despair brimmed in Chloë's eyes, the tears quivering on the brink before hurling themselves in cascades down her swollen cheeks. 'Wh-why?' She darted glances from Taz to Ted and Pauline.

Ted actually had the crassness to laugh.

'Because you're a thief,' he replied simply.

'Now hold on Ted . . .' began Taz. Her mind was working overtime, trying to think of good reasons why the police shouldn't be brought into this. She couldn't think of one, not one.

'Naturally you're anxious to protect your *friend*,' he said pointedly, 'but it's company policy to prosecute *all* shoplifters. Surely you know *that*, Taz.'

Damn you Ted Williams, cursed Taz silently. Damn you for being right.

'There there, sweetheart, Mummy'll make it all better.'

At three o'clock in the morning, the very darkest, coldest, most pessimistic time of the night, Taz was sitting on the edge of her bed, rocking Jack to sleep in her arms. The poor mite couldn't help being restless and fretful, he was cutting a tooth; and in a funny way Taz was almost grateful for an excuse not to lie in bed, staring blankly at the ceiling.

She was bone-tired, but peculiarly wakeful. What with Mandy's disappearance, Binnie's bombshell, skulduggery and incompetence in the food hall, Isobel's constant comments about unbaptised infants going straight to Purgatory, and now Chloë, Taz had more than enough worries to prevent her getting a good night's sleep.

'Oh Jack, what *are* we going to do?' The glow-worm night-light softened the blackness to a friendlier dusk, but it was still a bit chilly, not that Jack felt cold; in fact she had a suspicion he might be running a slight temperature. 'Poor little chap, never mind, soon be off to sleep again.' She hummed to him, some half-remembered lullaby her mother had sung to her when she was little.

It was about twenty minutes before Jack's eyes closed and she felt his body relax in her arms. Hardly daring to move in case she woke him up again, she tiptoed across to his cot and bent over to lay him on his back.

The door to the hall opened a couple of inches, and a familiar voice whispered, 'Taz, is everything OK?' Adam peeped into the room. 'Not ill is he?'

Taz shook her head and put her finger to her lips.

'Just teething. It's taken me ages to get him off.'

'Poor chap. Poor you, you look whacked.' Adam held out a mug. 'I couldn't sleep either, made you some hot chocolate.'

'You think of everything.'

'God, I wish I did. I'm so overworked at the moment I even forgot to buy my mother a birthday present. Can you imagine . . .?'

Taz could, only too well. She took her mug and slid under the bedcovers, motioning Adam to join her. It felt good to have the comforting warmth of another body, filling up the emptiness of her double bed. The glow from the night-light seemed to add an extra cosiness to their cuddling.

Adam slipped his free arm round her waist and pulled her close, but strangely there was nothing really sexual about it, even though they supposedly fancied each other like mad. Taz wondered if that was a good sign rather than a bad. After all weren't long-term relationships supposed to be based on companionship, trust, affection, not raging lust? Sex could be so confusing – although sex was the least of her worries at the moment.

Adam yawned and stroked her bare flank through her pyjamas. That was another funny thing. She wouldn't have been seen dead wearing pyjamas in the days before Jack; then again, who'd've thought she could ever feel comfortable breastfeeding in front of her brand-new lover? Or letting him sterilise her nipple shields?

'Why couldn't you sleep?' she enquired sleepily.

'It's that harassment case I'm working on. It just seems to go on for ever, and I feel so sorry for the poor family – and there's hardly anything I can do for them until it comes to court.'

Taz wriggled her toes under the duvet.

'Adam. I've been thinking – about Chloë. They're going to prosecute her, you know.'

'Hardly surprising, is it?' pointed out Adam. 'I mean, she stole three designer shirts and destroyed two of them, she assaulted a security guard . . .'

'But she's got such terrible problems at home,' said Taz, searching for the right words that would make Adam understand. If anyone could he could, he spent his whole life working with dysfunctional families.

'Then they'll be taken into consideration when her case comes to court. But you have to admit, she's not exactly behaved like an angel. From what you've told me she's even rejected her own child. It doesn't look good, does it?'

'Which is why she needs somebody good to defend her. Somebody who cares.' Taz's mouth was dry. 'I was wondering . . .'

Adam stopped her short. She felt his body stiffen against hers.

'No, Taz.' His voice was gentle but firm. 'Not even as a favour to you.'

'But . . .'

'This isn't my scene, Taz, you know that. I work with people on legal aid, people too poor to afford anyone better. Your friend Chloë can get Mummy and Daddy to buy her the best QC in the country if that's what she wants. All she's done is nick a few shirts, it's her first offence, they're hardly going to send her to Holloway, are they?'

Silence fell. Taz felt the distance between them grow, almost imperceptibly.

'I thought you'd understand,' she said.

'I do understand. But do you? Look Taz, I'm sorry, I really am. But if I take on some poor little rich girl who ought to know better, I can't take on people like Mandy and Dave and the battered wife who's terrified her thug of a husband's going to find out where she lives.'

'No. No, I'm sorry.' Taz cupped her hands around her mug of chocolate, seeking out the vestiges of warmth she so needed. 'But I really don't know where else to turn.'

Adam laid his head on her shoulder.

'Chloë's a grown woman,' he said. 'She can fight her own battles. It's time you stopped feeling responsible for the whole world's problems, and thought about what *you* need for a change.'

What Taz needed was to feel that she'd actually achieved something. And that meant that she had to stop running round in circles, take three deep breaths and plunge in at the deep end.

Starting with the food hall.

Theresa Carvell was cashing up when Taz sought her out at the end of the day.

'Can I have a word?'

'I'm a bit busy now, can't it wait?'

'No, I'm afraid it can't.' Theresa's over-made-up face registered a twitch of consternation. 'So if you'd just hand over to Mark, I'll see you in my office in two minutes. That's *two* minutes,' she added as a parting shot over her shoulder. 'Not five.'

Theresa arrived at Taz's office with much bad grace, but at least she was unusually punctual. So far so good.

'So. What's this about then?' Without waiting to be asked, Theresa plonked herself down on a chair and took out cigarettes and a lighter. Taz responded by taking them off her and putting them on the desk. Theresa gaped like an injured goldfish, her henna-red curls quivering with outrage.

'No smoking *anywhere* on S&G premises, remember?'

'Oh. Yeah. Sorry. Look, what did you want to see me about?' Theresa was talking too quickly now, almost gabbling, her nervous fingers fidgeting in the absence of a comforting fag. 'Only that Mark's flamin' useless on his own, if he adds the till roll up twice he gets three different answers.'

'Then it's about time he learned how to do it properly.' Taz sat herself on the corner of the desk, giving herself the advantage of a little extra height. She inspected her nails, smoothed down her skirt, let Theresa sweat a little before bothering to continue. 'I'm a little concerned, Theresa.'

'What about?' The lips fairly quivered with apprehension.

Taz consulted a folder of papers on her desk.

'Let's just say that certain items of stock have been turning up in places where they really oughtn't to be. Expensive items of stock.'

Theresa looked almost relieved.

'Oh, you mean that caviare and stuff I turned up in the stockroom, when we were making up the harvest hampers? Amazing that, wasn't it? I can't think how it got there.'

'No?' Taz let the question resonate a little before proceeding. 'Then maybe you have some idea how a quantity of Grape Harvest stock could find its way into the fuse-cupboard at the back of the stockroom?'

It could have been imagination or wishful thinking, but

Theresa seemed to turn a shade or two paler beneath her orange-tinged foundation.

'Did it?' Theresa shuffled her bottom on the chair, trying ineffectually to tug down her skirt over the hem of her black petticoat. 'God, no, I had no idea.'

'Really? You're absolutely sure about that?'

Theresa squirmed. Taz had to force herself not to feel sorry for her. After all, she might turn out to be pure as the driven snow, and Taz had never shared Ted Williams's appetite for wilful sadism.

'I really don't know, Ms Norton. You see . . . Ken Harris, he was always rearranging the stock, and he was so disorganised, you could've lost an elephant in that stockroom.'

'Perhaps.' Taz had to admit that Ken's managerial skills left a lot to be desired. 'But wouldn't you still know that the stock was in there?'

'Not if I'd lost the stock card,' replied Theresa, playing her trump card. 'Everybody knows the stock control system in the food hall's out of the ark. Now, if they'd brought in proper computerisation like in the rest of the store . . .'

'OK, OK. Point taken. But wouldn't you *remember* that there was a box of booze in there worth seven hundred and eighty pounds?'

Taz waited for Theresa to whack the ball back into her court; but Theresa's bottom lip was visibly quivering.

'I don't know what you're saying, Ms Norton, I really don't,' she said, not very convincingly.

Taz moved in for the kill.

'Don't worry, Theresa,' she said with a magnanimous wave of her hand. 'Nobody's blaming you.'

'No?' There was real wonderment in the gaze that met Taz's. 'Really?'

'Really. But we do need to avoid costly mistakes. You understand that, don't you Theresa?'

It was obvious from the look of apprehension on Theresa's face that she did.

Chapter 24

The sudden news that Marion Grey's mother had died came as less of a shock to Taz than the invitation to attend the funeral.

'Ten o'clock, October 3rd, Municipal Crematorium. Donations in lieu of flowers to Alzheimer's Relief.' Taz shuddered. She thought of all the many and valid reasons why she couldn't go, but she knew in her heart that she would end up going, simply because Marion had begged her to.

On a dingy October morning, she found herself standing in drizzle outside the crematorium, huddled among the pathetic straggle of Marion's nearest and dearest. They were a sad bunch: a couple of aunties Marion hadn't seen for decades, a scarlet-suited cousin from Toronto who Taz suspected was here only for the reading of the will, and Marion's brother Walter with the three small daughters from his late marriage, the children holding hands and whispering to each other in the uneasy atmosphere of solemnity.

Taz slipped her arm round Marion's shoulders.

'It was a nice service anyway,' she lied.

Marion sniffed away the last of her tears and dried her eyes, tucking her lace-edged hanky up her sleeve.

'Nice? That vicar didn't know the first thing about Mother,' she retorted. 'He might just as well have been talking about a stranger. Then again,' she sighed, getting into the car as the undertaker's assistant held open the door for her, 'Mother *was* a stranger at the end, wasn't she? It was only her body we buried, she went away a long time ago.'

'I'm sure she still loved you.' Taz squeezed in next to Marion, wedging the cousin from Toronto into the angle of the door. 'Even if she couldn't show it any more.'

'Perhaps.' Marion let herself sink back as the black limousine turned and glided soundlessly away from the crematorium. All her acquired stiffness seemed to be melting away, leaving her somehow smaller and much more human. 'It's all over now. Thank God it's all over.'

Taz squeezed her hand sympathetically, imagining how she'd feel if one of her parents had died.

'She's not suffering any more, that's the main thing,' offered the cousin from Toronto with a degree of insincerity that would have done credit to Ted Williams. 'She's at peace now.'

'And so am I,' replied Marion, in a small but steady voice. 'For the first time in a long, long time, so am I.'

If Taz had expected Marion to fall apart at the seams, her preconceptions were dented by the ritual tea and sandwiches back at the house. Marion carried herself with dignity, a great deal more dignity than Cousin Jane, who scarcely took the time to offer condolences and down a glass of sherry before ransacking the contents of Marion's mother's dressing table.

'Harriet wanted me to have these,' she announced, flouncing back into the sitting room with a cut-crystal scent bottle and a silver-backed hairbrush. 'You don't mind, do you? Only I'd like to have a memento of her.'

'Really?' replied Marion coldly. 'Funny you should want to remember her now, seeing as you hardly sent her a Christmas card in twenty years.'

Cousin Jane's pale porcelain cheeks flushed underneath her broad-brimmed hat. She laughed nervously, noticed all eyes on her and turned it into a cough.

'Really Marion, dear, you know that's not true. Your mother and I were always . . . very close.' Her fingers clutched the silver hairbrush with vampiric determination.

'Take what you like.' Marion's pale lips tightened in

disciplined anger. 'It's all you'll be getting anyway, she wrote you out of her will years ago.'

It was worth being there, just to see the expression on Cousin Jane's face, thought Taz, silently cheering Marion on. Who'd have thought that Marion had so much pure bitch in her, now, when her entire world was dismantling itself about her ears?

When Jane had stalked off to the solace of the sherry bottle, Taz chatted to Walter for a little while. Then she looked around for Marion to make her apologies; by her reckoning, it was time to make an exit. To her surprise, she found Marion had taken refuge in the kitchen, her eyes pink-rimmed but dry; the sleeves of her black dress rolled up and her arms plunged to the elbows in the sink.

'Marion – whatever are you doing?'

'The washing up, I have to keep on top of it. Just because Mother's gone, doesn't mean I'm going to let things slide.'

'But shouldn't you be taking a rest? It's been a difficult day for you, it'll take a lot of getting over. Why don't you sit down and let me make you a cup of tea?'

'Believe me, Taz, this is the best thing for me. Work.' Marion scrubbed energetically at stubborn fragments of burnt sausage roll, blackly welded to their baking tray. She looked across at Taz. 'Thank you for being here.'

'It was the least I could do.' Taz thought of simply saying a polite goodbye, but there was a tea-towel lying on the worktop and it seemed rude not to pick it up and pitch in. 'Here, let me help. You wash and I'll dry.'

'I wasn't sure you'd come,' said Marion, rinsing the baking tray and slotting it into the drainer. 'I could hardly blame you if you didn't, what with me being so horrible to you.'

'That was a long time ago,' protested Taz. 'I've forgotten all about it, besides, you were under a lot of stress.'

Marion shook her head.

'It wasn't stress that made me the way I was. It was . . . jealousy I suppose. I couldn't bear the thought of you – you know – having everything. Goodness knows why you didn't sack me.'

'Oh, you know me.' Taz dried an ivy-patterned cup and put it back into the wall cupboard. 'I like a challenge.'

Marion grunted.

'Then you ought to come back to menswear. That Ted Williams . . .'

'Ted? What about him?' asked Taz, pricking up her ears.

'Well, it's not my place to tell tales . . .' Marion's lips pursed. 'But I'll just say he's not the easiest person in the world to work for. And all that new merchandise we've been getting! It's impossible to take proper care of, it's so fragile and it gets so much handling. I keep telling him it makes no sense to stock it.'

'Oh? And what does Ted say?'

Two tea plates joined the baking tray on the drainer.

'I don't know why I bother saying anything, he doesn't listen. And in any case he already knows – I've lost count of the number of times he's had to take damaged stock out to the incinerator.' She plunged a handful of teaspoons under the soapy waves. 'Terrible, I call it. A criminal waste of good clothing.'

Criminal. The word stuck in Taz's head, setting a starburst of coloured lights flashing on and off like Blackpool illuminations. Steady on though, it would be only too easy to jump to the wrong conclusion.

'So,' Taz said, casually polishing a sherry glass. 'It's a big problem in menswear, is it? Damaged stock?'

'It's dreadful! I've never seen so much soiled merchandise being written off. The last stocktake we had, practically the only things left that weren't damaged were the cufflinks!'

It was agonisingly tempting to probe a little deeper, but this was neither the time nor the place. Taz went on drying dishes and putting them away, letting Marion lead the conversation back to Harriet.

'Mother liked you, you know,' said Marion, soap-suds dripping off her hands as she lifted out an oval serving dish.

'Liked me? We only met a couple of times. And even then . . .'

Taz recalled the two occasions on which she'd accompanied Marion to the nursing home. Harriet couldn't have been much more than seventy, but sitting slumped in her chair, dribbling into a bib as *Going for Gold* blared mindlessly from the TV set on the wall, she'd seemed little more than an empty shell.

'She *did* like you, Taz. She wasn't that way all the time, she had moments when she was almost her old self again. And she told me once, "I like that girl with the baby, you can bring her again if you like."' Marion wiped her hands on her apron, then dipped into the pocket of her dress. 'Then she said I was to give you this.'

Taz looked down as Marion opened her fingers. There, lying on the open palm, was an oval locket, very old by the looks of it, its engraved decoration worn faint from years of wear. The gold gleamed a buttery yellow against Marion's pink-white skin.

'Marion!'

'Please, Taz, she really did say you were to have it. Besides, I shan't have any use for it, shall I?' She prised it open and it revealed two empty oval frames, waiting to house two small photographs. 'It's meant for lovers so it's a bit late for me!'

'I'm very touched.' Taz took the locket, turned it over in her hand, imagining her own photograph in one of the ovals, and another opposite it – a portrait of Adam? 'But I can't accept it.'

'Tasmin, please!'

'No, Marion, I can't.' Taz replaced the locket in Marion's hand and curled her fingers over it. 'Your mum was confused, she didn't really know me, it was you she wanted to have it.'

'What use can it possibly be to me?'

'Who knows?' Taz smiled encouragingly at Marion, willing her to see her mother's death not just as a bereavement, but as the chance for a new beginning. 'Who can tell what's just around the corner?'

'I'm not too early am I?' Leroy hovered on the threshold

of Taz's flat, a leather document wallet tucked under his arm.

'No, of course not, come in.' Taz bounced Jack on her hip. 'I'm a bit behind, what with the funeral . . . Actually I was just about to give Jack his bath, but it can wait till later.'

Leroy tickled Jack under his arms. Jack giggled and writhed like a bag of eels.

'Hello there Jack. Remember me?' Leroy pulled a series of comical faces which enthralled Jack and frankly astounded Taz. At Seuss & Goldman, Leroy McIntosh did not project the image of a man who liked to stick out his tongue and flap his hands like elephant's ears.

'If the wind changes you'll stay like that,' commented Taz, trying to keep a straight face.

'Then I'll fit in perfectly in the food hall,' replied Leroy, returning to his usual deadpan self. 'We only employ gargoyles. Look, if it's Jack's bathtime, I can wait . . . I know babies need a regular routine.'

'Now what could somebody like you possibly know about babies?' teased Taz, ushering Leroy into the living room.

'I told you, I'm an uncle three times over,' replied Leroy indignantly, perching on the edge of the sofa and unzipping his document case. 'Yes I am Jack, don't look at me like that! Whenever I stay with Janis in Canterbury – she's my older sister – I get landed with babysitting.'

'Babysitting – you!'

'Well . . . all right it's more like zoo-keeping. The trouble is, Janis is great on love and cuddles but the discipline thing is taking some working on. Everett bit my leg once . . .'

'Speaking of work.' Taz placed Jack on the floor and gave him his plastic building blocks to play with. He promptly jammed the yellow one into his mouth and started chewing. 'We need to decide exactly what we're going to do about the food hall – and Ted.'

'We can't be absolutely sure Ted has anything to do with this,' cautioned Leroy. 'I mean – are we suspecting him just because we *want* to? What evidence do we have?'

'Not that much. Mainly supposition. All the goods we found hidden in the stockroom were damaged in some way. Nothing major, just enough for it to be classed as "soiled and damaged" if it turned up on the balance sheet. And now Marion Grey tells me stock's disappearing from menswear too.'

Leroy whistled.

'Bingo.'

'Yeah, expensive stock, it's being written off and taken out to be destroyed. The question is, has it actually been making it to the incinerator, or has somebody been creaming it off en route, for his own purposes? Naming no names, of course.'

'As if I would. But I do think maybe it's time you had a confidential chat with Diana Latchford about this, don't you?'

Taz nodded. She wasn't looking forward to this, not one bit, but the bullet had to be bitten.

'I wish we had a few more facts but yes, you're right. I'll make an appointment to see her. In the meantime, we'd better keep this close to our chests.'

Leroy pushed aside his papers, hitched up his trousers and got down on the floor with Jack, hoisting him up onto his fat little legs until the two of them were eyeball to eyeball. 'Now listen to me young man. If one word gets out about this you're looking at a ten-stretch and no rusks. Got that?'

Taz rocked with silent laughter. Jack stared back, blinked and gave a conspiratorial burp.

The following evening, Taz and Adam dropped Jack off at Painswick then drove on to Clive's.

'You're sure he invited me too?' Adam peered through the windscreen of Taz's car at Clive and Chloë's villa, its elegant bulk impressive even in the darkness.

'Positive. Cheer up, Clive's a nice bloke.'

'Ah. But can he cook?'

'Food – is that all you ever think about?'

'Not quite,' said Adam with a wink.

Inwardly Taz was telling herself to cheer up, too. Dinner

with Clive Baxendale wasn't exactly her idea of a fun Saturday night out, particularly as Adam had had the promise of theatre tickets for Stratford. But something – guilt about Chloë she supposed – had driven her to accept Clive's invitation before she'd even asked Adam if he was free. Which possibly accounted for Adam's less than sunny frame of mind.

Clive was already waiting for them on the doorstep, his obvious pleasure in seeing them quite painful to behold. What did Clive have to be grateful to Taz for? If anything, her efforts at mediation had made the stand-off with the Barstowes even worse.

'I hope you like fish,' said Clive, taking their coats. 'It's the only thing I can cook properly.'

Taz gave Adam a look that forestalled his protest of 'actually I'm a vegetarian'. Adam was only *almost* a vegetarian. They both knew that Adam ate fish sometimes, when he was in the mood, so he'd just have to be in the mood tonight.

'Thanks ... yes. Great.' Adam unfastened another button on his shirt. 'It's quite warm in here, isn't it?'

'Oh, sorry, is it too hot for you? I can turn the thermostat down a bit if you like – it's just Ayesha, she's had a chill, you know. The health visitor said to keep her warm.'

'We're fine, really,' cut in Taz as Clive led the way into the huge yet cosy kitchen, where an oak refectory table nestled under hanging copper pans. 'But how are *you*?'

'Oh, you know. Managing.' He didn't sound like it.

'And Ayesha?'

'She'll be fine now she's over the chill. The nanny's taking care of her but I'll pop up and see her after we've eaten.'

Clive poured wine and fiddled about with the stove. Taz spotted the soup-pan boiling over just in the nick of time, and whisked it off the hob, burning her finger in the process, much to Clive's chagrin.

'Oh dear, I am sorry, did you hurt yourself, there are some plasters here somewhere ...' Drawers were pulled out and rummaged about in, revealing crumpled plastic carrier bags and lots of string, but no plasters. 'Oh God Taz, I'm so sorry, Chloë used to . . .'

He clammed up. Taz calmly closed the drawers and turned on the tap.

'Don't worry, I'll just hold my finger under the cold water for a bit, it'll be fine. It's only a little burn, honestly.'

It was an inauspicious start to the evening, and things didn't get noticeably better. The sauce got spilt into the pudding, Taz had to rescue one of the trout before it turned to a chargrilled cinder, and conversation – always difficult with Clive – was near-impossible with Adam there as well. It was depressingly obvious that they had nothing to say to each other.

'Have you heard from Chloë?' enquired Taz, her nerve finally giving out as the kitchen clock measured out a whole sixty seconds of silence.

'We spoke for about five minutes on the phone last week, but that's the closest I've got to her in ages.' Bitterness infected his normally affable tones. 'Her parents . . . well, you know what they're like. The Gestapo with Range Rovers.'

'But I thought you got on so well with them.'

'That was before.'

Taz looked at Adam. Adam looked at his dinner. It was obvious that this was something he didn't want to get dragged into.

'And the court case? Has Chloë heard anything about that?'

'Her parents are trying to get her to plead guilty and keep the whole thing quiet.'

'Sounds sensible,' commented Adam. The first time he'd really tried to contribute to the evening's conversation, thought Taz, mildly encouraged. 'After all, she *is* guilty, there doesn't seem any doubt about that.'

'I know, but – ' Clive waved his hands about, trying to pluck the right words from the smoke-tinged kitchen fug. 'I know she stole those shirts, but she wasn't herself . . .'

Adam sighed.

'Look, this is none of my business Clive, but it's a first offence, it shouldn't go too badly with her. A fine, probably. And if there are any extenuating circumstances, the court will want to hear about them.'

Clive hung on to Adam's words like the edge of a very deep precipice.

'You really think so? You think they'll understand – about her being ill?'

'Ill? I don't know about that, I'm no medical expert – get her to see a doctor,' Adam said, shrugging.

'But she won't! She says she's all right.'

'Then there's nothing more you can do. Perhaps she isn't ill at all. Perhaps you're just imagining it.'

'But she *is* ill,' protested Taz. 'It's so obvious. She's not been behaving rationally ever since Ayesha was born.'

'Isn't there *anything* we can do, Adam?' pleaded Clive. 'Couldn't you advise her, take on her case?'

Adam wearily laid down his fork.

'I'm sorry Clive, I really am, but Taz should've explained. This isn't my type of case, I only do legal aid work. I'm afraid if it's a solicitor you need, you'll have to look elsewhere.'

'Oh.' Clive got up, scrunching his damask napkin and dropping it onto the table. He seemed to have aged ten years since Taz had first seen him at Steffi's; and she noticed that his jumper had a hole near the shoulder seam, a hole that Chloë would have darned for him in five minutes if she'd been here. 'Look, if you'll excuse me I'll just go up and check on Ayesha.'

His slippered feet made a soft scraping sound on the terracotta tiles, then a muffled thump-thump-thump as he climbed up to the nursery.

'You had all this planned, didn't you?' said Adam, his usual good humour markedly frayed around the edges. 'You brought me here just so Clive could emotionally blackmail me into taking on his wife's case!'

'Come off it, Adam. I wouldn't do a thing like that. And if you think I would, you really don't know me very well.'

They glared at each other for a few moments, then Adam held up his hands in defeat.

'OK, maybe I was wrong, I'm sorry. Well, wrong about

you anyhow. But I'm one hundred per cent certain Clive only invited us to dinner so he could pick my brains about the court case.'

'You're wrong,' snapped Taz, suddenly not at all pleased with Adam or his ridiculous suppositions. 'Completely wrong. It's not legal advice Clive's after. That poor sod's been living here all on his own for weeks now, he's lonely, he's frightened, his wife's walked out on him, he's hit rock bottom. It's not a lawyer he needs. It's a friend.'

By Monday, Taz and Adam had mended fences and agreed to differ about Clive Baxendale – though it still rankled with Taz that Adam could be so immune to Clive's obvious distress. On the other hand, as Adam kept pointing out, it wasn't Taz's job to sort out the whole world's problems, just her own.

She got Theresa Carvell into the office straight after the flash meeting.

'We need to talk again. About these discrepancies in the stock.'

'I've told you, Ms Norton, I don't know anything about it.'

'OK then, let me jog your memory. I'll remind you how this little scam might work, *in theory*. Let's say you – accidentally or otherwise – drop a tin of caviare and it gets dented. What's the company procedure?'

'If it's very badly damaged, it's written off and has to go to the crusher or the incinerator to be destroyed.'

'Correct. But what if it's only a little bit damaged?'

'We might mark the price down . . .'

'But it'd stay on sale?'

'Yeah. Course.'

'Unless, of course, you were to write it off anyway, then substitute it for something of lesser value, take that to the incinerator and destroy it instead. Which would leave you with a nice little thirty-nine pound tin of caviare all for yourself. I wonder how much you could sell it on for if you knew the right people.'

'How should I know?'

Theresa was worried, it was patently obvious from the

341

way she was frozen to her chair, her high-heeled shoe dangling ludicrously from one stockinged toe, her mouth hanging slackly open.

'Well, Theresa? Anything coming back to you yet?'

'No, Ms Norton. Nothing.'

'And what if I suggested that it wasn't you who did it anyway, but somebody else? Somebody you're protecting? What if I suggested that this lucrative little enterprise could transfer just as well to another department . . . say . . . Menswear?'

Taz held her breath, willing Theresa to break down and confess that she was nothing but Ted Williams' stooge. But Theresa was either very loyal or very stupid, or both.

'Like I said, Ms Norton, I don't know what you're talking about. In fact, I don't know anything at all.'

It was Wednesday afternoon before Taz managed to get an appointment with Diana Latchford; ample time to prepare what she needed to say. But even so, her heart pounded as she waited in the outer office, dreading the royal summons. It was no use reminding herself that she was simply doing her duty, it didn't make her feel good to know that she was grassing up her own colleagues.

The door to the inner office opened, and Diana Latchford ushered Taz inside.

'Come in, Tasmin. I can spare you twenty minutes or so. As a matter of fact, I was going to ask you to come and see me anyway.'

'You were?' This threw Taz. She looked into Diana's face; it seemed somehow less open than usual, less easy to read, though everything else about Diana was as immaculate and unruffled as it always was. The black patent shoes with the subtle gold trimming, the dark burgundy suit, the Chanel scarf. 'What about?'

'You first.' Diana indicated a chair. 'Take a seat. Coffee?'

'N-no. No thanks.' Taz folded her hands in her lap. They felt sweaty and cold, she was absurdly nervous, like a kid on a first job interview. 'It's about stock which has been going missing from the food hall. And . . . menswear.' She cleared her throat. 'I have reason to believe that Ted Williams is behind a large-scale fraud. He's been deliberately damaging stock, writing it off and then selling it on to line his own pockets.'

Diana stared at her, apparently poleaxed with astonishment.

'Ted Williams?' She sat down slowly behind her desk. 'I think you'd better explain. In detail.'

Taz proceeded to do exactly that, detailing the interviews she'd had with Theresa, the hidden goods discovered in the stockroom, Marion's comments about menswear, the quantities of merchandise written off and sent to the incinerator. Diana listened impassively, making no comment until Taz had finished.

'So. You're saying that stock was written off, cheaper stock substituted and that this was destroyed while the more expensive goods were sold on? And you're alleging that Ted Williams is behind it all?'

'I'm certain he is.'

Diana gave an impatient snort. Sliding open her top drawer, she took out two pieces of paper and handed them to Taz.

'Theresa Carvell's letter of resignation, we received it first thing this morning. You'll see she admits to stealing from the food hall over a period of several months, and takes full responsibility for what happened. The second letter is an apology from Grape Harvest, admitting liability for Theresa's actions. We'll be agreeing a financial settlement with them in due course.'

Taz's hands shook with shock and disbelief.

'But she's covering up for Ted, he's her boyfriend . . .'

'As a matter of fact,' said Diana. 'It was Ted Williams who brought this whole sorry affair to my attention. Apparently Theresa went to him, confided in him what she'd done, and naturally he advised her to make a clean breast of it.'

'Naturally,' murmured Taz. Trust Ted to be one step ahead of her. Again. 'But surely, don't you believe what I'm saying?'

Diana folded her arms.

'I believe the evidence of my own eyes. And as far as I can see you have no evidence at all but your own suspicions.'

Taz hung her head.

'No.'

'I thought as much. And I have to say, though it gives me no pleasure to do so, that your own behaviour falls far short of the standard I would expect from you. How long have you known about thefts from the food hall? Why didn't you bring your suspicions to me sooner?'

'Because,' said Taz in desperation, 'that's all they were. Suspicions.'

Diana stalked across to the window and threw it open, letting in a gust of chill, damp air and startling the pigeons into flight.

'For God's sake, Tasmin, sometimes you're your own worst enemy. First Angus Cornforth, now Henry Goldman. Who are you going to wind up next?'

She didn't wait for a response, gripping the windowsill with both hands and declaiming to the empty air above Imperial Gardens.

'Listen to me for once in your life. Henry Goldman hates all women on principle, and Henry Goldman has a lot of power around here. He is also on *very* good terms with Ted Williams, and with all this business in the food hall, right now all of Henry's prejudices are being confirmed.

'If I were you, I would strongly suggest that you avoid saying one word against Ted Williams unless and until you have concrete evidence – and plenty of it – that he has done something seriously wrong.'

'But I can't just . . .'

'Get your head down Tasmin, work hard, prove yourself. And do it quickly. While you've still got the chance.'

Chapter 25

'I'm never going to get the hang of this,' whinged Vernon, Theresa Carvell's temporary stand-in at the Grape Harvest concession.

'Yes you will,' Taz said firmly. 'Let's just go over it one more time.'

Secretly, Taz knew just how Vernon felt. He wasn't the only one who was having trouble coping. Still reeling from Diana's tongue-lashing, still trying to decide whether she loved or hated Sushil's conceptual sketches for the revamp, she was becoming more and more despondent about the long-term future of the food hall. For the first time, she was beginning to understand why Ken Harris had decided to roll over and play dead.

'I don't understand,' moaned Vernon. 'About booking in the new stock . . . Theresa always used to do it.'

Taz closed invisible fingers about Theresa Carvell's throat. Why oh why had that stupid girl chosen to sacrifice everything for the sake of a toerag like Ted Williams? There really was no accounting for tastes.

'Well you'll be doing it for the foreseeable future.' She fixed Vernon with the brightest and most insistent of smiles. 'Who knows, if you do the job well, maybe the promotion will be made permanent.'

Vernon positively quivered with horror.

'God, you don't really think so do you? All I've ever wanted is an easy life.'

Lord bless us and save us, thought Taz as she crossed to dry goods, pausing briefly at the cheese counter to reprimand Mark for sticking his finger up his nose.

Thank heaven for Leroy McIntosh, patiently supervising the latest junior as she restacked a perilous mountain of Petticoat Tails.

'Leroy, sorry to drag you away when you're having fun, but you couldn't just go over and calm Vernon down could you? Only he's having one of his crises.'

'If I have to keep on holding his hand like this, people will start to talk.'

'Do your best. You know how busy it gets round lunchtime, and the state he's in I wouldn't be surprised if he bursts into tears over the Veuve Cliquot.'

Leroy's eyes drifted briefly heavenward; then he strode off purposefully towards wines and spirits. Taz turned her attention to the junior, tongue-tip clenched between her teeth as she balanced another gift-pack of shortbread on the top of her pyramid.

'How's it going, Louise?'

'All right I s'pose.'

'What about the day release course, are you getting much from it?'

Louise couldn't have looked more dumbfounded if she'd been asked for the square root of a hundred and twenty-six.

'Dunno. S'pose.'

It really was one of those days, thought Taz. One of those days when nothing went quite right; when you had to expect the unexpected.

And here it came, strolling casually past the wet fish counter, one hand slipped lazily into the pocket of an exquisitely tailored navy-blue suit. A neutron bomb in pinstriped gabardine.

'Ms Norton,' came a plaintive voice. 'Miss, do I put this here or there – or what? Ms Norton?'

'What?' Shaking and icy cold, her eyes still fixed on the slowly-approaching figure, Taz forced herself to take notice of Louise. 'What did you say?'

'This.' Louise waggled a tin of Scottish tablet under Taz's nose. 'Does it go here, or what? Is it a luxury biscuit or a confectionery?'

Taz's mind reeled. She pushed the tin out of her way.

346

All at once it didn't seem to matter very much in the grand scheme of things.

'Ask Mr McIntosh, he'll know.'

The figure in the blue suit walked right up to Taz and greeted her with a dazzle of perfect teeth.

'Well, well. Long time no see.'

Every droplet of blood froze to ice-crystals in Taz's veins. When she tried to speak, there was a pathetic tremble in her voice, and she hated herself for being so feeble.

'Gareth.'

'Missed me?' enquired the handsome face, as ever framed by thick, dark hair that was only just beginning to grey at the temples.

'Gareth, what the hell . . .?'

Taz looked around her, suddenly realising that her voice had risen almost to a shout. Louise was kneeling on the ground at her feet, staring fascinatedly up at her. Spotty Ian was transfixed behind the cheese counter, Wensleydale in one hand and a paper bag in the other. Even one or two customers were pausing to peep over the top of the biscuit rack, ears pricked for any juicy snippet of scandal. Taz promptly grabbed Gareth by the sleeve and pulled him into the relative privacy of an alcove by the display window.

'Steady on, Taz,' winked Gareth. 'I know you're pleased to see me but let's take this slowly eh?'

Taz longed to pick up a five-pound tin of teatime assorted and smash it over Gareth's head. She contented herself with a hiss of barely-controlled fury.

'What the bloody hell do you think you're doing here, Gareth?'

'I'm back,' he replied, calmly extricating his sleeve from Taz's grasp and tweaking the crumpled fabric back into shape.

The words didn't register, they scarcely even touched the protective shell of disbelief which Taz had thrown up about her.

'You're what?'

'Back. In Cheltenham, well, Swindon actually. Henry

347

Goldman asked me to come back as senior financial adviser to the board, and frankly the package was so good I couldn't turn it down. So here I am.'

'That doesn't explain why you've come back to plague me. Why, Gareth? Why now?'

'Why? Because we need to talk. But you know that already, don't you?'

'Talk? What the hell would I want to talk to you about?'

'About the baby of course. My son.'

Taz gasped, took a step back, reached out for the pillar by the window to stop herself falling. Gareth peered quizzically at Taz's ashen face.

'Your little friend did *tell* you I paid him a call while you were away? He didn't forget to mention it?'

Taz took a ridiculously early lunch. In the circumstances there wasn't much else she could do. Gareth Scott had come rampaging back into her life, acting like he owned it and her and Jack – and there was no way she was letting him get away with it.

'I'm sorry if I gave you a shock,' said Gareth, perusing the menu at the café bar. 'But it's nothing to the shock I got when I came to see you. Why don't you try the linguie?' he added. 'It looks like the only edible thing on the menu.'

'I'm not hungry.' Taz took a slug of rosé from the glass in front of her. Normally she wouldn't have touched alcohol during working hours, it dulled the brain and made her sluggish, but there was nothing normal about today. Her pulse raced, she felt sick to her stomach with the horror of this one thing she had really dreaded happening coming true right in front of her eyes. She forced herself to look at Gareth, though it made her faint with apprehension and loathing. 'I want to know why you're doing this to me, Gareth.'

'Doing? Doing what? All I did was come round to your flat on the off-chance you'd cooled down enough to let Melanie have her stuff back.'

'Oh, right. Melanie.' Taz spoke the word with a whole

year's worth of accumulated rancour. 'How *is* Melanie these days?'

'We got married last August,' replied Gareth indifferently.

'So you actually went and did it. Not still with her are you? My God it must be a world record for you. Mind you, I expect you've got a spare waiting in the wings . . .'

'I'm not here to talk about my sex-life, I'm here to talk about my son.'

Taz felt a violent stab of protective anger. Her fingers tightened abruptly about the glass; a fraction more and it would have shattered in her hand.

'Don't you *dare* talk about Jack as if he has anything to do with you!'

'Come on, Taz, I can do simple arithmetic. The boy's mine, we both know that.'

'Oh we do, do we?' Taz's lip curled into a sneer. 'So what makes you so sure I wasn't two-timing you the way you were two-timing me? Tell me that.'

'You're not like me, Taz.' Gareth seemed mildly amused by the suggestion that she might be, which only made the insult worse. 'You wouldn't do a thing like that.'

'You don't know that,' Taz insisted, her mouth dry as dust and her heart pounding against her ribs. 'Jack's not your son, Gareth, he has nothing to do with you and he never will have, so just piss off out of our lives and leave us alone.'

'Look me in the eye and tell me he's not mine.'

'I don't have to do anything, I don't have to say anything.'

'OK.' Gareth relaxed back in his chair with a glass of wine. 'Have it your own way, we'll get DNA tests done. Apparently they cost about three hundred pounds, but don't worry about that, I'll foot the bill. After all, Jack is my son, I want to pay my way.'

'You're not laying one finger on Jack!'

Taz's fists clenched on the table-top. A couple at the next table, sticky-lipped from feeding each other spoonsful of sherry trifle, paused in their giggles to turn and stare.

Gareth shook his head sadly.

'I don't understand, Taz. All I want is for us to discuss *our* son like civilised human beings, make sensible arrangements about who takes care of him, how he's going to be provided for. All I want to do is spend time with my son. Why can't you just accept that?'

The waiter chose that moment to glide across with Gareth's steaming plateful of linguine al funghi.

'Your pasta sir ... you're sure madam wouldn't like something with her wine?'

Taz stood up, pushing the table away from her so hard that one of the legs caught in a gap between the tiles, sending Gareth's glass of wine flying into his lap.

'No,' snapped Taz. 'Madam would *not* like anything with her wine, thank you very much. In fact, the only thing madam wants right now is for sir to get the hell out of her life.'

'Taz, for pity's sake,' growled Gareth, seizing the white towel from the waiter's arm and using it to swab spilt wine from his suit. 'Come back here and stop behaving like a spoilt brat.'

But the fire-doors were already swinging shut, with a violence that suggested Taz had no intention of going along with any of Gareth's wishes.

Ever.

It wasn't like Taz to take the afternoon off sick. But when she got back to S&G from the café bar she was in no state to do anything but sit in the office and stare into space. She wanted to cry, but she couldn't. She wanted to ring Melanie up and scream at her, but she didn't even know where she lived. She wanted to ring Adam's neck for not warning her; to do something mad, anything, pour maple syrup all over Gareth's car ...

Anything that would make her feel better for a few minutes, stop her from dwelling on the fear.

In the end it was Leroy who made the decision for her, finding her sitting there not answering her pager; sorting everything out without asking any questions, ordering a taxi and telling her not to come back 'until everything was sorted out'. She made up her mind to thank him sometime, later when Gareth was a long way away, Jack was safe, and she could start thinking rationally again.

Jack. The thought of him obsessed her all the way home. What if Gareth had gone straight to the flat, sweet-talked Adam again, conned him into handing Jack over? What if he'd taken her son, kidnapped him? What if she never saw him again?

She almost fell out of the taxi, stuffing a ten-pound note into the driver's hand and telling him to keep the change. She cursed herself for not going straight home to him, as soon as Gareth had staked his claim. Oh Jack, Jack, please forgive me, I should never have left you on your own . . .

Fumbling in her bag for the key, she dropped it three times before she finally managed to get it into the lock and open the door.

'Adam . . . Adam are you there, is Jack all right?'

Jack seemed pleased but rather baffled to see his mother so early in the afternoon. He was bouncing up and down in his baby-walker, shrieking and gurgling happily as Isobel and Adam huddled round the coffee table, talking in smiley whispers.

'Tasmin!' Isobel looked up from next year's calendar, a pencil in her hand.

'What's wrong?' demanded Adam, jumping to his feet. 'You're not ill are you, you look terrible!'

Isobel sniffed the air.

'Can I smell drink? Tasmin dear, you've not been *drinking*? At lunchtime? You know it always makes you sick.'

Taz grabbed Jack and hoisted him onto her shoulder, snuggling him as close as she could without squeezing all the breath out of him.

'Jack, oh sweetheart, I've been so worried!'

'Worried? What about?' demanded Adam.

'There's not a thing to worry about,' cut in Isobel. 'He's absolutely fine, aren't you Jack? He's even tried a little mashed potato today, and you know how difficult it is to get him to eat anything but avocado.'

Taz hugged Jack and let relief flood into her, pushing out the dreadful, irrational fear.

'I won't let anyone take you away from me,' she whispered, very softly, into his tiny pink ear. 'Nobody, you're Mummy's boy and nobody else is having you.'

'Actually dear, I'm glad you're here,' commented Isobel with a wink and a smile at Adam. 'Adam and I have been sorting things out for you, haven't we Adam?'

'Things?' Taz looked suspiciously at her mother, then at Adam. 'What things?'

'The christening, dear. I know you've been too busy, so we thought we'd do the work for you. Now, I've had a quiet word with Reverend Burke, and he thinks he could fit Jack in on the third Sunday in January. Of course, you'd need to attend church for a few weeks beforehand, to show willing . . . still, that's not too much to ask for Jack's sake is it?'

Taz blinked, hardly believing she was hearing this.

'Look, Mother, I don't have time for this at the moment, any of it.'

'But Tasmin!'

'Jack and I will *think* about it, OK? Adam – in that kitchen, now, I want a word with you.'

Adam threw Isobel a baffled look over his shoulder as Taz hauled him into the kitchen and banged the door shut.

'What's this all about? We were only trying to help you out . . . with the christening. Do you mind if I just fetch my cup of tea from the sitting room?'

Taz plastered herself across the door in a human barricade; he wasn't going anywhere until they'd had serious words.

'Oh yes, the christening. I suppose you and Mum have already chosen the godparents and a nice robe for Jack to wear and baked two dozen fairy-cakes and bunged them in the freezer for the christening tea – not to mention sending out invitations to half of Gloucestershire!'

'Taz! You don't think you're over-reacting – just a teensy weensy bit?'

'Over-reacting? Yeah, maybe I am. Oh, and while

you're at it, why don't you choose Jack a nice middle name. How about Gareth?'

'Gareth?' Adam wrinkled his nose in puzzlement.

'Gareth *Scott*?'

Adam clapped his hand to his forehead in delayed recollection.

'Oh God, *him*. Yeah, I clean forgot, this guy called to see you while you were in Scotland, something about collecting some stuff? Didn't much care for him. I've got his number somewhere. What's all this about, anyway?' He rummaged in the pile of bills and junk mail by the toaster. 'Here it is.'

Taz snatched the card and shoved it into her pocket.

'For God's sake, Adam, why the hell didn't you tell me before that he'd been here?'

'I . . . I forgot.' Adam looked really sheepish under his sporty tan. 'You know what it's been like at work. How was I to know it was important, he just said he'd get in touch.'

'Oh, he got in touch all right,' hissed Taz. 'This morning, at work.'

'So what's the problem?'

'The problem? You really want to know? OK, I'll tell you. I work all the hours God sends to bring in enough money to take proper care of Jack. My son, the person I care about more than anything else in the whole world. Then, out of the blue, Jack's father turns up and wants to take him away from me . . .'

The mists cleared slowly. 'You mean . . . this Gareth character? He's Jack's *father*?'

'Got it in one. And then, when I get home half out of my mind in case Jack's been kidnapped, I find that somebody's already trying to steal my son away from me. And do you know who that somebody is?' She didn't bother waiting for a reply. 'It's you, Adam. You and my sainted mother.'

The next couple of days were strained and stressful, with Adam tiptoeing around the flat as though he was trying to avoid landmines, and Taz hardly daring to leave Jack when she went to work, for fear that Gareth would swoop like a pantomime villain and whisk him away to his lair.

By the third day Taz was finally beginning to believe that maybe, just maybe, Gareth had got the message. Maybe tomorrow night, if they were still getting on OK, Taz would invite Adam back into her bed. It was about time they sorted things out between them.

She was awoken just before two a.m. by something shrieking insistently over the tranquil hum of the central heating boiler.

Taz rolled onto her side, squinted at the fluorescent hands on the alarm clock and groaned. Two o'clock, it couldn't be time to get up yet. Her fingers fumbled for the button on the alarm clock, but it wasn't the clock that was making the noise. It was the phone. Panic clenched her stomach-muscles steel tight.

Jack grizzled and whined as she got wearily out of bed and pushed her feet into her slippers.

'Hush sweetheart, Mummy'll be back in a minute.'

Where was the cordless phone? Damn, she'd forgotten to bring it to bed with her, it must still be on the table in the hall. Oh hell, why bother anyway? It'd be just another of those wrong numbers, she told herself as she headed down the hallway; in fact it probably wasn't even worth getting out of bed for. But she was out of bed already, and her stomach kept on tightening; she could hardly breathe as she clicked on the wall-light and picked up the receiver. What if it was . . . Gareth?

'Hello?'

'Taz, oh Taz, it's you, it *is* you isn't it?'

There could be no mistaking that breathless, high-pitched voice.

'Mandy! Do you know what *time* it is?'

'Course I bleedin' do, it's the middle of the flamin' night. Look, don't go ballistic, OK? but I'm stuck down the cop shop with PC Plod.'

'The police station? Mandy, you've not got yourself arrested? Tell me you've not done anything silly.'

'Relax, I'm not in trouble. Well yeah, OK, I am in

trouble, but not that sort of trouble if you get what I mean . . .'

Adam's head stuck out of the spare room. There were dark purplish shadows under his eyes and his hair was sticking up on one side of his head. He yawned blearily.

'What's going on?'

'It's Mandy. She's at the police station.'

'I don't want to know what she's done,' groaned Adam. 'I don't want anything to do with this, do you hear?' But he came out of his room and shut the door. 'Go on, tell me the worst.'

'Mandy – Mandy are you still there?'

'I'm not goin' anywhere, am I? The thing is, there's been a bit of trouble at the place where we live, an' . . . well, we've not got anywhere to live no more. That's why I'm down the police station. I couldn't think of anyone else to ring but you.'

'What about her social worker?' hissed Adam, listening in with his head next to the receiver.

'That cow?' retorted Mandy. 'She'd make them take Dylan off me, I'm not havin' her anywhere near me, Taz, don't let him tell her . . .'

'I won't,' promised Taz. She picked up a pencil. 'Tell me where you are, Mandy.'

'I'm in Branch Street nick. In Gloucester.'

'Right.' Taz grabbed her car keys, pulled on socks and shoved her feet into boots. 'You stay right where you are and don't move. I'm coming to get you.'

Taz burst in through the double doors of the police station like an extra from *NYPD Blue*. The desk sergeant looked quite taken aback at the sight of a young mum in an anorak, nightie and wellington boots, hotly pursued by a slightly older bloke in dressing gown and slippers.

'So. What can I do for you?' enquired the sergeant, pen poised over a pad of complaint forms. An old woman with a shopping trolley stuffed full of grubby carrier bags, a teenager in fishnet tights and a drunk with a black eye watched sullenly from a row of plastic chairs.

'Mandy Robson, is she here?' demanded Taz breath-lessly.

'And you are – ?'

'Tasmin Norton, a friend of hers. She rang me up, told me there'd been some kind of trouble.'

The sergeant nodded.

'It's a bad area, that. No end of trouble with break-ins and arson and God knows what. She and the nipper are in the interview room, just on the right down the corridor.'

'But they're all right?' ventured Adam.

'Right as rain. Never heard language like it from a girl her age, mind, and I've been on the force seventeen years.'

They found Mandy sitting with a young policewoman in the interview room, Mandy rocking Dylan in his buggy while munching on a jumbo-sized bacon sandwich. Bread-crumbs spattered in all directions as she leapt to her feet.

'Taz, Taz, you came!'

'Oh Mandy, I'm so sorry. What on earth's been hap-pening to you?'

Taz handed Jack to Adam and the two women hugged like long-lost sisters. Mandy snivelled a little and it was all Taz could do not to join in. Taz was shocked to discover how thin Mandy had become, every bone easily countable beneath the three layers of thick woolly jumper.

'Somebody fire-bombed the chippy under my bedsit. I only just got Dylan out before the windows blew.'

'But why?'

'Landlord wants 'em out, don't he? That or he wants the insurance money. Any rate, me an' Dylan had to get out an' we've got nowhere else to go since Mam slung us out the flat.'

'We thought it was best if Mandy stayed here tonight,' explained the policewoman. 'Until we can get Social Services to find them somewhere else to stay . . .'

'No – Taz, don't let them ring the Social! They'll take Dylan away from me.'

'They won't, I'm sure they won't.' Taz looked over Mandy's shoulder at the young WPC, hoping for easy reassurance. 'They wouldn't would they?'

The policewoman shook her head non-committally.

'I really can't say what they'll do. It's up to them to decide what's for the best.'

'That settles it,' said Taz, making a snap decision. 'Mandy's coming home with us.'

Adam looked nonplussed. But Mandy's hollow-cheeked face lit up like a Christmas tree, her eyes unnaturally large and dark against the undernourished whiteness of her skin.

'Really? You mean it? I can stay with you?'

'For a few days, yes. Till you get back on your feet.'

'Fantastic! Oh Dylan, did you hear that? Your Auntie Taz is pure dead brilliant isn't she?'

The look of tearful gratitude on Mandy's exhausted face was enough to convince Taz that she'd made the right decision.

First they had to drive over to Mandy's bedsit and salvage her meagre possessions.

By the time they got there, the worst of the fire was out and a column of acrid black smoke was hanging in the air above the parade of shops. Three fire engines were parked along the roadway, one with its ladder still up against the first-floor window above what remained of the Chinese chippy. A dozen or so sightseers straggled behind the blue and white police tape, weary of nothing much happening but reluctant to go home in case they might miss something.

'It was the oil, see,' Taz heard somebody say. 'Went up like a Roman candle. Miracle nobody was killed.'

'So what if they were,' sniffed his companion, a small round woman in a check coat. 'They're scum anyway, we don't want their kind round here.'

It was the smell that hit Taz first as she stepped down onto the pavement, the all-pervading odour of charred wood, that caught chokingly in the back of the throat. And then she looked down at her feet and saw that she was standing in a miniature river, murky water flooding out of the open door of the gutted chip-shop and fanning out across the pavement to form a shallow delta.

Mandy leapt out of the car and pushed her way through

to the front of the gathering, grabbing herself the oldest and most sympathetic-looking firefighter.

'Can I go in an' get my stuff now then?'

'No chance. It's not safe in there.'

'But everythin' I've got's in there – my clothes, the baby's food, my books, everythin'.'

'Mandy,' urged Taz, 'If it's not safe . . . come on, you can come back in the morning.'

Mandy shook her head vigorously. The smears of dirt on her white face looked like warpaint.

'No way, I'm not leavin' till I've got my stuff. You don't know what they're like round here,' she added, offering venomous looks to the woman in the check coat. 'Turn your back for five minutes an' they'll have the food from out your baby's mouth.'

The firefighter gave in gracefully.

'Well all right then. But you're not going in on your own. Steve, take this young lady up to get her stuff will you?'

'Right you are, chief.'

'And don't let her out of your sight.'

Adam stood holding Jack, Taz soothing Dylan in his buggy as Mandy disappeared up the blackened stairs into the shell of her home.

'It's OK Dylan, your Mummy'll be back soon. God, but it's awful here,' shivered Taz, gazing not just at the burned-out chippy but the boarded post office, the graffiti picked out like dark scars under the yellow streetlights, the big black bulk of the abandoned factory looming over the darkened horizon.

'I know . . . but Taz.' Adam paused, choosing his words carefully. 'Look, I know I'm not exactly in your good books and Mandy and I haven't always been the greatest of friends, so maybe I should keep my big mouth shut, but are you sure you're doing the right thing? Taking Mandy in like this?'

'The right thing? Of course I'm doing the right thing – have you seen the state of Mandy? She's all skin and bone. God alone knows how she's managed to keep Dylan so happy and healthy, she must've been starving herself to provide for him. Are you suggesting I should throw her out on the street?'

'Of course I'm not. But they wouldn't be on the street, would they? Social Services would find them somewhere ... and what with Jack, and me in the spare room, it's not as if we've got room for them at the flat.'

'Listen, Adam. "We" doesn't come into it. This is about *my* flat, *my* life, *my* baby, *my* friends. And this is *my* decision. Got that?'

Adam nodded dumbly. At which point Mandy came stumbling down the stairs from the bedsit, a carrier bag of books in one hand and a giant, homemade-looking teddy bear tucked under her arm.

'Quick, Adam, open the boot – there's loads more to come, Steve's bringing down a suitcase. Look Dylan, I found Big Ted!'

She bent lovingly over her son, waggling the teddy bear's arm in a jaunty wave. And Dylan gurgled back, merrily oblivious to everything but the smile on his mother's face.

Chapter 26

Isobel took off her gloves and tucked them neatly away in her handbag. She checked her watch. Half past eight on a fine, crisp October Sunday morning: just the right time to pay a surprise visit to Tasmin.

The poor girl was looking terribly tired and drawn these days, hardly surprising when you considered she was trying to do the work of two parents *and* hold down a job that would have challenged any man. Isobel was proud of her daughter's achievements, of course she was, but it wasn't natural driving yourself like that, not with little Jack to think about.

Isobel fished in her bag for the front doorkey to Taz's flat. It would be such a nice surprise for her and Adam, having Granny turn up out of the blue to babysit Jack while they went off and had a lovely day to themselves. That was what those two needed; small wonder their romance wasn't progressing as quickly as it ought to, with all these pressures and anxieties on them both. Isobel was here to play the fairy godmother and make sure that the path of true love ran smooth.

Turning the key, Isobel gave the bottom of the door a delicate kick – the only way to make sure it opened without juddering. She really must tell Bill to come and plane down the door to stop it sticking.

'Tasmin dear . . . oh!'

In the semi-darkness of the hallway, rendered gloomy by the still-drawn curtains, stood a small figure with electric-shock hair, arms and legs like blanched twigs and a ring through its nose. It was wearing Taz's best nightie, the one Isobel had bought her from Rigby & Peller, but it definitely wasn't Taz, since the nightie was teamed with boot socks and a knitted tank-top. Brandished above its head, clenched in plaster-white fingers, was a cast-iron doorstep in the shape of a pig.

'Oh God, is that you Isobel, you could've knocked.'

The pig sank slowly to hip-level. Isobel took a couple of seconds to compose herself and think of a suitable riposte. It came in the form of a single word.

'You.'

Mandy rubbed her nose with the back of her hand. A multi-tinted dreadlock slipped down over one eye.

'Look, I'm sorry, I didn't mean nothin'. I thought you were, you know, a burglar or somethin'.'

'Oh yes, well, your sort would know all about burglars wouldn't you?'

'What's that?' demanded Mandy, her hackles rising. 'You callin' me a criminal or what?'

'Where's my daughter?' enquired Isobel stiffly.

'Asleep, it's Sunday.'

'And Adam?'

'Where do you think?' Mandy gestured towards the living room. 'He's on the sofa bed.'

'Why isn't he in his room?'

'Because *I'm* in there,' replied Mandy with growing impatience. 'Me an' Dylan.'

Isobel felt her entire soul tense with horrid expectation. Not again. Not *that girl*, back in Tasmin's life, making everything cheap and grubby. But perhaps she'd got the wrong end of the stick.

'Don't be silly, what would you be doing in Adam's room?'

'We're stayin' here, me an' Dylan. I told you.'

'You can't be!' Isobel gestured around the cluttered hall, taking in the two bin-bags by the telephone table, the huge, slightly damp teddy-bear sitting on top of Taz's handwoven Peruvian laundry basket, the rainbow-coloured rucksack with one broken strap. 'There isn't room!'

'Taz said we could crash here for a few days,' replied

Mandy, hitching up one of her socks. 'She came an' fetched us last night. From the police station.'

The conjunction of the words 'police' and 'station' was sufficient to give Isobel the vapours. Angry panic sent her handbag tumbling to the floor; Isobel was prepared for most things, but not for Mandy Robson.

'The police station! What have you done, you wicked girl? What have you got my Tasmin mixed up in?'

'I've done nothin'! The flat burned down, that's all . . .'

'What! And who burned it down? If you meddle in my daughter's life and ruin everything . . .'

'Meddle? What, like *you* you mean?'

'How dare you speak to me like that!'

From behind the door of the spare room came the cry of a frightened baby.

'Now look what you've done, you've upset Dylan,' said Mandy, bristling.

Taz stumbled out into the hallway, awakened by the commotion outside her door. Mandy was standing with the doorstop in her hand, Isobel scooping the contents of her handbag off the carpet. They were bawling at each other like fishwives.

'Mummy! Mandy – what's going on?'

The living room door opened and Adam emerged, naked save for a pair of boxer shorts and looking very designer-rough.

'What the . . .? Oh, Isobel, I didn't know you were coming.'

'Obviously not,' replied Isobel icily. 'Would somebody like to explain to me what is going on?'

'I've got to see to Dylan,' said Mandy, pushing past Isobel and disappearing into the spare room. Taz thought she just caught the muttered word 'cow' as the door thudded shut.

'Calm down, Mummy, Mandy and Dylan are just staying here for a few days, they had nowhere else to go. That's right isn't it Adam?'

'Yeah,' agreed Adam reluctantly.

'There was a fire at the place where they lived, they would've been on the street if I hadn't said they could stay here. It's not for long, just still they get sorted out. Adam said he didn't mind sleeping on the sofa for a few nights.'

'That girl is taking advantage of you, Tasmin,' warned Isobel, snapping shut the catch of her handbag and swinging it back onto her shoulder. 'She'll bring you nothing but grief.'

'Calm down, Mummy, I know you've never liked her, but she's been a good friend to me.'

Isobel shook her head uncomprehendingly.

'You just don't see, do you Tasmin? You can't have a girl like that as a friend. A . . . a . . .' Isobel fought to get the words out. 'A common little trollop.'

'What!' Taz could hardly believe her ears. For all her softly-spoken embarrassment, Isobel was every bit as bad as the yobs who'd sprayed graffiti on Mrs Norton's front door.

'I don't suppose she even knows the difference between right and wrong. She just wants you for what she can get. She's wrapping you round her little finger . . .'

'It's not like that. Is it Adam?'

Taz turned to Adam for support, but Adam had retreated back into the living room. She heard him switch on the TV set and then a two-second burst of *The Perils of Penelope Pitstop* blared out before he closed the door.

'See?' declared Isobel in triumph. 'He knows what I mean, he's a sensible boy. You should listen to Adam, Tasmin, he's good for you – not like *her*.'

'I'll choose my own friends, Mummy, I'm a big girl now.' Taz righted the pig doorstop and placed it back against the wall. The pig was smirking. 'Tell you what, let's all calm down and have a nice cup of coffee. I've got some Bourbon creams in the kitchen cupboard.'

'Why don't you share them with Mandy?' sniffed Isobel, and before Taz could open her mouth to reply, she was gone.

Over the days that followed, Taz had to fight to keep her mind on her work. It wasn't just the tensions between Isobel, Mandy and Adam – which had at least achieved a kind of uneasy balance. It wasn't just the fact that there was always somebody in the loo, and never enough milk in the fridge. It was all the other anxieties which crowded in on her; the feeling that she was trying to juggle twenty different balls at once, and in imminent danger of dropping them all.

Gareth, Mandy, the food hall, Diana's report, Ted Williams, Henry Goldman ... the list of troubles seemed endlessly self-renewing. Just when she thought she'd sorted out wines and spirits, the manager of the bakery concession went down with shingles. Then, when she'd sorted out that crisis, along would come another to take its place: a customer complaint, a late delivery, a consignment of defective crisps.

And then there was Jack, the biggest of all her joys and the most constant of all her worries. She was sure he was sickening for something, though Isobel and Adam kept reassuring her that he was perfectly all right. He seemed niggly, faddier than usual, not interested in his food – it was nothing you could really put your finger on, he just didn't seem himself. Perhaps Adam was right, and he was just unsettled by having so many people around him. Whatever the cause, Taz felt guiltier than usual about leaving him when she gave him a kiss and waved bye-bye.

'Don't you worry dear, he's fine,' Isobel assured her as she bundled Taz out of the door. 'He'll take his food as soon as you've gone, just you wait and see. He always takes his dinner when his granny feeds him, don't you sweetheart?'

As if that was calculated to make her feel any better, thought Taz, finishing off the weekly sales returns and rubbing her aching head. Eleven thirty. Time to get back on the sales floor and check that everything was running smoothly. Well, as smoothly as the food hall could ever run.

Just then she spotted something rather odd going on at the Bonbon Box, the confectionery concession.

Wasn't that Sushil, wandering about with a pencil and a sketch pad? But what on earth was he *doing*?

Des, the manager of the Bonbon Box, peered at Sushil over the top of his till.

'Excuse me.'

Sushil didn't respond. He scribbled something on his sketch pad with a flourish of his pencil, then whirled round, craned back his head and peered up at the ceiling.

'Hmm. Right.'

'*Excuse me*,' repeated Des, coming round from behind his counter. 'Can I help you?'

Sushil shook his head, waving Des aside.

'Can't talk, got to let the ideas flow. Yes, yes, I can see it ... here ... and here ... and here ...' More squiggles appeared on the sketch pad.

Sushil started pacing out the length and breadth of the Bonbon Box, twice almost colliding with a couple who were selecting multicoloured cubes of Turkish delight.

'Look,' said Des, exasperatingly falling into step with Sushil. 'I don't know who the heck you are. Haven't I seen you around the store? Do you work here or what?'

'Fourteen by twelve-six,' murmured Sushil. 'Nope, can't do it.'

'Can't do *what*?' demanded Des, by now well and truly irritated. He'd lost a sale, people were staring at this weird guy like he'd just broken out of the local loony bin, and for all Des knew, he had. 'Look, would you mind getting out of the way, you're disrupting my business.'

Sushil wheeled round, his eyes alive with artistic inspiration.

'Smaller, you must be smaller ... and over there.' Sushil indicated the far corner of the food hall, currently occupied by the wet fish counter. 'It's obvious really, I don't know why I didn't see it before.'

Oh damn, thought Taz, arriving on the scene just in the nick of time.

'Come on Sushil, sorry Des, he's one of Patros's new designers, he gets a bit carried away.'

'Yes,' said Des with feeling. 'And by the look of him, he ought to be.'

'Excuse me, Ms Norton.' Taz spun round. Des's assistant Rhona was offering her the phone. 'It's Mrs Latchford's office. They say could you go straight up, she wants to see you right away.'

'Please, let me have a go,' pleaded Mandy, doing her absolute best to be polite to Taz's mother – not for her own sake, or even for Taz's, but for Jack's. Poor little chap, he was red in the face, fretful, he'd hardly slept all night – no wonder he wouldn't eat his dinner. Anyone with half a brain could see that something was wrong.

Isobel turned, a spoonful of baby-food poised in the air above Jack's protesting face.

'And what makes you think you could do any better?'

'Well, for a start off I wouldn't try stuffing it halfway down his throat.'

'As if . . .!'

'An' it's obvious he doesn't want it, look at him, he's sobbin' his little heart out . . . an' he's all hot.'

'He'd soon settle down if you stopped distracting him,' retorted Isobel, making another futile attempt to get Jack's dinner down him. 'And if you stopped filling his mother's mind with unnecessary worries.'

Adam picked up Jack's training cup and tried to tempt him with a drink of juice.

'Come on little feller, just a sip eh? For Uncle Adam?' Jack turned away his face and gave a high-pitched, wailing cry.

'See?' said Mandy, itching to grab Jack from his high chair and give the poor child a cuddle. 'He's not well. I think we ought to ring Taz.'

'At work? No need for that, he's just a bit warm,' said Adam. 'Isobel's right, he's probably just cutting another tooth.'

Mandy bounced Dylan on her knee. He bounced like a spacehopper, not like poor Jack, who was all floppy and listless and didn't seem to care about anything that was going on around him.

'He's *ill*,' repeated Mandy. 'For God's sake Adam, how can you be such a bonehead? Just look at him!'

Adam put down the cup and made himself take a long,

hard, impartial look at Jack. 'I suppose he's a little bit pink.'

'He's fine, she's talking nonsense,' insisted Isobel. 'I've brought up a baby, remember . . .'

'Yeah,' commented Mandy, 'Twenty-six years ago.'

' . . . and I'm telling you, he's just playing us up because of all this extra disruption.'

The last word was accompanied by a hard stare at Mandy, but Mandy was past caring about hard stares. She set Dylan down in the playpen, went to the kitchen cupboard and took out the thermometer.

'All right, if he's not ill he won't have a temperature, will he?'

There was no answer to that. Even Isobel couldn't object to Mandy sticking the strip thermometer on Jack's forehead; and even she couldn't deny the evidence of the digital numbers, counting way up beyond thirty-six, thirty-seven, thirty-eight . . .

'God no,' gasped Isobel, clapping her hand to her mouth. 'Thirty-eight point five! Oh Jack, poor Jack . . .'

Mandy didn't say 'I told you so,' there was no point in wasting time scoring cheap points. And she was already on the telephone to the doctor's surgery.

Henry Goldman was not an impressive man. In appearance, he was rather like a moth-eaten spaniel, with wavy brown-grey hair that had to be tucked behind his ears because it always needed cutting, and cheeks that puffed out whenever he was stuck for something to say. Which he often was. Henry had not been endowed with the gift of eloquence. He was, thought Taz, very much the sort of man who would have spent forty years as a junior invoice clerk if his father hadn't been chairman of Seuss & Goldman.

Taz sat on one side of the desk, Diana on the other, next to Henry Goldman. She had the definite sensation of being on trial.

'What exactly . . . am I supposed to have done?'

Henry Goldman puffed out his cheeks, threw his pen onto the desk, sat back in his squeaky leather chair.

'This . . . Sushil Gupta.'

'Patros's assistant? I asked him to rough out some ideas for revamping the food hall.' Taz's eyes searched out Diana, hoping for a nod of agreement, but Diana seemed to be looking right through her. The message wasn't difficult to interpret. Unofficially, Diana might be backing her all the way; officially, this was something she knew nothing about. For whatever reasons, she couldn't afford to. 'Improvements that would cost hardly anything, but make a real difference to presentation. We have to do *something*. Don't we?'

'This . . . Sushil,' repeated Henry mechanically, as though he hadn't heard a word Taz had said, 'has been annoying people. A lot of people.'

'Oh,' said Taz. She saw Diana flinch slightly, avoiding looking at her. 'Who, exactly?' Though she could guess who. Des hadn't been exactly thrilled by Sushil's flamboyant presence, and no doubt he wasn't the only one.

'The concessionaires. Grape Harvest, Bonbon Box and The Butler's Pantry have all made complaints about him. To head office.'

Now it was Taz's turn to flinch. Why couldn't they have made their complaints to her? It made no sense.

'Which is why Mr Goldman is here today,' said Diana. 'He has made a special trip to Cheltenham to have frank discussions with you about this problem.'

'Frank discussions' – as in 'bollocking', thought Taz with a familiar sinking feeling. Something clicked and whirred inside her head. Complaints made to head office by the concessions – not just one, but several – that smacked of an orchestrated campaign against her. And she knew she wasn't without enemies at S&G. Was Ted behind this? Or could it be Gareth? Or even both?

'I am not pleased,' intoned Henry Goldman. 'In fact I am extremely angry. As you are no doubt painfully aware, the concessions bring in most of our income from the food hall, we absolutely cannot afford to alienate them in any way . . .'

This was almost too much for Taz to bear.

'Excuse me, Mr Goldman.' Astonishment flicked across

Henry's face at this unheard-of interruption. 'But what about Theresa? What about all the stock that was stolen from the food hall?'

'What about it?' demanded Henry drily. 'As I recall you were somewhat compromised by that incident, I wouldn't have thought you would wish to draw attention to it.'

'What I want to *draw attention to*,' said Taz, 'is the fact that these beloved concessions of yours are robbing you blind.'

'I *beg* your pardon!' Astonishment turned rapidly to anger. 'May I remind you who you are speaking to?'

Taz took a deep breath and plunged in.

'If I wasn't speaking to you, face-to-face, I wouldn't be saying this; I've been waiting long enough and it needs to be said.'

Out of the corner of her eye, Taz saw Diana's head sink, very slowly, into her hands. But she wasn't going to stop now.

'Is that so?' Henry's politeness was chilling, a warning sign that said 'stop now or you'll regret this'.

'Yes. Look.' She leaned over the desk, her hands forming white-knuckled fists on either side of the silver-topped inkwells. 'I'm trying to stop these people stealing from you, in fact I'm working my butt off to get the food hall back on its feet, but I can't. Why? Because you won't bloody well let me!'

'Tasmin,' said Diana. 'I'm not sure this is either the time or the place . . .'

But it was both. In fact it was now or never.

'And why won't you let me? I'll tell you. Because you'd much rather spend your money lining the pockets of the creeps who pretend to be your friends – and who won't tell you what's going on because they're a part of it.'

'Miss Norton, you do realise the implications of what you're saying?' The phone rang at Henry's elbow. He picked it up and dumped it in front of Diana. 'Answer that. Well, Miss Norton, do you?'

'Yes, Mr Goldman. I'm saying that you trust the wrong people, people who flatter your ego. And sooner or later you're going to realise that's a big mistake.'

Diana coughed. She looked shocked, almost frightened. The invisible bond of loathing which held Taz's gaze locked to Henry's was dissolved in the space of a few small words.

'It's for you, Tasmin, somebody called Mandy Robson? She's at the hospital. With Jack . . .'

Taz felt every ounce of bravado evaporate from her body, leaving her small and weak and afraid.

'J-jack? He's in hospital?'

'They say can you get there right away . . .'

'It can wait. She'll sort it out later,' Henry snorted contemptuously.

He took the receiver from Diana and was about to jam it back onto the hook, but Taz snatched it from him with an energy that took him unawares.

'Oh no she won't,' snapped Taz. 'Because right now my son needs me, and if you can't accept that, you can go to Hell.'

She shouldn't have been driving.

Taz's hands were shaking so badly that she could scarcely hold the wheel, her brain was reeling, she couldn't see the other cars, only the agonisingly endless grey ribbon of the road ahead. Later, she couldn't even recall how she'd managed to get between S&G and the hospital car park.

Parked outside accident and emergency, she sat frozen to her seat, her breath coming in short, staccato gasps; too afraid to go in, too terrified to walk those last few yards to the reception desk and find out what terrible thing had happened to her son.

Shock turned her welling tears to a kind of dry, hacking laughter. Henry Goldman. Well that was the end of her career at Seuss & Goldman. Bound to be. Then again, there were thousands of jobs in Cheltenham, in Gloucestershire, in the world. But there was only one Jack.

She imagined him, lying screaming in the arms of some stranger; wanting his mummy, not understanding why all these bad things were happening to him. He needed her, needed her more than any other person in the world.

A moment later she was running towards casualty. She didn't even remember to lock her car.

Chapter 27

'Your sister did absolutely the right thing,' said the young Irish doctor, ushering Taz into the relatives' room, followed by a student nurse carrying two cups of brick-red tea. 'Getting Jack to hospital so quickly.'

'My sister? Oh, you mean *Mandy*' Taz tried to concentrate, her thoughts, but they returned time and time again to the tiny pink body lying in the hospital cot, naked save for a nappy and the forest of tubes sticking out of it. 'She's my friend.'

'Oh? Sorry, I just assumed . . . Anyway, Mrs Norton . . .'

Taz didn't bother correcting him. What did social niceties matter when your baby was lying in hospital?

'What's wrong with Jack, doctor? Is he going to be all right?'

Dr Quinlivan drew up a chair and sat down. The student nurse placed the cups on the low table and left, closing the door very carefully behind her. The waiting was unbearable.

'I'll be absolutely honest with you, Mrs Norton, when Jack was first admitted I thought we might be looking at meningitis.'

Taz gasped and pushed her fist into her open mouth, the knuckles grating against her teeth.

'He was running a very high temperature and giving us some cause for concern. But now that we've run some tests and got his temperature down, I'm almost one hundred per cent certain that Jack's going to be absolutely fine.'

'Then why is he . . .?'

The doctor folded his arms. He was so young, thought Taz, even younger than she was; in fact, this was probably his very first appointment as a qualified doctor. Did he really know what he was talking about? Could she allow herself to believe him when he told her that Jack was going to get better?

'Why did he become so poorly so quickly? Hard to say. Probably a virus infection, these things often look a lot worse than they are. High temperatures sometimes lead to other problems, and while I was examining him your baby had what we call a febrile convulsion.'

'Convulsions! Isn't that the same as epilepsy?'

Dr Quinlivan shook his head kindly.

'Not at all. Febrile convulsions are quite common among babies of Jack's age, and they're rarely a sign of anything sinister.'

'You're sure about that?' Taz scanned the doctor's face for any trace of a lie. She knew what these people were like, sometimes they'd lie to you just to spare your feelings. 'If there's something bad . . . I want to know.'

'Nothing bad, Mrs Norton, I promise. Jack's going to be fine. We'll keep him in overnight, just to make sure, but if he continues to improve at this rate he'll be able to go home tomorrow.'

Isobel, Adam and Mandy were sitting at far-distant corners of the largest table in the hospital canteen, as far apart from each other as they could manage to be without actually moving to separate tables. Adam looked like the last stray in the dogs' home on Christmas Eve, Isobel was staring down at her neatly-folded hands, and Mandy, sitting with Dylan on her knee, was mechanically pulling a polystyrene cup to bits. She looked even more shocked and frightened than Taz felt.

'Tasmin – Tasmin, how is he?' Isobel rose slowly to her feet.

Taz sniffed back the last of her tears; Jack was going to be all right now and so was she.

'The doctor says he's going to be fine, it's just a virus. They've taken him up to the ward.'

373

'A virus,' said Isobel faintly.

'Thank God,' said Adam with a long, shuddering sigh of relief.

'Can we go up and see him? I *must* go up and see him.'

'No Mum, not just yet. They want to get him settled.'

Isobel didn't look very pleased, but sat down again at the table.

'I really can't see the problem, we *are* family.'

It was Mandy who got Taz a cup of coffee, spooned three sugars into it and set it down in front of her, sweeping aside the snowdrift of polystyrene fragments.

'Drink it.'

Taz stared blankly at the cup.

'What?'

'Go on, drink it.' Mandy wrapped Taz's fingers round the cup and watched as she lifted it to her lips. 'All of it, it'll do you good.'

'Thanks,' said Taz, feeling the hot liquid burn its way down to the pit of her frozen stomach. She smiled at Mandy. 'I mean, *really* thanks.'

'It's only a cup of coffee,' sniffed Isobel.

'Not for the coffee.' Taz cradled the cup between her hands, craving the warmth. Mandy looked at her, head on one side, the dark circles of her eye make-up giving the general impression of a startled panda. 'For what you did for Jack. Getting him to hospital so quickly.'

Taz could have sworn she saw Mandy blush under the off-white panstick. The rainbow dreads swished embarrassedly against her cheek as she turned away and fiddled with Dylan's knitted hat.

'All I did was call the doctor.'

'Yes, but just think what could have happened if you hadn't.' Taz looked briefly at Isobel. Isobel was looking daggers at Mandy. 'Dr Quinlivan says things could have been a lot worse if you hadn't done it so promptly.'

'You'd've done it for Dylan,' replied Mandy with a dismissive shrug.

'Of course,' said Isobel, 'I knew straight away that there was something wrong with Jack, the poor child hasn't been himself in days.'

'What?' Mandy stared incredulously at Isobel, then turned away in disgust. 'God, I just can't *believe* you, I really can't.'

Neither could Taz.

'Mother – what exactly are you saying? I mean, correct me if I'm wrong, but haven't you been telling me all week that there's nothing wrong with Jack and I'm just an over-fussy mother?'

'Nonsense, dear, didn't I say he was looking peaky on Monday? And if you ask me . . .'

'As a matter of fact I'm *not* asking you, Mother,' snarled Taz.

'Calm down Taz,' said Adam, touching her hand. 'I know you're stressed out but there's no sense in taking it out on Isobel.'

Taz punched his hand away. Isobel, blissfully ignorant of the look she was getting from Taz, just went on giving the world the benefit of her expert opinion.

' . . . if you ask me, it's no wonder the poor child is ill. Babies need peace and quiet and hygienic surroundings – not overcrowding, noise and . . . and . . . visitors.' If Isobel had said 'bed bugs', she couldn't have invested the word with more venom.

Mandy's panda eyes narrowed to vehement slits.

'What you gettin' at?' she demanded.

'Yes,' echoed Taz. 'Why don't you say exactly what you mean, Mother?'

'I've said my piece dear, I think you know what I mean.'

'Yeah,' said Mandy, 'She's sayin' me an' Dylan are dirty and Jack's caught somethin' off us.'

There was street-sharpened anger in the strident voice, but Taz knew Mandy well enough not to be fooled by the hard outer shell. There were unshed tears in those flashing eyes, just waiting to spill down the white cheeks in black mascara rivers.

'If the cap fits,' replied Isobel with cattish imprecision. 'Now, shall I get us all another cup of tea, or shall we go up and see Jack?'

'I told you, Mother,' said Taz with fraying patience,

'the charge nurse wants to settle him before he has any visitors.'

'But they won't turn me away, dear. I'm his granny. Granny knows best.'

That was the final straw, the last tiny shove that pushed Taz over the brink of impatience and frustration into blind fury. Perhaps if Bill had been there he'd have found a way to avert disaster, but she couldn't always rely on Bill to fight her battles for her.

'Shut up, Mother.'

'I *beg* your pardon?' gasped Isobel, her eyes saucers of incredulity.

'I said, shut *up*.'

'Taz . . .' hazarded Adam. 'I don't think . . .'

She rounded on him, all guns blazing.

'And you can shut up too. I'm sick of what you think, and what Mum thinks, and what everybody in the bloody world thinks. What about what I think? I'm Jack's mother, for God's sake, not you!'

Isobel swallowed, too utterly shocked to do any more than open and close her mouth. A girl clearing tables nearby calmly went on swabbing down the melamine, not so much as batting an eyelid. Here, in this theatre of human tragedies and dramas, she had seen and heard everything a hundred times before.

'I'm sick of your interference, Mother. Sick of you poking your nose in where it's not wanted. Sick of your christenings and your babysitting rotas – and your match-making,' she added with a glance at Adam, who was desperately trying to get a word in edgeways. 'This is my life, I'm going to live it the way I choose, not the way you've decided to plan it out for me. Got that?'

'She's upset,' cut in Adam as Taz paused to draw breath. 'She doesn't know what she's saying.'

'Oh yes she does.' Isobel was shaking all over as she pushed back her chair and pulled on her coat. 'Don't you?'

Taz couldn't deny it. Every word was true.

'I'm sorry, Mum, but not for what I said. Only the way I said it.'

'Right. I'm going then. It's obvious I'm not wanted here, I'm nothing but an impediment.'

'She didn't mean it,' protested Adam, pursuing Isobel across the canteen to the door. But it was the feeblest of protests, all of them knew it wasn't true. 'Come back.'

Head held high, nose in air, Isobel pushed open the double doors, not even bothering to step aside for the man in the wheelchair who was trying to get into the canteen. He stared after her, provoking a comment from the pretty girl by his side.

'Christ, the manners of some people. You'd think she'd know better.'

'You're kidding. Her sort are the worst.'

Adam returned to the table. Taz was still standing there, gazing at the empty doorway.

'Now look what you've done,' he sighed. Taz ignored him so he glared at Mandy. She put out her tongue at him.

'Don't you look at me, it's not *my* fault.'

Taz peered into the murky dregs of her coffee-cup. Her own reflection stared up at her, and for the first time she realised that her fringe was sticking up in a mad, ridiculous spike. She couldn't be bothered to do anything about it. What was the point? She'd thrown away her job, practically told her mother to butt out of her life, her seven-month-old son was lying in hospital, and in some way she couldn't quite define, it was all her fault. All of it.

'What am I going to do?' she said dully.

'Taz, you've got to get a grip on yourself – go after her, apologise,' urged Adam.

'I can't. Like I said, I meant it. Every word.'

Adam threw up his hands.

'Oh brilliant. Now who's going to look after Jack when you're at work and I'm at the law centre? Just when you really need people who care about you, you spit in their faces.'

'Adam, please . . .' She squeezed his hand. A dry sob escaped from her throat. 'What *am* I going to do? I just don't know.'

'I do,' said Mandy. Two pairs of eyes focused on her. 'I

know what you're goin' to do. You're goin' to leave Jack with me an' Dylan.' Her smile was bright, optimistic and dismissive of any doubts. 'Obvious, innit? Now, who wants another cup of coffee?'

It was two days before Taz felt able to leave Jack at home and go back to work, even though he had Adam *and* Mandy to look after him, and seemed almost as rosy-cheeked and healthy as Dylan. Waving goodbye to him was the most awful wrench, worse even than saying goodbye to him on her first day back after maternity leave. Having almost lost him once, Taz found it impossible not to imagine it happening all over again.

Diana had been very good about it, all things considering. But now was the time of reckoning. Taz couldn't help expecting the worst as she climbed the stairs to administration. So this was it then. This was what it felt like to get the sack.

The interior of Diana's office seemed gloomy, even for a late October morning, almost as if someone had subtly altered all the lighting, turning it into the set from a *film noir*.

'Coffee and biscuits in ten minutes, Nikki. And see we aren't disturbed.'

The door closed. Taz was alone with Diana. Peculiarly, Diana seemed almost human – more approachable than she'd ever been, except perhaps for the moment when Taz had told her that she was pregnant with Jack.

'How's Jack?'

This took Taz by surprise. Diana's rule about not allowing personal concerns to invade the sacred domain of S&G tended to leave babies way down the list of conversational priorities.

'He's . . . much better, almost well again. It was a close shave though.'

'Yes.' Diana contemplated the skyline for a few seconds. 'Well I'm glad he's all right, it must have been a terrible shock for you.' Diana sat down and folded her hands, her elbows resting on the desktop. 'I expect you've worked out why I sent for you?'

Taz nodded.

'I'd like to apologise.' She looked into Diana's eyes. 'For embarrassing you, and for behaving so unprofessionally.'

'But not for what you said?'

'No.'

'I thought so.' Diana rubbed the end of her nose with a manicured fingertip. Only Diana Latchford could contrive to look dignified while scratching her nose. 'Your report. On the food hall. Have you finished it yet?'

This was another unexpected turn. The night before, Taz had been on the verge of tearing up her notes and using them to line Minky's litter tray.

'Almost,' she said. 'I've been waiting for Sushil Gupta to finish off a design – I had wanted to do things properly.' It sounded absurd now, in the light of what she'd done. Bawling out Henry Goldman could hardly be described as 'doing things properly'.

'Well, I'd like two copies of it as soon as possible, shall we say first thing Monday?' Diana consulted her desk diary. 'I make that the twenty-seventh. Now – your department. Are there any new developments to report?'

'Only the new training scheme Leroy and I have been discussing with the local college. And that's still at the preliminary stage. Oh, and there's a slight improvement in takings on the fish counter since we changed our supplier.' She hesitated, then went on. She might as well be hanged for a haddock as a fish finger. 'The thing is . . . it's like I told Henry Goldman, the concessions are ruining everything – it's like the Mafia. And Ted Williams . . . I know you think I should keep my mouth shut, but how can I? He's on the take, Mrs Latchford, he's stealing from the company right under Henry Goldman's nose.'

Diana Latchford's response came like a bolt from the blue.

'I know, Taz,' she said quietly. 'I don't have the slightest doubt.'

'Then why . . .?'

'There are some things even a junior board member can't do anything about. You have to understand that,

Taz, you can't always fight the system and expect to win. There are some things that are never going to change.'

'You mean we should just give up trying? Let people like Ted and his cronies get away with it?'

'I know it doesn't sound very heroic, but there's not much point in personal crusades if you end up losing your job. Which brings me to the reason why I asked you to come and see me.'

Taz felt herself freeze to her chair. This was it.

'I'm being sacked, aren't I?'

Diana cleared her throat.

'I don't know, I honestly don't know what Henry Goldman has in mind. Technically speaking, all you've done is be extremely rude to him – effectively, you've ignored two verbal warnings.'

'Which is enough to get me sacked?'

'It might be.'

Taz felt less dreadful than she'd expected to. Somehow, now that it had come to the crunch, the one thing she really wanted more than anything else was to get it over with.

'So what are you saying? Where do I stand?'

There was no readable expression on Diana's face, only a kind of melancholy blankness.

'I'm afraid it's not good news. As from today, you're suspended from your job on half pay. Pending a final decision by the board. I honestly can't tell you what that decision will be.'

'I think I can guess.' Taz got to her feet. 'And how long will I have to wait for this decision?'

'I'll let you know as soon as I hear anything. Try not to worry too much.'

'Right. I'll wait to hear from you then.'

It was a curious anticlimax, walking out of Diana's office into limbo, no longer knowing whether she had a job or not, yet certain that she had crossed the Rubicon and life would never be quite the same again.

As she stepped out of the inner office and into the corridor outside, she heard the intercom on Nikki's desk crackle into life, and Diana's voice filling the room.

'Page Leroy McIntosh, will you Nikki? I need to speak to him right away.'

If anyone deserved to be acting DSM in the food hall, it was Leroy. That at least was some consolation to Taz as she sat alone in the flat. Adam was at the law centre, Mandy and Dylan had gone off looking for somewhere more permanent to live. As soon as they found somewhere they'd be leaving, and then she really would be all alone.

She was sitting on the carpet with Jack, watching him making determined attempts to crawl.

'Oh Jack,' she murmured. 'Oh Jack, you've got such a silly mummy, what *are* we going to do?'

Poor us, she thought. And poor Leroy. She couldn't think of anyone less like Ted Williams. He was horrified to discover that Taz had been suspended, and had flatly refused to take over the food hall until Taz had begged him not to be so stupid, to take the job for the sake of his own career. Leroy had replied that he'd take care of the food hall, but only until Taz got back. She hadn't had the heart to explain that she wouldn't be coming back, not if Henry Goldman had anything to do with it.

As though sensing that his mummy needed cheering up, Jack rolled onto his back and started sucking his own foot. Taz couldn't help smiling at his cheery little face, and the corkscrew of brown hair which stood up from the middle of his head like a question mark.

'I'll have to tell Mum and Dad soon,' she whispered to Jack, dreading the moment of truth. 'But I can't. What'll they think of me?' But Jack just grinned at her, proudly displaying the single tooth which had appeared in the middle of his gummy mouth.

When all was said and done, however, she was more than the sum total of her job. She was Jack's mother.

And that was the one good thing in her life that she must hold onto.

Chapter 28

'So,' said Mandy at breakfast a couple of days later. 'You decided what to do then, or what?'

'If you've got any sense,' observed Adam, looking for his tie and finding it in the bread bin, 'You'll tell him to go to hell.'

Taz glanced at Gareth's torn and crumpled letter, painstakingly rescued from the bin, Sellotaped back together, smoothed and staked out on the pinboard. According to Gareth, they 'needed to talk'. About 'his' son. Her blood boiled just thinking about it.

'I don't know,' she replied, lifting Jack into his high chair and tying on his bib. 'I can't decide.'

'You'll have to decide soon,' Mandy pointed out. 'He wants you to meet him on Thursday, that's only two days away.'

'I'm sure Taz can count up to two,' commented Adam as he fiddled his tie into some semblance of a knot. 'Is this OK Taz, I can't tell without the mirror.'

'Bit more to the left – fine, that'll do.' Despite everything, it still made Taz smile to see Adam's sheer helplessness in the face of a suit and tie. 'You look good.'

'No kidding? This collar's strangling me to death. I still don't see why people have to get all dressed up to go to court. Look Taz, this thing with Gareth. He's got no right to come swanning back into your life and interfere with the way you bring up your son.'

'Jack's his son too,' remarked Mandy, touching a raw nerve that made Taz wince with emotional hurt.

'Oh yeah, *biologically* maybe. But who gave birth to

382

him, who's taken care of him since day one? Who's nurtured him and bonded with him in a way Gareth Scott never could?'

'Christ Adam,' said Mandy drily, 'anybody'd think it was a flamin' virgin birth. You did sleep with the guy didn't you Taz? I mean, there weren't any angels or nothin'?'

Taz stirred Jack's porridge with his bunny-rabbit spoon. Jack waved his arms enthusiastically, and formed his mouth into a pink O of expectation.

'I can't wish I hadn't ever met Gareth,' she said. 'Because then there'd be no Jack. But I don't want him anywhere near my baby.'

Her heart ached with love for Jack, more than ever now that she felt so threatened by this man from her past who was insisting on forcing himself into her future.

'Then tell him to get lost,' said Adam simply. 'He's sold you down the river every inch of the way. Why should you believe a word he says now?'

'Sounds like sour grapes to me,' said Mandy. 'Just because he had you fooled.'

'That's got nothing to do with it,' snapped Adam.

'No?' Mandy spread strawberry jam on a slice of thick white toast. 'Well how would you feel if you found out you had a kid, an' you weren't allowed to see it?'

'It just so happens,' replied Adam flatly, 'that I know exactly how that feels. And just because your precious Dave doesn't want anything to do with you or Dylan . . .'

Taz felt the words pierce like knives. A horrible, stilted silence fell over the breakfast table, punctuated only by the goos and gaas and squeals of small children at feeding time. On the radio, some junior minister or other was ranting on about the Child Support Agency.

'Are you working today then?' she asked Mandy, doing her best to be positive.

'Not till this evenin'. And then I'm on earlies for the rest of the week.'

'I can babysit Dylan if you like, it's no trouble.'

Mandy shook her head.

'Thanks, but I'll take him with me, he likes it there an' I can keep an eye on him.'

Adam made a disapproving sound in his throat.

'Are you sure he wouldn't be better off here, with Taz?'

'Yes. I'm sure. Ta very much.' The flare of contemptuous anger animated Mandy's tired, thin face. 'Or don't you think I'm capable of lookin' after me own kid?'

Adam squirmed uneasily under Mandy's searchlight gaze. She had called his bluff and there wasn't much he could do about it. Nobody could say Dylan Robson was suffering in any way; he was happy, healthy, rosy-cheeked, chubby-limbed and precocious – hardly deprived by anybody's standards, unlike his mother.

'No, of course not. But this cleaning job of yours . . .'

'It's not a bad job,' said Mandy defensively, taking another slice of toast from the rack. 'An' the money's OK.'

Taz paused in feeding Jack to look across the breakfast table at Mandy's hands. They were red-raw and scaly with dermatitis, the skin cracked and weeping in places. Mandy's new cleaning job at the Megaplex might pay a regular wage for regular work, even offering a tenuous kind of security, but the *kind* of work horrified Taz. She wondered if, when Henry Goldman could be bothered to get round to sacking her from S&G, she too might end up scrubbing floors for pennies.

'You can do better,' she suggested, not really believing what she was saying. She was a realist; not everybody would view Mandy Robson as the ideal employee.

'Oh yeah?' Mandy stuffed toast into her mouth while doing up Dylan's dungarees with the other hand. 'Like what?'

'What about hairdressing? You could go back to that.'

'I only did six months, remember? Besides, I can earn more cleanin'. Can't I, Dylan? Yes, I can.' She kissed and tickled Dylan and he crinkled his button nose in giggling delight. 'I'm good at it.'

'I know, but . . .'

'Anyhow, don't worry, soon as I can I'll be out of your hair. I'm no scrounger.' She was looking at Adam as she spoke, but Adam was busy sorting papers on the kitchen floor, and stuffing them into his bulging briefcase. 'An' you know what they say, three's a crowd.'

'There's no need to go,' said Taz. 'You can stay as long as you like. Can't she, Adam?'

'What's that?' asked Adam, looking up.

'Mandy. I told her, she can stay as long as she needs to. There's no rush for her to leave, is there?'

'Well. No. I suppose.'

'See?' Mandy licked the last of the jam off her fingers. 'He can't wait to see the back of me.'

'I didn't say that,' protested Adam.

'You didn't have to.' Mandy dampened a square of kitchen roll and started wiping the Milupa from Dylan's mouth. 'I'm not blind *and* stupid you know.'

'No, just paranoid,' muttered Adam. Mandy looked daggers at him. Taz felt like knocking their heads together.

'Anybody want more coffee?'

Her enquiry went unheeded, so she just poured herself another one. Her third. Not that she was counting – now that she was on an enforced holiday from S&G there was nothing to stop her mainlining caffeine twenty-four hours a day if she wanted to. Nothing to think about but what a mess her life was in. She tried again.

'Look Adam, can't we at least try to get on? You know Mandy and Dylan have nowhere else to go.'

Mandy got up from the table, popped Dylan into the baby bouncer and made a start on clearing away the dishes.

'Actually we've been offered a place. Just a couple of rooms over a junk shop. I meant to say only there wasn't much point.'

'What do you mean, not much point?' asked Taz, stiffening.

'I'm still a few quid short of the deposit. Well...' Mandy looked sheepish. She dumped the plates into the sink and squirted Fairy Liquid all over them. 'Two hundred.'

Two hundred! Taz did a quick mental calculation. The figures frightened her so she ignored them.

'I guess... I could...'

But Adam cut in, shoving the last sheaf of papers into his overstuffed briefcase and persuading it shut.

'I'll lend you the money,' he said.

'You what?' said Mandy staring at him.

'I'll lend you the deposit.'

'Are you serious?'

'Of course I am.' A tiny hint of exasperation crept into Adam's voice. 'Is a cheque OK or do you need cash?'

Taz smiled encouragingly at Mandy. She had serious doubts about Adam's altruism, but what did the motives matter if Mandy got what she and Dylan needed: a home of their own?

'That's kind of you, Adam.'

Adam shrugged. Mandy grunted dismissively.

'Kind! Come off it, he's only offering 'cause he can't wait to get shot of us.'

'Oh Mandy, I'm sure he's not . . .' protested Taz.

'What if I am?' said Adam quietly. 'Look, the money's there if you want it. And face it, we'll all be better off if we're not at each other's throats all the time.'

Mandy looked at him steadily. Taz wondered what was going on behind those intelligent, shadowed eyes.

'All right then,' she said abruptly, plunging her hand into a rubber glove. 'You're on. But I'm payin' you back, soon as I've saved up.'

The delight on Adam's face was impossible to mask. And naturally Taz was pleased for Mandy and Dylan. But there was a feeling of sadness inside her, too; and the wistful resentment that just as things were starting to look up for Mandy, Taz's life was spiralling downwards, ever more out of control.

Diana Latchford was in the middle of reading Taz Norton's report on the food hall when a call came through on the intercom.

'Call for you, Mrs Latchford. On line one. It's Binnie Lethbridge for you, from Edinburgh.'

Edinburgh? Diana's brow furrowed. She'd been under the impression that Binnie and Jim had settled somewhere off the beaten track, to the north of Inverness.

'Binnie? How are you, it's lovely to hear from you again. How's Jim? And little . . . what's her name?'

'Amy.' Binnie paused, as though searching for the right words. 'Actually, Jim and I . . . we're having a trial separation.'

'No!' Diana flopped back in her chair, genuinely stunned. Binnie and Jim Lethbridge must have been together for a good ten years; everyone at S&G Cheltenham knew them as the perfect couple. 'Oh Binnie, I'm sorry to hear that.'

'It's not permanent,' said the voice at the other end of the line. 'Well, not yet anyhow. In fact, we're getting on better now we're living apart, but we've got things to sort out between us.'

'So where are you living?'

'Jim's at the house, I'm in Edinburgh. I'm working as a part-time senior sales consultant at S&G.'

'Part-time! But I'm sure we could find you something a little more challenging than that. I thought there was a DSM's post going in men's accessories.'

'Thanks for the vote of confidence,' laughed Binnie, 'but I'm afraid I won't be going back full-time just yet. You see, I'm expecting again. It wasn't planned.'

Babies, thought Diana, absent-mindedly patting her hair back into its customary perfect waves. All they ever seemed to bring into people's lives were complications, heartache, discord. Funny how she'd longed to start a family of her own. Maybe she'd made the right decision after all.

'I'm on my tea-break at the moment,' Binnie went on. 'I just called to have a chat with Taz Norton, only they told me on the switchboard that she's not around. And I couldn't reach her at home. Not ill is she?'

Diana exhaled slowly and painfully. This sort of thing was never easy.

'Binnie . . . I shouldn't really be telling you this, but Taz has been suspended pending a disciplinary hearing.'

The silence seemed to last for ever.

'But I don't understand . . .'

'No,' sighed Diana. 'Neither do I, not really. And I can't go into the details, I'm sure you appreciate that.'

'Y-yes. Do you think I should call Taz – or leave well alone?'

'If I was Taz I'd be glad to hear a friendly voice.' Diana tapped her pen on the desktop, recalling the dozen or so times she had almost picked up the phone to call Taz herself. 'Binnie – there is just one thing you might be able to help me with. When you were at Cheltenham, did you ever meet a man called Gareth Scott? He used to work in financial services.'

Even before Binnie answered, Diana knew that the answer must be yes. The pause was so heavily laden with emphasis.

'Yes. Why?'

'I just wondered if perhaps Taz knew him too.'

'It's possible. Why do you ask?'

Well, Mr Scott has recently returned to S&G Head Office as senior financial adviser, and . . . let's just say . . . Tell me, Binnie, can you think if Taz has ever done anything to annoy him?'

Making up her mind to see Gareth again wasn't easy. Steeling herself to take Jack with her was unimaginably painful. Just letting Gareth see his son felt tantamount to sharing him; and her love was so jealously possessive that she couldn't imagine ever sharing Jack with anyone, most especially not Gareth Scott.

They'd argued on the telephone about where to meet. Gareth and Melanie's nice new house? No way. Taz's flat? Forget it. No, it must be somewhere neutral, and the kind of place you could take a small child and feel at home. They argued for half an hour, plunging Taz deeper and deeper into despair. Adam was probably right. She should just have told Gareth to go to hell and stuck to it.

Ridiculously, they ended up fixing on a dreadful new burger joint on the outer ring road; a palace of primary-coloured plastic, baseball-capped assistants and seats in the shape of giant toadstools, gathered into 'fairy rings' about fake tree-stump tables.

It was Thursday morning, and the Burgerstop was virtually empty, save for the odd trucker and a party of French schoolkids stopping off on the way to somewhere more interesting. As she pushed Jack's buggy up to the doors, Taz bent over and whispered to him.

'Jack, I promise you, I won't let any harm come to you. I promise.'

Tears of apprehension pricked the undersides of her eyelids. Why was she doing this to herself, to Jack, to them both? Only Gareth deserved to suffer.

Gareth was already there, sitting at a table with his briefcase on the floor beside him. He looked almost as apprehensive as Taz felt. Old too. Taz felt a sneaking satisfaction as she glimpsed the slightly larger patch of thinning hair on the top of his head, gleaming pinkly under the fluorescent lighting.

The moment he set eyes on her he leapt to his feet, the old smile switching itself back on. The old charm too, though these days Taz was immune to it. Or at least, hoped that she was.

'You came then.'

'Obviously.'

It was then that Taz realised Gareth wasn't looking at her, he was staring in complete rapture at the pushchair. No, at *her* son. All at once, Taz wanted to snatch Jack up and run full-tilt out of this horrible restaurant – and never stop until she was somewhere Gareth would never find them.

'Hello Jack. You don't know me, do you?'

'Hardly surprising, is it?' commented Taz. 'I mean, you were too busy two-timing me with Melanie to even notice you'd got me pregnant.'

She said it loudly, in the hope of embarrassing Gareth, but the truckers were too engrossed in their burgers to listen in, and the French kids were squabbling over the video machine.

'Look. Taz.' Gareth touched her hand. She drew it away as if it had just met something unspeakably cold and slimy. 'I really appreciate your agreeing to see me – and to bring Jack.' His eyes met hers. 'Mind if I hold him?'

'Yes. I do.' Taz drew the buggy a little further away from Gareth, and sat down. Unbuckling Jack, she lifted him up and sat him on her knee. 'He doesn't like being held by strangers,' she lied, knowing full well that Jack was the sort of baby who'd quite happily let himself be carted off by the gypsies with not even a squeak of protest.

'Oh.' Gareth's face fell. There was a weird look in his eyes, a kind of schoolboy fascination; and he couldn't seem to stop staring at Jack. 'Well, if we can sort something out between us we won't be strangers for long, eh little chap?'

He stroked Jack's mittened hand, and Taz's heart lurched painfully at the sound of Jack's interested gurgle. Why oh why couldn't he scream and cry and want his mummy, instead of being perfectly delighted to meet this rat who wanted to play happy families because he was bored with breaking them up?

'I'm not sure why I came,' began Taz. 'Because if you think I'm letting you anywhere near my son . . .'

'Steady on.' Gareth, the very soul of reasonableness, put up his hands to ward off Taz's anger. 'All I'm asking is to spend a little time with the boy. He is my son, after all.'

Inside her head, Taz heard echoes of Mandy's words: 'He is Jack's dad'.

'I told you, your name's not on the birth certificate. As far as I'm concerned you've nothing to do with Jack.' She was shaking slightly, but managing to keep her self-control.

'We've been through all that, I don't want to fight. All I want to do is make up for the past – do the best for my son. Besides which,' Gareth's eyes flicked back to Jack, placidly playing with his mother's car-keys. 'It would mean a lot to Melanie.'

'What!' This time, the sound of Taz's exclamation did make a couple of heads turn, albeit briefly. 'What the hell has this got to do with Melanie?'

'She's always wanted a family, you know that. And the doctor says she'll never have children of her own . . .'

'Well she's not having mine!' Taz's arms curled protectively around Jack's waist. 'Why should I let you within a mile of him?'

Gareth paused, weighing up his words with the utmost care.

'Because you love him. Because you want the best for him.'

'Oh. And you think that's the best thing that could happen to Jack, do you? To get to know his lying, cheating scumbag of a father?'

Gareth shook his head sorrowfully.

'Please, Taz. Listen. I know you think I'm the devil incarnate, but not everything I do is bad. I'm just a guy who . . . makes mistakes. Like everybody does.'

'So Jack's a mistake now is he?'

'Far from it. The way I see it, he's just about the best thing I've ever done. You have to give me the chance to take some part in my own son's life, surely you can see that!'

'I don't have to do anything, Gareth. Except look after my son and give him the love and stability he needs.'

The moment she'd spoken those words, Taz sensed that she had played the ball right into Gareth's court. He smiled. A smile that chilled her blood.

'Exactly. You want a good, stable home life for Jack and so do I. But things aren't good for you right now, are they? What with troubles at S&G, money must be tight . . .'

Taz shivered. Everything Gareth was saying was horribly true.

'Yeah, right. And I suppose you're going to tell me you've got nothing to do with these "troubles"? You, with your nice new job on the board?'

Gareth sighed.

'If you mean, did I get you suspended, then no, of course I bloody didn't. If you mean, am I the one who's stopping Henry Goldman coming to a snap decision about your future, then perhaps I may just have something to do with that . . .'

'What!'

'It just so happens I've been trying to put him off

coming to a final decision, hoping he'd cool down a bit. Hell, Taz, I've been trying to save your job for you!'

'I don't need your help, Gareth. I don't need anything from you.'

'Well I think you do. And more to the point, I think Jack does.' Gareth contemplated the baby, offering him his signet ring to play with. 'I hear he's been ill.'

'What about it?'

'And you've got some kid and her baby staying with you, not to mention lover-boy . . .'

'This is nothing to do with you, Gareth,' warned Taz, but there was no shutting him up.

'All in one small flat? It's not a healthy way for a baby to live, Taz.'

'Butt out, Gareth.' She was sounding angry now, and she *was* angry, but more than that she was covering up the guilt of knowing that maybe, just maybe, she alone might not be able to give Jack everything he needed in his life. 'I've told you, we don't need you. For anything.'

Gareth shrugged. He wasn't going to push the point, not this time.

'Think about it, Taz. I could help you. And Jack. And isn't Jack the one who matters most in all of this?'

The weekend came and Taz was still feeling threatened. Dark imaginings assailed her in the middle of the night, when she hugged her knees under the duvet and imagined terrible scenarios which invariably ended with Jack being stolen away from her.

Adam's paranoia didn't help: anyone would have thought *he* was the neurotic parent, not Taz. Nor did Mandy's announcement that she had paid the deposit on her new flat, and would be leaving on Sunday. Taz's world seemed smaller, and more frightening, than ever before.

On Sunday night, when Mandy had cleared out the last of her possessions and Jack was sound asleep in his cot, Taz and Adam ate a monosyllabic supper in the kitchen.

'More bread?'

'No thanks.'

'Cheese?'

392

'What? OK. Just a bit.'

They chewed in silence for a bit.

Adam downed a mouthful of wine.

'Why don't you call Dee?'

'Dee!'

'Yes, Dee. I know she behaved appallingly, but she's really sorry. Go on, call her – mend a few fences. She's good fun, and you could do with cheering up.'

'Oh, I don't know. Maybe.' Taz drew patterns in the tomato ketchup on her plate. 'I don't know if I could ever trust her again.'

'You don't have to trust her, just have a laugh with her.' Adam peered earnestly into Taz's face. 'It's ages since I saw you smile.'

'It's ages since I had anything to smile about. Look – would you mind doing the dishes? I think I'll go and call Binnie, it sounds like she's having an even worse time than I am.'

Binnie's letter had come as something of a bolt out of the blue. Taz had long suspected that all was not quite sweetness and light chez Binnie, but marital squabbles were hardly in the same league as a trial separation, were they?

Lying on her bed with just the nightlight on, so as not to disturb Jack, Taz poured out her heart to Binnie and listened to Binnie's tale of woe.

'But I thought Jim *wanted* loads of children.'

'To be honest, Taz, I don't think he's got a clue *what* he wants any more. If he had a magic wand, I think he'd whisk us back to Cheltenham the day before we decided to start a family.'

'Poor Binnie. And what about you, do you wish you'd never had Amy?'

'Are you kidding? She's the only intelligent conversation I get these days. It's going to be hard going with two though, if Jim and I don't get back together.'

'You will. You're made for each other.'

'Maybe. And if we don't I suppose there's always S& G. There's a lot to be said for having a career.'

'Yeah.' It wasn't so much a word as a long sigh. Somewhere in the distance the doorbell sounded, followed by the sound of muffled voices. Taz wondered idly who it was, maybe her father delivering an olive branch from Isobel.

'Oh Taz, I'm sorry, I wasn't thinking. Is there any news about your suspension?'

'Not a word. And Gareth had the cheek to tell me he's been trying to delay the disciplinary hearing! He *says* it's to give Henry Goldman time to simmer down, but I can't believe that. And I don't want him anywhere near Jack, I just can't bear the thought of it, you understand don't you?'

At that moment the muffled voices increased in volume to acrimonious shouting – and it was only too easy to identify the owners of the voices.

'If you think I'm letting you anywhere near that baby . . .'

'My son, lover-boy, that baby is *my son*, remember?'

'Oh God Binnie, it's Gareth! I've got to go, ring you back later, bye.'

'Piss off and leave us alone, you creep.'

'I've brought a present for my son, I'm not going till I've given it to him. Get out of my way!'

'Get your filthy hands off me!'

'Your sort are all the same . . .'

Jack began to sob quietly in his cot.

'Hush, sweetheart, hush, Mummy'll make the bad things go away.'

She leapt off the bed and wrenched open the door. Across the hallway in the living room, two men were standing eyeball to eyeball, a gift-wrapped package lying on the carpet at their feet.

This was Gareth and Adam as she had never seen them before. Brawling. Blood was dripping from Gareth's nose onto the carpet, and there was a darkening swelling on Adam's left cheekbone.

Two shocked faces snapped round to look at her, Gareth hastily staunching the flow from his nose with the end of his tie.

'This ... thug ... *hit* me,' he gasped between gulps of air. 'He bloody *hit* me.'

'Yes I bloody did. And you bloody deserved it.'

Taz stared at Adam's right fist; the knuckles scraped and smeared with blood that was not their own. Could this be the same Adam who saved the whale on alternate Sundays, who ate nothing that wasn't dolphin-friendly and who rescued drowning earthworms from puddles?

'I do not believe this,' said Taz, her head moving slowly from side to side. 'I just don't *believe* it.'

'He wanted to see Jack, I told him he couldn't.'

'Oh you did, did you? You should both be ashamed of yourselves.' In that moment, Taz hated the two of them so much she could scarcely find words adequate to express her loathing.

'I'm sorry Taz,' said Adam, rather feebly now. 'I was only trying to protect Jack and I got carried away.'

'Oh really.'

'And that gorilla ...'

'Come on Taz,' urged Gareth, 'let's forget about this and calm down.'

'Oh? And why should I want to do that? You barge your way into my flat, you brawl in my living room, you drip blood all over my fitted carpet.' And what exactly are you brawling about? A baby, *my* baby. My son Jack, who is now crying his eyes out in there because two grown men are behaving like animals.'

'I'm sorry,' muttered Gareth, who looked like it almost killed him to get the words out.

Eyes blazing, no longer sure which of these two overbearing idiots she hated more, Taz almost spat out the rest of the words.

'Let me just ask you one question. Both of you. And think before you answer. Just whose baby do you think Jack is?'

By way of reply, she stalked off back into her bedroom and closed the door; shutting out the kind of obscene world where two boneheaded men could fight for possession of somebody else's child.

Chapter 29

Taz had time on her hands. All these years she'd been working eighteen hours a day, dreaming of having unlimited time off to do all the things she wanted to do, it had never occurred to her just how unnerving it might be if it ever actually happened.

She'd given up ringing Seuss & Goldman every morning. Diana had made it clear that, as soon as she knew anything about the disciplinary hearing, she would be in touch. Until then, Taz was to sit back, stop worrying, and 'enjoy being with Jack'. The truth was that, much as she adored him, she'd have enjoyed him a lot more if she could be sure she'd got a job to go back to at the end of it all.

Mandy's invitation to visit her at her new flat came as a relief, though Taz felt more than a twinge of apprehension. What if the new place turned out to be even worse than the last one? A one-bedroomed flat above a junk shop, at the arse-end of the industrial estate, didn't sound exactly promising.

At first sight it didn't look promising either. Plastic carriers from the local supermarket were blowing around among the discarded Coke tins and up-ended trolleys, with the odd tattered black bin-bag caught up in the almost leafless trees, flapping about disjointedly like disabled crows. Taz parked up, locked the car, then as an afterthought went back and took out the radio. Probably a paranoid thing to do, but you couldn't be too careful.

Or maybe you could. As Taz rounded the corner into Bletchley Street, she counted the numbers along. Twenty-four, twenty-four A; a dry-cleaner's, a fruit and veg shop with mangoes and people actually buying them; thirty, thirty-two; a cake shop with some really nice-looking almond croissants. On impulse, and celebrating her near-victory over postnatal flab, Taz dodged in and bought six: two for her, two for Mandy and two to fight over.

Thirty-six, thirty-six A, thirty-six B, an architectural salvage merchant . . . hang on, this was it, thirty-eight A, Bletchley Street: a small blue door set into the wall at the side of the architectural salvage shop. So, not really a junk shop after all: rescued marble fireplaces, Victorian tiles, a fox weathervane, oak and pine floorboards, a couple of pews and an old harmonium. Taz quite fancied the weathervane; pity she had nowhere to put it and no money to buy it with.

'Oh Jack, look at the lovely fox – can you see him? And that big bath, wouldn't it look gorgeous in Mummy's bathroom?' She planted a big kiss on the top of Jack's head, making him wriggle and screw his head round to look at her.

'Ma-ma-mam?'

'Come on Jack, let's go and see Dylan shall we?'

The door was already ajar. As she stepped inside, she was instantly engulfed by a great waft of pine disinfectant. It was rather gloomy and windowless inside the entrance, the only light provided by a sixty-watt bulb, but there was enough to pick out the narrow staircase leading up to the flat above the shop, and the figure of a girl in jeans and a jumper frantically bobbing up and down as she scrubbed at the bare lino.

'Mandy?'

The head popped up, its crowning glory dyed a virulent shade of orange and tied up in a pink bandana.

'Taz! Hang on, I've nearly done.'

'Mandy, what are you *doing*?'

'Scrubbin' the stairs, what does it look like?'

'But they're spotless already,' protested Taz, thinking how lucky she was not to have any stairs, since if she did they'd be covered in half an inch of cat-hair and biscuit crumbs, like the rest of her flat. Even houseproud Adam hadn't managed to reform her slovenly ways.

'Can't be too careful with babies around, can you?' pointed out Mandy, getting to her feet and dropping her scrubbing brush into the plastic bucket. 'I'll do the rest later, mind you shut the toddler gate, Dylan's gettin' into everything.'

Mandy led the way into her flat. It wasn't a bit like Taz had expected it to be. True, it was small and it wouldn't make the cover of *Period Homes and Gardens*, but it was spotlessly clean, bright, and it would have been tidy too except for the snowdrift of toys littering the threadbare carpet and the pile of library books stacked against the wall. Taz bent down to look at the spines.

'*Sophie's World*?'

'It's good, it's about philosophy. Read it, have you?'

'You're kidding, Enid Blyton's more my level these days.' Taz scanned the rest of the pile: *Foucault's Pendulum, Remains of the Day, Accordion Crimes, Finnegan's Wake*, not a copy of *Hello!* or *Inside Soap* in sight. '*Mathematics for the Million* – have you actually read this?'

'Course I have,' replied Mandy indignantly. 'Twice.'

Taz shook her head in wonderment.

'God God,' she said. 'I'm turning into a vegetable.'

Mandy laughed, unstrapped Jack from his buggy and gave him a big, big hug.

'How's my boyfriend today then, huh?'

'He's a naughty boy, he won't eat his carrots.'

Mandy tut-tutted in Jack's bemused face.

'Did you hear that, Dylan? Jack doesn't like his carrots. You do though, don't you?' Dylan chuckled happily, squishing his squeaky duck between his strong, fat fingers. 'He'll eat *anythin*',' Mandy confided. 'He'd have the lino off the floor if it wasn't nailed down, that's why I have to keep everythin' so clean, see. Now Jack, you goin' to behave yourself for your mummy, or what?'

Jack responded by grabbing a handful of orange hair and stuffing it into his mouth.

'Ow!,' winced Mandy, half laughing. 'Oi Jackie-boy, that's not a carrot!'

'Oh Mandy, I'm sorry, he will keep doing that. Naughty boy Jack, spit it out.' As she prised the hair from Jack's vice-like grip, Taz carried on talking. 'Of course, he'll take carrots if Adam gives them to him . . .'

Mandy gave Taz a sideways look.

'I thought you an' Adam had a big bust-up.'

'We did. Sort of. He hit Gareth, you know – and I was that angry, I went right off the deep end.'

'Angry? I'd have thought you'd give him a medal, the way you go on about Gareth.'

'I know. But it wasn't just Adam, it was both of them – they were behaving like kids, fighting over Jack like they owned him or something. Anyhow, Adam's apologised and we've made it up, thank goodness.'

Mandy grunted non-committally.

'Look, Mandy, I know Adam's not your number one favourite person . . .'

'He's not even my millionth favourite person.'

'But I do like him. I mean, he can be pig-headed and possessive sometimes, but . . . I can't help it, I *like* him!'

'I know.' Mandy relented with a toss of her carroty spikes. 'It's none of my business who you shag anyhow.'

'I'm not . . . !'

'Oh come off it, course you are. Good is he?'

'Mandy!' Taz felt her cheeks burn.

'OK, OK, I'm just jealous right?'

'Jealous – of me and Adam?' This was a thought so ludicrous that it simply hadn't occurred to Taz before. 'You mean you fancy Adam?'

Mandy practically exploded with laughter.

'*Me*? Fancy *him*? Do me a favour. No, I'm just jealous of you . . . you know, havin' somebody.'

Taz took Jack and sat down on Mandy's sofa. It was old, battered and had *War and Peace* where the fourth leg should be, but it was comfy and it did the job.

'You've got Dave,' she pointed out.

Mandy seemed not to have heard what Taz had said, or at least did a good job of pretending she hadn't. She pounced like a tiger on the carrier bag dangling from the back of Jack's buggy.

'What's in here then?'

'Almond croissants – want one?'

'There's six in here,' said Mandy as she peered in.

'You can have all six if you want,' laughed Taz.

Mandy's face assumed the familiar sharp, slightly wary look that Taz knew so well.

'I don't need food parcels you know, I'm not a charity case.'

'I never said you were. Last time you came to me, you brought doughnuts. So I thought I'd bring croissants.' Taz winked. 'More for me if you don't want any.'

Mandy snatched the bag from her half-hearted grasp.

'I'll get a plate. D'you want lemonade or tea?'

'Lemonade's fine.'

They ate sitting on the floor, watching Dylan and Jack learning noisily about 'sharing' their toys.

'Ayesha must be nearly walking by now,' commented Taz, sneezing as she accidentally breathed in a puff of icing sugar. 'Poor Chloë.'

'Poor kid you mean.' Mandy swallowed the last of her second croissant, licked her fingertip and dotted it around the plate, gathering up all the crumbs. Taz couldn't help noticing how ravenous she seemed, and still scarcely more than skin and bone under that baggy jumper. 'Wonderin' where her mummy's gone.'

Taz thought about Chloë, waiting for her shoplifting case to come up, her mother keeping her incommunicado from everyone who really cared about her. What on earth must be going on inside that desperately unhappy head?

'Still, at least Ayesha's got her daddy. Clive loves her to bits.'

'Yeah. But he's not her daddy, is he?'

'No, but he loves her just as much as if he was. It's hard on him, though, he loves Chloë too.'

'God knows why, she's bin horrible to him.'

'I know. Adam's doing his best to cheer Clive up, you know, taking him down the pub and press-ganging him into the darts team, but it's not easy . . .'

'It's not the same for a kid, is it?' said Mandy out of the blue. 'Not the same as havin' a real daddy.'

'Better than having a bad one,' replied Taz, shuddering at the thought of Gareth and his demands. 'A lot better.'

'I guess.' Mandy's finger circled the third croissant, lying untouched in the centre of her plate.

'You don't get on with your dad, do you?'

'Neither would you if you met him. I hate his guts. But he's still my dad, isn't he? An' Clive's not Ayesha's dad, even if he wants to be. It's some other bloke she'll probably never meet . . .'

'What's this all about?' asked Taz, giving Mandy a good, hard stare.

'Nothin'.'

'Come on, Mandy, it can't be nothing. Is it something to do with your dad? He's not come looking for you and hit you again? He's not done something to hurt Dylan?'

'No!' Mandy's whole body became rigid, from the tips of her pointy-toed boots to the ends of her spiky orange hair. 'Nothin' like that, I'd slit his throat if he laid a finger on Dylan.'

'So what's wrong?'

'If you must know, it's Dave. You know his case is goin' to appeal?'

'Aren't you pleased?'

Mandy shrugged.

'Yeah. Course. Anyhow, I took Dylan to see 'im last week. At the prison.'

'And it was upsetting for you?'

Mandy laughed humourlessly.

'It might've bin, if we'd got to see him. Turned us down flat, didn't he? Said he didn't want to see us. Not then, not next week, not never.'

'But I thought he was standing by you,' said Taz, shocked.

'Changed his mind, hasn't he? Fed up with bein' a dad, says he's too young to be bothered with a kid. 'Sides, things haven't been right since before he went down. You know,' the brown eyes darted to meet Taz's then darted away again, 'since he wanted me to give him an alibi an' I wouldn't.

'He didn't do them break-ins, none of 'em. But he had

401

no alibi, did he, an' he's got a record long as your arm. He couldn't see why I wouldn't lie to keep him out of jail. Then there was all that trouble with his brothers. Anyhow, it's over now.' She looked at her son, placidly crawling about with Jack in his wake, chubby bottoms waggling in the air and nappies at half-mast. 'We'll not be seein' him again.'

Taz felt Mandy's pain acutely, perhaps because it was the exact inverse of her own. Gareth was trying to force his way into Jack's life; Dave simply didn't want to know.

'Maybe he'll change his mind,' she suggested.

'He won't. He's even started sayin' Dylan's not his.' Mandy's eyes mirrored the angry betrayal in her voice. 'He's scum, Taz.'

'I don't know about that, but he's not worth upsetting yourself about.'

'No, Taz, you don't understand. Dave's scum, but he's still Dylan's dad.'

It was the week for heart-to-heart chats. First Adam, then Mandy . . . and now Bill.

He called up early in the morning, hissing down the telephone in a kind of stage whisper. Adam handed Taz the phone with a baffled shrug.

'It's for you. Sounds like a heavy breather – or a bad case of bronchitis.'

'Tasmin, is that you?'

'Dad? Dad, is there something wrong with your voice?' The voice became very slightly louder and clearer.

'Is that better? I can't speak any louder, your mother's in the kitchen. Listen, she's going out later, are you free sometime today?'

The calendar on the wall spelled out the thrilling story of Taz's packed social whirl: Tuesday, take Jack to baby clinic, Wednesday, clean bathroom, Thursday, buy more bin-bags.

'Yes, but why?'

'Can't speak now, see you later. About eleven thirty OK?'

Before she could answer, her father had put the phone

down, leaving Taz baffled. Adam came back into the room with Minky balanced on his shoulders, and handed her a mug of tea.

'What was all that about?' he enquired.

'Good question.'

It came to something when you had to creep around like a catburglar, terrified of bumping into your own mother. Taz drove into Painswick half expecting an ambush of hostile ladies from the WI, brandishing egg-whisks and lobbing jars of home-made jam at the car. But the village lay tranquil and timeless as ever, troubled only by the occasional drone of a tractor rumbling down the narrow lanes, or the lone bleat of a doleful sheep.

She parked up and walked round to the back door of the house. It was open but there was nobody in the kitchen, and a trail of bootprints led down the path to Bill's beloved shed.

'Dad?'

'Come in, the door's open.'

An invitation into Bill Norton's shed was a rare privilege. It was years since Taz had been into her father's inner sanctum, yet the smell was as distinctive as ever: a blend of old pipe-tobacco, turps, tomato fertiliser, creosote and two-stroke.

'Hello Daddy.'

'Hello Kitten. Close the door, it's chilly out there.'

She closed it, shutting out the whip and whine of the November wind, which was stirring up leaves into brown and gold eddies under the apple trees.

'What are you doing?'

'This?' Bill paused in his sawing. 'It's a Christmas present for Jack – a push-along cart for when he's learning to walk.' He winked. 'But don't tell him, I want it to be a surprise.'

'Dad!' laughed Taz, 'I think he's a bit young to understand about surprises!'

'Just my little joke.' Bill put his free arm round his daughter's shoulders and gave her a hug. 'But he's not too young to notice that his granny's not around, is he?'

Taz's face fell.

'No. Dad, I know I was a bit hard on Mum . . .'

'It's not me you need to say that too, it's your mother. She's not angry, you know, she's hurt.'

'But I meant it, about her interfering I mean. Sometimes she makes me feel like Jack's her baby, not mine, and she's trying to run both our lives for us.'

'Then explain it to her. But gently. Shouting at her doesn't do any good, you know it doesn't, she's stubborn as a mule and it only makes her worse. Doesn't it?'

'Yes,' sighed Taz. 'You're right.'

'And believe me, it takes one to know one. There aren't many people around who can give Bill Norton lessons in how to be a pigheaded old sod. Listen, Kitten, your mum had a tough time accepting Jack and everything, what with her lofty principles and me behaving like an idiot, but she got her head down and just got on with it, not like me. I was acting like a big kid, she was the sensible one.'

'But you came round, Dad. The minute you saw Jack. And you don't tell me how to live my life, even though you can't stand the sight of Adam.'

'Now hang on, I never said . . .'

'You don't have to, I know you don't like him, but you've tried to get on with him for my sake. Thanks Dad.' She kissed him on the cheek; it was bristly and rough, and smelt of carbolic. 'So what do I do about Mum?'

'Have a chat with her. Say you're sorry even if you're not. Then explain how you feel. She'll listen, if you do it right.'

'I'll try.'

'That's my girl.' Bill finished sawing and put the saw aside. 'Hand me that tin of knotting will you? And the half-inch brush.' He prised off the lid and started dabbing the varnish-brown fluid onto the bare wood. 'I know things are hard for you just now. Any news about work?'

'Nope.'

'That's a terrible way to treat people, it's bad management you know. I'd never have kept anyone waiting the way they've done to you. Never,' snorted Bill.

'I know Dad, but you're not Henry Goldman. He hates

me, he just wants to make sure I suffer before he gives me the sack.'

Bill dabbed thoughtfully.

'So don't give him the satisfaction. Look for another job. Get yourself fixed up, resign before he gives you the push.'

'Wouldn't that be like giving up?'

'Looking out for yourself isn't giving up. And if that Diana Latchford's the kind of woman I think she is, she'll want to help you. You've got talent, Kitten, don't waste it.'

Taz smiled at her father. He winked back.

'Thanks, Dad. You've got more sense than I'll ever have.'

'Rubbish. Go out there and prove me wrong.'

He squeezed her tight and she knew he wasn't just talking about fighting for her future at Seuss & Goldman. Before she tried to save her career, first she needed to salvage her relationship with her mother. And if anything, that was going to be even more of a challenge.

By way of escape, Taz and Mandy decided to take Jack and Dylan to the new soft-play centre; a paradise of foam-rubber cubes and tunnels, where babies could crawl and tumble in perfect safety and harassed parents could relax while somebody else took charge for half an hour.

'Dylan's going to give you the runaround when he's older,' giggled Taz, watching Dylan crawl determinedly around the softly-padded floor, hotly pursued by a nursery nurse with a beachball under her arm.

'What do you mean, when he's older? Just look at him now!'

By contrast, Jack seemed content to crawl into one of the squashy foam tunnels and lie there on his tummy, watching the world go by with open-mouthed astonishment.

Some of the babies had both parents with them, most were with mums, a few with lone dads. Taz watched the tender way that huge, brawny-armed men cradled tiny babies, soothing imagined hurts, and wished with all her heart that Gareth Scott could never have existed – or far better, that he could have been somebody completely different.

'What are you thinkin' about?' demanded Mandy after Taz had been silent for a long time.

'Oh nothing. I was just wondering . . . If Dave wanted to see Dylan again, what would you do?'

'Take him down the prison.'

'You wouldn't mind?'

Mandy squatted down on the floor, tucking her feet underneath her.

'Course I'd mind, but he's Dylan's dad, isn't he?'

'Oh.' Taz watched Jack wriggle out of his protective tunnel and into the arms of one of the helpers.

'What's up? It's Gareth, isn't it? He's been on at you again.'

'I met up with him last week.' Taz swallowed down the lump of fear that was filling her constricted throat. 'He wants to see Jack, you know, spend time with him.'

The uniformed helper came smiling across to Taz, Jack balanced on her hip.

'Mrs Norton? I think he needs changing.'

'Oh, thanks.' Taz took Jack into her arms, automatically sniffing the seat of his pants as she did so. 'Uh-oh, who's gone and filled his nappy then?' She grimaced. 'Again.'

'Come on Dylan.' Mandy scooped up the wriggling, protesting bundle of her son. 'Your friend Jack needs his nappy changing.'

In the mother and baby room, Taz eased off Jack's trousers.

'You couldn't hand me some of those wipes could you? He's got himself into a right old smelly mess, haven't you sweetheart?'

Jack didn't reply in words, but his bottom emitted a sonorous burp and the atmosphere in the room became slightly more fragrant. Mandy coughed. Taz's eyes watered.

'You did that deliberately, didn't you?' Jack smiled proudly. 'And I bet you're going to wee all over me just because I haven't got a spare tee-shirt with me!'

'What did you tell Gareth then?' demanded Mandy, bouncing Dylan on her lap.

Taz felt the pain of anxiety creeping back, enclosing her heart with its cold, black fingers.

'I told him no.'

'Why?'

'Because I don't want him to be part of Jack's life.'

'But Taz, he's Jack's dad. He *is* part of Jack's life.'

Taz wiped Jack's bottom and dropped the soiled cotton wool into the rubbish bin. She didn't respond. She couldn't.

'At least he *wants* to get to know his son, not like Dave.'

Taz selected a clean nappy from the supply in Jack's changing bag.

'Why should I, Mandy? Why should I let Gareth anywhere near Jack, after what he did to me? He's got no right . . .'

'No. But Jack has. How's he goin' to feel if you don't give him a chance to know his dad?'

Those were the words that really hit home. This wasn't about Gareth's right to know Jack, it was about Jack's right to know that he had a dad, not just some faceless genetic contributor whose role had ended at conception.

Mandy put her hand on Taz's shoulder.

'Why don't you let him spend a bit of time with Jack – you know, take him out for the day or somethin'? Why not?'

For a few moments, Taz stood paralysed, every dreadful imagining crowding into her brain. If she let Gareth have Jack, even for ten minutes, he'd run off with him and she'd never see him again. She knew that Gareth wasn't really like that, yet she couldn't take the risk.

'I'm afraid,' she confessed.

Mandy hugged her.

'I know. But think about it, you don't have to decide now do you? Let him sweat a bit.'

Taz contemplated the sheer mass of stuff that surrounded her: the filthy, smelly nappy, the three bulging bags, the buggy, and last but not least the cheerfully wriggling form of Jack, who liked nothing better than to play hard to get when his nappy was being changed. Maybe if Gareth was to find out what being a parent was really like . . .

She dried and powdered Jack's bottom, and did up his fresh nappy.

'There, all done and dusted.' Taz slipped Jack's feet back into the legs of his clean trousers. It was quite a fiddly job if you weren't used to it. Frustratingly impossible if you were a forty-six-year-old man who didn't know one end of a baby from the other. She picked up Jack's discarded nappy between finger and thumb. 'You know Mandy, if Gareth really wants to play daddies . . . I think he ought to start with *this*.'

It was almost eight o'clock and Leroy was working late. Not that it was anything unusual; he'd been working late practically every night since Taz had been suspended as DSM.

Responsibility sat heavily on Leroy's shoulders, and it was more than just a question of proving his own ability. When Taz came back to S&G – and he refused to believe that she might not – he was determined to show that he had taken good care of the department. *Her* department. He wanted to succeed in his own career, of course he did; but not at Taz Norton's expense.

As he rubbed the drowsiness out of his eyes, he forced himself to concentrate on the figures in front of him. Party-size mini-quiches, brie and asparagus brioches, monkfish patties and oak-smoked Cheddar swam before his eyes, resolving themselves into something almost meaningful before turning back into an amorphous muddle.

He yawned. Coffee, he needed more coffee. Time to fetch another cup from the vending machine.

But he didn't make it to the vending machine, because just as he was getting up from his chair there was a knock on the office door. Must be one of the security guards, checking if anyone was still around before locking up for the night.

'Come in.'

The door opened, but it wasn't Brian from security who hovered on the threshold. It was Theresa Carvell.

Leroy's eyebrows hitched up a fraction of an inch, then recovered their composure.

'Theresa. What a surprise.'

Taking this as encouragement, Theresa stepped inside and shut the door. She was the same tarty Theresa as ever, but something was missing; in place of the cocky defiance of old, a brittle bitterness animated her every gesture. Theresa was undeniably unhappy. Leroy watched her grab a chair and position herself on it with angry precision.

'I'm glad you're still here,' she said. 'I've got something to tell you.'

'Really?' Leroy finished scribbling on his sheaf of papers, then covered them with his blotter. You had to take precautions – everyone knew Theresa had been sacked for stealing from S&G, and had been lucky not to find herself in court as well. 'What about?'

'Ted.' Theresa enunciated the word with venomous dislike. 'He's a cheating bastard.'

Leroy bit his lip, sorely tempted to make some facetious remark.

'You don't say.' He folded his hands. 'But why would you want to talk to me about Ted Williams?'

Theresa leaned forward, her rather scraggy cleavage very visible but not very tempting through the V-shaped plunge of her blouse.

'I lost my job because of him,' she hissed. 'I owned up to save his rotten stinking skin – and what does he do? He dumps me.'

'Oh.' Light was starting to dawn for Leroy. 'I *see*. So . . .'

'So I'm here to put the record straight, Mr McIntosh. I've got one or two interesting things to tell you about Ted Williams.' Theresa opened her handbag, took out several folded sheets of paper and laid them in front of Leroy. 'And in case you're wondering, I've got the evidence to back them up.'

Chapter 30

Diana Latchford was not in the habit of inviting junior managers to her house at all hours of the day or night. It was well after eleven, she was dog-tired and she'd just run herself a bath. But as soon as she'd received the telephone call from Leroy, she knew he would have to qualify as a special case.

Leroy sat at her dining-room table, carefully laying out papers on the polished surface. He looked perfectly at home in elegant surroundings, not in the least overawed by Diana or her home. He sat back to contemplate the effect.

'So you see, Mrs Latchford, Theresa Carvell has provided us with some impressive evidence. And she let me tape her statement. It's all on this audiocassette.'

Diana looked impressed – but wary. She fingered the corner of a stock record form.

'Is there a problem?' enquired Leroy, impatient for something good to come out of this horrible mess.

'This could be down to sour grapes,' Diana pointed out. 'Ted dumped her, she's bound to want her pound of flesh.'

'Oh, she wants her revenge all right,' agreed Leroy. 'But you know as well as I do that she couldn't have fabricated all this if she'd tried.'

'No,' conceded Diana. 'She couldn't, could she?' And then, quite unexpectedly, her face was lit up by a broad smile. 'So, all in all, I think it is quite in order for us to proceed.'

'You're going to contact the police then?' said Leroy, his spirits soaring.

'Not just yet. First, have a discreet chat with someone in menswear. Someone you can trust – Marion Grey perhaps.'

'And then?'

'Get back to me. The next time Ted makes one of his little visits to the incinerator, I want to know.'

Isobel was less than delighted to see Taz's old brown car bumping to a halt outside her cottage. If her heart leaped a fraction at the sight of her small grandson, being carried by his mother up her garden path, she showed no outward sign.

'Someone at the door,' observed Bill from behind the kitchen door, where he was putting on his wellies. 'You get it, eh, I'm just off to the allotment for some sprouts.'

Isobel could only marvel at Bill's escapology act. He was out of the back door and halfway down the path to the gate before the doorbell had sounded a second time.

From behind the curtains in the front room, Isobel could see without being seen. Taz was standing on the doorstep, hugging Jack to her, swaying from one foot to the other as she waited. That hat didn't suit her, it made her look a fright, not that it was any of Isobel's business what her daughter wore. Tasmin had made that abundantly clear. Maybe she'd pretend she wasn't in, all she had to do was not open the door. But oh! Didn't Jack look sweet, in his quilted suit with the furry hood, and the mittens his granny had knitted him . . .

Taz was glancing up at the windows, peeping through the fanlight at the top of the door, calling through the letter box.

'Hello – anybody home? Oh Jack, we should have called first, shouldn't we? They're not in.'

Something tightened in Isobel's stomach as Taz turned to walk back to the car. A few seconds later, she opened the door.

'I thought you weren't in,' said Taz, relieved.

'Really? Well I do have more to do than sit around waiting for you to call.' Isobel looked her daughter up and down, doing her best not to smile as Jack woke up and rubbed his sleepy eyes with his little fists.

'Can we come in?'

'I suppose so. If you're quick – I was just going out.' That last bit was a lie, but she didn't see any reason why Tasmin shouldn't feel a little more guilty. Reaching the front room, she untied her apron and folded it with meticulous, irritable precision before putting it away in the top drawer of the sideboard. She picked up a duster and a can of spray polish. 'So – what is it this time?'

'Pardon?'

'What do you want?' She gave the sideboard a quick squirt of polish and started rubbing at it with short, bad-tempered strokes. 'That girl Mandy let you down has she? I told you it was no use relying on her sort . . .'

'Mum! Please don't.' Taz's voice tailed off from a shout to a near-whisper. 'Please. Nobody's let me down, I just came to say I'm sorry.'

Isobel stopped in her tracks, the duster skidding to a halt on the over-polished wood.

'I beg your pardon?'

'Don't sound so shocked, Mummy. Even I sometimes admit it when I'm wrong.' Taz touched her mother lightly on the shoulder and she froze at the sudden contact. 'Mummy, I'm really sorry I hurt you, I didn't mean to.'

'You have a funny way of showing it,' commented Isobel frostily, recommencing her obsessive polishing with a pair of glass swans.

'I know, I was tactless. That's me all over. You've been so good to me and Jack, and I really appreciate that. But . . .'

'Oh, so there's a but is there? I might have guessed you couldn't simply say sorry.'

'I can't help wanting to bring up Jack the way I see fit, after all he is my baby, Mum. Can't you remember what it was like when you had me and everybody wanted to tell you how to look after me?'

'I only wish they had,' replied Isobel softly. 'I wish my mother had been around to give me the benefit of her advice.'

And that was the crux of it all, she thought to herself as her fingers scrunched the duster into a yellow ball of tension. Losing her mother when she was hardly more than a child herself had made her bossy and over-protective towards her own daughter; she knew that in her heart of hearts though she didn't like to think about it.

Her face turned away to avoid betraying any telltale emotion, Isobel rearranged the ornaments on the mantelpiece. She listened to Jack grizzling in his mother's arms, and the soft, kind way Taz soothed him back to chuckles and smiles.

'Mum . . .'

'What?'

'When I was little, I really missed having a granny.'

'You had Bill's stepmother.'

'Yes, I know, and she's lovely, but she's not really like a proper granny is she? I used to wonder what it'd be like, and I don't want Jack to have to wonder the way I did.'

Isobel straightened up, clicking the top back onto the can of polish.

'I don't follow.'

'Yes you do, Mummy, I know you do. Jack loves his granny, he misses you so much. Look – he wants to give you a cuddle.'

Isobel pivoted slowly round to face her daughter. Jack was reaching out his arms to her and smiling. Isobel caught Jack's mittened hands and felt them curl determinedly about her index fingers.

'So do I, Mummy, we both do,' pleaded Taz, putting her free arm about her mother's shoulders. 'And I've got something to ask you.'

'Oh?' So this was it, thought Isobel with cynical sorrow. All this was just Taz's underhand way of softening her up to scrounge a favour.

'You really do want Jack to be christened, don't you? It means a lot to you.'

'You know it does. But as you said, it's none of my business.'

413

'Well, Mummy, I think it is. And if you still want to help organise it . . .'

'Me? You want me to help you organise Jack's christening?'

'Only if you don't mind.'

Isobel wondered if she was hearing things. Taz smiled.

'Why on earth would I mind? Jack's my grandson.'

'Exactly. And you're his granny. And I want to make sure that Jack's never short of people he can care for and people who care about him.'

Ted Williams nodded briefly to the man on the desk as he passed through the security lodge.

'Just on my way to the incinerator with these.' He raised his hand to reveal three carrier bags, full to bursting point. 'I've signed the forms, they're on their way down to you.'

The security guard peered over the desk at the bags.

'More damaged stock?'

'You know how it is, they don't make things like they used to. Cameras switched on are they?'

'They're always switched on, Mr Williams. Half the stock in this place'd go walkies otherwise.'

'Know what you mean. Comes to something when you have to film people to stop them nicking the stock.'

Ted whistled merrily as he went through the door at the side of the desk, and down the narrow corridor which led to the crusher and incinerator situated at the rear of the goods loading bay.

At the end of the passageway, he passed through another door into the open air. Above his head, three security cameras whirred into action, tracking him as he walked the twenty or so yards across to the crusher. His hand was poised above the button, ready to consign all three bags to oblivion, when another hand came down. Right on his shoulder. He nearly jumped out of his skin.

'I'll take those, Ted. If you don't mind.'

Ted turned round in horror-stricken slow motion. Diana Latchford was standing right behind him, flanked by Brian from security and some gorilla from goods inward.

'Mrs Latchford . . . Diana.' He retrieved his slipping

smile and stuck it back in the middle of his face. 'Is something wrong?'

'Brian, take those bags off Ted, will you? Before he does something we'll all regret.'

It was useless Ted protesting, Brian had already relieved him of the three carrier bags. The three bags which were supposed to contain nine damaged Dior shirts . . . 'I don't understand.'

'No?' Diana smiled at him, coaxingly. 'Come now, I think you do. Let's just take a look inside these bags shall we?'

Ted stood frozen in paralysed horror as Brian opened one of the bags and took out . . . several other bags, rolled up and stuffed into the bag with a couple of torn tee-shirts, to pad it out.

'Well, well, well,' said Diana, looking long and hard at Ted. 'Who'd've thought it?'

'I can explain,' gasped Ted, as the gorilla's paw closed around his elbow.

'You'll have to,' replied Diana.

'I can explain,' protested Henry Goldman, his eyes sweeping the boardroom for some small sign of support.

There was none. Diana Latchford was grim-faced, Angus Cornforth pale with anger, the human resources director was muttering to himself, and young Daniel Seuss looked utterly appalled by the whole business. Nikki, Diana's PA, who had always seemed so very pleasant and personable, resolutely refused even to look at Henry and scowled, head down, as she scribbled down the minutes.

'Look . . .' he went on, hope fading fast. 'Look, all I did was . . .'

'All you did,' snapped Angus Cornforth, 'was allow your personal judgement to be severely compromised by your susceptibility to empty flattery.'

'Quite,' agreed the human resources director sourly. 'Which allowed one departmental manager to rob this company of God knows how many thousands of pounds. You're a prat, Goldman, a pompous inadequate prat.'

'Now just hold on!'

'No, you hold on, I haven't finished yet. A pompous, inadequate, self-obsessed prat who'd never have made it past sales assistant if his father hadn't owned the company.'

'You can't speak to me like that!'

One glance at the stony faces surrounding him was enough to show that he could.

Diana Latchford watched with a degree of smug satisfaction which almost ashamed her. But it was all she could do not to punch the air when the board voted unanimously to dismiss Henry from the board, appointing Angus Cornforth as acting chairman and co-opting Daniel Seuss as a permananent board member.

Diana wholeheartedly approved. Angus Cornforth was crusty but sound. Daniel Seuss, a graduate of Manchester Business School, was young, keen and morally unimpeachable – the perfect antidote in fact to Ted Williams, who was likely to be helping the police with their enquiries for some time to come. Thanks to Theresa Carvell, Leroy McIntosh . . . and of course Taz Norton.

Taz was very much on Diana's mind as she caught up with Angus after the meeting.

'Bad business that,' he remarked as he packed up his papers. Still,' he went on, snapping shut his case, 'at least it's over now.'

'Not quite,' Diana corrected him. 'There's one very important aspect of this case that we haven't even discussed.'

Cornforth's brow furrowed.

'I'm sorry, you've lost me.'

Diana slapped Taz's report on the boardroom table, right under Cornforth's nose.

'The food hall.'

'Ah.' Diana could tell from the expression on Cornforth's face that this was something he'd rather have put to the back of his mind.

'That's right. Tasmin Norton, you do remember her?'

'How could I forget?' His fingers smoothed the cover of the report. 'She's still on suspension you say?'

'And we need to do something about that. Soon. But first, can I suggest you take a look at her report? It makes interesting reading.'

'This way?' Gareth held up a disposable nappy. Taz shook her head.

'No, not that way, that's upside down. The padded bit goes at the front, see?'

Gareth scratched his head.

'It looks the same both ways to me. So tell me again, what do I do with this?'

'That's zinc and castor oil cream, you rub it on his bottom to stop him getting nappy rash. Have you been listening to *anything* I've been saying?'

'Of course I have, anyhow I'll soon get the hang of it, won't I Jack?'

Jack looked thoroughly bemused by all the fuss, perched in his high chair and waiting for his lunch while two grown-ups argued the toss about how to put on his nappy. The third grown-up was sulking in the corner, pretending to read *BBC Wildlife*.

Taz was beginning to wonder who was the child around here. Did Adam think she actually *liked* the idea of letting Gareth take care of Jack for five minutes, let alone a whole day out? Well, if it was going to happen she was going to make sure Gareth was thoroughly prepared for it. Dirty nappies and all.

The kettle switched itself off and Taz stirred a little hot water into the pulpy mess that called itself Jack's dinner.

'There, now we let that cool down.'

'Ugh, what the hell is *that*?'

'Lamb and swede risotto apparently,' shrugged Taz. 'My mum cooked it for him.'

'You've tasted that?' Gareth looked quite green. 'Tasting's not compulsory is it?'

'No, but you'll find it easier if you do. Jack likes to see you eating before he has a taste. Don't you Jack?'

By now, Jack was banging his fists impatiently on the tray of his high chair. He was also getting in some singing practice. In between shouts and bangs he snuffled, two parallel threads of snot dribbling onto his upper lip. Even from a doting mother's perspective, it wasn't a pretty sight.

'Go on then, put his bib on. No, not like that, you'll strangle the poor child. That's better, good boy Jack, try not to wriggle. Oh, and you can give him a bit of bread to chew on, it helps with the teething.'

'This much?' asked Gareth, breaking off half a French stick.

Taz cast a look at Adam. He was cringing in the corner, one hand over his face to blot out the awful sight.

'Oh yeah, definitely,' commented Adam with heavy sarcasm. 'And why don't you fill it with garlic mushrooms and gravad lax while you're at it?'

'Shut up Adam. Look Gareth, Jack's only a little baby, he doesn't eat much – and he wastes most of what you give him. This much will do.' She broke off a couple of inches of bread and gave it to Jack, who promptly tried to stuff it in his ear. 'His dinner should be cool enough now, you can bring it over if you want.'

Gareth brought over the plastic bowl containing the beige-coloured mush. Unfortunately he chose to put it down in front of Jack at precisely the same moment that Jack decided to bang his piece of bread down on the tray. One small but determined fist caught the side of the dish, it flew sideways and landed, upside-down, in the middle of the kitchen floor, splattering Gareth's very nice three-hundred-pound shoes.

'Shit,' said Gareth. 'Now what do we do?'

'We clean this up,' said Taz serenely. 'Then we make Jack some more dinner. Go on then – fetch the floor cloth.'

'What about my shoes?'

'Never mind your shoes, Jack's hungry.'

'Cretin,' muttered Adam.

'What?' demanded Gareth, in the middle of rolling up his shirtsleeves.

'You heard.'

'Now look here, lover-boy . . .'

'Oh shut up!' Taz grabbed the floor cloth from Gareth

and started wiping up the mess herself. 'Both of you. Damn, isn't that the phone?'

'I'll get it,' volunteered Adam, looking like a drowning man who had just spotted a life-raft.

'I thought you had better taste in men,' commented Gareth, ruffling Jack's silky brown hair.

'Obviously I can't have,' replied Taz. 'Not if I ever fancied you.'

'It's S&G. Sounds important,' said Adam from the doorway.

Something turned a triple somersault inside Taz's stomach. She grabbed the phone from Adam.

'Taz? It's Nikki here. Diana wants you to come in right away.'

'But . . .' Taz surveyed the dreadful mess of her kitchen, the baby rubbing breadcrumbs into his hair, the lover and the ex-lover glaring each other to death across the quarry tiles.

'It's important. I mean, *really* important.'

'Well – hang on a minute.' Taz put her hand over the mouthpiece. It's Diana Latchford's PA, apparently they want me in urgently. But I can't go . . . unless . . . Adam?'

Adam was about to open his mouth but Gareth got in first.

'I'll take care of Jack for you,' he volunteered. 'It's a great chance to spend some quality time with my son.'

'Gareth. Are you *certain* you want to do this? I might be gone a few hours.'

'Relax, we'll be fine. Won't we Jack?'

Jack contrived to look truly angelic, despite the snot and the breadcrumbs and the faint smell wafting from the seat of his pants.

'Well . . . if you're sure.' Taz's eyes sought out Adam, refusing to let him look away. 'I suppose not too much can go wrong. And if you're really stuck Adam'll be here to give you a hand, won't you Adam?'

Adam responded with a Neanderthal glare, which seemed hardly nice coming from a Friend of the Earth.

'Don't fucking count on it,' he replied, and stormed out of the kitchen, crashing the door shut behind him.

419

Taz hardly knew which to be more nervous about: leaving Jack with Gareth or going to see Diana Latchford.

This was it, it had to be. Her death sentence. There was no other reason why Diana would drag her in to S&G at five minutes' notice. The clock on the dashboard was ticking its way towards twelve o'clock. What was the betting that by half past she'd be out of a job?

Nikki wasn't at her desk; she must be at lunch. The door to Diana's office was ajar, and Taz could see Diana inside, working at her PC. She tried to judge her mood from the set of her head, the angle of her shoulders and back, but it was impossible. There was only one reliable way to learn her fate.

She knocked. Diana looked up.

'Come in.' She said the words very gently, as though dealing with someone extremely fragile, or someone who was about to receive bad news. 'You managed to get a babysitter then?'

'Oh . . . you know. People help out.'

'Right. Take a seat, will you?' There was a marked awkwardness between them, an emotional thickness in the air that made it difficult to breathe, harder still to communicate.

'I'd rather stand, if you don't mind.'

Standing up, with Diana in her stockinged feet, Taz had a slight height advantage. That was some comfort; at least she didn't feel completely belittled. She decided she might as well take the initiative.

'I suppose you're going to sack me now, are you?'

'As a matter of fact I'm not.'

'Oh.' This rather took the wind out of Taz's sails. 'What then?'

Diana took a sealed envelope from her out tray and offered it to Taz.

'What's this?'

'It's a written apology and a letter of resignation. From Henry Goldman.' Seeing the reaction on Taz's face, she nodded ruefully. 'Actually I think we all owe you an apology. You were right to make a fuss about Ted Williams.'

420

'I *know* I'm right, but . . . being right isn't enough is it? There's no evidence.'

'Theresa Carvell has just given us all the evidence we need. Besides which, I caught Ted red-handed, trying to dispose of some fake damaged stock. We sacked him yesterday.'

Shock flooded Taz's system, paralysing her, tearing her up by the roots and carrying her away.

'You. Sacked. Ted.'

'There are going to be some other changes around here too, but I'll fill you in on those as you go along. Right now, I guess you'll want to get straight back to your department.'

The words made perfect sense, but they refused to penetrate her skin and enter her soul.

'My department? You mean – you're reinstating me?'

'Of course, didn't I say? I'm sorry, everything has moved so quickly I'm having difficulty keeping up with it all myself. Are you all right, Taz?'

'Er . . . yes. Sorry.' Taz flopped down onto the chair she had scorned only minutes ago, landing on it with all the grace of a sack of potatoes. 'This has come as a bit of a shock.'

Genuine concern registered on Diana's professionally pleasant face.

'Yes, of course, I'm rushing you aren't I?'

'Well yes. A bit.'

'Look, Leroy's doing a good job of keeping things ticking over. Take a couple of days' leave to sort yourself out. But we'd like you to get back to the food hall as quickly as you can.'

'We?'

'The board. Angus Cornforth was particularly impressed by your report, he wants to talk to you about some of your proposals. Did I mention he's standing in as acting chairman?'

If Taz had been surprised before, she was frankly astounded now.

'Angus Cornforth? The same Angus Cornforth who

wanted to rip my throat out over that kiddies' painting competition?'

It all seemed so far away now, so long ago and ludicrously far away. Diana laughed. She looked, thought Taz, surprisingly human when she laughed; more like a woman and less like a retail icon.

'We can all make mistakes,' Diana said. 'And that includes me.'

Chapter 31

Hang on, thought Taz, racing up the passage to her flat. I know that baby buggy.

OK, so it seemed to have acquired a new plastic hood and a coat of paint, and it wasn't held together with sticky-tape and string any more, but it was definitely Mandy's buggy, parked outside the front door of Taz's flat.

Mandy and Gareth and Adam, all in the same flat. The thought made Taz walk even faster.

She turned the key and nudged the door open with her toe. Minky darted out, wound herself round Taz's legs and mewed lovingly.

'Hello Minky, where's everybody got to?' She stepped inside, nudging the cat ahead of her, and closed the door. 'Gareth? Adam? Hello, anybody there?'

There was a funny smell in the flat, or rather, all the right smells were present, but in the wrong proportions. Lamb stew, baby lotion, soiled nappies, Toilet Duck, disinfectant . . . a *lot* of disinfectant. And good God, whatever was that noise? It sounded like an animal in pain. Faintly alarmed for no good reason, Taz dumped her things on the hall table and hurried into the living room.

'Hello? Mandy? What are you *doing*?'

Mandy, swathed in a black and white bedspread, was crawling around on knees and elbows, making mooing noises. Her little fingers were sticking out on either side of her head, making small pink horns. Dylan was sitting on his bottom on the carpet, happily banging two plastic bricks together and being very blasé about it all, while

Jack giggled as he crawled for all he was worth in Mandy's wake.

'What does it look like?' replied Mandy cheerfully. 'I'm a Friesian cow.'

'Oh. Well that's all right then.' Hands on hips, Taz surveyed the scene. Everything was as neat and clean and tidy, as a room could be when it had two nine-month-old babies in it, plus all their impedimenta. 'Don't take this the wrong way, Mandy, but what exactly are you doing here?'

'Mindin' Jack.' Mandy got up, swinging Jack into the air and making him squeal with delight. 'Gareth phoned me.'

Taz put her hand to her forehead, not quite adjusting to this unexpected turn of events.

'But Gareth said he could manage . . .'

Mandy gave a snort of laughter.

'Did you ever meet a bloke who said he couldn't cope? I'm not kiddin' Taz, there was dinner all up the walls an' you've never seen anythin' like the state of Jack's bottom. Gareth's in the kitchen now. I told him I'd mind the babies while he cleaned up.'

Gareth – cleaning? The image was so incongruous that Taz's mind instantly rejected it.

'Well I'd better have a word with him then,' she said.

The reality surpassed anything Taz's imagination could have dreamed up. Gareth was balancing on a kitchen stool, stretching up to swab blobs of lamb mince from the ceiling. There was bread and butter stuck to the floor, spilt baby-juice on the table, and a pebbledash of dinner up the one tiled wall that Gareth hadn't already managed to wash. And as for Gareth himself, those expensive leisure clothes would never, ever be the same again, no matter how many times Melanie might get them dry-cleaned.

'What in God's name have you done to my kitchen?' squeaked Taz.

Gareth got down from the stool, sponge in hand. There was a brown smear up one side of his face. Taz had never seen him look so utterly dejected.

'Oh God, Taz – this is . . . not as bad as it looks.'

'It looks like an explosion in an abattoir.'

'I know.' Gareth threw his sponge listlessly at the wall. It bounced off and fell soggily to the floor. 'I really fouled up here didn't I?'

'Looks that way,' agreed Taz, wondering how on earth anyone could get stew onto the ceiling and make it stick.

'I had no idea, Taz. Absolutely no idea it could be so difficult, looking after one little baby.'

'You don't say.'

'The minute you walked out of the door, Jack started screaming his head off – and naturally your precious Adam decides he has somewhere really important to get to in five minutes' time.'

'Naturally.' Taz smiled to herself, but didn't let Gareth see her satisfaction. She didn't want him to think he might be off the hook.

'Smug bastard.'

'You were the one who said you could manage on your own, remember?'

Gareth heaved a sigh of capitulation.

'OK. So I was wrong. When it came to the crunch I couldn't get anything right – not even changing his nappy.'

'But we went through that three times!'

'Tell me about it.' Gareth sat down wearily, easing the fabric of his trousers away from the skin where they had adhered to his legs. 'He wouldn't eat, he wouldn't be quiet, and when I managed to get his nappy off he weed all down my trousers . . .'

'So I see.'

'For God's sake Taz, stop laughing at me, it's not funny!'

'No.' She made a determined effort to keep a straight face. 'No, it's not funny at all, I'm very angry with you Gareth. What if something had happened to Jack?'

'Don't remind me,' groaned Gareth. 'All the time he was screaming, I was thinking, what if there's something wrong with him, what I've hurt him, what if he's ill? How do I tell?'

'It's a big responsibility, looking after a baby.' Taz wiped off another stool and sat down opposite Gareth. 'I should know, Jack's turned my whole life upside down. He's not just a fashion accessory, you know, you can't just walk into his life and expect him to love you – you have to work at it.'

'Maybe I'm not cut out for this fatherhood thing then,' said Gareth dully. There was something that looked like melted chocolate in his greying hair; Taz rather hoped it wasn't chocolate.

'Maybe,' she said, as gently as she could. 'Only you can decide that.'

In the silence, Taz heard the sounds of play and laughter coming from the living room.

'He loves *her*,' observed Gareth, with a resentful nod in that direction.

'Mandy? Yes, he does doesn't he? But then she's great with kids, a real natural. Not like me.'

'You?' Gareth looked up sharply. 'But you're a first-rate mother.'

'So? I still had to learn to be a good mother, Mandy didn't. It's all instinct with her, she's a natural. Look, it's early days, don't be too hard on yourself.' She wondered why she was being so charitable towards Gareth, who, when all was said and done, was still a piece of slime. 'Did you know – about Henry Goldman?'

Gareth flinched slightly, then nodded.

'Well thanks a bunch. You might've told me. I went there this afternoon thinking I was going to be sacked!'

Gareth managed to look defensive and self-righteous at the same time.

'OK, here's the bottom line. There were rumours that there was going to be an emergency meeting of the executive committee – and the word was that Henry was going to be asked to go. But there was nothing concrete; besides it was confidential, I couldn't tell you could I?'

'You're not usually so scrupulous.'

'No. No, I suppose you would think that. I haven't treated you very well, have I?'

'Does the phrase "like shit" mean anything to you?'

Gareth coughed.

'I've been thinking,' he said. 'About the future.'

'Oh?' Taz felt the hairs rise on the back of her neck. Whenever Gareth started talking about the future, he invariably included Jack in his plans.

'Now Henry's gone, things are going to change at S& G. I've had one or two offers, and to be honest Melanie's not really that keen on Swindon.'

'Get to the point, Gareth.'

'I've had the offer of a couple of lucrative directorships in London. It would mean moving down there of course, and I wouldn't be able to see much of you and Jack if we were in London. But now I'm wondering if maybe that's not such a bad thing. I'm not really bringing anything to Jack's life that he can't get more of from you . . .'

'You're his father, Gareth.' It astonished Taz to hear herself say so, but the words just came out. 'He can't get that from anybody else.'

'I know.' A trace of wistfulness passed across Gareth's eyes, then it was gone. 'But let's be honest, Taz, I'm really not cut out for this. I'm unreliable, I'm selfish, I'm useless at relationships.'

'But you care about Jack. Don't you?'

'Yes. Yes, I do.' For once, Taz found herself believing him. 'I really do, and that's why I think he'll do a lot better without a guy like me screwing up his life.'

Taz felt a kind of dull ache weighting the pit of her stomach; not so much anger as frustration.

'And so you're running out on him – again.'

'No!' There was real passion in his eyes, the kind of genuine emotion he had never displayed when he and Taz had been together. 'Listen Taz. I may not be around all the time, but I'll never let the boy down. Anything he needs – you only have to ask.'

'Fatherhood's about more than money, Gareth,' Taz warned him. 'You can't buy his love.'

'And I won't try. Look, the trouble is, I've never got on with anything I couldn't hold a conversation with. And I don't think I should be doing this just because Melanie wants to play mummies and daddies. You're Jack's mother, Taz, I think I lost sight of that for a while.'

'And you're his dad. Whether I like that or not. You have a right to see your son.'

Gareth shook his head. He looked quite sad, thought Taz; sad but single-minded.

'When Jack's old enough to ask who his daddy is, and if you think I'm worth knowing, I'll be there for him. Any time. I promise. I'll make sure you know where to find me.'

Now that the air had been cleared, Gareth and Jack seemed to get along much better, as if each sensed relief at not being forced to enjoy each other's company every alternate Saturday for the next eighteen years.

Mandy and Taz sat at the kitchen table, Mandy occasionally craning her head round the door to steal a glimpse of Gareth playing peep-bo with Jack in the living room. It was a rather heavy-handed kind of playing, but Jack seemed to put up with it remarkably well.

'Gareth's not got much idea has he?' remarked Mandy. 'Still, at least Jack's stopped screamin'. An' Dylan's not bitten him yet. It must be love.'

'Well, it's a start anyhow,' laughed Taz. 'Do you want another chocolate finger?'

'Go on then, seein' as you're celebratin'. Just one mind.'

They munched their way through the rest of the packet before they paused for breath.

'I'm going back to work on Monday,' said Taz casually.

'Yeah? Adam lookin' after Jack is he?' Mandy didn't even bother to disguise the disapproval in her voice.

'When he can, yes. The thing is, Mum's great but I don't want to rely on her, besides, she's got enough on her plate organising the christening. I'm looking for someone who wouldn't mind taking Jack for the odd hour now and then . . .'

'I'll do it if you like.'

Taz's heart soared. This was going just as she'd hoped it would.

'Really? You wouldn't mind taking Jack occasionally?'

'I said, didn't I?'

'That's wonderful! Of course, I'll pay you the going rate, the same as I used to pay Dee.'

Mandy's smile sagged into a frown.

'No way are you payin' me, Taz.' The stubborn jaw jutted, the orange-glossed lips pouting defiantly. 'I thought we was friends.'

'Of course we are!'

'Then I'll take care of Jack for you, to help you out, but I don't want nothin' for it.'

'But I thought . . . couldn't you use the extra money?'

Mandy drew herself up to her full five foot three inches of pigheadedness, her electric orange top-knot straining to sweep the cobwebs from the ceiling.

'Me an' Dylan are gettin' by, thank you very much. We don't need charity.'

Oh shit, thought Taz. I've gone and offended her again.

'Mandy, I never meant . . .'

'I know what you meant. But it's still not right. I'll look after Jack but I'm not takin' your money, and if you don't like it you can lump it!'

The first day back at Seuss & Goldman felt like the first day at big school. All Taz needed to complete the sensation was a satchel, squeaky shoes and a brand new blazer.

But as she addressed the Monday morning flash meeting in the food hall, she realised that she wasn't the new girl, she was the new teacher; the rookie form mistress egging on her pupils to bigger and better things. And she'd need to be Miss Jean Brodie and more to get anything much out of this lot.

Still, they seemed pleased to see her – or at least Leroy did, and the others weren't scowling as much as usual, though Gloria's first words to Taz were: 'There's no paper in the staff bog and I want tomorrow afternoon off for my bunions.'

Nothing much had changed. But it was going to – and soon.

'Right, first of all I'm really glad to be back.'

'And we're glad to see you back,' cut in Leroy, eyes sweeping the semi-circle of overalled figures. '*Aren't we?*'

A low murmur ran round the staff; more of a grunt than a yes, but it was a start.

'Second, good news from head office. Mr Cornforth and the board have OK'd the proposals I submitted to them last week, and we've been allocated additional funds to update the food hall.'

The grunt became a murmur, this time identifiably positive.

'Do we get paid more then?' demanded Mark.

'Not unless you sell more.' Taz ignored the mutinous groans and disappointed whines of 'bloody typical'. 'And that goes for all of us, we're still going to be paid by results – only it's going to be easier to achieve those results, because we'll be working in a modern environment, selling products that people actually want to buy. Leroy – the provisional schedule?'

Leroy stepped forward.

'We now have a firm date from head office. As from six p.m. this Friday, the food hall is closing down.'

'Completely,' confirmed Leroy. 'And it will stay closed for five working days for complete refurbishment, reopening the following Friday.'

'But,' spluttered somebody at the back. 'What about us? What are we supposed to do?'

'Do we get paid while all this is going on?' demanded Gloria. ''Cause if not, I'm taking it up with the union.'

'If you listen,' said Leroy, 'you might find out. Ms Norton?'

'What we're all going to be doing for the next five days,' explained Taz sweetly, 'is training. And don't look at me like that Mark,' she added, turning him red with embarrassment. 'Frankly, we could all use a little retraining, me included. This food hall has been at death's door for years and it's going to take more than a fresh coat of paint to revive it.

'So first thing on Saturday morning, we are all going to report to human resources. Aren't we, Mark?'

'Yes, Ms Norton,' replied Mark with less than white-hot enthusiasm.

'Good', nodded Taz. 'Because I'd like to think we *all* have a future with Seuss & Goldman.'

The long-term future might be bright, but waiting for the refit to begin was one of the toughest weeks of Taz Norton's life.

Watching the guts being ripped out of the food hall on Saturday morning was far more traumatic than Taz had imagined it would be. After all, she'd loathed the place since the day she'd joined S&G; she ought to be glad to see it dismantled before her very eyes.

'Frightening isn't it,' commented Leroy as they stood in the middle of what had been the bacon counter. 'Seeing it like this.'

'Let's just say I never thought I'd feel nostalgic about the festering old rat-hole.' Taz stepped aside to dodge a sheet of plate glass which was being manoeuvred into position. 'And I keep wondering if Sushil really knows what he's doing.'

'It's a bit late if he doesn't.'

'What do we do if it all goes horribly wrong?'

'Emigrate.'

'Ha ha.' Taz craned her neck to gaze up at the ceiling, re-emerging after more than half a century under plaster-board. It looked disgusting: lumpy, brown and dingy with sticky accretions. It bore little resemblance to the rococo delight Sushil had promised. 'Don't suppose you're any good with a paintbrush?

Sushil sashayed past with an armful of fabric swatches.

'Taz, what do you think – the pink or the green? The green is more cosmic, but then again . . .'

Taz and Leroy looked at each other.

'We could go with the pink and a hint of alabaster . . . or maybe I should stick with the fresh and natural look . . .'

Then Sushil was gone, a ponytailed phantom in silver trousers, wafting insubstantially between a row of builders' bums.

'That boy is weird,' observed Leroy.

'Patros says he's a genius.'
'Patros wears open-toed sandals. In January.'

On Thursday, the eve of the grand reopening, Taz and Leroy reported to Diana Latchford's office for an evening meeting. Diana was talking over some NVQ reports with Paul Logan, the human resources director.

'Taz, hi, come in. And Leroy, good to see you. How are the refurbishments coming along?'

'Just putting the finishing touches to the paintwork.' Taz hoped it was true; the last time she'd seen the place it had been crammed with shouting men in overalls.

'Excellent. So – ready to give us a guided tour?'

Taz nodded. She felt ridiculously anxious about this, a bag of nerves. Only Leroy's deadpan stoicism had kept her from going barmy, these last few days. That, plus endless cups of coffee.

'Before we go down, perhaps you could talk us through the new layout?' suggested Paul Logan, indicating to Taz and Leroy to sit down. Taz was grateful to have something solid underneath her backside; it was hours since she'd snatched a sandwich and she was feeling slightly faint.

'Well, as you'll have seen from the report,' explained Taz, 'I regard S&G essentially as the kind of store where customers can buy a total lifestyle experience – from interior design to clothing to food, we can provide them with all they need to create a fashionable way of life.'

'Sushil has carried that idea through into the Food Hall,' continued Leroy, unrolling the plans and spreading them out on the desk. 'Basically, he's eliminated the old layout completely and gone for themed areas instead: breakfast, dinner, drinks parties, outdoor dining and so on.'

'I see.' Logan followed Leroy's finger as it moved from square to rectangle to circle on the sketched floor-plan. 'So what about the concessions?'

'We're severing our connection with them,' cut in Diana.

'But what about our contractual obligations? I thought we were committed until well into next year.'

'Oh yes, we were.' Diana seemed mildly amused. 'But as soon as they realised we were going to take a microscope to their accounting practices and insist on strict adherence to the terms of their contracts, they were only too happy to terminate those contracts a little early.'

'I've instructed Mr McIntosh to line us up some new suppliers,' broke in Taz. 'With our new emphasis on superb quality, it's essential to have excellent lines of supply. Leroy?'

'To date, we have agreements with major suppliers of Indian, Thai, Middle Eastern, Scandinavian, Tex-Mex and Italian products . . .'

'And Caribbean,' added Taz. 'Leroy has connections there.'

'Er . . . quite. New stock will be coming in over the next fortnight, and we're taking charge of fresh produce ourselves: principally fruit, vegetables, meat, fish and cheese.'

'Good. Splendid, it sounds as if you have everything well in hand.' Paul Logan nodded, evidently impressed. Taz felt a rush of confidence.

'I think you'll be surprised by what Sushil's done. It's very . . . interesting and innovative.'

'Is that a way of telling me I'm not going to like it?'

'On the contrary, I think you'll be impressed.'

Hell, I hope so, thought Taz; because it's my neck that's on the block. More to the point, tomorrow's grand reopening of the food hall was going to be covered live on both local TV news programmes, and if the watching millions weren't equally impressed the whole exercise might turn out to have been an expensive waste of time.

'Then perhaps we should go straight down and take a look.' Logan grabbed his jacket and slipped it on. 'Lead the way.'

'There is only one thing that really concerns me,' said Diana as they headed for the stairs. 'And that's the calibre of staff working in the food hall.'

Taz felt a little of her euphoria evaporate. Diana had hit on her Achilles heel. Diana seemed not to notice.

'So how has the retraining programme been progressing?'

'Better than expected. But not quite as well as I'd

hoped. Some of the food hall staff are rather resistant to change, particularly customer-oriented working practices.'

'Some of them,' said Logan drily, 'are straight out of *Titus Groan*. I've never seen such grotesque specimens in all my life.'

'We've decided to advertise locally for additional staff,' nodded Diana. 'What's needed is new blood. It's all very well refurbishing the food hall but if we can't provide the level of service people expect . . .'

'They'll go on shopping elsewhere,' Logan concluded for her.

Taz led the way down the escalator into the foyer, and stopped at the doors which opened into the food hall. There was a moment's hesitation, then she pulled every scrap of her courage together and cleared her throat.

'OK folks, this is it.'

The moment she stepped inside, she knew she'd been foolish to have doubts. What Sushil Gupta had done to the food hall was indeed a work of genius, and she could read the appreciative surprise on Paul and Diana's faces.

Somehow, against all the odds and without spending vast amounts of company money, Sushil had transformed a dark, depressing, almost windowless hole into a palace of light and pastel colour. Eyes gravitated naturally to the rediscovered ceiling, the exposed plasterwork picked out in what seemed like miles of metallic foil, turning it into a gorgeous inverted wedding-cake iced in pure silver. Second-hand chandeliers, bought up cheaply from a local hotel, flooded the hall with airy grandeur, and picked out the vibrant colours in the Victorian tiled walls and pillars.

It was open, spacious, inviting. All the old partitions had been torn out, to create one opulent space in which floated variously-shaped islands of smooth pine, screened from each other by climbing plants which lent everything a hint of the exotic.

Paul Logan whistled. Taz knew exactly how he felt.

With all the fuss about reopening the Food Hall in time for the Christmas rush, and the sheer complication of trying to organise a childcare rota without upsetting

Adam, Isobel or Mandy, Chloë and Clive had gone right out of Taz's mind. It wasn't until her next afternoon off that they came thundering right back into it.

Half an hour late, she bounded down the corridor from the security lodge and escaped into the crisp December air. Adam was waiting for her in the staff car park, tapping his fingers impatiently on the steering wheel of his van.

'Oh damn I'm late aren't I?' she apologised breathlessly as she opened the passenger door. 'We ran out of that Brie again, had to ring round to get some more for tomorrow.'

She wriggled into her seat and breathed in to do up the seat belt. Adam put on his stern uncle face.

'No excuses, Taz. Two o'clock you said, you can't let yourself be a slave to that shop.'

'It's in the blood, Adam. And I can't just dump on poor Leroy every time something goes wrong, can I?' Taz smiled winsomely.

Adam gave her a sideways look as he turned the key in the ignition.

'Poor Leroy? He's twenty-five years old, Taz, he can cope on his own. The way you talk about him, anybody'd think you two had a thing going.'

'That's rubbish!' Taz wished she didn't blush so easily. 'He's my assistant, we work well together that's all.'

'Hmm. I believe you, thousands wouldn't. Now, where are we going? Gloucester? Oxford?'

'Anywhere I can find my mother a Christmas present. She's had everything there is to buy in Cheltenham.'

'Oxford it is then. There's bound to be something she'd like in a place that size.'

Taz was about to counter with 'don't you believe it' when a young man came hurtling out of the security lodge and across the car park towards them, waving his arms and mouthing at them to stop.

'What's that bloody idiot playing at, he'll get himself run over.'

'Adam, stop, it's Clive!'

She didn't need to hear Adam's barely-audible groan as he stepped on the brake to know how he felt.

'Clive? Oh God, what does he want *now*?'

435

Taz wound down her window. Clive, hands on knees and panting like a winded gelding, gasped out the words he desperately needed to get across.

'Thank . . . God. I . . . thought I'd . . . missed you. It's . . . Chloë.'

'Might have guessed,' muttered Adam with a fatalistic detachment, switching off the engine with an ominous clunk. 'What's she gone and done this time?'

'Oh shut up, Adam!' Taz glared at him. 'Can't you see Clive's upset? Go on Clive, what's happened?'

'You've got to help me, Taz. I d-don't know what to do.' Clive gulped in a draught of autumnal air. 'She's been arrested.'

'Shoplifting? Again?'

Clive shook his head. He was shuddering with emotion now, the shock hitting him and making his legs buckle underneath him.

'N-no, not that. She was arrested in the arcade. She tried to steal a baby.'

Chapter 32

Taz had never seen the inside of a psychiatric ward before, and to judge from the look of absolute terror on Clive's face, he neither had nor wanted to. Adam followed three or four paces behind, as though he hadn't yet quite decided whether or not he wished to be associated with anything around him.

Taz felt sick. It wasn't that the ward was a frightening place per se; in fact it looked bright and cheerful, with yellow walls and floral curtains around beds with plump duvets and cuddly toys. But you couldn't pretend not to notice the lock on the door, or the uniformed nurses, or the poor girl who paced endlessly up and down clutching a headless doll.

'What's happening, doctor?' demanded Taz as they were ushered into the ward office.

'Anything you tell me you can tell Taz,' broke in Clive. 'She's my wife's best friend.'

And that was perhaps sadder than anything, thought Taz. When all was said and done she still felt she hardly knew Chloë. If she'd known her better she might have guessed that Chloë was going to do something very, very unfortunate.

'As you wish. Well, I'm Dr Patel and I'm taking charge of Chloë's case. As you know, she has been referred to us by the police who arrested her and we are detaining her under section twelve of the Mental Health Act . . .'

'Detaining her?' Taz looked at Clive. His eyes seemed glazed over with unshed tears, and he was holding baby Ayesha tightly to him, as though afraid that someone

437

would steal away this last vestige of his lost happiness. 'You mean she's been sectioned?'

Dr Patel leaned forward, hands clasped between his knees.

'I'm sure you'll appreciate, Miss . . .?'

'Norton. Taz Norton.'

'Miss Norton. I'm sure you'll appreciate that a prison cell is no place for someone as ill as Chloë. That's why she's here. Now, Mr Baxendale, you say she has already received some treatment for depression?'

'Our GP prescribed her something, anti-depressants I think. I'm not sure that she took them.'

'I see,' nodded Dr Patel.

'But she said she was getting better.' The unshed tears spilled out onto Clive's cheeks as Ayesha babbled contentedly, blissfully unaware of the drama unfolding around her. 'Ayesha's only a baby, doctor, she needs her mother.'

Taz turned to put her arm round Clive, but to her surprise Adam had already laid a hand on his shoulder. He didn't say anything, but Taz could tell from his face that he was moved by Clive's distress.

'Of course,' said the doctor. 'But it's early days, Mr Baxendale. First we have to stabilise her condition, then we must prepare psychiatric reports for the court.'

'She's to be charged then?' asked Adam.

'That's not for me to decide. But attempting to abduct a child is a serious offence.'

'What's wrong with her doctor, what's wrong with my Chloë?'

'As I said, Mr Baxendale, it's early days. But at this stage I believe she is suffering from a severe depressive disorder related to childbirth, possibly postnatal psychosis.'

'Psychosis.' Adam whispered the word and the whole room seemed to shiver.

'It sounds worse than it is,' said Dr Patel gently. 'Most patients make an excellent recovery. It can be caused by a simple hormonal imbalance.'

Clive wiped his nose and drew himself up straight.

'Can I see my wife?'

'Of course you can. But you'll understand... she's under sedation, she may not respond as you expect her to.'

'Will you come in with me? To see her?' Clive asked Taz and Adam.

'Surely you don't want us in there,' said Adam uncomfortably. 'You'll want to talk to her on her own.' But Clive grabbed his hand and crushed the fingers.

'Please.'

Taz could only imagine how Clive must be feeling as they walked between the beds towards the side ward at the end. There was something about the smell of this place, the sounds, the unnatural quietness. Something that made you want to turn tail and run away.

'She's in here,' said the charge nurse, opening the door. 'I'll be back in ten minutes, just give a shout if there's any problem.'

Chloë was sitting on the edge of her bed in a pink nightdress, a crocheted bed-jacket about her thin, white shoulders. Her eyes looked like blue saucers in her porcelain face.

'Chloë?' Clive could hardly get the word out for the tears he was choking back. 'Chloë sweetheart...'

Chloë stared blankly at him for a few moments, as if trying to remember exactly who he might be. Taz held her breath, glad for the warmth of Adam standing at her back.

'Why, sweetheart?' Clive sat down on the bed next to her, Ayesha on his lap. 'Just tell me why.'

'I... I just wanted to make things all right,' said Chloë, faintly and hesitantly.

'But how?'

'I thought if the baby was white...' Her eyes begged for understanding. 'It's all I ever wanted... a baby. But it wasn't white, so everything was wrong.'

'Ayesha's your baby', said Taz softly. 'Isn't she Clive?' As soon as she's spoken the words she wished she hadn't; for all she knew it might be the very worst thing to say, with Chloë in such a state.

'Ayesha,' said Clive, taking Chloë's hand and placing

439

Ayesha's within it. 'This is your baby, Chloë. Ayesha. *Our* baby.'

'Ours?' The blue eyes blinked, astonished.

'Ours. Because I love you Chloë, and I love Ayesha too, and all I want in the whole world is for us all to be together.'

It was almost Christmas again. As Taz stood in the food hall and watched her last-minute customers scurrying about like manic ants, she thought back to the same time the previous year, when things had been so different, so frightening, so uncertain.

The food hall was picking up nicely, and might even nudge into credit by the end of the month; giving staff their very first bonus since Old George was in short pants. That side of Taz's life was working out better than she could have hoped a few weeks ago, when her job was on the line and it felt as if everyone at Seuss & Goldman was against her.

But there were other things in life besides work, as her mother was always reminding her. First there were friends, most of them with even more complicated lives than her own: Binnie, resolutely determined to manage without Jim and hating every moment of it; Chloë, recovering slowly in hospital and Clive, still terrified that a court would send her to prison and throw away the key. Dee's love life was in its usual disarray too, and as for Steffi Parkes . . . Only Mandy seemed to be getting her head together, scrimping and saving and winning against all the odds; and forcing her life into the shape she wanted it to be, for Dylan's sake if not her own.

Then there was Taz's own life. On the face of it things looked so settled and so secure. She had a nice flat, a nice boyfriend, a nice job and a wonderful son. Was it only guilt that stopped her from wanting more?

Leroy stopped her train of thought before it reached its destination.

' "Severn Vale Tonight," ' he announced, arriving with his arms full of panettone.

'The local TV programme? What about it?'

'One of their researchers has just been on the phone to Diana Latchford. They want to do another feature on us. A TV guide to Christmas gourmet food shopping. Oh, and they want Old George in it, apparently he's going to be the next Fred Dibnah. Shall I tell them yes?'

Taz recalled the televised reopening of the food hall, and Old George's impromptu performance of 'Roll Out the Barrel'. Against all the odds, it had been a big hit with the viewers.

'Well all right then, I guess we can use the publicity. But tell George no monologues – or we'll have to sit through the whole of "Christmas day in the Workhouse".'

Leroy arranged the panettone into a fat, glossy pyramid.

'I love this stuff. Dad runs a deli, so we always have it at Christmas. How about you, doing anything special?'

'Oh, you know. Just staying at home and pigging out, it'll be nice to have a couple of days off before the sales. And it's Jack's first Christmas – I want to make it really special for him. Mind you,' she laughed, 'I think he's a bit young to understand all the fuss.'

'You think so?'

'I took him to see Santa last week and he burst into tears when he saw the elves. Then when we got home Minky'd eaten half the tinsel off the tree and I had to rush her to the vet for an X-ray. It's chaos! And I haven't even thought about buying Adam a present yet. Nothing's ever quite the way you plan it, is it?'

'No.' Leroy's kind brown eyes looked at her over the top of the panettone. 'Unfortunately not.'

She reached up to readjust one of the boxes and their fingers met, very briefly. And then the moment was gone.

By three o'clock on Christmas Day, everyone was too full of pudding to take much notice of the Queen's speech.

Bill snoozed on Taz's sofa, under a paper crown which fluttered with each sonorous snore. He didn't even notice Isobel hoovering round him, picking up tattered sheets of paper and bits of string as she went.

'Mum,' protested Taz, 'It's Christmas Day, why don't you put your feet up and have a rest?'

Isobel switched off the vacuum cleaner briefly.

'Rest? Oh I couldn't possibly dear, I'd get terrible indigestion. Why don't you two take Jack out for a walk? It's a lovely afternoon and you'll need an appetite for your tea.'

Taz thought she would probably never have an appetite ever again, not after a massive roast turkey dinner, an EU sprout mountain and half a box of Thornton's Continental. But there would be sherry trifle and Isobel's home-cured ox-tongue for tea, and hell to pay if they weren't eaten.

As though reading her mind, Adam held out Jack's brand-new snowsuit.

'Rise and shine, shake a leg.'

They weren't the only people wandering about aimlessly in the watery sunshine, occasionally squinting up at the snowless sky. As Jack's buggy trundled up the road they nodded and smiled at half a dozen other exiles from the festive fun.

'Race you to the top of Ham Hill?' suggested Adam.

'Not unless I get to drive up,' replied Taz, picking up Jack's favourite fluffy duck and tucking it back into the buggy for the umpteenth time. 'Adam . . .'

'Hmm?'

'Thanks for taking on Chloë's court case, I know it's against your principles to work for people with a lot of money . . .'

'Maybe I was just being pigheaded about Chloë,' Adam replied, shrugging. 'It really shook me up, seeing her in hospital like that.'

'And you think you'll be able to get her off?'

'Let's just say no jury in their right mind would send someone that sick to prison. And the psychiatric reports are pretty conclusive.'

Taz groped around for the right thing to say.

'Is there something wrong? Only you've been a bit quiet all day.'

'No, not wrong exactly. But there is something I've been meaning to tell you.'

'Go on.' Taz's legs moved mechanically, the buggy jarring slightly as it bounced over a stone, making Jack

442

whimper. 'It's all right Jack, all right sweetheart, Mummy's sorry.'

'You know I told you I was looking to buy a flat? Well, I've found one.'

'Oh, I see.' The buggy trundled on, Taz not really seeing where she was going. 'You might have told me.'

Adam sighed and hung his head. He thrust his hands deep into his jacket pockets.

'I know. I just couldn't bring myself to tell you, I tried a dozen times but I always chickened out. I couldn't be sure how you'd take it, you see. The thing is . . .'

'Go on.'

'You don't need me any more, do you Taz? I mean, you used to, but not any more. You like me – or at least, I hope you do . . .'

Taz felt something stir within her. Was it sadness, shock – or relief?

'Of course I like you. I fancy you too – and you've been wonderful to me and Jack.'

'But you don't need me. Admit it. You've got Isobel and Mandy looking after Jack now; and Jack's the one thing we've always had in common, isn't he? You've always liked me Taz, sure, but you've never really *loved* me, have you?'

Taz shook her head. It felt like ingratitude, but it was a relief to come clean.

'No. Not love.' She smiled up at Adam. 'But we came close, didn't we?'

'Closer than you'll ever know.'

'So when will you be moving out?'

'Would three weeks from now be OK?'

'Fine. Why not?'

'You'll have enough money to manage?'

'We'll manage. I'm back on my feet again now.'

They trundled on in silence for a few more minutes, lost in their own thoughts.

'I suppose we'd better go back,' said Adam, looking at his watch.

'Yeah. Mum's going to be upset, she really likes you, you know.'

'I know. But that's not enough to base a future on, is it? This has to be about me and you. And we'll always be friends, won't we?'

'Always,' echoed Taz, but already she could see Adam Rolfe slowly receding from her life.

The January sales started the day after Boxing Day; Taz hardly had time to take her coat off before Diana Latchford paged her.

'If you could just come up to my office, Tasmin.'

'Now? But we're just about to open the doors . . .'

'I realise that, but I'm sure Mr McIntosh can hold the fort. This won't take long.'

Taz ground her teeth in frustration as she made her way upstairs. That was the trouble with retail work, you never had time to do something properly before something else more urgent turned up. And with Gloria and Mark both off with flu, and customers falling over each other to get at the bargains, the food hall needed all the staff it could get.

'Come in.' Diana showed Taz into her office. 'Take a seat. I'm sorry to drag you away on the first day of the sale, but I've got something rather important to tell you.'

'Oh? I'm not sure I like the sound of that.' The last time Diana had used that tone of voice, it was to tell her that she was suspended.

'Well I'll get straight to the point. I think it's high time Leroy McIntosh got his own department. What do you think?'

Taz hoped her relief didn't show.

'Yes of course. I agree. But he's doing such a wonderful job in the food hall . . .'

'Precisely. Which is why I've decided to promote him. To departmental sales manager in the food hall.'

Taz's jaw hit the deck. A turmoil of emotions whipped up into a miniature tornado in her stomach.

'In . . . the *food hall?*' She swallowed, anger surfacing out of the turbulence. 'And just exactly where does that leave me?'

'I realise you may be a little upset . . .' began Diana.

'Upset? Look, I'm sorry if I'm speaking out of turn, but you took me out of menswear and dumped the food hall on me when it was on its last legs. And now, just when I'm starting to turn it around, you tell me you're moving me on to God knows where!'

'Only because the food hall doesn't need you any more,' replied Diana patiently. 'Whereas I do.' Diana smoothed a hand through her hair. 'You'll no doubt have noticed that Gerry Rothwell hasn't yet returned from his placement in the USA?'

'Yes.' Taz shifted irritably in her seat. 'But I don't see what that has to do with me . . .'

'Quite a lot as it happens. The fact is, Gerry has applied to remain in the USA to manage the new Chicago store, and that leaves me without an assistant store manager. I need someone with proven managerial skills in more than one department. Someone who isn't afraid to tell me when I'm wrong.

'If you want the job, Tasmin, it's yours.'

Isobel couldn't have looked more stunned if she'd tried.

'You're going to be . . .?'

'Assistant store manager,' beamed Bill, grabbing his daughter in a big bear-hug as he danced her round in circles. 'Well done, Kitten, well done, I always knew you could do it!'

'Dad, Dad, let go, I can't breathe!'

Isobel let herself collapse into Taz's second-best armchair, the one with the dodgy webbing. Her bottom immediately sank into a deep, stuffingless well, but she was far too dazed to care.

'But you *can't*,' she exclaimed. 'You've got a baby!'

'Congratulations, Taz,' piped up Mandy, unzipping Jack from his snuggle-suit and easing off his mittens. She paused, and looked down at her feet. 'I s'pose this means you'll be gettin' a full-time nanny now.'

'Of course she will,' interjected Isobel. 'You can't possibly manage without a proper trained nanny, Tasmin, and of course money won't be a problem now you're in *senior* management.'

445

'Mum,' said Taz. 'I'm only going to be assistant store manager, I won't be buying any luxury yachts. Actually,' she went on, 'I was wondering if Mandy would like the job. She and Dylan could come and live here now Adam's moving out.'

Isobel clapped her hand to her mouth. There was a look of complete panic in her eyes.

Mandy said nothing, but kept on staring at the ground.

'Mandy, what do you think?' asked Taz. Mandy raised her head slowly.

'I've got a job,' she said bluntly. 'Cleanin'.'

'I know, but you don't like it much, do you? And you said you liked looking after Jack.'

'I do.' Mandy wrestled with the emotions inside her, feeling her way into the right words to express them. 'The thing is . . .'

'If she doesn't want the job,' said Isobel triumphantly, 'don't push her. You'll be much better off with somebody qualified,' she added.

'Let the girl speak for herself,' said Bill with unusual sharpness. 'Go on Mandy love, spit it out.'

Mandy sat down on the settee, with Dylan on one side of her and Jack on the other.

'What I've got I've had to work for,' she said. 'I had nothin' till I got me flat an' me job. But I'm savin' up, makin' things nice for me an' Dylan. I'm independent now, aren't I? If I give it all up to work for you, I'll have nothin' again.'

Taz nodded. She understood; in fact she'd already thought about what Mandy might say.

'What if you kept on your flat and just slept here when I was working late?'

Hostility moderated to doubt on Mandy's face.

'Well . . . I dunno . . .'

'And what if I gave you time off to go to college?'

Doubt turned to astonishment. Isobel snorted her complete disbelief.

'College? Her? Oh Tasmin, really.'

'I know it's what you really want, Mandy, you talk about

446

it all the time. You know, going to college and getting your NNEB.'

'But I can't. I can't afford to go to college.'

'Yes you can. All this time you've been taking care of Jack and not accepting any money for it, I've been putting that money away for you. It should just about cover your tuition fees, and with your salary from working as Jack's nanny . . .'

'Well, well,' said Bill, nodding approvingly. 'Seems like a sound idea to me.'

'Sound!' Isobel looked horror-stricken.

'But what really matters,' pointed out Taz, 'is what Mandy thinks. What's it to be, Mandy, yes or no?'

'You're not just offerin' it 'cause you feel sorry for me?'

'I'm not stupid, Mandy. I'm offering you the job because you're wonderful with kids, you're totally reliable and Jack thinks the sun shines out of your backside.'

A light seemed to switch on behind Mandy's brown eyes. Her orange hair bounced to jaunty attention.

'Well. If you're sure.'

'Great! That's settled then.' It was Taz's turn to hug Mandy.

'Hang on though,' said Mandy reflectively, 'if I'm goin' to college part-time, who's going to mind Jack while I'm there?'

'Don't you worry about that, Mandy,' said Bill, winking. 'Isobel and I will help out. Won't we dear?'

The look on Isobel's face could have made an angel weep.

Two Months Later

'Happy birthday to you,
Happy birthday to you,
Happy birthday dear Ja-ack –
Happy birthday to you!'

Jack, one whole year old today, sat in his high chair and clapped his hands in delight. The birthday cake was rather strange – Taz had insisted on making it herself – but it was vaguely steam-engine shaped, with blue and yellow icing, 'Jack' picked out in silver letters and one big silver candle.

'Shall we blow the candle out now?' Taz kissed her son on the velvety, fragile skin of his cheek and he giggled and kissed her back, a big wet slobber of a kiss that she never wanted to wipe away. 'One, two, three, everybody, blow!'

They were all here to celebrate Jack's first birthday: Mandy of course, Mum and Dad, Binnie (minus Jim but perhaps not for too much longer), Steffi and even the still-apologetic Dee. Dee had turned up with the twins and someone who looked like Lorenzo's twin brother but wasn't. Apparently his name was Laszlo and he was booked in for a vasectomy next Tuesday. Taz knew she must be dreaming when Dee confided in her that 'you can have too many children, don't you think? I reckon five's enough for anybody to cope with.'

Clive and Chloë were absent, but on the mantelpiece there was a teddy bear with a red bow-tie, and a card from Clive, Chloë and Ayesha. Next to it rested a plain brown envelope, containing the cheque Gareth had sent Jack for his birthday. No card, no cuddles, just a cheque. Some people would never change.

'I think we'd better shift some of these dishes,' commented Binnie, steering her very pregnant stomach around the table and gathering up a couple of sticky plates from the carpet.

'I said we should have bought disposable ones,' commented Isobel, but nobody was listening.

'You're not shifting anything,' said Taz, whisking the plates out of Binnie's hand. 'You're going to sit down with Amy and have a nice rest! Tell you what, I'll get these washed and then bring you a nice cup of tea, OK?'

Taz breezed off into the kitchen, pursued by Mandy bearing armfuls of dirty cups.

'You wash, I'll wipe,' said Mandy, grabbing a tea-towel.

'It's all right, you go back to the party, I can manage.'

'You're payin' me, remember? I'll wipe.'

But Mandy had scarcely dried half a plate when the kitchen door opened and a head popped round it. A beautifully-groomed, exquisitely good-looking head with café noir skin and close-cropped black hair.

'Am I too late? I got held up at S&G.'

'Leroy!' Taz knew Mandy would read the excitement in her voice. Her hands trembled so much that she dropped the cup she was washing and splashed herself with soapy water.

A purple velvet elephant pushed its trunk into the kitchen by way of response, and waggled its ears.

'I brought this for Jack, do you think he'll like it?'

'He'll love it to bits, come in and show me.'

Leroy stepped into the kitchen. Mandy looked from Taz to Leroy and back again, and decided on a tactical retreat.

'I'll just go an' blow up some more balloons then, shall I?' She gave Leroy a wicked grin and threw him the tea-towel. 'Here, make yourself useful.'

Alone in the kitchen, Leroy and Taz stood looking at each other. Now that Mandy had gone they both felt awkward and rather silly, Taz conscious of the soapy splashes all down the front of her sweatshirt and Leroy in a suit, with a tea-towel in one hand and a purple elephant in the other.

'I'm glad you could come. Jack will love the elephant.' Taz took it from Leroy's hand and placed it on the kitchen table. It sat and looked back at her with a very knowing expression.

'You really think so? I wasn't sure what I should bring.'

'Just yourself would have been fine. Anyhow, you're here in time for jelly and cake.'

'I was thinking . . . after the party, are you free?'

Taz felt a warm thrill of anticipation.

'I suppose I could ask Mandy to stay on for a few hours. Why, what have you in mind?'

'I thought maybe we could go for a drink. Or something. If you like,' he added tentatively.

'Again?' Taz smiled. 'That's the third time this week.'

'I'm not counting.'

'People will start to talk.'

'They probably already are. You know what S&G's like.'

'Yes I do. And you know this is a really bad idea, don't you?'

Leroy sighed dramatically, a twinkle in his dark eyes.

'Don't tell me, your mother hates me?'

'Far from it. No, I mean I'm your boss, it can't possibly work out between us. And it's terribly unprofessional.'

'I know,' said Leroy softly. And taking Taz into his arms he kissed her, very tenderly and passionately, and not at all in the way a DSM ought to be kissing his line manager.

'Taz, have you got any kitchen roll, little Leonie's chucked up on the . . .' The door burst open and Binnie appeared, a crying baby on her hip. 'Oh! Sorry, I'll get some loo roll from the bathroom.'

'Don't be silly, you're not interrupting anything!'

'And if you think I'll believe that you must think I'm daft as well as fat. Good on you,' she grinned. 'But by God Leroy, you're a slow worker.'

There was to be no peace for the wicked. Isobel was right behind Binnie, with a stack of plates a foot high.

'Still not finished those dishes dear? Tsk tsk, they'll never get done if you just stand around chatting all day. Binnie dear, did you know that child's been sick? Here, stand back and let me do the washing up.'

Taz, Leroy and Binnie exchanged glances as Isobel rolled up her sleeves and hunted out the rubber gloves from under the sink.

'We were just saying how well it's all going,' said Leroy, for want of anything better to say. 'The party I mean.'

'And what a wonderful job Taz has made of bringing up Jack,' enthused Binnie. 'He's a super baby, so placid and happy.'

'Oh, he may be good *now*,' Isobel chuckled, 'But just you wait till he gets older, Tasmin. The first year is the easy one.'

'Easy?' Taz wrinkled her nose in dismay.

'Oh yes, dear. You were no trouble at all till you were twelve months old, then it was one thing after another. Believe me, dear, from here on in it just gets harder!'